MOKELUMNE GOLD

A NOVEL BY

MAJOR MITCHELL

Mokelumne Gold

For information contact: Shalako Press
P.O. Box 371, Oakdale, CA 95361-0371
http://www.shalakopress.com

ISBN: 978-0-9846811-0-5

Cover design: Karen Borrelli
Editor: Judith Mitchell
Cover photograph by Major Mitchell

PRINTED IN THE UNITED STATES OF AMERICA

Dedication

To Vickey Ruiz, the first of our children to realize her father's talent and passion for writing.

Acknowledgments

This book, similar to all others I have written, is the combined effort of many people. Without them, this book would have been most difficult.

I would first like to thank Anna Collier for correcting my *gringo* Spanish.

Thanks to Jamie Hood for her critical eye and input, which is always appreciated and much needed.

Thanks to the entire Phillips family, who not only read the manuscript, but helped school a Protestant in Catholicism. This effort helped immensely in creating a believable and factual story.

A huge thanks to my brother, Jerry, in whose fertile mind the original story of *Doña* Leonida was created.

And most of all, hugs and kisses to Judy, my editor, partner, friend, and wife. Without her, this would be almost impossible.

As usual, if the reader should happen to discover any mistakes in the text, they are the sole responsibility of the author, and do not reflect on the above-mentioned people.

Chapter 1

Leonida looked up from the needle work in her lap as Woodrow's buggy stopped at the stables. She frowned at the shapeless pattern in her hands once more as the big man handed the reins to one of the stable boys. He eased himself to the ground and swatted the dust from his jacket and pat-legs before offering a hand to his wife, Susanna.

"Maria?" Leonida tossed the sewing aside with a sigh. Needlework was not one of her stronger points. "Maria?" she called louder as she stood to brush the wrinkles from her dress.

"Si, señora?" The maid poked her head through the doorway.

"We have company. Señor Black and his wife have come to pay us a visit."

"Bien, I will put water on for tea." The maid disappeared back into the kitchen while Leonida positioned herself at the edge of the steps to welcome her guests.

"Buenos dias, Señor Black." She took his extended hand and leaned to kiss Susanna on the cheek. "Señora, Dios ben'decir. Thank you for coming. We do not get enough visits from the people in town."

"God bless you too, Mrs. Garcia." Susanna hugged her and placed a kiss on her cheek in return. "I do miss seeing you. I wish you'd come to town more often."

"Sí, but the court hearings in San Francisco concerning our rancho have been taking much of our time." She took them both by the arm and nodded toward the open door.

"Come, I think Maria is making tea. We shall discuss what it was that brought you here over some refreshments."

"That is kind of you." Susanna smiled. Woodrow paused at the doorway to glance around.

"Is Hanky anywhere around?"

"Señor Russell? Yes, he is with my father at the creek. The Indians are building a dam to water the cattle and horses during the summer months. Do you wish to see him?"

"Yes, if it's possible. I have a message for him."

"Ah," she nodded, "then make yourselves comfortable at the table, and I'll send someone to tell him you are here."

"Come." Maria met them at the door with a matronly smile. "Sit." She motioned toward the walnut table surrounded with leather-backed chairs. "Maria has made you a special treat this morning."

"Excuse me for a moment please. You are in good hands, now." Leonida's skirt swished as she turned to cross the porch. "Julio." She shaded her eyes against the sun. "Julio?" she called again. The heels of her high-top shoes clicked against the bricks as she crossed the patio. A wooden boat abandoned by one of the children danced happily in the fountain, giving her a quick sense of melancholy.

"Julio Ramos!" She shouted, a bit aggravated.

"Sí, Doña Leonida?" The barefoot stable boy rounded the tack house at a dead run.

"Why didn't you answer me when I called?"

"Perdon, Doña Leonida, but I did not hear you." He jerked his sombrero from his head and studied the bricks at his feet.

"That's okay. You're forgiven, this time."

"Sí, gracias."

"I need you to do me a favor." His eyes darted upward, but quickly returned to the bricks. "Do you know where my father and Señor Hanky are working?"

"Sí, by the creek," he pointed.

"Bien, I want you to go tell Señor Hanky he has visitors from Dogtown, and that he is to come to the hacienda immediately. Bueno?"

"Sí, Doña Leonida. Gracias." He bowed and turned away.

"Julio?"

"Sí?"

"Come here." The top of his head nearly reached the level of her chest as he shuffled closer. "How old are you now?"

"Eight years...I think."

"Bien, I get so busy, I forget sometimes." She caressed his glossy black hair and cheek with her palm. "I don't spend enough time with you children anymore. Now, go get Señor Hanky." She smiled and swatted him on the bottom.

"Sí, Doña Leonida." He grinned and darted across the bricks.

Leonida watched as the boy passed the open gates to disappear behind the adobe wall surrounding the hacienda. There was little danger of attacks by Indians or marauding bandits these days, so the gates were left open at her order. This offered those inside the hacienda a clear view of the rolling, grass-covered hills, dotted with oak and scrub pine trees. A line of trees bordering the Mokelumne River snaked a dark green line accross her property toward the east. Don Rudolfo's cattle grew fat on the northern California grassland, and only seemed to tolerate the occasional human that happened their way. She had no idea how many cattle or horses she actually owned. She only knew that more than three hundred people, counting women and children, currently claimed her rancho as their home. That number would decrease in the winter, when some of the Indians would migrate south to find warmer climates, but jump again the following spring. Leonida heaved a sigh and turned back toward the hacienda.

It was all changing too fast with the influx of people coming to the gold fields. A great percentage of these were hard cases who had found nothing but more poverty; and while she had helped many of them, others were claiming she owned too much land. They demanded that she abandon her home and return to Mexico. If it were not for the memory of Rudolfo, and those like Maria who truly depended on her, she might have given in to their demands long ago. After all, what business did a childless widow have trying to run a seventy-five square mile rancho?

The kitchen was filled with the rich smell of chocolate and cinnamon when Leonida stepped through the door. Maria smiled and set a steaming cup at the head of the table as she held the chair for her to be seated.

"My word, this is heavenly. What is it called?" Mrs. Black asked.

"It is atole." Leonida sipped the thick chocolate in her cup. "Maria fixes it on special occasions. Evidently, you are special." She grinned and took another sip.

"Sí, anyone who is nice to my Doña is special." Maria slid a plate piled high with fruit-filled turnovers onto the table. "She may be the Doña, but she is like one of my daughters."

"And you're more than special to me too." Leonida patted the maid's hand.

"Well, this drink is divine. Thank you, Maria. Thank you very much," Susanna said.

"Oh, forgive me." Leonida motioned toward the plate. "Those are called empanadas. I was able to buy a crate of apples on my last trip to San Francisco. Try one. I believe you will like them as much as the atole."

"Don't mind if I do," Woodrow said, reaching for the plate. "By the way, how's that court battle going, anyway?"

"Not well." Leonida crinkled her brow. "They keep postponing our hearing for one reason or another. I have given our solicitor, Señor Sattler, everything he needs, but, he doesn't seem to be making much headway."

"Hmmm." Woodrow munched thoughtfully on one of the apple turnovers. "I'll just bet you've given him a lot of money too, haven't you?"

"Sí, the señora has given all the gold that was left from the matanzas." Maria scowled.

"Maria, remember your place."

"Sí, señora." The maid bowed and backed away.

"Well," Woodrow cleared his throat, "what I meant was, I hear lots of things. And one of the things I've heard is, there's a lot of those city lawyers handling land disputes like yours, who are getting rich, and most of the Mexicans are still losing their land."

"Sí, we have heard those rumors also. I stay in touch with some of the other ranchos, so we know of their troubles. But, Señor Sattler comes with a high recommendation. I'm sure he's an honest man." She turned to her maid and patted an empty spot by her chair.

"Maria, come, por favor. Perdon my abruptness, mi campañera." She leaned and kissed Maria's cheek as the maid seated herself.

"I pray he's honest. You've had enough trouble for ten lifetimes," Woodrow said. They were interrupted by Josiah Russell stamping his boots on the porch. Maria jumped up to fill another cup with atole.

"Well, hey, Woody. How y'all doin'?" The Texan had to stoop as he came through the doorway. He grabbed Woodrow's hand and gave it a vigorous shake.

"About as good as can be expected, Hanky. Yourself?"

"Fine, fine. And you, Mrs. Black? This old buzzard been treatin' ya kindly?"

"Oh, yes, Mr. Russell. He's been quite an angel."

"Now, why do I doubt that?" He seated himself as Maria set the cup on the table. He grabbed the maid's hand as she turned away.

"Hey, woman. Is that the type of greetin' yer supposed tuh be givin' a hardworkin' man like me?"

"Señor Hanky!" She jerked away as he puckered his lips. "Caramba, you're such a crazy gringo." She returned to the stove shaking her head. Leonida set her own lips in a thin line and nodded.

Woodrow chuckled and cleared his throat. "What I wanted to see you about, Hanky, isn't actually funny."

"Guess someone's gotta be the one to break the party up. What's eatin' at yer craw?"

"Someone killed Ambrose Brice last night."

"Don't say?" He took a sip of atole. "Got any idee who and what for?"

"No. Ruby burst into my office just after I got there this morning, yelling to beat the band. I followed her down to The Rusty Rail, and there he was on the floor with his own butcher knife stuck in his chest. Been dead some hours, from what I take." Leonida shuddered while Maria crossed herself and mumbled a prayer.

"Waal, that's all interestin'." Josiah shifted in his chair as he dug the makings out of his shirt pocket. He took his time rolling a cigarette. "But seein' as Ambrose weren't no brother of mine, and I ain't a gonna shed no tears over the buzzard, what's this gotta do with me?" Woodrow folded his hands and leaned his elbows against the table.

"Because you were a Texas Ranger once upon a time, and we don't have any proper law in Dogtown..."

"Never did." Josiah struck a match and lit his smoke.

"Yes, we can agree on that. But, seeing as Angel's Camp doesn't have a justice at the moment, I sent one of my men over to Columbia to see Judge Hansen..."

"Lloyd Hansen?"

"Yes, Judge Lloyd Hansen. He claims to know you."

"Hope to shout. Met him over Arzonie way. Good man."

"Good, I'm certainly glad you approve of him," Woodrow said. "Because," he added after taking another sip of chocolate, "he said he's willing to hold court right here in

Dogtown whenever we find out who killed Ambrose, and he wants you to investigate Ambrose's murder."

"What? That old coyote is up to his tricks again, ain't he? Well, you can tell him this ranger ain't takin' the bait. He can play his trick on someone else."

"I'm afraid it's no joking matter. He was dead serious, and here's your commission as a California lawman to prove it." He pulled an envelope from his coat pocket and handed it to Josiah. "You'll find the badge inside."

"Naw, I've been out of the law business some three or four years now. Besides," he slid the envelope back to Woodrow, "Tommy was a Texas Ranger too. What's wrong with him nosing around?"

"Because, that letter has your name on it, and you know as well as I do that Tex had as much reason to kill Ambrose as anyone else." He gave the envelope a shove and it landed in Josiah's lap.

"Say, you're not insinuating that my boy had anything to do with killing that skunk, are you?"

"No, I don't believe he did. But others might take it differently if someone with a grudge against him the size of Texas was investigating his murder."

"What if I don't wanna do it?" Josiah slid the envelope toward Woodrow.

"Take that up with Judge Hansen. It's out of my hands. I just delivered the message." He shoved the envelope to the center of the table where Leonida grabbed it.

"Besides, there's other things to consider." Josiah crossed the room to toss his cigarette in the wood-burning stove. "I've been living here most of two years now, eating these good folks' food and sleeping in their bed. And the only excuse I got for doing such a thing is what little work I get done around the place. You and Lloyd Hansen better take it up with Mrs. Garcia before talking to me."

"It's okay, Señor Hanky," Leonida said glancing up from reading the papers she had removed from the envelope. "As for your staying here, you are family now. There is no need to question that any further." She waved the back of her hand as if she were shooing a fly. "But I think you should look at these papers before refusing. It says you not only have the power to investigate Señor Brice's death, but you are to enforce the law, and you will prosecute whoever is guilty when it comes to trial."

"Huh, ain't askin' for much, is he?" Josiah flopped in the chair and folded his arms. "Besides, if I do decide to do what he says in that bunch of chicken-scratch you got there, who says I'm gonna find anything? Hell, half the state wanted to croak that skunk. Pardon me, ladies," he nodded to the women, "but, I'm surprised they ain't holding some celebration on top of his grave."

"Perhaps you are right, Señor Hanky." Leonida shuffled the papers into a neat stack in front of her. "But I think you should go ahead and do it."

"Yeah, and why's that?"

"Because you're a good man with a good heart, and I know you'll be fair."

"Huh, little do you know." He shifted to stare out the open door.

"But mostly, because I believe that in doing so, you will clear all the names of those who did not kill Señor Brice."

"How do you argue with that, Hanky?" Woodrow snickered.

"Don't know. Here," he leaned across the table, "let me see that." She slid the envelope and papers toward him. Josiah Russell, retired Texas Ranger, held the silver star in the sunlight and rocked it back and forth.

"I always knew women were nothing but trouble." He studied the shiny piece of metal a long minute before pinning it on his vest.

Chapter 2

Clara Baker whirled across the stage and leaped gracefully into the air. The calves of her tiny legs beat against each other as she performed a perfect entrechat. She then bounced feather-light from one foot to the other to complete a jeté. A wisp of her golden-red hair fell from the bun on the back of her head to tickle her freckled nose as she extended one leg backward in a straight line and leaned forward. Her extended hands gracefully told of the overwhelming love the happy bride felt as she waited for her groom. Her face beamed as applause from the tiny rehearsal audience drifted to her ears.

"Wonderful, darling. Simply marvelous." Michelle LeVoe paused clapping, long enough to toss her a kiss.

Clara had been dancing ballet from the moment she could walk. Her mother, Dorothy, had been one of Boston's premier dancers and had given up her career in order to become a full-time mother, but ballet had never left her blood. She had made sure her daughter knew the proper attitude, the art of extending one leg forward or back with bent knee, before she even knew the proper way to hold a fork. Clara took to ballet as naturally as eating, which delighted her mother even more. She taught her to fouetté at age three. And while most young women were not given lessons until at least eight or ten years old, Clara had already learned to pas de deux, partner with a male dancer, by that time. The girl loved her dancing more than anything in her young life, and eight years of training were starting to pay off. She had already landed one of the leading rolls in an previous production of Beethoven's Die Geschöpfe des

Prometheus, which thrilled her. But in a few short months, all eyes in the San Francisco Opera House would be turned toward her as she danced the part of the bride in Johann Sebastian Bach's The Wise Virgins. She would become one with the audience and hold them in her hand, making them understand what the master was trying to convey with each note of music.

"Alright, my darling, that's enough." Michelle tossed another kiss. "Take a little break. I want you to give these other girls a chance to catch up with you."

"Okay." She danced her way to her mother waiting behind the drawn curtains and bowed gracefully.

"How was I, Mommie?"

"Exquisite, my dear." She leaned to kiss her daughter's cheek. "Now, be a good girl, and go get some rest."

Clara couldn't help but make one or two more fairy-like turns as she descended the steps. It was on the sixth step that Clara's toe caught in the loose carpet and she was catapulted headlong into the air. A rending pain shot through her right knee as she landed on the hardwood floor.

"Clara! Are you alright? Are you hurt anywhere?" Her mother hovered over her as Michelle LeVoe yelled and ranted like she was possessed. She knelt close to the girl who was writhing in pain, before turning to beat the stagehand with her director's copy of the ballet.

"I told you to fix that carpet. Now, see what you've done?"

"First you tell me to fix the carpet. Then fix the lighting and the curtain. There is only one of me to go around." The old man with gray stubble bent over Clara.

"My leg..." She tried sitting up. It was more her mother's reaction than the sight of her twisted leg that caused her to scream. She was only ten years old and her career was already over.

~   ~   ~

By one o'clock that afternoon, Sean Kilkenney had already tended to more than a dozen patients, including one knifing victim who had taken most of an hour to stitch up. His medical practice was booming in a way that did not speak well of San Francisco. Gold fever had peaked to a boil, flooding the crowded city with greedy men and women. The bustling shipyards had become a circus of sailing vessels that arrived in the harbor carrying supplies and passengers, but never left. Crew members, having spent weeks listening to the talk of the passengers they carried, abandoned their vessels in search of gold. Only a few captains like Jonathan McDougal, who kept a tight rein on his crew and paid them well, could muster enough men to sail back out to sea. Other ships lay silent like decaying carcasses waiting to be buried by the garbage and sludge being constantly dumped into the bay. Some entrepreneurs had opened businesses in some of the abandoned vessels, while others sold parts of their ships, such as canvas sails and brass lanterns, to those heading for the goldfields.

Sean waved off protests from the patients in his crowded waiting room on Hyde Street.

"I've been up half the night, and haven't even stopped for breakfast. If I don't have something to eat and get a little rest, I'll become a patient myself."

"You can't leave, Doc. I've been waiting for over an hour," the large bearded man in bibbed overalls whined.

"And you'll have to wait a little longer, or go find another doctor. I'm sorry, but I must get a few minutes rest." He closed and locked the door to his examination room and bounded down the stairs two at a time. He had just stepped into the cool salty air when he was accosted by a well-dressed man in a top hat and cloak.

"Doctor Kilkenney?"

"The office is closed." He tried brushing past, but the stranger drifted in front of him, blocking his way.

"I'm sorry, doctor, I know you're a busy man."

"Then you'll be good enough to take your illness someplace else."

"It's not for me, sir. Judge Samuel Baker would like to see you immediately at his residence."

"Judge?" Sean ran a hand across his tired eyes. "What about?"

"I'm not at liberty to say, sir. I'm only Arthur, the butler."

"Well, Arthur Butler, can't this wait awhile longer?"

"Not Arthur Butler, sir," the man chuckled. "I'm Arthur, the butler. My full name is Arthur Farnsworth."

"Okay, Arthur The Butler Farnsworth. You still didn't answer my question. Can't Judge Baker's problem wait awhile longer, while I get something to eat and rest?"

"I'm afraid not, Dr. Kilkenney. I have orders to bring you as soon as possible. I have a cabby waiting." He motioned toward the shiny black carriage parked at the curb. "You may rest as we travel, and I'll personally see to it that you receive all the refreshment you need."

"I don't suppose I'm going to be able to ignore you or your judge, am I?"

"Hardly, sir."

"Then, let's go get this over with." Sean headed toward the curb.

"Ah, excuse me, sir. I would suggest that you retrieve your medical kit first."

"Oh, would you, now?" Sean stood with his hand on the door staring at the man.

"Yes sir, I would."

"All right, Arthur The Butler Farnsworth, I'll tell you what. You go up to my office and retrieve my kit yourself. Because the dozen or so angry patients in my waiting room will more than likely kill me if they know I'm not returning this afternoon. Some of them have been waiting all morning to see me."

"I wouldn't know where to locate it, sir."

"Sure you would." He handed Farnsworth a key ring. "Open the door to the examination room, and you'll find it on the bottom shelf of the supply cabinet."

"Very well, sir." Farnsworth bowed. Sean glanced up at the driver as he cracked open the carriage door.

"Know where we're supposed to be heading?"

"Yes, sir. To Judge Samuel Baker's residence. Why do you ask?"

"Because that damned-fool butler may not be coming back." He glanced over his shoulder at the man climbing the stairs.

~   ~   ~

"This way, sir." Arthur Farnsworth led Sean to a bedroom at the end of the second story hallway. Sean could hear the whimpers of a young girl as the butler rapped softly on the door.

"Yes?" a booming male voice drowned out the girl's voice. Farnsworth stuck his head inside.

"Doctor Kilkenney is here, sir."

"Took you long enough. Get him in here."

"The Judge will see you now, sir." Farnsworth bowed gracefully and swung the door wide for Sean to enter.

The room was a pink wonderland filled with dancing dolls and lace curtains. The canopied bed was surrounded by two uniformed maids and an attractive woman in her late thirties. The short, stocky man with a ruddy complexion had almost chewed the stem of his unlit pipe in two.

"It's my daughter, Doctor. She caught her toe on a piece of loose carpet at that flea-bag of a theater downtown and almost tore her leg off. I don't care what it costs, just fix it where she can walk again."

Sean set his bag on the dresser beside a ballerina music box and bent over the bed to study his patient. The frightened girl stared at him with huge eyes.

"Good morning, young lady. I'm Sean. What might be your name?"

"I'm Clara. And it's afternoon."

"Oh, so it is," he said, glancing at his watch. "But it doesn't matter much, does it?" He gently brushed one of the maids aside with a smile and sat on the edge of the bed. He held her arm to check her pulse.

"I hear you are a pretty good dancer. Is that right?"

"My daughter is the best," Dorothy Baker said.

"Aye, I'm sure she is, Mrs. Baker. Young Clara has the perfect build for a ballerina. Please allow her to answer as many questions as she can for herself. It will help calm her," he smiled. The woman backed to her husband's side with a helpless expression.

"That was insulting, Doctor," the judge growled.

"Aye, I agree. And so is being shanghaied when you're only wanting to get a bite to eat. Now, are we going to argue, or see if we can't do something for the young lady here?"

"I offer my apologies, Doctor. It's just that we are so concerned about Clara," Dorothy said.

"No apology needed, ma'am. I would be concerned too. In fact, I am concerned." He scowled at the girl. "Here lies the prettiest dancer in San Francisco, and she tried to hurt herself before I got the chance to see her perform. Now let me see your leg, young lady." He frowned slightly as one of the maids pulled the bed sheet away from the swollen knee.

"Okay, now I'm going to push and squeeze it some, just so we can find out exactly where it hurts the worst. So you let me know, all right?" She nodded and Sean began his examination. "I want you to tell me exactly what happened every second before and after you fell and hurt yourself. All right?" He waited until she nodded again. "Because I need to know in order to figure out what is wrong inside this knee."

"Well," he said after a few minutes, "are you ready for the bad news?"

"Oh!" Her mother stifled a cry as Clara nodded.

"You're going to have to dance again, whether you like it or not."

"Really, Doctor?" Her mother grabbed Sean's shirt sleeve. "We were so afraid when Doctor Thornton said..." Her fingertips fluttered to her lips.

"And, what did Doctor Thornton say?" Sean grinned.

"He said that Clara may have damaged her knee beyond repair," Judge Baker answered for his wife. "He claimed she might never walk normally, let alone dance again."

"Hubert Thornton's a good man, and I respect his judgment, but he treats mostly gunshot and knife wounds and the like. I could be wrong, but I don't believe that there is anything broken, or damaged to the degree he described. My guess is that Miss Clara Baker will once again grace the stage. That is," he touched the tip of the girl's nose with his finger, "if she'll be good and do exactly what I say. Will you, young lady?"

"Oh, she will, Doctor. She will..." Dorothy Baker gripped his shirt sleeve.

"That's fine, Mrs. Baker. But I'd rather hear it from your daughter, because she's the one who's going to have to work at getting well. Will you?" He stared Clara in the eye.

"Yes. It's just that it hurts," she whimpered.

"I'm afraid it's going to hurt a whole lot worse before this is over. I'll help you all I can, but it's up to you. Now," he turned to Arthur Farnsworth who had been keeping a silent watch by the door, "what I need is a pot of coffee...black and no sugar. And plenty of ice, chipped fine and placed inside a water bottle."

"Yes, sir. Right away, sir." Farnsworth bowed and disappeared.

"What in the world do you need coffee for? How is that going to help my daughter's leg?" Judge Baker scowled.

"It's not. The coffee is to keep me from passing out. The ice is for your daughter's leg."

~   ~   ~

Two days later Sean Kilkenney returned to the Baker house with a present for the young dancer.

"It's a brace. I had a lormer at the blacksmith's shop make it for you." He strapped the soft leather contraption around her leg. "It will allow you to bend your knee back and forth like it was meant to do, but it will keep you from twisting or hyper-extending sideways like it did when you hurt yourself."

"Am I going to have to wear this thing for the rest of my life?" Clara frowned.

"No, not at all. Just until your knee is better. Especially while you are practicing."

"She can practice, Doctor?" Dorothy Baker said.

"Certainly. In fact I want her to. A little at first, and then rest when it starts hurting too badly. You see, if you don't use your leg while it's mending, it might stiffen, and that would be bad for a dancer. So, I want you to wear this brace while you walk around and practice your dancing. I also want you to exercise, to build up your muscles. One hundred leg-lifts a day with each leg. Now, get up and try out your new dancing partner."

Clara walked gingerly around her pink bedroom staring at the shiny buckles holding the brace snugly against her leg.

"How does that feel?" Sean said.

"Cold and funny."

"The brace will warm up, and you'll get used to the feel. Now," he held her right hand, "try putting all your weight on your leg. Slowly..." Clara gripped his fingers and raised her left leg high in the air.

"Ow!" She lowered it again. "That hurts."

"Sure it does." He knelt in front of her and smiled. "But the most important thing is, you did it. I'll bet that two days ago, you would have thought that you would never do that again. And, in just a matter of a few more weeks, you'll be dancing all over the stage. Now, let's see you walk around a little." Sean stood beside Dorothy Baker as her daughter moved slowly around the bedroom.

"Only let her do this a few more minutes today, and increase it a little each day for a week. Then let her go, but try to keep a tight rein on her for awhile. I'll keep checking in every chance I get."

"She said her knee still hurt. Can't you give her something for the pain?"

"Heavens no, Lady. If she's going to be a dancer, she's going to experience some pain every now and again, and she'll have to deal with it. I've already seen too many people in this city addicted to laudanum. Your child is too important to get her started down that path. You, being a pretty good dancer yourself, should know about that." He glanced at her and grinned.

"Yes, but it's been so long, I'm afraid I've forgotten."

"Forgotten? Now don't tell me you've given up on dancing entirely? That would be a gross sin for a woman of your talents."

"No, not entirely. I still dance some, but not on stage. That's reserved for Clara now. Tell me Doctor," she took a picture of a young ballerina from the shelf, "when did you ever see me dance?"

"That you?"

She nodded.

"I didn't actually see you on stage. We were poor Irish immigrants, and I don't know if they would have allowed us inside the theater even if we could have scraped the money together. But I remember seeing your picture plastered everywhere the time you came to New York. Dorothy Mitchell was the talk of the city."

"I'm flattered someone remembers. But as I said, Clara is the great love of my life now, and dancing has become second."

"And where does your husband fit in?" Sean raised an eyebrow.

"Most anywhere he wants." Dorothy giggled and returned the photo to the shelf. "Are there any special instructions about helping Clara recuperate?"

"No." Sean shook his head. "Keep using the water bottle with ice when she's not wearing the brace. Right now, the pain's a good thing, and it will eventually go away."

~ ~ ~

"Hey, Sawbones." The gruff voice caused Sean to jump. "I'll be damned; it is you. Sean Kilkenney." The slap on the back almost drove him to his knees. "I thought it was you from way yonder across the street."

"Bear!" He eyed the huge man in the tailor-made suit up and down.

"Didn't recognize me, did you?"

"No. Last time I saw you, you were wearing buckskins and spitting tobacco juice in the streets of Dogtown."

"Naw, them bumps on your head made you plumb forget. Last time I seen you, you was laid up in that purdy woman's bed, licking your wounds."

Sean raised his eyebrows and cocked his head to one side. He had somehow pushed the beating he had received at the hands of George Bidwell and his friends from his mind. If the big man standing in front of him hadn't rescued him and taken him to the Garcia Rancho, he might well have died in the streets of Dogtown that night. In an odd sort of way, the violence he had received at the barber's hands had a pleasant memory connected with it. The vision of Leonida hovering around the bed as she nursed him back to health suddenly rushed inside his head. Her gentle touch, her golden hair, green eyes and warm smile. The thrill of her moist lips as they brushed against his under the moonlight by the fountain, and the smell of her perfume as he held her trembling body against his. But the lifeless body of Judge Henry Baines hanging from the livery stable in Dogtown had cast a pall over the pleasant memories of Rancho Manantial Escondido and had driven Sean to San Francisco.

"I don't know how that could have slipped my mind. Come on." He returned the slap on the back. "I was just going inside to get myself something to eat. I'll buy you a steak."

"No, you won't. I'm gonna buy you the biggest steak in town." Bear grabbed his arm and began ushering him toward a carriage parked across the street. "Besides, no telling how long some of those critters they cook inside that place have been dead."

"Albert, please take us to The Comstock," Bear said to the driver as they took their seats.

"Yes, sir." The man touched the brim of his top hat and started the vehicle forward.

"Damn, but it's good to see you, Doc." Bear swatted him on the shoulder. "Tell me, what have you been doing with yourself?"

"Oh, just doctoring." Sean shrugged. "I've got my own practice now, down on Hyde Street."

"And the way you had your nose stuck in them books all the way out to Californy, I'll bet you're a good one too, ain't you?"

"Well, yes, I guess you can say I am." Sean glanced at the throngs of people and lighted buildings as the carriage wove its way through the crowded streets. "If you count working from sunup to the middle of the night as being successful. This is actually the first night I've had free in weeks."

"Well, that's 'cause you're a good sawbones, and honest as the day goes by. You can't find folks like that everyplace you look. Know that, don't you?"

"Yes, I'm beginning to find that out," Sean chuckled. The carriage slowed to a stop in front of the nightclub. "Ah, Bear," he glanced from the smartly dressed doorman to his smiling friend, "I hate to mention this, but The Comstock is rather expensive. We don't actually have to eat here."

"Aw, no need to worry about that none. I already told you this was on me. I'm gonna get you the best steak in town."

"Good evening, Mr. Walker." The doorman bowed as the carriage door swung open. "I hope you and your guest have a pleasant evening."

"I'm sure we will, Chad." The big man shoved some paper money into the hands of both the doorman and the driver. "This here is an old friend of mine, Doctor Sean Kilkenney, who I come out to Californy with. Now, I ain't seen him for a million years. So y'all just sort of hang around and help us back into this contraption in case we have too much of a good time."

"Yes, sir. We will make sure you and your friend are both taken care of." Chad bowed gracefully before ushering them inside.

"Mr. Walker?" Sean snickered as they were seated at one of the best tables.

"Yeah," Bear shifted to make himself comfortable, "guess you never knew me by my full name, did you?"

"I never knew you by your real name at all."

"Well, it happens to be Francis Allen Walker. And I'll whollop you right here and now if you laugh."

"Francis?" Sean tried his best to hide the grin that kept tugging at the corners of his mouth.

"Yeah, that's the handle my pa nailed on me. And keep in mind what I told you about laughing."

"Oh, no. I think it's a fine name. I just think 'Bear' suits you better, that's all."

"Yeah, I guess it does at that. The boys I grew up with started calling me that. I kind of liked it, and just sort of kept on calling myself Bear." The maître d' arrived, and Bear ordered steaks, pasta, salads and champagne for both of them.

"I had trouble getting them funny little things called noodles on my fork first time I tried, but I got to liking the taste, so I keep ordering 'em. They kinda remind me of my ma's dumplings, only skinnier and longer."

"Bear," Sean leaned across the table. "I want you to allow me to pay for part of this dinner. I don't think you have any idea how much this is going to cost."

"I don't, huh?" Sean shook his head. "Well, let me tell you something, Mister. I've been eating most my meals right here at this table since I got here, 'cause when I find something I like, I don't see no need in changing. In fact, I liked it so much I bought the danged place."

"You what?"

"I said, I bought the danged place. Me, Charlie and Frank made us a pile of money hauling freight over the mountain to Nevada, just like I said we was gonna. Then, I run into some folks who needed some money 'cause they was gonna dig a big hole in the ground. Well, I loaned them some money, and they gave me a bunch of paper they called stock in return. I just sort of forgot about it for awhile, and done the same thing for several other folks. Well, them first fellers I was telling you about hit a bunch of silver and started calling their hole The Comstock Mine. That's where I got the idee for renaming this place. Then, some of the others did the same. Well, because I was nice enough to loan them the money, they made me rich too. So, now that I've got more money than I can ever spend in a lifetime, I thought I'd start letting folks kind of wait on me for awhile."

Sean kept his open-mouthed stare directed at this friend while the waiter popped the cork on the champagne and filled their glasses.

"Here's to ya Doc." Bear lifted his glass. "Damn, but it's good to see you."

Sean had no idea how hungry he was until he took his first bite. He had to agree with Bear; it was the best steak in San Francisco. He stuffed himself on the steak, pasta and salad, then watched in amazement as Bear polished off a huge piece of chocolate cake. They were on the second bottle of champagne when Bear's conversation turned serious.

"Guess you know that woman's about to lose all that land, don't you?"

"What woman?"

"Mrs. Garcia. The one I took you to when you got yer brains kicked out."

"No." Sean shook his head. "I've been so busy with my practice, I've kind of lost touch with everyone. How?"

"Well, it seems a lot of folks are taking all the Mexicans who own land to court. They's claiming that since they got the land when Californy belonged to Mexico, they don't really own nothing now that we're part of these United States."

"They can't really do that, can they? What about the Treaty of Guadalupe Hidalgo?"

"What's that got to do with anything?" Bear's laughter caused the people at the next table to stare. "Hell, when's a treaty ever stopped anyone from taking some land they wanted? They've broken every treaty they had with the Injuns. Look," Bear stared at Sean over his champagne glass, "most of these Mexican folks are gonna lose everything they've got. You ought'a know that as well as I do."

"No, I had no idea that was happening." Sean rolled the empty glass back and forth in his hands aimlessly while staring at the white tablecloth.

"Well, no matter." Bear refilled both glasses. "We're both here now, and got our own businesses to attend to. Does kind of make you wonder though. What's gonna happen to all them folks? I mean, she did seem to love that ranch of hers a whole bunch, and she had all them folks she was taking care of. Those vaqueros and Injuns and their families. One can't help but wonder where they're all gonna go." Sean grew silent and morose as Bear continued.

"I thought a time or two about riding out there myself and checking up on her, but I never knowed her that well, and I got things to attend to here. I been hearing that she's been coming all the way to San Francisco to attend those court hearings of hers. I'm kind of surprised she didn't look you up on one of those trips of hers."

"Probably doesn't even know I'm here. Like I said, I haven't kept in touch."

"Well, that's too bad." Bear shook his head. "But it's probably better that way. I mean, a man can't go around worrying about everyone, now can he? Come on." He rose from the table. "I'm gonna show you a couple of other favorite places of mine."

The conversation and sights became a blur as they bounced from one nightspot to another. Sean, for the most part, sat at the table and drank while Bear laughed and danced with the ladies. It was at The Silver Slipper that Bear brought Loretta Stewart to their table. "Kinda took my eye. Tall and pretty, with yeller hair, and eyes like a cool mountain lake. She sorta reminds me of that young Mexican widder we was talking about earlier."

Sean smiled silently. His alcohol-numbed mind was miles away from the noisy San Francisco night club. He had been thinking of the clean mountain air of Rancho Manantial Escondido with its crystal clear streams. He longed to hear the soft lowing of cattle and smell the smoky campfires of the vaqueros as they held their matanza. He had tired of the tinny sound coming from the honky-tonk piano in the corner and longed to hear happy guitar music as brown-skinned maidens danced. He missed Leonida. It was well after midnight when he paid for another bottle at the bar and staggered toward the door. He had no idea where Bear had gone. The last thing he could remember was leaning against Loretta Stewart as they climbed the stairs to his hotel room.

Chapter 3

Josiah Russell struck a match against the plank siding of The Rusty Rail and lit his cigarette. There was little else to do but wait for Woodrow Black to return with the buckboard and haul Ambrose Brice to his final resting place. He had started his investigation early that next morning and had run smack into a dead end. He had the knife, a body and some blood stains on the wood floor, but little else to go on. No one claimed to have seen or heard anything.

"So, what are your plans, big guy?" He turned as Ruby pushed her way through the swinging doors. She leaned her shapely form against one of the posts and took a drag from her cigarillo, propping one foot on top of the pine box holding her former boss. "You really going to try and find out who killed him?" She grimaced with a cough.

"Reckon that's what Judge Hansen wants me to do. Tell ya the truth, I don't much care myself. I figure the world's a better place no matter who or what kilt that snake."

"Then why bother?" she shrugged.

"Because upholding the law's all I've ever done. If a man ain't got respect for the law, then he ain't got much else."

"Like Ambrose," Ruby snickered.

"Yeah. Only I kinda figure he was worser'n most. He weren't like no honest thief or rustler that you could put a finger on." Josiah paused at the sound of metal-rimmed wheels and shod hooves grinding against the rocky ground. The black buggy rolled past Carpenter's General Store at a fast trot and stopped in front of The Rusty Rail. A pregnant

Rosa Burwell climbed out of the passenger seat and scampered to the crude coffin.

"Is it really true?" She glanced up at him.

"Yessum, I'm afraid so."

"Open it up."

"Beg yer pardon?" He glanced toward Tex, Rosa's husband seated inside the buggy.

"I want to see. Open it!" She motioned impatiently.

"Crack the lid, Hanky, and give her a peek," Tex said with a tilt of his head. "You know she ain't gonna be satisfied until you do."

"Aw, hell, Tommy. She's carrying my grandbaby." Josiah scowled as he tossed his cigarette into the street.

"It's my kid too, old man. But one of us had better do it before she hurts herself." Tex climbed to the ground as Rosa started tugging against the coffin lid with her fingers.

"Oh, you dad-gum women are the hard-headest critters anyway. Cut that out." Josiah grabbed Rosa by the wrists. "Ruby? You got anything inside that we can pry this lid off with?" Ruby tossed her smoke into the street with a laugh and pushed her way back through the swinging doors. She returned with a hammer and crowbar.

"There you are, you little hell-cat." He gave the lid a final tug. "He don't look so purdy. He's been croaked most of two days now."

"He never did look pretty, Papa. Especially when he beat me." Rosa leaned to stare a long minute before spitting and calling curses down from heaven in Spanish against his soul.

"I felt the same way when I found him on the floor with the knife stuck in him." Ruby laughed as Rosa climbed back into the buggy. "Only difference is, that Texan took you the hell away, and I'm still stuck here."

"Well, be seeing you, old man." Tex gave Josiah a slap on the shoulder. "You wanna come out to the place tonight for some vittles?"

"That's what you come all the way here for? Just so she could see him in his coffin?" He pushed his hat back and scratched his head.

"Wouldn't you, if you had been one of his girls?" Tex grabbed the reins.

"Nope. I'da kilt him myself. Hey," he grabbed his son's arm, "you doing the cooking tonight, or Rosa?"

"Rosa. Why?"

"Good, I'll be there then. 'Cause I ain't ridin' ten feet to eat nothin' you whip together." He waited until they were out of sight before nailing the lid back on the coffin.

~   ~   ~

The small crowd gathered at the cemetery consisted of Josiah Russell, Ruby, Aurie Templeton, Mr. and Mrs. Black and Alice Carpenter from the general store. It was Josiah himself that gave the final prayer, but only after hearing Woodrow's remarks that it wouldn't be fitting for a Mormon to give a grave side blessing over such a pagan gentile. No one, outside Alice Carpenter, bothered to shed a tear.

"That's because we all loved the sonofabitch so much." Ruby smirked after Josiah mentioned the fact.

"I'll admit, I had my differences with the man." Alice dabbed her eyes. "I still believe him to be a totally despicable character. But it is sad to see him in that condition, knowing his soul is lost forever."

"It was lost long before whoever it was stuck him with that knife." Josiah adjusted the neckerchief that had given him his nickname.

"Well," Ruby hugged one of Josiah's arms as they walked back toward the center of town, "are you still gonna try and find out who killed him?"

"Guess I gotta. That's what Judge Hansen wants me to do."

"I was hoping you would forget the whole thing," Alice Carpenter said, giving her eyes one last dab with the handkerchief. "There's been too much sadness around here as it is."

"Well, I'll grant you that." Josiah nodded. And I'll allow that things would have been easier if he'd a gotten croaked when Mrs. Garcia brought her army of vaqueros into town and cleaned this berg up. But the law is still the law, and you can't let someone go around sticking folks with knives, no matter who they are." They stopped in front of The Rusty Rail.

"I suppose you're right, but I still wish you would forget the whole thing." Alice set her lips into a thin line and glared at him. "Now, if it isn't against the law, I'd like to take this child home to stay with me, while you settle this matter." She took Aurie Templeton, who had been one of Ambrose's girls, by the arm.

"No, that would be just fine, ma'am." Josiah tipped his hat and stared until they disappeared inside the store. "Now, don't that just beat all."

"What's that?" Ruby said.

"You would've thought she'd be the first one calling for Ambrose's killer to be caught, knowing how upright and Christian she is."

"Yeah, but maybe she's right. What's it going to matter, one way or the other?" Ruby raised her eyebrows and grinned. "Come on, I'll buy you a drink. I own this place now...I guess."

Chapter 4

James Sattler stood inside the massive study grinning as Leonida pointed out certain books and reminisced about how her husband, Rudolfo, loved to sit in his favorite leather chair for hours and read.

"He must have been a great man."

"He was, Señor," she slid the book of poetry back on the shelf, "and I loved him very much."

"I'm sure you did. No one blames you for what happened in that mining camp a year ago. Judge Baines would have certainly been hung if the whole thing had been tried in a court of law."

"Yes, that is what I keep telling myself." Her hand trembled as she moved one of the papers on her desk.

"But that happens to be one of the things that concerns me. I hate to say it, ma'am, but they are not going to look too favorably on your case when it finally comes to a hearing."

"What you are saying, Señor Sattler, is that we're going to lose all our land anyway, even though I have given you proof that my husband owned it?"

"No, I'm not saying that at all. I'm just saying that...well, the court might not look too favorably on you as a person. You were the one who ordered the hanging of Judge Baines, if I'm not mistaken."

"You're not mistaken. But I suppose that your court in San Francisco would look favorably on the murderers who killed my husband and his brother and a half a dozen other people, including our priest."

"Yes, well...I did say that you had every right to do what you did, under the circumstances."

"Yes, you did." She folded her hands on top of the desk to study him. "But you didn't come all the way from San Francisco to discuss my guilt or innocence regarding Judge Baines. What is it you need?"

"Actually, that is one of the reasons I came." He took a chair opposite her and leaned against the desk to match her stare. "I have heard, from a reliable source, that the court is taking a stern look at what happened in Dogtown. So I'd like to build a good, reasonable case to present to them. If we don't, I'm afraid it's going to be difficult to talk them into ruling in your favor."

"I have already given you all the facts concerning what happened in writing. Names, dates," she shrugged, "I even gave you a copy of the letter I sent ahead to warn the citizens of my intentions."

"Yes, and that's all well and good, but it's going to take more than that. It's going to take witnesses who were actually there when it all happened. People who knew what Henry Baines and Pod Randell were doing that caused you to take the action you did. It might even take you getting on the witness stand yourself."

"I see no problem in that, Señor. I can produce as many of my vaqueros as witnesses as you wish. I'm also sure Señors Russell and Tex will do the same."

"What about that doctor friend of yours? Will he testify on your behalf?"

"Señor Kilkenney?"

"Yes, the one you said lived here at the rancho during that time."

"I don't know. I haven't seen or heard from him in almost a year." She turned in her chair to stare at the window.

"It would be nice if you could talk him into it. The word of a medical doctor might go a long way in convincing the court. Do you have any idea where he might be located?"

"I don't know if he would be a good witness, Señor." She shook her head. "The reason he left Rancho Manantial

Escondido was because he did not like the hanging of Judge Henry Baines. He thought I should have...I don't know," she gestured in the air, "locked the man in jail. The last I heard, Señor Kilkenney was headed toward your San Francisco to set up a practice."

"That's too bad." James Sattler frowned. "He would have been a good witness. I'll see if I can locate him and talk him into cooperating. In the meantime, this is going to take a lot of work. I will actually have to write a book on the matter, and have several copies printed. And I'm afraid it's going to be quite expensive."

"How expensive are we speaking of? I've already given you a large sum of money."

"Yes, but that was used in filing the petitions and writing reports."

"How expensive are we discussing here, now?" She tapped the desk.

"Oh, I'd say around ten thousand dollars."

"There is no way I can possibly give you that kind of money right this moment." She shook her head violently and got to her feet.

"I thought that might be the case, Mrs. Garcia." He pulled a stack of papers from his briefcase. "A lot of landowners are in the same situation. What they have chosen to do is, use their land as collateral. I've taken the liberty of drawing up the papers giving me power of attorney in order to make a loan, large or small...whatever you choose, against your land." Leonida stared at him a long minute.

"Very convenient of you, Señor, but that is not a decision I'd wish to make at this moment."

"I don't see what other option you have. Think of this as another battle to keep your ranch. It's like the one in Dogtown, only this time you're going to use money instead of bullets."

"I don't I care for your choice of words, Señor." She almost hissed the words. "What happened in Dogtown is something I would like to forget."

"Yes, it was a poor analogy. Please accept my apology." She gave a curt nod, and he continued. "We are going to have to trust each other if we're going to win this battle, and one of the things you are going to have to trust me on is this." He tapped the papers.

"I think I am trusting you, Señor. I'm trusting you with the future of our rancho...all 50,000 acres, everything I have, including the lives of the people living and working here. Yes," she nodded, "I would call that trust. I've given you all that responsibility, plus every cent of money my husband had saved. Now, I'm asking you to trust me a few days longer to get your ten thousand dollars in my own way."

"Alright, Mrs. Garcia. I get your point." He stuffed the papers back into the briefcase. "When do you think you can scrape the money together?"

"I have no idea. Perhaps a week or two."

"That should pose no problem. I'll try to schedule the initial court hearing around that time. Do you think you could meet me at my office in San Francisco around, say," he glanced at a pocket calendar, "May 3rd?"

"Sí, I will do my best."

"Well, try very hard. These things take time, and I have other cases I'm working on besides yours."

Leonida saw John Sattler to the door and watched until his buggy had disappeared beyond the gate and down the road toward the river.

"I do not like that man." Maria glared as she vigorously dried the coffee cup in her hand.

"Neither do I. I find him arrogant and offensive. But he is supposed to be one of the best solicitors in San Francisco." Leonida sat at the table and covered her face with her hands.

"What am I going to do, Maria? I'm afraid we're going to lose this rancho. He says more money is needed to handle our case, and I don't have any. I'll have to sell some of the land. I don't see any way out of this."

"Mi niña," Maria wrapped the Doña in her arms and caressed her golden head, "it will be okay. I asked the Holy Virgin when I was praying this morning to take care of you and give you wisdom. And I asked for her son to send some one to help us like the last time when we had troubles."

"Oh, Maria," she hugged the maid, "you are so good to me. You're just like my mother."

"Sí, Doña, you are my niña, and it will be okay. You'll see. I will get everyone on the rancho to pray for you."

~   ~   ~

"Well, good morning, sleepy-head." Sean had to shade his eyes against the sunlight peeking through the half-drawn curtains before he could focus on her face. She was sitting in his swivel chair at the desk with a cup in her hands, smiling. Every inch of her was beautiful, from the blond hair cascading across her shoulders to the shapely limbs peeking through the split in the bathrobe she was wearing. It was his robe.

"Ohhh," he grabbed his head as he tried to move, "what time is it?"

"Almost ten o'clock."

"Ten o'clock?" He jerked up, only to fall back to the pillow as the inside of his head exploded. "Dear mother of Christ! I'm dying."

"Got a good one, huh?" She filled another cup with coffee from a silver pot on the tray sitting on top of his desk. "Take anything in your coffee? Milk or sugar?"

"No, just black. I've got to get to my office." His stomach churned as he tried to move, causing beads of sweat to break out on his head.

"Not in that condition, you're not. You'd be a whole lot worse than your patients, if you did." She sat on the edge of the bed and held the cup for him. "Here, take a sip of this. Careful now, it's hot."

"Thanks." He lay back to study her. "I'm sorry, but who are you, and what are you doing here in my robe?"

"Now, I really am offended." Her laughter lilted like soft bells as she set the cup on the night stand. Her bare feet moved silently as she retrieved a cool washcloth from a ceramic washbasin on the dresser.

"My name is Loretta Stewart, and I'm here, in your robe, because you brought me here last night."

"I did?"

"Yes, you did." She lay the washcloth across his eyes and brushed his hair back with her palm. "Just relax and let me take care of you. You know, Dr. Kilkenney, most men would remember bringing me to their room and what we did, even if they couldn't remember my name."

"I didn't take advantage of you, did I? Where did you sleep?" He jerked the cloth away to stare.

"No," she giggled and patted his chest. "I slept right here in your bed, and you were the perfect gentleman...for someone who was drunk out of his mind. But, to ease your conscience, I usually get paid for being compromised. But you didn't." She gave a huge sigh. "You just talked my ear off. Now, finish your coffee. I'll get you some toast." She removed the lid on a large serving tray and began filling a plate with scrambled eggs, bacon and toast.

"I hope you don't mind, but I happened to catch the bellboy on my way to the ladies room and took the liberty of ordering breakfast. I paid for it with some money out of your billfold. The rest is all there. You can check, if you want." She handed him the plate.

"No, I believe you. I would have bought you breakfast anyway. What did we talk about?"

"You talked, and I listened. Mostly about some ranch you used to live on, and the bad guys who were trying to steal it away from the owners. You told me all about the people who live there and how happy they were, even though they were starving because all they had was burnt cows to eat." Sean almost choked on a mouthful of egg laughing.

"I said that?"

"Oh, yes. But mostly, you told me all about the lovely widow who owns the place. Is she really that pretty, Doctor?"

"Um-hum." He nodded.

"Then why did you leave her?"

"I have no idea." He let the fork fall to the plate with a clank as he stared into her eyes. They were crystal like Leonida's, only blue and darker.

"It was the look she had when she ordered the vaqueros to hang Judge Baines. Every time I saw her, that picture would flash to my mind. I couldn't shake it."

"I don't know how much of what you told me last night was true, but if they killed her husband and all those people, you can't blame her. It's a wonder the poor woman didn't go insane." Loretta held a piece of bacon with her fingers for him as if she were feeding a child.

"I know you're right, and the crazy thing is, I can't get her out of my mind. All the good about her. Her laugh, the way she looked, her smell as she entered a room. I can still feel her body against me on those few occasions I was able to hold her. Maybe I'm the one who's insane."

"No, I'd say the Doctor's in love." She dabbed his lips with a napkin and gave him a little kiss, then carried the plate back to the desk. "Why don't you go back to her? That would be the smart thing. You know that, don't you?"

"Yes, and believe me, I've thought about it...a lot. But it just wouldn't be the same. I've been gone a long time."

"Well, we'll never know until we've tried. Will we?" She cocked her head to one side with her hands on her hips.

"We?"

"Yes, I'd like to go with you and see if that place is really as pretty as you described. It can't be any worse than that smoky old dance hall with its smelly men. Can it?"

"No." He shook his head slowly. "But..."

"Good." She tossed him his pants and shirt. "Get dressed. We've got a lot of things to do."

"Ah, Miss Stewart?"

"Oh, okay." She turned to face the door. "But hurry. I've still got to get my things, and we've got to go by your office."

"That's what I was going to say," Sean said as he pulled his trousers on. "I have a medical practice with responsibilities. I just can't pick up and leave, no matter how good it might sound to you."

"No?" She helped button his shirt. "And why not? There are plenty of other doctors who can look after the ailing people in San Francisco, but there is only one real love for Sean Kilkenney."

"And what's in it for you?" He cupped her hands in his and studied her face. "Why are you so set on giving up everything to go with me?"

"You are sweet." She laughed and stood on her tiptoes to give him another kiss. "Just call me a romantic, but I really don't have anything to give up, except the dance hall. And," she paused to give him a crooked grin, "believe me, I've got my reasons. Now, it's your turn to turn your back while I get dressed."

Chapter 5

Josiah Russell drummed his fingers on the table and stared at the two girls sitting opposite him. He had taken care in positioning the chairs so the dark blood stain on the floorboards could be seen. The butcher knife that had killed Ambrose Brice lay in the middle of the table between them.

"The bar's closed," he said as the swinging doors creaked open.

"I was just wantin' one drink," said the roughly clad miner.

"And I said the place is closed. You deaf?" he yelled.

"Okay, don't get so het up." The miner shuffled back through the door.

"Oh hell, Hanky." Ruby raked her chair against the floor. "Quit acting like a damn lawman for a minute and let the man have a drink." She leaned across the bar to retrieve a bottle and glass.

"Well, for your information young lady, I AM a lawman, duly appointed by Judge Lloyd Hansen of Columbia."

"Well, la-te-da." She wagged her head and pushed one of the doors open. "Here." She handed the miner the full shot glass. "It's on the house. Just leave the glass when you leave."

"Thanks. You're a real lady, Ruby."

"Yeah, well tell that to mister lawman here." She swung her hips as she crossed the room and took her seat at the table.

"Now, can we continue our investigation?" Josiah growled.

"I don't know what difference it makes. You've been sitting here for most of an hour and haven't said a dozen words. What are you investigating? The color of mine or Aurie's hair? Think that knife's gonna jump up and tell you who stabbed Ambrose?"

"It just might. What I've been doing is cogitating the situation here, and the way I see it, Aurie here is the one with the most reason to kill Ambrose Brice."

"No!" The young girl shook her head violently and started from her chair.

"You're crazy." Ruby clamped a hand on Aurie's wrist. "Nearly everyone within a hundred miles had one reason or another to cut his heart out. Now, what makes you so sure Aurie did it?"

"Because of the way he was treating her. Buying her from those folks like she was some sort of slave. Then, you yourself told me how he was beatin' and taking advantage of her in that back room. Now, if that ain't reason enough to kill the man, I'll eat my hat."

"Yeah? Well then every girl that ever worked here had reason enough to kill him, including Rosa and myself, because he used to treat us all that way. It was his way of teaching us the proper way to treat a man. Huh." She struck a match against the table and lit her cigarillo. "As if that's something hard to figure out." She took a drag and coughed violently.

"That might be true, but Aurie's the one he was treating that way when he got kilt. So I say she had the best reason to do it."

"And you're full of horseshit, because I know she didn't." Josiah grinned as her face flushed.

"Now, how do you know that, young lady? You've been telling me you was asleep the entire time, and didn't know anything until you found his stiff body lying there next morning." He motioned toward the stain. "If what you're saying is true, you couldn't possibly know that Aurie didn't kill Ambrose."

"Well, she didn't." Ruby took an angry puff and blew a cloud of smoke in the air.

"And how do you know that?"

"Because...because I did."

"No!" Aurie knocked the chair over as she jumped to her feet.

"Shut up, Aurie! I'm the one telling this story. I killed Ambrose Brice with that butcher knife."

"Why? What was your reason?" Josiah crossed his legs and leaned back in his chair.

"So I could have The Rusty Rail. He owed it to me. I've been working here a long time, and he owed me money."

"He owed everyone money, including Alice Carpenter at the store. But that don't mean she kilt him." The two girls glanced at each other as Josiah continued.

"You know what you're saying, Ruby. You're confessing to killing a man."

"Yeah, so? He needed killing."

"That might be true. But Judge Hansen says this case needs to come to trial. They're trying real hard to bring some law and order to California, now that she's become a state. You confessing that you stuck Ambrose in the gizzard with that knife means they are going to try you for murder, unless you can prove otherwise. Know what they do to folks that kill someone? They hang 'em. You want that, Ruby? To get hung? Ever see someone get hung?"

"Yeah, I saw Henry Baines get his just desserts over at the livery." Her skin turned pasty white as she leaned over to wipe some dust off her slipper with her hand. "But it doesn't matter much, does it?"

"And what makes you say that?"

"Because I'm just a whore who's dying anyway." Ruby clutched her chest as she coughed. "Damn, that hurts. Better hurry and start you trial, Big Guy, or, I might not be around for you to hang."

"Aw, hell, Ruby," Josiah shifted in his chair, "you're lying through your teeth. We both know you didn't kill Ambrose. Now, come on, tell me the truth. If Aurie here didn't kill him, who did?"

"I already told you, I did."

"You're lying, 'cause it ain't your style. You might've beat the hell outta him to see him suffer a little bit. But you would've never kilt him right off like that."

"I was angry, 'cause he was trying to replace me with Aurie."

"Likely story. My boy Tex tells better yarns than that." Josiah grinned as he licked the paper on the cigarette he'd been rolling.

"You can't prove I didn't kill him."

"Okay, Ruby, have it your way." He lit his smoke and got up from the table. "I'll send for Lloyd Hansen and we'll get this whing-ding underway, but if you wind up getting hung for something you didn't do, you can't say it was my fault." He grabbed the butcher knife from the table and used it to point at Aurie.

"And you, young lady. If you know the truth, you'd better speak up before your friend here gets herself hung. It wouldn't set too well with The Maker if you let someone else die for something you'd done yourself." He pushed his way through the swinging doors and stood on the edge of the sidewalk smoking his cigarette. He tossed the butt into the dusty street as Tex came out of the general store with a roll of chicken wire slung over his shoulder. He could hear the girls arguing in hushed tones as he strode toward the buckboard parked in front of the store.

"How'd it go in there?" Tex dropped the wire into the bed and glanced up at him. "Learn anything new?"

"Naw." Josiah shook his head. "Ruby's claiming she done it, but she's trying to cover up for someone else."

"Maybe she did croak him."

"Yeah, like them beeves of your'n drop gold patties."

"Well, I wouldn't write her off too quickly, Hanky. You can't never tell what a woman critter's gonna do. You told me that yourself. Remember?"

"Na-uh." He frowned and leaned against the wagon wheel. "I still think that young girl Aurie done it, but I can't prove it."

"So, what are you gonna do now?"

"Send for Lloyd Hansen and get the show started. Then get them girls out at the ranch to praying real hard so's the truth will come out at the trial. It goes agin' my grain to do it this way, but I ain't got much choice."

"Anything I can do to help?" Tex pulled a couple of cigars out of his shirt pocket and handed one to his father.

"Yeah." Josiah nodded. "You can keep your eyes and ears open, and let me know if anything pops up. And send Paco into town to keep an eye on them two girls in there." He nodded toward the saloon. "I reckon I'm supposed to lock 'em up until this thing goes to trial, but that kinda goes again' my grain too. Besides, neither of 'em has any place to go, and that vaquero's slicker'n any snake I've ever seen. Maybe he'll be able to worm something outta them females I wasn't able to." He paused to light the cigar. "I'd shore hate to hang Ruby for something she didn't do."

~   ~   ~

"Yes ma'am. I sunk my shovel right there and out it come." The egg-sized nugget in Vernon Blackstone's hand caused a tingling sensation to sweep across Leonida's spine. Paco had dashed into the kitchen where she was having tea with her father and almost drug her physically through the door, yelling about their discovery. It was almost one week to the day since her conversation with Maria about the financial difficulties of the rancho. The maid had indeed gathered the women for prayer inside the tiny chapel daily, asking for a miracle from God, and now, she was witnessing it with her own eyes. "Here. Take it." He dropped it in her

40

palms. "It's rightfully yours. The land you sold us is on the other side of the river."

"Why were you digging on our side of the river?" Jose stared over Leonida's shoulder.

"Like I was telling your daughter, Paco thought it might be good to grow some extra hay for the horses come winter. So we was gonna dig a ditch and build a bucket lift to pull water right out of the Mokelumne to irrigate with. I've seen it done in other places. But as you can see, I didn't get very far before I started coming up with these."

"You mean there are more?" Leonida's eyes grew large as she stared at the huge man.

"Oh, hell yes. Begging your pardon ma'am." He ran to retrieve a small box from under a tree. "See, I come up with four or five more small ones. And Paco did a little panning with some of the dirt and come up with a lot of color. You're standing on a gold mine, ma'am. And it's all yours."

"No, it belongs to everyone. Maria has had everyone praying that we might find the means to pay our legal bills in order to keep this land. The gold belongs to everyone including you, Señor Blackstone. Your family shall share equally with the rest of us."

"Do we have anyone who knows how to mine the gold?" Jose took another look at the nugget.

"Sí, Armando and Arturo Ortega have both worked for Señor Black at the Three Mile Mine," Paco said. "They can teach us."

"And I've done a little prospecting myself, ma'am. I can teach 'em what I know," Vernon grinned.

"Bien." Leonida nodded. "We shall take from the ground what Dios has provided. But it shall be divided equally, with ten percent going to Rancho Manantial Escondido. Paco and Señor Blackstone shall be in charge. I will inform Father Ramon of our discovery, and we shall have Mass tomorrow morning right where we are standing to thank Dios for his kindness and mercy."

"Begging yer pardon, ma'am, but there's one important thing y'all's forgetting." Tex plucked a blade of tall grass and propped it between his teeth.

"And what might that be?"

"Just that y'all better keep this good and quiet. We've already had the dickens keeping nesters off yer land, and you know what come down after them Mormons found gold in Dogtown. You'll have to hire the whole Yankee army if the word gets out."

"Señor Tex is right. This is just between us, bien?" Jose studied each face.

"Sí." Leonida smiled as she rolled the nugget back and forth in the sunlight. "Between us and Dios."

~   ~   ~

"What was that all about?" Emery Hawkins nodded toward the black horse with its female rider leaving town. She was flanked by several heavily-armed vaqueros.

"That was Mrs. Garcia. She owns that big cattle ranch bordering the Mokelumne River." Albert Miller closed and locked the door to the Dogtown Assay Office.

"Yeah, I know who she is. I've seen her before. I was just wondering what she'd be doing inside your office. She ain't having you tell her how much her cattle are worth, is she?"

"No." Albert chuckled. "Seems some of the men working on her property found a little color. Actually," he shrugged, "from the looks of what she brought in today, it might be quite a bit of color. It seems that some people have all the luck."

"Yeah, seems that way." Emery struck a match and lit his smoke.

"Well, maybe I'll get lucky and my wife will have cooked something edible tonight. See you later."

"Sure, see you 'round, Al." Emery waited until Albert Miller was out of sight before tossing his cigarette into the street and heading the opposite way toward Costello's Lucky Ace. It wasn't his favorite saloon and gambling hall, but it was the only one left since the closing of The Rusty Rail.

"Yeah, some people have all the luck." He gave the door a shove and pushed his way up to the bar.

Chapter 6

"I have the money you requested, Señor Sattler." Leonida pulled a large envelope from her handbag.

"Thank you, Mrs. Garcia." He snatched the envelope from her hand and opened it. "I just knew you wouldn't let me down. I know it's a sad state of affairs," he paused in the middle of thumbing through the stack of bills, "but money is, as they say, what makes our modern world go around."

"Sí." Leonida allowed her eyes to drift around the room. The cramped third floor office was nothing more than a studio with a small wood-burning stove, a sink and a bathroom. There were stacks of papers on the two spare chairs as well as the floor and desk. The sweaty man counting the money left her and Juan to stand instead of removing the papers and offering them a chair. "It is indeed sad when pieces of paper become more important than people," she said as she ran her fingers across some of the books stacked inside a bookcase.

"Well, it seems to be all here." He scribbled a receipt and ripped it from the book. "I'll get started filing your petitions immediately."

"And when might that be, Señor? I would like to be there when the papers are filed, but I can only spend a few days in San Francisco. I must get back to my rancho and attend to affairs."

"Mmmm, that might pose a problem." He frowned and squinted at his calendar. "The earliest date I could get with Judge Samuel Baker is two weeks away, on May the 15th. Were you able to talk to Josiah Russell and his son Tex?

Now, what's his real name?" He tapped the desk. "Tommy? That's it, Tommy Burwell."

"Sí." Leonida nodded.

"And what about that doctor friend of yours? Have you contacted him yet?"

"No, you were going to do that. He lives here in San Francisco. Remember?"

"Oh, yes. I'm sorry." He scribbled something on a piece of paper. "I'll get on that right away. I'll see if I can't get him to meet with us when we go to court on the 15th."

"I can't wait that long." Leonida's blond hair bounced as she shook her head. "Can't we see the judge sooner, while I'm in town?"

"I'll see what we can do, but I'm afraid his calendar is full. The courts are having to decide the fate of five hundred and twenty cases like yours, involving some two and a half million acres." Sattler rested his elbows on the crowded desk and tapped the fingers of both hands together.

"Sí, and I realize that is a huge problem, but I'm not really concerned with the whole two million acres, Señor. I'm only concerned with our case, and what is going to happen to the people living on our rancho."

"Yes," he nodded, "I can appreciate your concern. I'll see what I can do. Now, if you'll excuse me," he glanced at his pocket watch, "I just might be able to catch Judge Baker at the noon dinner break. I'll have to hurry though." He stuffed the envelope containing the money into his coat and ushered them toward the door. Leonida paused as he held the door open.

"When might we be able to find out if we can see him while we are in San Francisco?"

"Check back with me this afternoon. Say, around three o'clock. I should know by then. Now," he made a sweeping motion with his arm, "if I don't hurry, I'll never be able to catch him today."

"Bien." She agreed. "I'll be here at three."

"Perdon a me, Doña, but I do not like that man." Juan Gonzalez shook his head as they descended the stairs.

"Neither do I, Juan. But I don't see that we have any choice. The others were too busy to represent us, and he did come recommended as a hard man to beat inside the courtroom."

The cool air felt good on her face as they stepped into the busy San Francisco street. Her very presence turned heads and brought several hoots and whistles from the hardened miners and merchants as they wove their way down Market Street to where they were to meet the others. She was certain it was only the sight of the heavily armed vaquero at her side that kept some of the men from accosting her. Her heart sank when they reached the corner of Lombard and Gough and stood staring at the busy street.

"Where are they, Juan? They were supposed to meet us here."

"Hay, over there, Señora." He pointed toward Angela and Pablo leading a large bearded man across the street.

"Mrs. Garcia." Jonathan McDougal clasped her by the shoulders and grinned. "By heavens, it's good to see you again."

"We found him in there." Angela pointed toward a building across the street with a huge canvas sign draped across the front.

"Yes, can you believe it?" McDougal shook his head. "They have the head of Joaquin Murrieta and Three-Fingered Jack's hand pickled in brandy. They're charging folks a dollar to see them."

"Madre de Dios." Leonida crossed her breast as she glanced toward the building.

"It is not Joaquin." Pablo sneered and shook his head. "I see him well at the rancho and that is not him. Juan would know."

"Que?" Leonida said.

"That's what he's been saying, Mrs. Garcia, and he caused such a ruckus, they ran us out of the exhibit." McDougal laughed and clapped Pablo on the back.

"Que terrible, it's a sinful waste of money to pay to see such a thing." She glanced at the building once more and shuddered. "But it is so good to see you, Capitán McDougal." She took him by the hands and kissed his cheek. The action brought whistles from the onlookers.

"Hey, you filthy barnacles, get out of here and leave us alone," McDougal yelled, as he waved his arm. The men laughed and moved on down the street.

"Come on." He took Leonida and Angela by the arms. "Let's get off the street and find some privacy. I know of a little place right down this way that has a pretty good galley."

~   ~   ~

Darrell was seated in the back of the courtroom when James Sattler stood before Judge Samuel Baker at one-thirty that afternoon.

"I'm sorry, your Honor, but I've just met with Mrs. Garcia, and my client has requested another postponement of her case. It seems she's having difficulty collecting all the documentation I've requested."

"This is the fourth time you've requested such a postponement, Counselor. Did you explain to her that we are very busy, and postponements such as this are not only time-consuming, but costly?"

"Yes, your Honor, she's very aware of that. But, and I hope I don't give the court the wrong impression of my client, as you well know, most of these people can't read or write. It seems that over a period of time, the thought of keeping such papers as legal documents in a safe place was not really a concern."

"Then, perhaps you should see to it they have some help in locating the items you need." Judge Baker stared over the rims of his glasses.

"I have, your Honor. In fact, I've personally been to her ranch twice."

"All right, Counselor, your postponement is granted. I'll notify you of another date when we reschedule our calendar." Judge Baker banged his gavel. "Next case."

Darrell Rodeen raised his eyebrows as he got up from his chair. The Doña Leonida Garcia he knew was not the same one he had just heard described inside the courtroom. As an amateur lawyer he had spent hours on end listening to legal minds argue their cases in front of judges and jurors. But as a full-time sailor aboard the North Star, under the command of Captain McDougal, he had become acquainted with Mrs. Garcia. The woman he knew was educated and in control of everything happening on her ranch, to the smallest detail. He smiled and held the door for a well dressed lady before leaving the building.

Darrell had been privileged to spend several days at the Garcia ranch during Juan and Angela's wedding fiesta. That was when those men hired by Pod Randell had broken into the Doña's bedroom and tried to kill her. She screamed like a woman all right, but instead of running, she fought them both off until help could arrive. That had been another battle over her land, and, like the others, she won that battle without backing an inch. No, he shook his head. Someone was passing that judge inside the courtroom a barrel of rotten cod. He found a table in a small pub three blocks from the courthouse and ordered a bottle of rum. This was going to take some contemplating.

~   ~   ~

"I'm sorry, Mrs. Garcia. I was able to catch Judge Baker as he was returning from his dinner break, and his calendar is filled. In fact, he was wanting to postpone our May hearing until July."

"What? That's impossible." Leonida shook her head before leaning across the desk to glare. "Señor Sattler, I have given you good money to represent me and my people, and our coming to San Francisco is a huge imposition. Now, I wish for you to explain all this to the judge and settle our case in a timely manner."

"Believe me, I have, and it isn't a matter of money, Mrs. Garcia, it's a matter of case-load. We're all doing the best we can, and we will settle your claim as fast as we can."

~   ~   ~

Jonathan McDougal talked Leonida into spending an extra day in San Francisco in order that he might take them sight-seeing. Pablo grumbled during the half-hour Omnibus ride from Portsmouth Plaza to the Mission San Francisco de Asis, that the fee of twenty-five cents per person was simply too much.

"That is an awful lot of money just to get packed inside a crowded stagecoach and drug over a rough plank road."

"Ah, yes," McDougal nodded, "but think of the atmosphere, my young man. Where else in the world can you experience something like this? No where but San Francisco."

"Sí, but at least on Rancho Manantial Escondido you can have your own horse and not have to breathe the smoke and dirt from these factories."

After visiting the mission, McDougal hired an open carriage to tour the rest of the city. They were on Lombard Street between Gough and Laguna when the carriage came to a stop to allow several Chinese women carrying loads of laundry to cross.

"This is known as Washerwoman's Lagoon," McDougal said. "Nearly all of the buildings on this block are some sort of laundry."

"There must be a lot of dirty clothes in San Francisco." Leonida grinned.

"Well, let's just say that most of these miners and businessmen think they're too busy to wash their own clothes. They pay these folks up to eight dollars for a dozen shirts."

"Que? I wash Juan's for nothing." Angela turned to glare at her husband.

"Sí, but you are my wife. That is what wives are supposed to do."

"Ah!" Angela swatted his arm.

"Anyway," McDougal laughed, "it's gotten so expensive, that some people are now sending their laundry aboard ship all the way to China. They might have to wait for several months for their clothes to return, but they say it's actually cheaper that way."

"Caramba." Juan shook his head. "Maybe we should start washing their clothes at the rancho. Eight dollars is a lot of money for a few shirts."

"Ha, I could see you washing clothes, Juan Gonzalez." Angela laughed. "That would be difficult to do from the back of your horse."

Leonida shook her head as the carriage started forward. "I'm afraid I would have to do my own laundry before I would pay eight dollars for twelve blouses."

"Sí," Angela nodded, "these people must have an awful lot of money."

"They only think they do, my dear." Jonathan chuckled.

"It isn't the money that bothers me. It's the sinful waste of it." Leonida craned her neck as they passed several saloons and gambling halls. "To pay that much for laundry or spend it in places like those...? I wonder what Dios must think?"

"I try not to think of things like that." Jonathan grinned.

They turned down Washington toward the bay. Both Washington and Clay streets were lined by flimsy shacks, canvas tents and mud huts. Angela covered her nose as the carriage wheels ground through the garbage-littered street.

"I'm afraid we won't be stopping to look around until we reach the dock. These people here are fairly destitute and have little to lose. Even with the efforts of the Vigilance Committee, you'll still find a lot of crime here." The carriage came to a halt on the long dock and its passengers got out.

"See? There she is." Jonathan pointed toward a ship anchored in the bay. "That's the North Star."

"Oh, it's beautiful." Leonida shaded her eyes against the glare off the water.

"Aye. Finest cargo ship on any water. I'd be proud to take you and some of your folks aboard one of these days. Maybe we could spend a few days and sail up the coast toward Oregon."

"Oh, I'd love to. Perhaps when this argument over our property has ended."

She took his arm as they wove their way along the crowded piers, stopping frequently to browse at the fish and produce stands. They had coffee and sandwiches at the Tadich Grill, a small canvas-covered stand. The owner, a Croatian immigrant, had fun teasing and bantering with Juan and Angela in his broken English.

"Yes, San Francisco, like any other large city, has her problems," Jonathan said as they climbed back into the carriage. "I don't believe that anyone actually knows the exact population, but I'd say a conservative figure would be around 120,000 and still growing. She's been burnt by six fires since 1849, but she's bounced back every time. Her population is more diverse than you'll find anywhere in the world. Her people consist of Indians, Mexicans, a whole city of Chinese, French, Italians and plenty of Germans, not counting the Russians and whoever else you might find. Yes, you'll have a hard time finding another place like San Francisco, and because of it, she has her problems. As you well know, it costs a small fortune to live here. A one-room shack costs eight-hundred dollars a month rent, and you'll pay approximately 300,000 to buy a decent place to live. Many of the streets aren't safe to walk down, and the iron foundries and lumber mills have turned the tide waters black with tar. But," he paused to smile, "that's what makes her what she is."

They were about to enter the Poulet Or, San Francisco's first French restaurant, when Leonida paused to stare at the strange little man strolling down the crowded street with two dogs. He was a bedraggled character dressed in a uniform complete with epaulets, but it was not his poor dress that caught her eye. His hat sat cocked to one side of his head, and he carried himself with an air of royalty, instead of shuffling like a beggar.

"That's Joshua Norton." Jonathan leaned close to her ear. "He's an English Jew who immigrated to San Francisco a few years back and assembled quite an amount of wealth speculating in the rice market. But for one reason or the other, he lost everything when the market bottomed out. Now, as you can see, the poor fellow seemed to go insane. He's proclaimed himself, Norton The First, Emperor of North America and Protector of Mexico."

"Really? How does he survive?" Leonida glanced at Jonathan and back again.

"Oh, he just signs chits for his meals and lodging," Jonathan chuckled. "The merchants seem to allow it. No one seems to... Leonida, wait!" he yelled as she scampered through the crowd after the strange man.

"Your Majesty," she bowed, "may I present myself. I am Doña Leonida Garcia." Joshua Norton stared for a long minute before glancing around at the laughing men and women gathered on the busy sidewalk.

"Are you addressing me, young lady?"

"Sí. You are Norton The First, Emperor of North America, aren't you?"

"And Protector of Mexico," he added with a nod.

"Sí, please forgive me for forgetting that part." She lowered her eyes. "I would like to introduce my friends." She motioned with her arm. "This is Juan Gonzalez and his wife Angela. Pablo Rodriguez," she paused as the men nodded, "and Jonathan McDougal, Captain of the North Star."

"Pleased to meet you." Joshua nodded to each one. "And what may I do for you and your friends, Miss....ah, what did you say your name was?"

"Garcia, Doña Leonida Garcia."

"Yes, Garcia. Now, what is your wish, Mrs. Garcia?"

"I was wondering," she turned away with a blush, "this is silly of me, Your Majesty, but this is my last evening in San Francisco, and I would like you to join us for dinner."

"Leonida." Jonathan gave her a strained grin as he motioned toward the restaurant with his head.

"Oh, perdon a me, Your Majesty, I'm sorry. You're probably not dressed for dinner. Let me see." She quickly glanced around. "Ah, yes. Come with me." She took the man by the arm. "Angela, could you and Juan watch his dogs while the Emperor and I visit the men's clothing store across the street?"

"Sí, but..."

"Take special care of these animals. I consider them part of the royal family, you know." He handed Angela both leashes. "This one is Bummer, and the brown and white one is Lazarus."

It only took a matter of minutes for Leonida and the owner of the clothing store to fit Joshua Norton with a new blue jacket, trousers, shiny black shoes and a top hat. His dislike with the jacket was quickly settled with the promise that if he returned the following morning, the tailor would fit the coat with matching epaulets. The transaction was complete with payment by Leonida and a promise from the owner to keep all of Joshua's old clothing stored in a bag for him to retrieve when he returned.

"Nice, very nice." Jonathan nodded his satisfaction as they rejoined the others in front of the restaurant. "I already have a table waiting inside."

~   ~   ~

"Doña Leonida?" Angela's soft voice followed the tapping on the door.

"Sí, come in. I'm not asleep." The young woman slipped inside the suite at the Union Hotel and pattered across the carpeted floor in her bare feet to sit on the edge of Leonida's bed.

"What is that you're reading?" she said as Leonida marked her place with a piece of ribbon.

"The House of The Seven Gables." She laid the book in her lap. "It is a scary mystery, but you did not leave your husband and come to my room in your nightgown to find out what new book I'm reading, did you chica? What's on your mind?"

"Why did you do those things for that man this afternoon?"

"Mr. Norton?"

"Sí. You spent a lot of money on a crazy man. I couldn't sleep and kept wondering."

"The money no es importante, chica. I find that with the money I give to people who are in need, Dios seems to return it with more than I need. As to why that man, I felt that it is something Jesus Cristo would have wanted. It did not take much of our time to show to someone a little kindness who had lost everything and become an object of ridicule.

"You know, chica," she rubbed Angela's cheek with her palm, "with the way things are going in the courts, we stand a good chance of losing everything we have. Perhaps I shall be in a situation like Señor Norton some day. I would certainly want someone to show me kindness if that happened."

~   ~   ~

Leonida stood frozen to the upper deck of the paddle boat as it pulled away from the port of Stockton. She had only caught a glimpse of the man helping a woman across the busy street, but it was enough to cause her heart to skip a beat.

"What is it?" Angela slipped her arm around Leonida's waist.

"Nothing, nothing at all. I just thought I saw Doctor Kilkenney crossing the street, but that was silly. The last we heard, he had become what he always wanted, a highly successful doctor in San Francisco." She gave Angela a crooked smile.

"Where is he? The man you saw?" Angela scanned the crowd.

"Oh, he has long disappeared into one of those buildings. Along with the woman hanging onto his arm." She stared toward the dock fading in the distance.

"Woman? Señor Kilkenney had a woman with him?"

"First of all, my little niña," she tweaked Angela's nose, "I'm not sure it was our doctor friend. I only said it looked like him, and why would it surprise you to know he had another female friend besides us? It wouldn't surprise me at all to find that he had met and married someone. He is a very attractive man."

"I was just thinking of you. I know how much you loved him."

"Gracias, but that is all in the past; is it not? Now come, my little worry-angel." She pulled Angela away from the railing. "We must figure out what to wear. You will find that Grayson is nothing like San Francisco or even Stockton. It is more like Dogtown, only ten or twenty times larger."

"Caramba." The girl glanced at her. "Then why do we go there?"

"Because, my dear one, your husband says it is easier to get to Rancho Manantial Escondido by taking the river boat to Grayson. From there, he claims the roads are better to Columbia and on to Angels Camp and Dogtown."

"And you believe him, Señora? I think that is an awfully long way around just to ride on a good road."

"I agree with you. I think the men just want to see some new and exciting sights. I also think it will be up to us women to protect them from the evils that lie ahead." Leonida paused to press her forehead against Angela's and grinned. "I hear Grayson has many cantinas and gambling halls."

~   ~   ~

It was eight o'clock that evening when James Sattler pulled his favorite chair from the card table and sat down.

"Sure you want to do this, Jim? You already owe us about four thousand." Ken Edwards chewed on the end of his fifty-cent cigar as he shuffled the cards.

"Got that much right here, and then some." Sattler dropped the envelope on the table. Ken couldn't help but notice the woman's name in neat handwriting on the front.

Chapter 7

"Cathy? What's wrong with her?" Sean glared at the smiling woman seated next to him as the buggy creaked its way down the rough trail. They had taken the ferry as far as Stockton, and had spent the next two days shopping and sightseeing. They were now making their way toward the Garcia hacienda.

"Nothing. I think she's a fine looking mule. I was just wondering why you went to all the expense and trouble of loading your own buggy and mule onto the ferry, when we could have bought another rig in Stockton for less money." Loretta shrugged.

"Well, I don't know if that's true or not. I've seen the time when you couldn't even find a spare horse or buggy available at any price. Cathy and I are old friends. I bought her from a miner in Dogtown when I first arrived in California. We've been through a lot together, and I wouldn't trade her for a million dollars."

"A million dollars." She raised her eyebrows and grinned. "Really, Doctor?"

"Well, I'd have to think about it awful hard. Speaking of old friends..." He grinned as he pulled the buggy to a halt. He sat for a long minute studying the cabin sitting off the roadway. The man on the front porch had a familiar swagger as he stepped into the sunlight and made his way toward the buggy.

"That's Tex, one of the best friends a man could ever have, and that woman in the doorway must be Rosa. This place is new." He glanced around. "It wasn't here when I left. Come on, I'll introduce you." He clucked his tongue and turned the buggy into the yard.

"Tex, by God, it's good to see you." Sean climbed from the buggy and extended his hand. The cowboy took one glance at Loretta before swinging a vicious right hand that knocked the doctor to the ground.

"What in the world?" Loretta jumped from the buggy to grab at the man's arm, but he brushed her aside to give the doctor a kick as he struggled to regain his feet.

"You sonofabitch! First, you run off, breakin' her heart into a million pieces. Then, you come around bringing this here woman to flaunt in her face."

"Stop it, you bastard!" Loretta hit at his shoulder with her fist. He gave her a shove that caused her to land on her rear in the dust. Rosa came running to the yard to grab hold of her arm and pull her away from the fighting men.

"Come on. Get up and get what's coming to you!" Tex held his fists high and kicked at the struggling doctor one more time.

Sean scrambled on all fours out of reach of the cowboy's long legs and spit blood from his wounded lips. "What the hell's the matter with you? You crazy?"

"No, you're the crazy one." Tex ignored Rosa's pleading and shook loose of her grasp on his arm to take another swing at Sean's head. The doctor danced easily away from the blow and put his own hands up for defense.

"I didn't come here to fight, you crazy Texan. I came because I love this place, and the people living here."

"You've got a funny way of showing it." Tex charged, swinging both fists. Sean ducked under the haymakers and snapped a left jab to the cowboy's chin, followed by a harder right. Tex's legs crumbled and he dropped in a heap at Sean's feet. He jerked the pistol from Tex's holster and handed it to Rosa.

"Now, maybe you can tell me what this is all about."

"Oh, he's angry because you brought your new woman for Doña Garcia to see." Rosa motioned with her head as she knelt beside her husband.

"Loretta?" Sean glanced at the ashen-faced woman standing beside the buggy.

"Sí." Rosa gave a nod as Tex moaned. "He says you come here with her to break the Doña's heart again."

"Aw, he's crazier than I thought. Here, give me that." Sean snatched the gun from Rosa's hand. "I wouldn't trust him being this close to a weapon if he's that insane. Loretta Stewart and I are just friends, and nothing more. I brought her with me because I wanted her to see what a beautiful place this is, and to meet people I consider to be my friends."

"Is this true?" Rosa glanced toward Loretta.

Loretta nodded.

"Well hell, Pard. Why didn't ya just say so." Tex struggled to his feet rubbing his chin.

"You wouldn't let me, and I'm keeping this until I leave." Sean stuffed the pistol into his belt.

"Naw, ya didn't need shootin', just a good beatin'. Damn, but you hit hard." He wiggled his jaw back and forth.

"You're not so bad yourself, in an awkward sort of way." Sean worked the pump handle to wash the blood from his mouth.

"Say, this place wasn't here when you left, was it?" Tex joined him.

"No. When did you and Rosa get married? Last I saw, you were running as fast as your horse away from the altar."

"Aw, I was only funning her. We got hitched about a month after you left. Come on, I'll show you around the place." Tex clasped an arm around Sean's shoulder and led him toward the corral, leaving the two women alone.

"Are they going to be all right together?" Loretta asked after a long minute.

"Sí, they really are good friends. Come, we'll make some tea." Rosa offered Loretta her hand. "You must tell me about yourself."

~   ~   ~

"When are you due?" Loretta studied the cozy little kitchen with its whitewashed walls and lace curtains. There were metal pots and pans hanging from pegs near the wood burning stove and a white washbasin on a long counter under the window. Rosa smiled as she retrieved the steaming pot of water from the stove.

"Maria Sanchez, Doña Leonida's maid, says two months from now. But I think sooner." She set the teapot on the table and held both hands on her stomach. "He's going to be big, like his father, and a fierce fighter too," she laughed.

"Kicks a lot, um?" Loretta dropped the fob filled with tea into the pot and replaced the lid.

"Do you have any children?" Rosa's dark eyes caused her to pause as she retrieved the cups from the counter.

"No." She shook her head. "I've never been so lucky as to have been married, or had anyone care about me like you say your husband does."

"Que? You are so beautiful, señorita. That seems impossible."

"Thank you. You are very beautiful yourself."

"Does Señor Kilkenney love you?" Rosa's stare caused her to shift in her chair as she poured the tea.

"No." She shook her head. "We are like he says...just friends. There are some things you must know about me. I'll tell you some day, but, I'd like to keep them a secret, at least for awhile."

"Bueno." Rosa held her cup in both hands and gently blew across the surface. "There are always some things no one needs to know. They are only for you and Dios, and maybe your husband." She cocked her head and grinned.

"Does your husband know everything about you, Rosa?"

"Sí, Tex knows me very well. He knows I was once a prostituta. But no more." She set the cup on the table and caused her mass of dark curls to bounce as she shook her head. "I am now the Señora Rosa Burwell."

"I beg your pardon, I don't understand Spanish very well." Loretta crinkled her eyebrows with a grin. "I might not have understood you correctly, but I could have sworn you just said you used to be a...prostitute?"

"Sí, a puta." She let the words roll off her tongue casually. "So was Angela Gonzalez. You'll meet her later. But we are both different now. Here," she patted her breast, "inside where it counts. Jesus Cristo changed us both and gave us good husbands and gave us babies. Me first. Angela is just a little pregnant." She held four fingers apart and grinned.

"Doesn't it bother you, for people to know what you used to do?"

"Sí, a little. But, señorita, everybody already knows about me. They know how Tex rescued me from that filthy cantina in Dogtown, and all the bad things that happened there. I think it is best you know also," she reached across the table and held Loretta's hand, "so you can know Dios changes lives." Loretta's bottom lip trembled as she stared into the dark eyes.

"How did you know?"

"I just know these things." Rosa shrugged. "Maybe it's the manner, or something in the air. Things are just different for us, señorita. Clothes look better when we wear them, and perfume smells better on us than other girls. Besides, being in such places with such men changes us. We even talk different. You might look like a lady, señorita, but a lady would not have called my husband a bastard, no matter what caused the fight in the yard." She cocked her head to one side and grinned. No importa, señorita, your secret is safe with me. But I also know something else about you that does bother me."

"And what is that?"

"That you love Señor Kilkenney more than your own life."

"Well," Loretta raised both eyebrows and laughed, "I don't know if it's all that bad yet, but he is all I think about. And would you believe it? He's the first man I've ever met that hasn't tried to paw or grope me. He treats me like a lady, but he doesn't even know I exist."

"You've never...?" Rosa cocked her head and motioned as if to grab the word out of the air.

"No." She giggled. "We spent the first night we met together in the same bed, and all he did was talk about this ranch and Leonida Garcia, whoever she is. Then we slept. That's why I wanted to come here so badly...to meet this woman. I feel like I hate her, and I've never met her yet."

"You will meet the Doña," Rosa said, "and that's what frightens me, señorita. Doña Leonida is a very beautiful woman, like you, but she is also a woman of many sorrows. Those men in Dogtown did many bad things to her. They killed her husband and his brother and many other people, including our priest. She hasn't told many, but those men also raped her before beating her very badly."

"Doctor Kilkenney mentioned something about that, but he was drunk and I thought it was the alcohol talking. Why? Why would anyone do that to her?" Loretta crinkled her brow.

"To steal her land, señorita, and now, others are trying to do the same thing. Only this time, they are doing it legally, through the courts, but, that is not what I wanted to tell you. The killings and beating were only part of the sorrows Doña Leonida suffered. There was another sorrow that came later. That happened when Señor Kilkenney left for San Francisco. You see, she came to love him very much, and his leaving caused her heart to break. I don't think it has stopped hurting yet." Rosa shook her head.

"I'm sorry for her, but why would my meeting her frighten you?"

"Because she will think the same thing. That you and Señor Kilkenney are lovers."

"I can't help what she thinks," Loretta snickered. "Besides, it will only take a few minutes before she realizes the truth."

"I don't think so." Rosa stared at her over the rim of her cup. "It will take more than words this time, and if you haven't noticed, Señor Kilkenney might say that you are only friends, Señorita, but you are special to him. I can see it in his eyes, and Doña Leonida will see it also."

"So, what are you trying to tell me, Rosa? Give up my own wishes and desires and hand him over to another woman like a Christmas package? I just can't stop what I feel. You know that, don't you?"

"Sí, and I'm not asking you to do that, señorita. Only be kind to her. I know the Doña, and she is a woman who loves very much. She loves me and Angela, even though she knows that we were once prostitutas, and she will love you for Señor Kilkenney's sake. You will think she is strong and nothing bothers her, but she is a woman who feels pain the same as we do."

"I don't know what you are insinuating. Do you think I came here with the intention of hurting her?"

"No." Rosa smiled, "I think you came here to protect your interest, the same as I would if it were Tex instead of Señor Kilkenney. I can't blame you for coming, señorita. I am glad you did. I think we will become friends. I only want you to understand that the Doña is not like you and me. She is innocent. We have our ways with men, and you can do things that will make Señor Kilkenney forget about her. All I ask is, let Señor Kilkenney make up his own mind. Bien?" She grabbed Loretta's hand and gave it a squeeze. "You'll be happier that way, señorita. If Señor Kilkenney chooses you, you'll know for sure he loves you more than the Doña."

"Talk about innocent." Loretta gave a crooked grin and shook her head. "I know what you're saying, and I'll try. But I don't know if I can really stand by and watch another woman take my only chance at getting out of the hell I'm in. You were lucky, Rosa. Look around you." She allowed her gaze to drift around the tiny kitchen. You've got a real nice place here, a good-looking husband and a baby on the way. I'd slit someone's throat to live like you. Men like your husband and the doctor don't happen by for women like us every day, you know."

"Sí, but it will happen for you, señorita. I will pray to Saint Joseph, and he will take care of you. Who knows," Rosa raised both eyebrows and shrugged, "Señor Kilkenney might be the one he sends."

Loretta tilted her head back and laughed heartily.

"Did I say something funny, señorita?"

"No...well, yes you did. Here we are drinking tea. One former whore talking to another whore about God and prayer. Doesn't that seem a little strange to you? I mean, I'm not even sure that God knows who I am."

"Sí, that might be strange, but Dios knows who you are, señorita. And you're here for a reason."

Chapter 8

James Sattler urged the tired team across the creek and down the road in a cloud of dust. He caught a glimpse of two men watching from the corral as he shot past the cabin with the black buggy and white mule tied in the front yard. He paid them little mind as he rehearsed the speech over and over in his mind.

Mrs. Garcia, things have gone badly. Gregory Stevenson, the prosecuting Attorney for the State of California, has been talking to some miners who were in Dogtown when all that trouble happened, and he is considering pressing charges. Do you know what that means, Mrs. Garcia? They are going to try you for murder. Now, I'm prepared to defend you, the same as I am defending your interest concerning your land, but, this is going to take a lot of time. It means I will have to drop some of the other cases I'm currently working on, and, it will also take a lot of money. I'd say another two thousand would be a good starting point. He nodded with satisfaction and shook the reins. Yeah, that should work.

The card game three nights earlier had gone bad in an instant, and before he had realized it the money in the envelope was gone, and he was signing notes just to stay in the game. Before the night was over, his debt had grown to five thousand dollars.

"Na-uh." Ken clamped onto his wrist as he reached for another i.o.u. note. "Game's closed Jim, and I want my money by the end of the month. That's almost four weeks. I don't care how you get it, but I've been carrying you long enough. Either I get my money, or I'll starting taking it out of your hide."

Sattler knew from experience that Edwards didn't make idle threats. He had been in the suite on the third floor of the Montgomery Building when Edwards ordered Frank and Black Jack, his two body guards, to break Clarence Adams' hands. Adams had been overdue on his two-thousand-dollar payment by two weeks. James had no desire to find out what might happen if he failed to come up with the five thousand he owed.

He smiled with satisfaction as the Garcia hacienda came into sight. Mrs. Garcia trusted him and had always been good about paying every time he asked for money. Besides, he had learned from listening to the conversations around the card table that the Garcias had discovered gold. They were keeping the whereabouts of their mine a secret, but someone had seen them cashing in some of the gold. Two thousand dollars shouldn't mean a whole lot to someone who owned a gold mine. He had already leaned on Francisco Lopez and Hector Ramos before coming to see Mrs. Garcia. The others didn't actually have the cash, but he was able to talk them into signing over part of their land grants, which he could use for collateral at the bank. He had brought the paperwork folded inside his coat pocket just in case it came to that here, but that shouldn't be necessary. He slowed the lathered team to a halt and handed the reins to the stableboy before climbing to the ground. He brushed the dust from his clothing as he walked toward the house. Jose Flores, Mrs. Garcia's father, stepped from the shaded front porch to greet him.

"Buenos dias, Señor Sattler." Jose extended his hand. "What brings you all the way to Rancho Manantial Escondido?"

"Oh, I'm afraid I have some more bad news, General." James shook his head as he gripped Jose's hand. He was momentarily taken aback by the retired general's strength.

"Que? I am no prophet, but I thought as much. You were here not three weeks ago, and my daughter met you in San Francisco just last week. No one would come all this way, unless they liked to travel a great deal. Now, what is it that is troubling you, señor?"

"Well, this might be better to say in front of your daughter. Is she inside?"

"Sí." Jose shrugged and opened the door. "I'll have Maria make some tea while we discuss what is bothering you." It took a couple of seconds for Jim's eyes to adjust to the cool dimness of the hacienda before he noticed the figure standing in the hallway.

"Come." She turned with a nod of her head before disappearing inside the study. Jim stared at the empty doorway as the general gave orders to the maid. No handshake, or smile? This was going to be harder than he had imagined.

~   ~   ~

"Well, niña, what do you think?" Jose Flores studied his daughter through a cloud of smoke as he lit his cigar. James Sattler had just given them his prepared speech, and finished by mopping his damp brow with his handkerchief.

"Let them go ahead with their charges."

"Mrs. Garcia, do you realize what you're saying?" James leaned forward in his chair. "They are going to try you for murder."

"Sí, I understood you very well, but I have already been cleared of such foolish charges last year by Judge Lloyd Hansen of Columbia, and unless I am mistaken, California has become a part of the United States. Am I not right?"

He nodded.

"Then, according to amendment five of the Constitution, a person cannot be tried twice for the same crime. So, let them go ahead with their silly charges."

"You've read the Constitution?" James snickered with a shake of his head.

"Sí," Leonida nodded. "Since we were suddenly to become citizens of the United States, I considered it wise to know the laws we were going to be governed by."

"My daughter and I both actually read and understood your Constitution before we left Mexico City, Señor Sattler." Jose smiled. "You see, we were at war with the United States at that time, and as a general, I thought it imperative to understand the people I was fighting. But as she just said, we both reread it after coming to California."

"Yes, I see your point, and hers. I had simply forgotten her telling me about Judge Hansen's hearing. Maybe I'll take a ride over to Columbia and have a chat with him and see if I can't get him to draw up a copy of his ruling to present in case it ever gets that far."

"There is no need to go to that trouble, señor. I have one right here." Leonida opened one of the desk drawers to retrieve a folded packet of papers. "You may keep this for your files, if you think it is necessary. I have others."

"Yes, that would save me a lot of trouble." He stuffed the packet in his coat pocket next to the blank deed.

"Is there anything else I can help you with, señor?" Leonida smiled.

"No, I don't think there is." James chuckled. *Not while you're holding four aces and I've only got a pair of deuces.* "I guess I was over-reacting when I heard of Mr. Stevenson's intention of charging you with murder. But this ruling," he patted the coat pocket, "should settle any argument he could mount against you."

"Bueno." Leonida took him by the arm. "It is too bad you had to travel all the way to our rancho for nothing. Perhaps some refreshments might ease that pain just a little. Come to the dining room, and I'll have Maria fix you something. Then we'll prepare one of the upstairs bedrooms for you to spend the night."

"The refreshments sound nice, Mrs. Garcia, but I'm afraid I must be heading back toward San Francisco as soon as possible."

"I know you always seem to be in a hurry, señor, but it would be impossible for you to reach San Francisco this evening." She crinkled her eyebrows with a grin.

"Yes, but I can reach Stockton and take a ferry on into San Francisco by midmorning. I do have to be in court day after tomorrow."

"It wouldn't be concerning our rancho by any chance, would it?" Jose asked as he poured several glasses of brandy.

"No, I'm afraid this hearing has nothing to do with any land grants at all. It's a simple matter of defending a client who happened to get into a drunken brawl." He lifted his glass and smiled. "To your health."

"And yours." Jose completed the salute. They were interrupted by squeals of delight as Maria rushed from the kitchen through the dining room and toward the front door.

"Maria, silencio, por favor." Leonida craned her neck to stare as the maid continued. "Maria, you are being..." She stopped as the door swung open. The sight of the tall man standing in the doorway caused her to grip the edge of the table.

"By all the saints of heaven, it's the return of the crazy gringo doctor." Jose set his glass on the table.

"Look, Doña Leonida, it's Señor Kilkenney." Maria giggled and threw her arms around the man.

"Yes, I see." Leonida steadied herself against the table before gliding across the marbled hall toward the door.

"Señor Kilkenney," she extended a hand, "it is indeed a pleasure. It has been a long time."

"Yes it has." He took her hand and bowed. "Too long, I'm afraid. But some things never change. You are just as beautiful as ever, ma'am."

"Ah, and you are still the great charmer you once were."

"Perhaps more so." The sharpness of her father's voice caused her to turn. "I have never seen such arrogance, even in a gringo."

"Papa."

"Nay, niña. See for yourself." He nodded toward the buggy parked by the fountain. "Only a gringo would come to visit one woman, and bring another with him." The sight of the elegantly dressed woman caused her to dig her fingernails into the doorpost for support. The beautiful blond was surrounded by barefoot children, all clamoring to get a better view of the stranger who had come to visit. Leonida had trouble finding her voice.

"Why don't you ask your wife to come join us, Doctor?"

"Wife? Oh, but I'm afraid you and your father are both mistaken," Sean laughed with a shake of his head. "Loretta and I are simply friends, and nothing more."

"Friends?"

"Yes."

"What type of friend? How close is your friendship with this woman?" Jose raised his eyebrows and studied the smoldering cigar in his fingers.

"Certainly not what you are implying. We are just friends, honest." Sean shrugged. "And after hearing me brag about how beautiful this place is, she talked me into bringing her for a visit. I hope you don't mind."

"No, you and your lady-friend are welcome here, but that is no way to treat a her." Leonida raised on her tiptoes for a better view of the buggy. It was now totally engulfed in noisy children. "Maria?" She glanced toward the maid. "You had better rescue that poor girl before they carry her off."

"Sí." Maria chased the children away from the buggy as though she were shooing chickens and returned with the smiling girl. Sean took her by the arm in order to make the introductions.

"Mrs. Garcia, General Flores, may I present a good friend of mine, Loretta Stewart of San Francisco."

"Welcome to Rancho Manantial Escondido, Señorita Stewart. I hope your visit here is a pleasant one." Leonida offered her right hand to the girl.

"Doña Leonida Garcia." Loretta held Leonida's hand lightly as she preformed a perfect bow. "I am humbled that you would allow me to enter your hacienda."

"Well," General Flores cleared his throat while Sean and Leonida stared open mouthed, "you have been keeping better company than I thought, Doctor. Allow me, señorita." He offered his arm to Loretta. "You must excuse my daughter. It is not often that one comes to our door who knows the proper way to greet her. This crazy doctor friend of yours has certainly never given her the respect she deserves."

"Perhaps not in her presence, General, but he described her to me as a queen, and I can see that it was no exaggeration. You are beautiful, Doña Leonida."

"Gracias. The compliment goes both ways, señorita. It seems our doctor friend has impeccable taste in women." Leonida glanced at Sean as he stuffed his hands in his pockets and stared into the distance. "By the way, Doctor, what happened to your mouth?" She cocked her head to stare at his swollen lip. "It looks as though you have been in a fight."

"This?" He touched his lips with his fingers. "No, just an accident."

"Really? Well, no importa. Come, let's join our other guest. I'm afraid we have been very rude to him." Leonida led the way into the dining room. James Sattler rose to his feet with a huge grin.

"Loretta Stewart! What in God's name are you doing here?" Loretta dug her fingers into Leonida's arm as the color drained from her face.

"Do you know this young lady, Señor Sattler?"

"Know her? I should hope so."

"Miss Stewart is a good friend of mine. By the way, I'm Sean Kilkenney." Sean stepped forward to extend his hand. "Doctor Sean Kilkenney. I brought Miss Stewart to visit Mrs. Garcia, thinking perhaps the country air might do her some good. She had developed this cough..." He paused to grin. "But you're probably not interested in such things. I also thought they might become friends. I find them both beautiful and elegantly charming, don't you?"

"Well, yes. I guess I do at that," James said as Sean continued to grip his hand.

"You were saying you know Señorita Stewart?" Leonida said as she filled two more glasses with brandy. She handed one of the glasses to Loretta and was stunned as the young woman drained it in one gulp. She handed Sean his glass before retrieving the decanter from the serving tray.

"Yes, she's a client of mine." James coughed and cleared his throat before handing his glass to Leonida. "If you don't mind."

"Certainly." She refilled his glass before making her way around the room. "You were saying she is a client of yours, señor?"

"Ah, yes. Nothing serious, you know. But I did have to represent her in court one time."

"Oh? And now you are representing me." Leonida turned toward Loretta with a smile. "It seems that we do indeed have some things in common. You must tell me, señorita. Is he really a good solicitor, or am I wasting my money?"

"Oh, he's good, all right." Loretta sighed. "I'm sure you'll be receiving your money's worth."

"And why did you have to go to court, niña? Or, is that too personal a question?" General Flores said.

"No, it's not too personal." She took a sip of brandy and shook her head. "I happened to witness a crime. Someone broke into a room at the hotel I was staying at and robbed an old man who happened to have a lot of money. He had invited me to dinner earlier that evening. So, they naturally thought at first, I had somehow taken his wallet."

She shrugged. "When I found myself sitting inside a cell with iron bars, I decided I needed an attorney."

"But you said you witnessed the crime." General Flores cocked his head to one side and relit his cigar.

"As it turned out I did, sort of. I remembered seeing a man watching us in the restaurant as we ate, and later in the hotel lobby. I noticed the same man again as I was entering my own room. You see, my room happened to be about three doors down from where this old man was staying. I told the police, and when they finally caught him, he admitted to having stolen the money."

"Lucky for you they caught that man," Leonida said.

"Yes, but I was also lucky to have James Sattler arguing my case in court. You see, they didn't actually catch him until later, after James had already gotten the charges against me dropped."

"It was my pleasure." James smiled and toasted Loretta with his glass. "By the way, Mrs. Garcia, if it isn't too much of an imposition, I would like to take you up on that offer to spend the night. I am rather tired, and it is getting late."

"It would be no trouble at all. I'll have one of the girls fix a room for you." She paused at the door to smile at Loretta. "And if you don't mind, I'll have them prepare the room next to mine for you."

"Thank you, I would appreciate it."

"Bueno." Leonida nodded. "Doctor Kilkenney may have his old room. It has been empty since he left." She glanced toward Sean. "You will find it much the same as you left it. The things you left behind are still there."

~   ~   ~

"All right, you can square with me, Loretta. What the hell are you doing here?" Loretta was seated in the cool night air having a cigarette when James Sattler decided to join her by the fountain.

"I'm here with a friend visiting, just like I said. Now, be quiet. You'll wake the others."

"I hardly think they can hear us inside the house," he snickered, "but I'll keep it down just the same. Now come on. Loretta Stewart doesn't do anything unless it benefits her. What's your game, girly?" He pinched her cheek.

"Dammit." She slapped his hand away. "I told you, nothing! Now, leave me alone."

"Whoa, hold on. We're on the same team, remember? You and me? I saved your bacon inside the house this afternoon. I could have told them what you really are. You want that?"

"Yeah, Jim, you're a real prince. And no, I don't want that woman and her father to know what I really am. But there really isn't any game going on this time. Believe me. I just wanted to be treated like a lady for once in my life."

"Huh, you're on the level this time?"

She nodded.

"Wow! I didn't think it was possible. That doctor knows something about you if I'm not mistaken."

"Yeah, he knows all about me...mostly." She crushed her cigarette under the toe of her slipper. "And you know what? It doesn't make any difference to him. He still treats me like a lady."

"Uh-oh." James shook his head. "You got a bad case, don't you?"

"Yeah, I'm afraid so."

"Well, don't get too respectable on me, not yet anyway. I need your help."

"You're not flimflaming these nice people, are you? Come on, Jim," she said as he grinned. "They've already been through hell and high-water. and this land's all they've got."

"I'm sorry about that, but, there is no way they are going to be able to keep it. You know that as well as I do, Loretta. I just figured on getting my share before everyone else does, and you're going to help me, now that you're here."

"Like hell I am." She stood to glare down at him.

"Yeah, like hell you are." He sprang to his feet and dug his fingers into her shoulders. "Because if you don't, everyone within a hundred miles of this place is going to know Loretta Stewart is nothing but a whore. And they'll know that you really did steal that old man's money and helped me pin it on some poor old drunk that never hurt anyone in his entire life. Want them to know all that, darling?"

"All right, what do you want me to do?"

"Actually, nothing much. Just make good friends with her and find out everything you can. I want to know where she keeps things. All the little secret hiding places. Because somewhere inside that house, she's got a whole lot of gold stored."

"You've been hanging around those Chinese opium dens too long." She shook her head. "What ever gave you that idea?"

"Just a hunch, my dear. I've spent a lifetime studying people, and she doesn't act like someone wondering where their next piece of bread is coming from." He grinned as he drew her close. "When she bought all those guns for that fight in Dogtown, she paid for them with gold. A lot of gold. And she has always been able to come up with the money to pay me, when the other Mexicans have to sign over deeds to their land. I also heard a nasty little rumor from a miner at a card table that they've discovered gold somewhere on this property. Now, when you find out where she keeps it, just let me know. That's all you have to do. I'll do the rest. Okay?" He turned and paused to glance back over his shoulder. "Oh, I'll make sure you get your usual cut."

Chapter 9

"All rise. Court is now in session. Judge Lloyd W. Hansen of Columbia presiding." Cary Jones pounded the whiskey-stained table with a clawhammer as Judge Hansen took his place behind a second table positioned to Cary's right. The graying judge cleared his throat and nodded toward the packed saloon.

"Be seated."

The room was instantly filled with random coughs and scraping chairs. Hanky was the last to be seated as he took his time scanning the faces of the spectators seated behind him. Every man, woman and child in Dogtown and the surrounding gold camps had packed inside the Rusty Rail hoping to get a firsthand view of the drama about to unfold. Leonida and her father had commandeered an entire corner of the room for a select few from the rancho, including Sean Kilkenney and the pretty woman seated beside him. Most of the jurors were Three Mile Mine employees, including its owner, Woodrow Black, who had been appointed as foreman. In Judge Hansen's opinion, it was the best way for Ruby to get a fair trial.

"They're all God-fearing folks. Mormons, who don't drink or smoke or chase women. You can't ask for a better jury than that," he had said after completing the selection process.

"Yeah, but they don't look too favorable on whores, Lloyd," Hanky said. "What's gonna happen when she gets up there and says she done it?"

"The same thing that would happen in any other courtroom. They'll pronounce her guilty and I'll have to pass judgment. Look," he said as Hanky shook his head, "you think I like hanging women? I hate it as much as you do. That girl's too young to die, but the law is the law, and it's our duty to uphold it as best we can. I've heard you say much the same thing."

"Yeah, but now I shore wish you'd of asked someone else to find out who done it. I don't mind hanging a horse-thief, but Ruby's just a kid who happened to kill a hydrophobied skunk. Besides, I don't believe she really done it."

"Bailiff, read the charges." Judge Hansen took his seat in the one and only padded chair in the room. Cary Jones stood to his feet and cleared his throat again. Hanky thought it was probably the first time the Three Mile Mine foreman had ever spoken in public.

"The State of California versus Ruby Fay Lang, charged with murder in the first degree in the death of Ambrose Brice, owner of The Rusty Rail, on the nineteenth of April, 1852."

"Marshal Russell, please bring the accused forward," Judge Hansen said.

"Come on, Ruby, let's go get this over with." Hanky took her by the arm. She was dressed in a modest gingham dress she had borrowed from Alice Carpenter at his request. Her red hair was pulled tightly in a bun and she had scrubbed all the makeup from her face, allowing her freckles to show. He thought she could have been easily mistaken for a housewife or store clerk anywhere. The judge took a deep breath and studied her over the rim of his glasses for a long minute.

"Miss Lang, you have entered a guilty plea. Do you understand what this means, young lady?"

"Yes, sir, I do."

"Are you aware of the penalty for murder in this state?"

"Yes, sir. I believe it is hanging."

"And knowing that, are you still willing to stand by your original plea?"

"Yes, sir, I am." The room was instantly filled with mumbles and scraping chairs.

"Order." Judge Hansen banged his wooden gavel. "Order in the court. May I ask why?" he continued as the room quieted down. "Why did you kill your former employer?"

"Because he wouldn't leave Aurie alone."

"And Aurie is that young lady seated beside Mrs. Carpenter in the back of the room?" Ruby glanced over her shoulder.

"Yeah, that's her, Aurie Templeton. He was beatin' and takin' advantage of her in that room over there." She pointed toward the door in the corner of the bar. "That was his way of teaching us girls how to be a good whore. Anyway, I told him Aurie was just a little girl, and to leave her alone. He told me...well, I can't say what he told me, because there are women and children in here."

"That's quite all right, you may skip that part. Go on." Judge Hansen nodded.

"Well, I got tired of hearing her cry and beg while that, that, what ever you want to call him kept hurting her. So I went into that room to get her. Then he got real angry and came at me. I thought he was going to hurt me real bad this time, so I ran out here and grabbed the butcher knife from the counter where he always left it. I was just trying to scare him, but he kept coming, so I stabbed him."

"Why didn't you tell the marshal that story when he first asked you what happened? If I remember right," he thumbed through a stack of papers, "you said you killed Mr. Brice because he owed you money. Is that right?"

"Yes, but that wasn't true. I mean, he did owe me some money. He owed everybody in town," she made a sweeping motion with her arm, "but that wasn't why I killed him. What I just told you was the truth."

"I see. Do you have anything further to add to your testimony?"

"No, sir."

"Then, I have no alternative but to ask the jury to adjourn and render a verdict." He shifted his gaze toward the row of chairs along the wall. "If you find her guilty, you will either give me a verdict of justifiable homicide or murder in the first degree." He raised the gavel but stopped as Aurie Templeton jumped to her feet.

"Wait! You can't do that!"

"And why not, young lady?"

"Because she didn't do it."

"Shut up, Aurie!" Ruby yelled.

"Order! Order!" Hansen kept pounding the gavel as the courtroom broke into pandemonium.

"Don't listen to her, your Honor. She's lying." Ruby yelled.

"No, I'm not." Aurie broke Alice Carpenter's hold on her wrist and scrambled through five rows of chairs to the front of the room.

"You are so. I killed Ambrose." Ruby pounded her chest.

"I said, order!" Hansen slammed the gavel and rose to his feet. "And Marshal Russell?" He pointed the gavel at Hanky. "If you can't keep these women quiet, I'll hold you in contempt."

"Here, now," Hanky said as Ruby tried to pull from his grasp. "If'n ya don't settle down, I'll turn you over my knee and paddle yer hide." He shoved her into a chair.

Hansen pounded the gavel once more as the courtroom erupted into laughter. "Quiet, or I'll clear the courtroom. Now," he glared at Aurie, "perhaps you can explain to me what in the world you've been talking about."

"Ruby didn't kill Mr. Brice." Her eyes darted around the room without finding a spot to light.

"And if she didn't kill him like she said, then who did?"

"Me. I killed him because he was hurting me." Aurie burst into tears.

"She's lying." Ruby jumped to her feet as the courtroom exploded again.

"Well, it's for certain that one of you is lying, and I aim to get to the bottom of this. And you, young lady, already had your turn," he pointed a finger at Ruby, "so you just sit yourself back down and let Aurie have her turn."

"But, she's lying." Ruby stomped her foot.

"I said, sit down." Hansen raised his voice and banged the gavel.

"Here, rest yer bones." Hanky pulled her into the chair. "You'll get another turn."

"Now, perhaps you can shed some light on the subject." Hansen directed his gaze at Aurie.

"You'll be wasting your time questioning these girls, your Honor," Alice Carpenter said from the back of the room.

"May I ask why, Mrs. Carpenter? And please don't tell me you killed Mr. Brice." She waited patiently for the laughter to subside before she spoke in an even voice.

"I'm afraid I have to. Otherwise, I'll be wasting your time also."

"The hell you say." Hanky jerked around as the courtroom erupted again.

"Dammit." Hansen ran his fingers through his hair before pounding the gavel one last time. "Court's adjourned until we can make some sense of this mess. Bailiff, Marshal, clear the courtroom."

"But she's lying. They're both lying," Ruby yelled.

"And I don't want to hear another word out of you until I ask, or I'll have you locked up in that little hole they call a jail. Is that clear?"

"Sit yerself, both of you." Hanky grabbed Ruby and Aurie by the arms, guided them to empty chairs and gave a shove. "I'm about to whup ya both, just because."

"Because why?" Aurie squinted up at him.

"Because you need it. You done told a big whopper in the middle of a courtroom. That's why."

"Mrs. Carpenter, come to the front of the courtroom, please." Judge Hansen waved toward the woman standing in the back of the room as he joined Hanky. He took his time glaring at the girls. "I ought to hold you both in contempt of court. Do you realize what a mockery you've made out of our justice system? Ruby and Aurie sat motionless.

"And you," he turned on Alice Carpenter, "I've known you for several years now. I met you and Ike when you first rolled into gold country, a year or so before he died. What's gotten into you? Standing up in court and claiming to have murdered a man."

"I said it, because it is true."

"Dammit, I don't want to hear that, Alice. It was bad enough hearing Ruby killed that man, then Aurie. But I know you."

"It's shore one big mess." Hanky shook his head.

"Yes it is. I appointed you Marshal to find out who killed Ambrose before we got to court, and look what a mess you've made of everything. I think I've got a simple case with a signed confession, and I wind up with three women claiming to have killed the same man. I ought to revoke that badge."

"Here," Hanky pulled the star from his vest, "you're welcome to it. I didn't wanna find out who kilt him in the first place."

"No, you're keeping it until this case is settled." He took a deep breath and exhaled slowly as Leonida joined Alice's side. "Don't tell me you killed that man, or I'm going to explode."

"I could have." She shrugged. "I certainly tried once. I shot at him three times, but I'm afraid my aim was too poor."

"Now, Mrs. Garcia, I know fer certain you didn't croak Ambrose." Hanky snickered.

"Really? Can you prove I didn't? I think not, señor. I could have ridden into town that night and done the deed and been back home in my bed before sunrise. But that is not what I came to say. I think you and Judge Hansen have a problem you wish to work out. Bueno?"

"Yer right there, lady." Hanky chuckled.

"Then I offer you the privacy of Rancho Manantial Escondido, if you wish. You may bring these ladies and try to figure out which one of us killed that man."

"Oh, for Pete's sake," Judge Hansen growled. "You're not serious in wanting to include your name in the list of killers, are you? Why?"

"Por nada." She raised her eyebrows and shrugged. "Perhaps I feel guilty because I failed to complete the task a year ago. If I had shot Señor Brice, or at least run him out of town, these young women would not have suffered. Maybe I heard what he was doing to them, and came into town that night to finish my mission. But either way, you are welcome to use my rancho in order to unravel your mystery. Come." She took Alice by the arm. "You and the girls need to do some packing. This could take a long time."

"Dammit, Hanky," the judge glared as the women left the room, "I don't like the feel of this. Maybe I should just rule his death a suicide."

"Thought about it myself a time or two. Ambrose shore needed killing, and I ain't in too big a hurry to hang anyone for doing it, regardless. But I'd shore like to know who done it, so's I can shake their hand. One thing's fer shure; you're gonna like staying out at her place. It's shore 'nuff purdy."

"Well, I can't stay but a day or two. I've court in Columbia Friday."

"That's all right. We'll have us a time anyway. And no matter what that bone-head Irish doctor says, Maria shore can whip up some vittles."

"Hey," Hansen jerked around suddenly, "aren't those women supposed to be under arrest? You just can't let them go running free like that."

"Why not? They ain't going nowhere."

"Because it doesn't look right."

"Paco?" Hanky poked his head out the door and yelled. "Keep an eye on them females and tie 'em to a post if they try to escape."

Chapter 10

Darrell Rodeen stood in the open doorway studying the interior of James Sattler's tiny office. Sattler dipped his fountain pen in the inkwell and glanced up at the man. "May I help you?"

"Kinda small for a busy man like you, isn't it?" Rodeen removed a stack of papers from a chair before scooting it closer to the desk. He sat down and stretched his arms with a huge sigh.

"Not really. I like it that way. Everything's close where I can reach it." He returned his pen to its stand and folded his hands. "Now, how may I help you, mister...ah?"

"Rodeen. Darrell Rodeen." He leaned back in the chair and crossed his legs as he rolled a smoke. "I'm a sailor by trade, Mr. Sattler. But I've also studied some law. And as kind of a hobby, I sort of hang around courtrooms while we're in port. I've been inside courts all over this world, watching what goes on inside."

"And you want a job in my office; is that it?"

"Well, sort of. But not what you think."

"Then, what?" James knocked the ashes from his pipe and retrieved his tobacco pouch from the bottom desk drawer.

"Well, it's like I said. I've been all over the world, and one of the places I've been is to Mrs. Garcia's rancho up near Dogtown."

"Really?" James studied Darrell through a cloud of smoke as he lit the pipe. "I hope you enjoyed your visit. It's rather a nice place, isn't it?"

"Yes, I did enjoy myself, and it certainly is beautiful. But what I really found interesting is how educated Mrs. Garcia and her father are. Did you know she speaks and reads three languages?"

"What are you driving at, Mr. Rodeen? I'm sure you didn't come here to discuss Mrs. Garcia's linguistic capabilities with me."

"No, I didn't." Darrell struck a match and lit his cigarette. "But I happened to be in the courtroom four or five days ago and heard you telling Judge Baker the lady is illiterate. You also told him she hadn't kept any records, and I know for a fact she's probably kept every scrap of paper since she was five years old. I've been inside her office. So, what I'd like to know is," he took a long drag off his smoke and blew a cloud in the air, "what kind of a scam are you pulling on her?"

"I don't have any idea what you are talking about. Just who do you think you are, coming in here and accusing me?"

"Sure you do." Darrell cut him off with a laugh. "You know very well what I'm talking about. Quit acting so righteous and offended. I've also done a little checking on you, and found that you're representing at least four others who have land disputes similar to hers. In all of the cases, except Mrs. Garcia, you've talked the people into signing power of attorney over to you concerning the deeds to their land."

"That's nothing new. Most of these people don't have any money to fight these long drawn-out cases in court. So nearly every lawyer has them sign something so we can take out loans against their land, or sell off portions to finance their court battles."

"Sure, I can understand that. But when an attorney starts lying to a judge about his client, I sort of get suspicious. Now, I'm sure that Judge Baker and Mrs. Garcia both would love to know what you're up to."

"So that's it, blackmail. Just how much am I supposed to pay you to keep you from telling them about this fantasy you've cooked up?" James snickered and retrieved a bottle from the bottom drawer.

"Oh, it's no fantasy. You and I both know that Mrs. Garcia is quite good at running her business. The ship I sail on delivers supplies to their rancho. She has a good head on her shoulders, I can tell you that. So did her husband, and she's got money; a lot of it. According to my sources, nearly every time you visit her rancho, you return with a rather large sum of money. You sort of figure if you drag this case out in court her money will soon run out, and she'll have to sign her land over to you. Now, isn't that the truth, Mr. Sattler?"

"Neither you nor anyone else could ever prove that, Mr. Rodeen, even if it were true. Now, back to my original question. How much are you requesting for your silence?" James pulled a leather bound checkbook from one of the drawers and laid it on the desk. "I've found that sometimes buying silence is cheaper than having one's reputation smeared. How much did you say?"

"Oh, you misunderstand my reason for being here. I don't want your money, Mr. Sattler."

"No? What, then?"

"I want a partnership. I want to be part of the team."

"The team? Impossible, I've always worked alone. Even my secretary is only part-time. Besides, what could you possible do?"

"Keep silent, like you said. I could also deliver papers, and I'm very persuasive in getting people to cooperate, when needed." He got up from his chair and crushed his cigarette in the ashtray on James' desk. "I just thought you'd like to know you hired a new partner, starting this instant. See you in the morning, partner." He reached across the desk and shook James' hand. James glared as Darrell opened the door.

"Oh, silly me," he closed the door again with a laugh, "I just remembered; I'll need an advance from the general fund. I have some obligations to take care of."

"I thought so. What if I refuse?"

"Then Justice Baker will suddenly discover he's being lied to."

"Is five hundred enough?" James grabbed his fountain pen and opened the checkbook.

"Yeah, that'll do for a starter."

~   ~   ~

According to his pocket watch, it was eleven thirty, and Captain McDougal was considering calling it a night. The only thing keeping him at his table inside The Silver Slipper was plain curiosity. Two tables to their left, Darrell Rodeen was entertaining two young ladies and tossing money around like it grew on trees.

"Sorry, what were you saying?" McDougal turned his attention to his two companions at his own table.

"I was saying, that I didn't mean for Irish to go hauling that purdy girl out to Mrs. Garcia's ranch with him." Bear raised his voice over the loud music and laughter. "All I was hoping was to make him lovesick enough to go see Mrs. Garcia hisself."

"Well, the stupidity of the Irish is legendary, and I'm afraid Doctor Kilkenney is no different than the rest. If he had any brains, he would never have left in the first place." He tilted his glass and drained the last of his rum before addressing the man seated on his right.

"Salty? You've known Darrell Rodeen almost as long as I have. Has he ever had more than two pence in his pocket at any one time you can remember?"

"No, not that I can say. He always loses his pay gambling with the crew before we hit port."

"That's what I was remembering. But there he is, with more money than I've ever seen him with."

"Maybe he had a lucky night at the wheel, or playing poker," Bear laughed.

"No, my gut instinct tells me different." McDougal shook his head. "Salty? I want you to keep your nose to the wind and a sharp eye on our mate. Keep me posted when you find out what's going on."

Chapter 11

"Looks like that old cayuse of Hanky's throwed you boys into a patch of cactus, and you can't find yer way out." Tex sniggered as he licked the paper on the cigarette he'd been rolling. "Ever see anyone get tangled up this bad, General?" The women had decided to take a walk in the cool night air while the men gathered inside Leonida's study for brandy and talk.

"No, Señor Tex, unless it was the time my Federales got surprised by a band of Yaqui Indians. They outnumbered us three to one, so the wisest thing to do at that moment was to run for cover. Well, one of my lieutenants decided to stand in his stirrups and lean forward, thinking his horse could run faster. Whether that is true or not, I don't know. All I know is that his rear end made a beautiful target for one of the Indians. When we got to safety, we had to dig that arrow out. I'll tell you one thing, señores, that lieutenant never made his rear a target again. He had to ride standing up, the whole thirty miles back to the fort the next day."

"Huh, guess I did kinda have my ass sticking out on this one," Hanky grunted. "But I badgered everyone in town and no one said a blamed word. No one seemed to know nothing. Then I get me a signed confession from Ruby, claiming she done it. What would you think?"

"Hell, no one's saying you didn't do your job, Hanky. I'd of probably done the same thing. Only thing is, you're the one with the arrow sticking in your rear end, not me," Tex said.

"Go ahead and have your laugh. Hope you can still laugh when I string one of them young girls up and stretch her neck."

"Aw, you're not serious about hanging one of them, are you?" Sean Kilkenney set his glass on the end table with a bang.

"Guess I'll have to, if Lloyd here orders me to." Hanky scowled.

"What would you want me to do, Doctor? Someone killed that man, and the law's the law. If you kill someone, you get punished. That usually means hanging." Judge Hansen studied the smoldering cigar between his fingers as he spoke.

"Well, I knowed Ambrose Brice pretty well myself, and I'll tell you what, I never run into a skunk that needed killing any more than him," Tex said. "In fact, I had every notion of doing just that when that little whing-ding come off in town awhile back. Only thing is, the general's daughter took a pot-shot at him first and missed. He run like a scared rabbit. If I'd knowed where he was hiding, I would have saved us all this trouble when I got through with Pod Randle."

"Perhaps I should have trained my daughter in how to shoot her derringer before we went to town. But there was no time," Jose Flores said.

"So, what she said in the courtroom was true? She did try to kill him?" Lloyd Hansen said.

"Sí, she shot two, maybe three times and missed. The vaqueros said he ran pretty fast."

"I'll be damned," the judge chuckled. "She's such a lady; I would have never thought... Still, I don't know what to do. I'll agree that from what I hear about the man, he should have been hung long ago. Anyone who would buy a little girl like Aurie Templeton and then misuse her deserves to burn in hell."

"Well, Aurie ain't the first one he's done it to, Judge. He done it to my wife, Rosa. That was before I met her. He claimed to have bought her off her pa and then turned her into a whore. That's why I was hopin' to give him a new belly button or two for his trouble." Tex tossed down the last of his brandy and refilled his glass.

"He's telling the truth, Your Honor." Sean nodded. "That poor girl went through hell ten times over. I had to piece her back together after she almost got beaten to death."

"Well, like I said, I have no doubt that the man deserved everything he got, but that still doesn't change things, does it? Someone killed him. Stabbed him with his own butcher knife. We have a signed confession by one of the girls who used to work for him, saying she killed him because he owed her money and refused to pay. Then, we have two others...pardon me, three counting your daughter," he nodded toward General Flores, " all claiming to have killed the man."

"You're not taking Leonida's confession seriously, are you?" Jose frowned.

"I have to. She admittedly had reason and had made an attempt on his life once before. You just said as much. In her own words, we can't prove she didn't ride into town that night and kill him."

"Yeah, but I ain't buying it," Hanky mumbled over the cigar between his teeth.

"I will admit it's as flimsy as a piece of paper, but as a judge I have to take it seriously. That badge says you should too."

"Maybe, but it ain't her style."

"Sí." Jose nodded in agreement.

"The hell it ain't." Tex snickered. "I seem to remember hearing how she beat the hell out of ol' Doc here one night in the corral 'cause he wouldn't let her go kill everyone in town."

"That was because she wasn't in her right mind then. She had just been violated and her husband had been murdered. Besides, she wasn't going to kill everyone. She was only after Judge Baines and Pod Randle," Sean said.

"What about Alice Carpenter?" Hanky said.

"What about Señora Carpenter?" Jose Flores snapped.

"Sorry, forgot you kinda got yer brand set on that filly. But she is claiming she did fer that skunk too. Now, ya gotta admit that her story is sounding mighty convincing." Hanky toasted the general with his brandy.

"I'm sorry. I don't understand. What did she do for Señor Brice?"

"She's claiming she kilt him. Same as them other skunks in Dogtown."

"Sí, but she is a fine woman. I can't believe she would do such a thing."

"Hell, so's your daughter. Hanky ain't claiming Mrs. Carpenter's anything but fine. But the fact is, she'd done it once before," Tex said.

"Done what before?" Lloyd Hansen crinkled his brow.

"Kilt someone. Remember? She blowed a hole in Hugh Zornes and Charlie Shavers both, big enough to drive a team of mules through."

"Sí, but that was in the heat of battle. A war." Jose creased his eyebrows. "We were all killing. Besides, she shot one of those men to save my life."

"I ain't saying no different." Tex grinned. "All I'm saying is, she done it once, so she could of done it again. Maybe she kinda felt like the rest of us, like the job wasn't finished. You know, ya kilt all the coyotes that's been chasing yer cattle 'cept one? Ya can't really rest until you hunt him down and nail his hide to the barn to dry."

"Okay, we all agree that all four women are suspect at this minute." Judge Hansen leaned forward as Jose refilled his glass. "The way things are going, there's a chance we might not even have the right person yet."

"What do you mean?" Sean asked.

"What he means is, all them women might be fibbing to cover up for someone else," Tex said.

"Na, that's too stupid to be true." Sean shook his head.

"Stupid or not, it's a distinct possibility. What if the women all think that one of them did kill Ambrose. Let's say that Ruby and Alice believe that Aurie killed the man. They might be lying to cover for Aurie. But maybe Aurie didn't kill Ambrose, but believes Alice did. Then she might be lying to cover for Mrs. Carpenter. In reality, someone else could have come into the saloon that night and killed him for an entirely different reason, and left without anyone seeing or knowing he had been there."

"Then, the girls would naturally start thinking that one of them had murdered Ambrose," Jose said.

"Exactly," Lloyd Hansen nodded.

"But I don't understand why they would say such a thing, when they know they might get hung for murder." Sean shook his head.

"Maybe they're hoping for some miracle, sort of like we're hoping for right this moment." Hansen smiled. "It's a hard thing for a man to condemn a woman to hang. There is a reason I chose the men from the Three Mile Mine as jurors, regardless of what Hanky might think."

"Yeah, well too bad whoever it was didn't plug him with a six-gun. That way, Doc here could dig the slug out and maybe we could trace who kilt him that way," Tex said.

"Ballistics?" Judge Hansen said. "You know something about ballistics?"

"Sure, I spent some time in the Army. I find things like that interesting." Sean raised his eyebrows with a shrug.

"I thought he was kinda nuts at first, but he sure convinced me that a feller can trace a killer down by looking at the bullets. He shore had Pod Randle pegged." Tex dug into his pocket for a match to light a fresh cigarette. "Only thing is, it all kinda blew up before we could find an honest judge like yerself to try them."

"I kept those bullets as sort of a reminder." Jose pulled an envelope from the desk drawer and smiled.

"Yeah, well it's too bad, but you can't tell much from a butcher knife sticking in a man's gizzard," Hanky growled.

"Oh, but you can." Sean said as he opened one of the envelopes and let the led balls drop into his hand.

"Can what?" Hansen said.

"Tell some things about how a man got stabbed with a knife."

"Like what? Who done it?" Tex crinkled his brow and lit his smoke. "No one seen him do it."

"Well, just maybe we can tell if one of the women really did kill him, or if it was someone else. Like for instance, how was the knife sticking in Ambrose? Low, below the rib cage, with the blade traveling upward? That's how a man who knows how to knife-fight would normally stab someone." He demonstrated by stabbing the air with Leonida's letter opener. "A woman, on the other hand, will normally hold the knife just the opposite, and drive it downward like she's hammering a nail. That would make the knife wound high, with the blade traveling in the opposite direction." He stared at Hanky for a long minute. "Think real hard now. How was the knife sticking in the body when you found it?"

"If I remember correctly, it was poking straight in through his left shirt pocket."

"Not pointing upward or downward?"

"Nope." He shook his head. "I could be mistaken now, but I'd swear it was poking straight as an arrow."

"Interesting." Sean raised his eyebrows and tossed the letter opener on the desk. "That would mean it was driven into the body like a sword." He stabbed the air as though he were fencing. "It could have been one of the women, but Ambrose wasn't very tall, if I remember right."

"Na, he was kinda sawed off, like Paco." Tex said with a snicker.

"That would mean, if the killer was someone as tall as Mrs. Carpenter or Leonida, the knife would have been driven downward," Sean rubbed his chin, "unless they did hold it like a sword."

"Ha, I told you." Jose held his brandy glass high. "Neither of them could have killed him."

"That would leave Aurie and Ruby," Judge Hansen said.

"Yes, but now we're dealing with the issue of strength. How deep was the knife?"

"All the way in," Hanky said.

"All the way?"

Hanky nodded.

"Wow." Sean shook his head. "That's what, a ten inch blade? I don't think that either one of those girls are that strong."

"Then, we're back where we started from." Judge Hansen frowned.

"Not really," Sean said. "Everything I said here tonight is just theory. You know, the rambling of a man of science? But with your permission, Your Honor, I'd like to study this case a little longer. I find it quite interesting."

"Study it? How?" Hanky said.

"Well, for one thing, you weren't quite sure exactly how the knife entered the body. That might be something you'd like to know before you hang someone. So, I'd like to exhume the body for starters."

"Exhume the body? What's that mean?" Tex said.

"Dig Ambrose Brice up," Judge Hansen said.

"Dig him up? Ewww." Tex screwed up his face.

"Santa Maria." Jose Flores crossed himself.

"Think it will actually help?" Judge Hansen asked.

"Positive."

"General, find me a piece of paper and a pen." Hansen rounded the desk to sit in Leonida's chair. "I'll write your order right now, Doctor Kilkenney, if it might prevent me from hanging a young girl."

Chapter 12

"I'm busy, Rodeen. I've got to be in court in an hour." James Sattler stuffed a stack of paper inside his briefcase.

"Now, that's a rude way to treat your new partner." Darrell drug a chair closer in order to prop his feet on top of the desk.

"That's highly polished walnut." James swatted the dirty boots to the floor and gave the desktop a rub with his coat sleeve. "Now, what do you want?"

"I just wanted to see how my partner is doing."

"Your partner is busy making money, if you don't mind." James wormed his way past Darrell and the desk. "Like I said, I'm due in court, so make your visit short."

"I was thinking we could have dinner at the Maison Dorée, that new French restaurant they just opened."

"Impossible. I'm meeting a new client concerning business at that time. Now, if there isn't anything else..." He motioned toward the door.

"Well, since you put it that way, yes there is. I'd like another advance from the treasury." Darrell propped one of his boots back onto the desk.

"Dammit." James swatted his leg this time only to have Darrell grab him by the coat collar.

"Let's not forget that I'm a major stockholder in this company, Jimmy-boy. I've got the evidence to send you on a long vacation, if it ever made it into the right hands."

"Yes, and I've been thinking about that too." He forcibly removed Darrell's grip from his collar. "I've been wondering just how much evidence you have, and just how good it is."

"It's good enough."

"Good enough isn't quite good enough, Rodeen." James straightened his jacket. "You see, it would have to be perfect. Because if it isn't, I would make you look so silly they would laugh you right out of court. In the first place, I'm a respected lawyer, and you're nothing but a wandering sea-tramp with a drinking and gambling habit. Oh yes, I've done a little background checking myself."

"That's very good, Jimmy-boy." Darrell grinned and nodded. "I'd hate to think I have a lazy partner. My evidence is more than good, and it's all written out and addressed to a federal judge in case of my early demise. But I'm happy to hear you have so much energy. I'm sure we'll have a fine working relationship."

"Yes, I'm sure we will." James took out his checkbook and began writing. "By the way," he paused to stare across the desk, "since we are going to be partners, I just might have a little job for you. You are planning on earning your keep, aren't you?"

"Certainly, Jimmy-boy. What do you take me for, a free-loader?" James tore the check from the book and waved it in the air to dry the ink.

"There's a certain family by the name of Ramose. It seems they have run out of money. They own a rather large spread in the Sacramento Valley, but I'm afraid I might have to foreclose on their property in order to pay their court bills. Don Ramos has already signed over most of the property to me, but his son, Manuel, has been raising quite a stink. He's claiming I didn't give them the proper representation in court, and he's actually been trying to obtain another solicitor with the intention of raising the question of fraud. I believe I can handle all the questions he might raise, but he could waste a lot of precious time. In the meantime, there is a large corporation thinking of building an entire community with housing, warehouses, and lumber mills right in that area. We are talking about a huge amount of money for a large amount of people. I don't believe it would be right for one angry Mexican to stand in the way of all that progress, do you?"

"No, it would be immoral," Darrell said as he folded the check and stuffed it into his pocket.

"I heard Manuel has taken a job aboard a steamer, hauling supplies to the gold camps in order to help support his family. I applaud his noble efforts, but have you ever heard of a Mexican sailor?"

"No, not too many." Darrell snickered.

"Well, I was kind of worried that his inexperience might cause him to have an accident of some sort. I'm not even sure if the lad knows how to swim." James crinkled his eyebrows and shook his head.

"Yes, that would be horrible, wouldn't it? I just might have to check into it for his safety. Do you happen to know the name of the steamer?"

"Yes, it's the Golden Bell. If I'm not mistaken, it sails day after tomorrow at daybreak out of Sacramento."

"You know something, partner? I've been yearning to feel a deck under my feet. I realize that sailing a steamer up and down a river isn't quite the same as being aboard a fast clipper with her sails billowing in the wind and the smell of salt-spray in your face, but it might be kind of nice for a change. If you're positive you won't be needing me around the office for a week or so, I just might see if I can accompany our Mexican friend aboard the Golden Bell for a few days."

"Now, that is quite thoughtful of you, Darrell. I hope you will be able to stay close enough to Manuel Ramos to prevent something bad from happening to him."

James Sattler waited until the echo of Darrell's boots disappeared down the hallway. "Better watch out for yourself, Rodeen. People who squeeze too tightly sometimes wind up getting squashed in the end."

~   ~   ~

Salty Moran watched Rodeen leave the office building from his table at the sidewalk cafe across the street. He had just enough time to toss down his drink, pay his bill, and grab his corned beef on rye from the plate before dancing through the traffic to the opposite side of the street. He could see the turned-up collar on Rodeen's blue jacket half a block ahead. Salty took a healthy bite of his lunch and wiped his mouth against his sleeve as he skipped past a fat man struggling against the hill. He had just about finished his sandwich by the time Rodeen turned into The Silver Slipper. He waited outside long enough to savor the last bite before entering.

Rodeen was seated at a table with a scantily-clad brunette hanging on his arm. Salty ordered a drink at the bar before shuffling toward Rodeen's table.

"Darrell, me lad," he slapped his shipmate on the back, "'tis good to see you again."

"Salty! Sit yourself down, old man." Darrell motioned toward an empty spot on the other side of the table. The brunette gave Salty an irritated glance as he pulled an empty chair around and leaned his elbows on the table. "Where have you been keeping yourself?"

"Oh, here and there." Salty shrugged. "Just waiting for the captain to set sail again. About spent all me pay these past few weeks in places like this." He tossed his head toward the card tables with a grin. "From the looks of things, you're doing okay."

"Me? Oh, I'm doing fine." Darrell laughed as he refilled Salty's glass from the bottle on the table. "In fact, you'll probably be sailing without me when the North Star leaves port."

"Is that a fact?" Salty leaned farther across the table.

"Yes," Darrell hugged the brunette closer and raised his glass, "I've gone into partnership with a successful law firm. I'll be making more in one month than you'll be making all year, slaving for Captain McDougal."

"Ya don't say?"

"Yes, I do say. Drink up, old man." Darrell tossed down his drink and refilled both glasses.

"That's bloody good for you mate. I always knew you was interested in courts and trials and that legal rot. I never realized you practiced law yourself."

"Well, I don't. Not just yet. I'm working on that. What I'm doing right now is the investigating, you know," he motioned with his hand, "the leg work. I look things up and keep tabs on people. In fact," he let go of the brunette and leaned close to Salty, "I'm working on a case right now that involves hundreds of thousands of dollars. I'll be leaving town first thing in the morning."

"No." Salty took a sip of his drink and hugged the table so their faces were only inches apart.

"Yes, I'll be working undercover, kind of like a spy. But you'd never guess how. I've got to act like a sailor. Can you believe it?" He leaned back and laughed.

"Well, that ought to be an easy one." Salty took the liberty of refilling Rodeen's glass from the bottle. "Any particular ship you might be sailing?"

"Na, not a real ship. That's the only kicker. I'm going to be stuck on the Golden Bell. She's one of those river boats. It's only for a week or two, then I go to my next case. You have any idea when the North Star might be sailing?"

"No, me thinks the captain is tiring of the sea. He's been spending a lot of time with some rich friends hanging around fancy places." Salty frowned. "If me luck don't change, I might be sailing the rivers with you." He chuckled and pushed away from the table.

"Well, it's been good seeing you, mate." He leaned across to grip Darrell's hand. "Wish me luck." He nodded toward one of the card tables. "I'm going to go see if I can't win back some of me pay."

Salty laid his money on the table as the dealer shuffled the cards. He positioned himself in order to see Rodeen's table from the corner of his eye. *Drunken bastard could never keep a secret any better than he plays cards. Some spy he'll make.*

~   ~   ~

Tex and Paco were working the range closest to the Mokelumne when Gonzalo Saldana found them.

"Four white mans with guns. They hurt big Blackstone and take gold." The Yokut allowed the white dappled mare to dance from side to side as he spoke.

"Where are they at now?" Tex automatically checked the loads in his pistol.

"Across river at Blackstone hacienda. They look for more gold."

"Go find Baca and the others. Paco and I will try to hold them." The Indian dug his heels into the dapple's flanks before Tex had finished speaking.

"Maybe he reads your mind." Paco chuckled. "Come on, before he beats us to the river."

Both men urged their mounts into a full gallop past the scrub oaks and manzanita. Paco took the lead when he chose to leap his horse across a wash instead of slowing to a walk. Tex finally caught up with him and dismounted behind a clump of brush and trees opposite the abandoned camp. Water, which ran freely through open troughs and into the sluice, fed the crude waterwheel that Vernon Blackstone had built. Shovels and picks lay strewn on the ground. They could see the men gathered in front of Vernon Blackstone's cabin across the river.

"Ain't no way of us getting across without them seeing us, pard." Tex nodded toward the footbridge spanning the river. The muffled sound of unshod hooves caused them to turn as Baca and a dozen Indians slipped past to disappear into another wash a hundred yards or more to the north.

"Let's follow them." Paco motioned with his head.

"Better hurry," Tex said as they scrambled toward the horses. "They'll have them scalped before we cross the river."

Both men pushed their horses hard through the wash and out onto the gravel sandbar that reached halfway across the river. The last two Indians were already urging their ponies up the opposite bank. Tex's horse snorted his disagreement as he urged him into the water. The cowboy caught his breath and issued his own disagreement in the form of a curse as the icy water filled his boots and swept up around his waist. Baca was already in the process of ordering his men to surround the cabin by the time they dismounted behind a clump of oak trees.

"Want me and Paco to greet them for you?" The Indian only shrugged. "Well, once yer men are in place, why don't we all three greet them together then?" He got another shrug followed by a nod. "Yeah, sounds like a good plan to me too."

"I think they're ready." Paco motioned toward one of the Indians who was waving a lance behind a clump of brush opposite the cabin. The men stepped into the clearing just as one of the bandits slapped Catherine Blackstone across the face. Her two children were crouched against the wall crying. Tex could see a prostrate Vernon Blackstone lying on the floor inside the open door.

"Hey, I wouldn't be doing that if I wuz you." Tex cocked the hammer on his .44. The men on the porch jerked around to stare. "My pa says there are only two kinds of critters that would treat a lady that-a-way. That either makes you a hydrophied skunk or a damned Yankee. Now, which one you claiming to be?"

One of the men raised his gun and was instantly propelled against the wall by a blast from Paco's .44.

"Coulda told ya that would happen. Both my pards here are more than fair hands at that game. Now, why don't you three drop yer irons and leave them folks alone? Ain't no way of you getting out of here in one piece. The brush around this cabin is crawling with Yokuts, and none of them's acting too friendly toward you right this minute."

"Emery?" One of the men stared at the man who had been hitting Catherine Blackstone.

"He's lying."

"Baca? Show 'em we ain't fooling." The Indian raised his lance in the air, and the Indians surrounding the cabin stepped into the clearing. "Better drop them guns or these men are gonna take yer heads off."

"Go to hell." Emery Hawkins grabbed Catherine Blackstone around the neck and pulled her against his body as a shield. "I'm taking this woman with me. You're going to stand back and let us go, or I'm going to blow her brains out." He shoved the pistol against her head.

Tex took a step backward as a huge hand shot from the open door to latch onto Emery's wrist. He could hear the bones snap as the gun-hand was jerked away from Catherine in a twisting motion. Emery's scream was cut short as a second arm swept around his throat to lift him off his feet. "Damn," Tex muttered as both men disappeared inside the cabin. The stunned bandits on the porch dropped their guns as the Indians charged. Tex paused at the cabin door to see Vernon Blackstone panting over the prostrate man on the floor. The huge farmer had a bullet wound in his left shoulder and a bloody knot on his forehead.

"Think you kilt him, Vern," Tex said, squatting to take a closer look.

"Didn't mean to, but he was hurting Cathy. No one hurts my wife. Not while I'm around." He was instantly surrounded by his wife and children, all clamoring for some sort of hold.

"Well, I wouldn't spend too much time repenting over him none. This feller was aiming to get hisself kilt one way or another." He stood to holster his gun. "If it hadn't been you, it would have certainly been me or Paco or one of the Injuns. What happened to the others who was working the claim?"

"Only had two with me today. They killed Mario, and Gonzalo got away."

"Yeah, he was the one to tell us about this little party. Well, guess we'd better start posting some armed guards around that claim from now on." Tex stepped out onto the porch to eye the two remaining bandits.

"Vernon tells me y'all kilt Mario. He was a mighty good vaquero and a friend of mine. Murder? Assault and armed robbery? Looks like my pa's gonna have hisself a little hanging party after Judge Hansen gets through with y'all."

~   ~   ~

It wasn't hard for Darrell to land a job as a deck hand aboard the Golden Bell. They were always looking for experienced sailors on the barges. It was even easier to pick out Manuel Ramos. He was a tall, good-looking lad of about twenty. Darrell thought it kind of sad, what was about to happen, but business was business, and the Ramos boy was an obstacle in the way of progress. Darrell gave a final tug on the knot to make sure the stack of supplies was secure, when someone called his name. It was Salty Moran waving from the pier.

"I had me a real bad run at the table last night. They got room for one more sailor aboard?"

"I don't know, mate. Might be. You'll have to check with the captain. He's over at the shipping office. Big man with a gray beard." Darrell watched as Salty disappeared through the crowd. *That'll put a kink in my plans, but a job is still a job.*

Chapter 13

"Hello." The sound of his voice caused Leonida to jump. She had come to the fountain by the cover of night, thinking she would be alone.

"Oh, pardon me, Doctor Kilkenney. I did not see you hiding there."

"I wasn't hiding." He came into the moonlight smoking his pipe. "Well, that isn't actually true. I guess I was, in a way."

"Sí, you were hiding from me." She laughed. "I looked to see if anyone was here and did not see you."

"Would you have come had you seen me?" Sean propped one foot on the edge of the fountain and leaned his elbow against his knee.

"Perhaps. Maybe not. I was hoping to be alone. I have been constantly surrounded by people lately."

"Yes, I know. I've been trying to talk to you for several days now."

"Talk? Señor, we have spoken several times since you arrived here. I thought we had a rather lengthy conversation at dinner just tonight."

"No," Sean shook his head, "we did not have a lengthy conversation. Everybody seated at the table had a conversation. The trouble has been what you first said. We, you and I, have barely spoken to each other. We haven't been able to sit down and have a conversation like we used to when I lived here."

"Well, okay señor." Leonida perched herself on the bricks and patted the spot beside her with her palm. "I seem toremember that we used to sit here quite frequently and talk. So tell me what is on your mind?"

"Oh, things," Sean took the place beside her. He leaned forward with his elbows on his knees to study the smoldering pipe in his fingers. "I was wondering how you have been doing."

"Me? I've been doing fine. Very busy, as you well know, with the court hearings in San Francisco, and now this robbery at the mine, and the murder trial in Dogtown. But me personally? I've been well." She folded her hands in her lap and smiled. "How about yourself, Doctor? How have you been?"

"Busy also. I started my own medical practice, you know." Leonida nodded. "Well, they've kept me going both day and night. I started feeling like I was going to smother. That's why I chose to come here on the spur of the moment. I guess I missed the open spaces and clean air."

"Oh, I was under the impression you came to see me." She stuck out her bottom lip and frowned.

"But I did come to see you." Sean clasped a hand on her forearm.

"Come, you don't have to pretend with me, Doctor. We've been friends a long time. She's rather pretty, you know?"

"Who, Loretta? No, you don't understand."

"What is there not to understand, Señor Kilkenney? You're a man, and Señorita Stewart is a lovely woman. You've been away from this rancho for a long time now. I don't blame you for finding someone else. It hurt me terribly when you left. I cried for days, but I'm past that now. I must admit, though, I was both shocked and hurt when I first saw her standing by your buggy. But I have spent some time visiting with her since, and find her to be a nice lady. I can't blame you for liking her, and I wish you both all the best."

"What in the world are you talking about?" Sean chuckled. "I told you, Loretta and I are just friends. Don't you believe me?"

"Sí, I think that is what you are believing now. I've seen the way you watch her while she is in the room, and I know for certain that she thinks of you as more than just a friend. That woman is in love with you, Doctor." Leonida turned her moist eyes toward the darkness and managed a laugh.

"That may be the way she feels about me, Leonida, but I promise you, it is entirely different as far as I'm concerned. You are the one I've thought about every night for this past year."

"Don't." She removed his hand from her arm and stood with her back to him. "Don't lie to me again."

"Leonida," he took her by the shoulders, "look at me." She shook her head vigorously. "Okay, I did leave. I was mixed up. After what I had been through in Dogtown, and when I saw Judge Baines hanged...I just don't know. Things where all jumbled inside my head. I had to get away."

"Those things happened to us all, señor. Everyone on this rancho was affected by what happened in Dogtown. You keep talking about yourself, but I was the one who was violated, and it was my husband and brother-in-law who were murdered, remember?" Her green eyes sparkled as she glared at him. "I was hurt and humiliated by those events, señor. I did what I had to do in order to stop those evil men from killing more people. I didn't like it any more than you did. I had nightmares about what happened for the longest time. I still do, sometimes." She turned her back on him and blew her nose.

"Yes, I know. I'm sorry." Sean nuzzled the golden hair flowing down the back of her neck.

"Not sorry enough to stay and help me through the bad times. You know who held me at night while I cried myself to sleep? Angela and Rosa. They took turns sleeping in my bed and sharing my sorrow. They chose to leave their husbands alone on those nights, because there was no one else."

"'Nida...?"

"Don't you ever call me by that name again." Leonida spun to glare at him.

"But, I thought you liked it."

"That is a special name Rudolfo used to call me before he died. I allowed you to use it because I thought you loved me, but no more, señor." She shook her head. "To you, I am Doña Leonida Garcia and nothing more."

"But, why? I don't understand."

"How can you not understand? When you were here, during the time of trouble, did I not allow you to hold me on several occasions?"

"Yes." Sean nodded. "But..."

"And did I not kiss you under that tree?" She pointed toward the ancient oak standing at the edge of the bricks. "I even gave you my husband's pistols. How could you not understand that I loved you more than my own life? I thought we would marry and have children. You were the one who was supposed to hold me at night, not Rosa and Angela. How could you leave me like that? I would never have hurt you that way."

"I don't know what to say." Sean choked on the lump inside his throat.

"There is nothing you can say, señor." Leonida's bottom lip trembled as a tear spilled over to trickle down her cheek. "You made that choice when you left. Buenas noches." She turned to walk briskly across the patio toward the hacienda.

"Leonida, wait," Sean called after her. She paused to glare back over her shoulder.

"Doña Leonida, señor, and I have nothing left to say to you." She snapped her spine rigid and disappeared into the shadows. Sean caught a glimpse of her dress in the lamplight as she opened the door, then it slammed shut.

"Chihuahua, Señor Kilkenney, the Doña is plenty angry with you." He turned to see Juan and Angela Gonzalez standing in the shadow of the oak tree.

"You heard?"

"Sí, how could we not?" The young vaquero shrugged.

"Yeah, the cows on the hillside probably heard also. Maybe you and Angela can tell me. How can a man be so stupid?" Sean stuffed his hands in his pockets to lean against the tree.

"I don't think it is just you señor. Angela thinks I am cursed sometimes too. She says most men are that way."

"Is that true?" He glanced at the pretty girl.

"Sí, pero no es importante." She smiled sadly. "Women can sometimes be locas en la cabeza too, but we don't tell you when. You and Doña Leonida are both loco. You love each other very much, but you also run away. You go to San Francisco to get away from her. That is dumb, Señor Doctor." She tapped the side of Sean's head with her finger. "When you come back, she tells you to go away. That is dumb on her part. This is not good."

"You're telling me. Well," he shrugged, "what do I do now? Go back to San Francisco?"

"Hey, I thought you were a great warrior." Juan laughed. "You beat up big strong men like Señor Blackstone with your hands and stand up to Judge Baines like a pistolero. Now you are going to run from a little argument with your woman? No, señor that will not do. You must stay and fight."

"Fight what? She can't stand the sight of me. I hurt her too badly."

"You do not know women, do you, señor?" Angela said. "Sí, you hurt her, and she is angry, but she still loves you. This I know, and I know her very well. It is up to you to make her see how much she does love you."

"How?"

"I cannot tell you. You must discover it for yourself." She smiled and patted his cheek with her palm. He was about to ask another question when she took Juan by the arm and disappeared into the blackness.

"Yes, Sean Kilkenney, General Flores is right. You are one stupid gringo." He sat on the edge of the brick fountain and lit his pipe.

~   ~   ~

"Quit bothering those women. You've asked them enough questions about the murder." Leonida glared at Hanky through the open door. The retired ranger was seated in her favorite leather chair in the study holding a glass of brandy. Alice Carpenter, Ruby and Aurie were on the sofa, while Judge Hansen, Loretta and Paco took up the remaining chairs.

"Well, we was just jawing, ma'am," Hanky drawled.

"Jaw about something else then. Ambrose Brice was an evil man who deserved to die. Leave these women alone." Her heels clicked against the marble floor as she brushed past Maria, who was coming from the kitchen with a pot of hot tea. The ranger's voice echoed after her as she bounded up the stairs.

"We weren't talking about no murder. We was discussing havin' another whing-ding like the one you threw when Juan and Angela got hitched up."

Leonida flung her door open and stared at the inside of her room for a long minute. Loretta Stewart's voice at the back of her ear caused her to jump.

"He makes you angry enough to spit, doesn't he?"

"Oh." Leonida held her breast. "I didn't hear you follow me up the stairs. I don't understand. Who makes me want to spit?"

"You really are a dear, aren't you?" Loretta eased them both inside and closed the door. "Sean. You just saw him outside, didn't you?"

"Sí, how did you know?"

Loretta tilted her head and laughed as she took Leonida by the hand. "Come here. I want to tell you a story." She pulled her toward the edge of the bed. "Come on." She patted the bedspread as Leonida stood staring.

"Bueno." Leonida folded her hands in her lap and studied Loretta's smiling face.

"Okay, where do we start?" Loretta took a deep breath as a sadness swept across her face. She took one of Leonida's hands and gently massaged the fingers.

"This is going to be hard, so just bear with me, okay?"

Leonida nodded.

"I only told you half the truth when I came here. I did want to see the beautiful ranch with this magnificent house and meet the woman who owned it all. But I also wanted to meet and understand the enemy."

"Enemy? I don't think I understand, señorita. What enemy?"

"I find it hard to believe you're really that innocent. You, Doña Leonida. You're the enemy." She smiled sweetly, before turning away to stare at Leonida's riding crop lying carelessly on the floor next to her wardrobe.

"You see, I fell hopelessly in love with Sean Kilkenney the first time I met him. I haven't been able to rid my mind of him since that moment. I came here with every intention of taking him away from you."

"That should be easy, señorita, since he doesn't belong to me. You may have him, if you wish." Leonida pulled her hand away and moved to the dresser where she removed her veil and began brushing her hair.

"No, that's not quite true, My Lady." Loretta took the brush from her hand and continued the brushing. "You might not have any legal claim to him, but you own his heart whether you know it or not." She paused to run her fingers along a strand of hair. "You have beautiful hair, you know that? You should keep it uncovered so everyone can see how pretty it is."

"Gracias, but that is impossible. I'm Catholic and a widow. I must cover my head by tradition. What do you mean I own his heart?" Leonida glared at her reflection in the mirror. "I was the one who gave him my heart, and he stomped on it like you'd squash a bug. Then he ran off to San Francisco to leave me crying. You'll never know how hard it was for me to love him when he was here the first time. I had just lost my husband and his brother. Rancho Manantial Escondido was not a happy place back then. Those men also killed our priest and many other people who were dear to our hearts." She shifted to look in Loretta's face.

"I don't know what you've heard, but I have never met such evil men in my entire life as Judge Baines and Pod Randell. Those men who worked for them even molested a twelve-year-old girl before killing her and her grandfather." She looked away with a shake of her head. "I had a difficult time loving anyone, including Dios. But our doctor friend persisted in making me love him. Then he ran off. It was like losing my husband all over again. Not many people know how much that hurt." She buried her face in her hands and leaned against the dresser.

"Yes they do." Loretta laid her head against Leonida's shoulder and hugged her. "At least your father does. He told me how he used to listen to you cry in the middle of the night, and how he would pray and thank God for Angela and Rosa being here. Most everyone knew about your pain. Tex certainly did. That's why he gave Sean that fat lip."

"Que?" Leonida crinkled her brow with a crooked grin.

"The one he had the day we arrived. We stopped at their house on the way here, and that cowboy punched Sean in the mouth for bringing me with him. He thought Sean and I were married or something." Loretta rolled her eyes. "He was under the impression that my being here was going to hurt you even worse."

"Bueno." Leonida nodded. "Good for my Texas vaquero. He deserved to get punched in the mouth, and yes, your being here did cause me pain, at first. But I've grown to like you, señorita. You are a good woman with a good heart."

"Oh, I'm not as good as you think I am," Loretta chuckled.

"Sí, I believe you are," she said matter-of-factly. "I've seen you singing and dancing with the children as they play. and I see how you help Maria in the kitchen and Evangelina with the laundry. These are not things guests normally do. But you do them because you want to, and that makes you unselfish, señorita. Perhaps you may have done some things in the past that make you unhappy, but I don't want to hear about them right now. They are between you and Dios. Now, what is this story you wanted to tell me?"

"Well, if you don't want to hear about my past, I guess I'll have to shorten my little speech." Loretta gave a crooked grin. "Like I said, the main reason I decided to come was to take a good look at the competition."

"Well, as far as I'm concerned, you don't have any competition, señorita."

"Mmmm, yes I do." Loretta nodded as she ran the brush through Leonida's hair. "You're still in the running, whether you like it or not. I have tried everything I know to get that man to notice me, and all he's ever wanted to do was talk about you. You don't know how that's made me feel. God, how I hated you. That's why I came. I had to see you for myself."

"Oh." Leonida frowned. "He might be a stupid gringo, but I guess I am a stupida Mexicana. I was starting to believe that he was telling me the truth about you being nothing more than friends. Maybe I just wanted to believe him. You do love him very much, don't you."

"I'm afraid so, but it doesn't seem to matter, does it? What he told you was the truth as far as he's concerned. He is just a friend to me. I don't know what made him leave, Doña Leonida, but he's in love with you. Believe me. I know that for certain." Loretta laid the brush on the dresser with a sniff.

"Well, I can see that we have a problem," Leonida sighed.

"I'll be returning to San Francisco as soon as possible. I'm sorry." Loretta's lip trembled as she smiled into the mirror.

"And why must you return. We've just become friends. Why can't you stay awhile longer?"

"Because, I just told you." Loretta raised her eyebrows and motioned toward the door with her head.

"Señor Kilkenney? I think it is time he had to suffer like he has made us suffer. I have been thinking as you were talking, señorita. I don't believe we are the only women that he has left with broken hearts."

"Probably not. I have a feeling that comes naturally with him. But I don't know if I could stand to sit by and watch him chase after you, knowing how I feel about him. I'm not as brave and noble as you. How would you feel if he suddenly decided he really did love me, instead of you?"

"I wouldn't feel any worse than I already feel, and you couldn't either, could you?"

Loretta shook her head.

"Besides, I will be praying and asking Saint Joseph to find us each a good husband, not one that will play with our hearts like our doctor friend. I will also pray to Saint Anne to provide him with a good wife. Then, perhaps, he will quit hurting women this way."

"Rosa was right about you." Loretta's stare caused Leonida to squirm.

"Que? What is it that my friend has been telling you?"

"That I'd wind up loving you. Dear God, I don't think I could ever just pray, then sit back and let things happen like that. I'd be fighting with everything I've got. What if he turns his back on you again?"

"Señorita, that is exactly what I intend on doing. I am going to be fighting for both of us. If Dios can't make the doctor love me, then I certainly can't. Besides, he might choose someone entirely different than both of us. But, would you honestly want to marry someone who you suspected might actually love another woman? I didn't think so," she said as Loretta shook her head. "When I married my Rudolfo, it was an arranged marriage. I had nothing to say in the matter, but I was confident I was the only woman in his life. So, come." She pulled Loretta's cheek next to hers to stare in the mirror.

"It is time for us to have some fun. We are going to hold our heads high and conduct ourselves as the beautiful ladies we are. We will smile and flutter our eyes, but keep our proper distance. The doctor can look, but he will never touch until Dios has made up his mind. It will be fun to see him so miserable for once." She smiled at their reflection.

~   ~   ~

Manuel Ramos was busy coiling a rope on deck of the Golden Bell when Salty first noticed the shadow. It flashed across the lights coming from Grayson as the paddleboat rounded the bend in the Stanislaus River. He could hear the whine of a fiddle and laughter over the chug-chugging of the steam engine. The cabin had just rung eight bells and the mining camp was in full swing. Nearly everyone coming or leaving the mining camps of Columbia, Angels Camp, Jamestown or Dogtown somehow passed through Grayson. The hundred-thousand plus population consisted of miners, storekeepers, whiskey-drummers and a sizeable stable of whores. They were, for the most part, transients who lived in tents or temporary housing. There was talk once of making Grayson the capital of California because of its large population but, like most folks, Salty only counted it as talk. If the truth were known, most of its citizens didn't give a rip. Whores didn't vote, and none of the miners would be staying long enough to care what happened one way or the other.

Salty kept hidden as the deck came alive with activity. The landing of a paddle boat against the river's current was tricky enough in broad daylight, but even with the modern lamplight provided by the Golden Bell the landing would be dangerous to say the least. The slightest miscalculation could either damage the ship and the dock or, as in some cases, crush a man between the two. The shadow moved more quickly now, passing from a stack of barrels to a load of dry goods, and on to a bundle of tent canvas. The dock was in sight, and Salty was close enough to see the brass buttons on the man's jacket in the light. The dark figure glanced quickly from side to side before rising from the canvas. His movements were quick and sure as he brought the club down across Manuel's head, then, one quick shove and the young Mexican toppled overboard. The shadow turned to glance around as the light from the dock passed over him. It was Darrell Rodeen.

"Hey, you down there," came a voice from the cabin, "toss that rope to the men waiting on the dock." Rodeen calmly picked up the coil and prepared to give it a toss. Salty slipped to the starboard side of the boat. It was evident that in all the confusion, he was the only one who had witnessed the murder. He took one second to stare at the black, churning water sliding past before climbing over the rail.

"Hey, you! What do you think you're doing?"

Salty only had time to glance at the sailor headed toward him before kicking away. He hit the icy water with a splash. The churning paddles threatened to suck him into their path as they passed dangerously close. He could hear the screaming of the steam whistle and shouts from the men on deck as he kicked against the current.

"Now, where the hell are you, mate?" He shook the water from his hair and scanned the blackness of the water along the riverbank.

Chapter 14

Jonathan McDougal dismounted the large roan and adjusted his captain's cap before handing the reins to Julio.

"Take good care of him, boy," he said, slipping a gold coin into the lad's palm. "He's brought me a far piece these past two days."

"Sí, gracias, señor."

He glanced back over his shoulder as he neared the hacienda to see the boy sharing his good fortune with his fellow stable hands. He was in the process of stamping the dust from his boots when Maria Sanchez burst through the front door to engulf him in her arms.

"Señor McDougal! Ahhh, it is so good to see you again."

"And 'tis good to feel your arms around me once again, Maria. Tell me," he held her at arms length, "have you been faithful to me while I was away?"

"Hay, you tease me, señor," she giggled. "You know Maria is always good."

"Ha, but not with that landlubber Texan close at hand. I know he had eyes for you. Tell me the truth now."

"Well, señor, what can I say? When he talks so sweet to me?" She shrugged.

"That's what I thought. I'll have him flogged and strung up by the yardarm."

"Oh, but Señor McDougal. Who would nibble on my ear in the moonlight? You just like my cooking, not my ears." She took him by the arm. "Come, Doña Leonida and her papa have ridden to Dogtown to watch the gringo medico dig up a dead man."

"What?" He stopped her in the doorway. "Dig up a dead man? What in the blazes are you talking about?"

"What she is trying to tell you is that Doctor Kilkenney plans on exhuming the body of Ambrose Brice, the man who was murdered a couple of weeks ago."

"Ah, yes." McDougal was stunned at the sight of the beautiful woman standing in the hall holding a cup of tea. "I caught that part. But why?"

"Because he is loco en la cabeza." Maria shook her head. "Jesus Cristo and the holy angels will judge him very harshly for this. He will catch a bad sickness."

"That may be a distinct possibility, if he is going to examine a decaying corpse. But I still don't understand why in the world he would want to do something like that. For what reason?" McDougal had trouble taking his eyes off the woman sipping tea.

"Because, he thinks he might be able to help determine who the murderer is, by how the knife entered the body. Or, so he says. By the way, my name is Loretta Stewart." She set the tea cup aside and held out a soft hand. "You must be Captain McDougal. *Sastipe, Vatave McDougal. Nos me baksheesh dik tu.*" She dropped her gaze and bowed low toward the floor. "I've heard a lot about you."

"*Gestena, endra. E ta'co baksheesh se me.*" Jonathan kissed her hand and returned the bow. "You may call me Jonathan, if you like. I haven't heard Gaelic since leaving the East Coast. Where in the world did you learn to speak it so perfectly?"

"My grandmother is Scottish. We used to speak it around the house when I was a child. It drove my father crazy."

"He must have already been insane, if he did not take pleasure in hearing God's own language flow from such beautiful lips." He bowed again.

"My, but I think I'm going to like this man." Loretta grinned at Maria.

"Sí, I don't understand what you say to each other, but he is an angel sent from Dios."

"Uh-oh." Loretta raised her eyebrows with a grin. "If he's a real angel, I'm in big trouble. I told him it was my good fortune to meet him, and he returned the greeting and called me his sister."

"No need to worry about me being one of the heavenly host, ma'am. I sometimes get the feeling that God has a hand in what I'm doing, but I'm certainly no angel." He took Loretta by the arm and followed Maria into the kitchen.

"Please pardon me if I stare," he pulled a chair out for her at the table, "but seeing such a lovely lady, other than Mrs. Garcia, grace the halls of this hacienda is a pleasant surprise."

"And, what about Maria? Isn't she lovely also?" Loretta gave him a crooked grin as she took her seat.

"Most beautiful, but that pagan Texan with the gray mustache has already claimed her. Now, you must tell me, lovely lady," he sat to stare across the table at her, "has anyone claimed you?"

"Not yet." Loretta shook her head. It had been a long time since she could remember blushing, but her cheeks burned as she sipped her tea. Maria nodded with a smile as she turned to fill two more cups with the hot liquid.

~   ~   ~

"Eeewee, shore ya wanna go through with this, Doc?" Hanky helped Sean drag the wooden box out of the hole.

"No, but I have to."

"Shore do stink. I can smell him right through the box," Tex said leaning on his shovel.

"Don't remind me. It's going to be hard enough as it is." Sean waited for Hanky to pull his scarf up over his nose. He could see Leonida and her father standing with the small crowd at the edge of the cemetery.

119

"Might not hurt for you to wear one of these," the ranger said as he hoisted his end of the casket.

"Does it cut down on the smell?"

"Can't say that it does, but it don't hurt none either."

"I'll wait until we pry the lid off," Sean said as they slid the box into the back of the buckboard.

"Where're we takin' him?" Hanky said as they climbed into the driver's seat.

"I don't know. Somewhere where people don't go too often. It'll take awhile to air the place out after we're through."

"How about the jail, then. Ain't been nobody inside there since Leonida's ball that I know of. Hiya, getup there." Hanky slapped the reins, and the buckboard gave a groan as the horses lurched forward. Sean could see Rosa cross herself and mumble a prayer as they inched their way past those gathered at the gate. The crowd followed, but stayed a comfortable distance back.

"That's nice," Sean said.

"What's that?"

"I said it was nice seeing Rosa pray for Ambrose's soul. I know how she hated the man."

"Hell, she still does. I seen her spit and call curses down on his stiff body myself. She ain't praying for him, she's praying for you and me, and Tommy."

"Praying for us? Why?"

"Cause we dug him up. Them Mexican and Injun folks been saying something bad's gonna happen to us ever since they heard what we was gonna do. They think that maybe Ambrose's ghost is gonna haunt us, or we're gonna get sick and die." Hanky stopped the buckboard in front of the jail.

"Well, I don't rightly believe in ghosts, but there is a big argument going on in the medical field about the possibility of catching some sort of disease from a cadaver."

"A what?"

"A cadaver. A body. Someone who's dead. So, when we get the coffin open, I want you to stand back and let me do the work." Sean climbed down and grabbed his medical kit and a carpet bag with extra clothing from under the seat.

"Well, you ain't got no argument from me there, Doc. I always thought he was kinda ugly when he was alive, and I ain't thinking he got no better looking stuck inside the ground. Hey, Tommy," Hanky said looking past Sean, "give us a hand carrying this here carcass inside the jail before some buzzards start collecting for dinner. This is where he shoulda been long ago." Sean waited until they had the coffin completely inside the building before approaching Leonida who had now joined the others in front of Carpenter's General Store.

"Doña Leonida?" He removed his hat and bowed.

"Sí, Señor Kilkenney?" Those standing nearby glanced at each other.

"I wonder if it would be possible to have someone in your company collect several buckets of hot water for me? I would like to wash and change my clothes after I complete the autopsy."

"Sí, I'm sure that is possible. Where would you like us to set them?"

"Anywhere. Right outside the door of the jail would be fine."

"Bueno." She nodded curtly. "It will be there With a bar of soap when you need it."

"Thank you, m'lady." He bowed again. "Ladies." He nodded toward the others and turned away. He could hear Rosa snicker as he crossed the street. Tex and Hanky had the nails loose and the lid ready to remove when he closed the door.

"Weren't inviting none of them over to watch, was you?" Hanky grinned.

"No, I was simply asking for some hot water so I could wash up when I'm finished. Your wife laughed at me as I was leaving." He glared at Tex.

"Rosa? What for?"

"I really don't have any idea, but I suspect Leonida told them about our little misunderstanding last night." Sean tossed his medical kit on top of the former sheriff's desk and opened it.

"Really? Now what could you two have to tussle over?" Hanky said.

"The fact that I left. I was trying to explain how I felt at the time, and how much I really care about her right this minute, when she told me it didn't make any difference. She said I hurt her, and she gave me strict orders to address her as Doña Leonida from now on. That's exactly what I did, and it brought a snicker out of Rosa, and sarcastic grins from everyone else."

"Well, I wouldn't worry myself too much about it, if I was you. Me and Rosa's always got something to argue about. But we always get over it. You and Leonida will too," Tex said.

"Tommy's right." Hanky licked the paper on the cigarette he'd just rolled. "But just to set the record straight, you did hurt her pretty bad, boy, running off like that, when everyone was expecting you two to get hitched. I'm surprised that her pa didn't shoot yer leg off when you come back totin' that pretty girl on your arm the way you did."

"Oh, to hell with it. I've already explained about Loretta a dozen times, and I don't care a whit what she told Rosa and the others. When I finish helping you figure out who killed Ambrose, I'm going back to San Francisco where I belong." Sean grabbed a notepad and pen from his bag and glared at the wooden box on the table. "You have the butcher knife that killed him handy?"

"Right here." Hanky handed him the knife wrapped in buckskin. "Careful, it's kinda sharp."

"Take the lid off and let's get this over with."

~   ~   ~

"What did you discover, Doctor?" Jose Flores glanced at Sean seated behind Leonida's desk as he lit a cigar. "Or, is that privileged information?"

"No." Sean looked up from his notepad. "I don't think it is anything we didn't already know. I'm certain that it was indeed the knife that killed him. It went almost straight in, as Hanky said, and exited through the back. In doing so, it punctured the left side of the heart. Ambrose couldn't have lived more than seconds with a wound such as that."

"So, you are saying we are right back where we started from?" Jose raised his eyebrows and frowned.

"Maybe. I need to think on this some more." Sean pulled his pipe from his coat pocket and began packing tobacco in the bowl. "Something isn't right. I'm not convinced that Ruby killed him."

"Then, why would those women lie about..." Both men turned as the front door opened. Leonida entered with the women in tow from their evening walk. Ruby stopped her giggling to stare at the men in Leonida's study.

"Buenas noches, Señorita Ruby. How are you enjoying your stay at our rancho?" Jose smiled.

"Fine. It's a whole lot nicer than my room at The Rusty Rail." She gripped the doorway and coughed violently. "Oh damn, that hurts." She clutched the front of her blouse.

"Why didn't anyone tell me about this?" Sean lay his pipe on the desk and crossed the room.

"We thought you knew," Alice Carpenter said from the hallway.

"Hardly." He tilted Ruby's pale face upward to study her eyes. "I've only caught fleeting glimpses of her in the past few days, and this is the first time I've heard her cough. He felt her forehead with the back of his hand before placing his fingers against her throat to check her pulse. "You're going to bed, young lady."

"Okay, but I usually get five dollars in advance." She grinned.

"That's not what I meant, and you know it. You're ill, young lady. Very ill."

"Aw, don't sweat it, Doc." She grinned and pulled away. "It's nothing you or anyone else can help."

"And what gave you that idea?"

"Because I'm dying. You recognize consumption, don't you?"

"Yes, ma'am. I do recognize consumption, among dozens of other diseases. Who told you that you had consumption?"

"Ambrose. He said he'd seen a lot of it before coming to Dogtown, and knew for certain that's what I had." Her eyes grew cloudy as she looked away.

"Well, I'm afraid that your former employer was either an adroit liar, or a horrible doctor. What I suspect you have isn't consumption." Ruby's head snapped upward.

"Really?" Alice peered over one of Ruby's shoulders. "What is it then, Doctor?"

"I don't rightly know at the moment, but I'd like for you to let me know when you've gotten her tucked into bed. I want to have a better look at her." He could see Leonida staring at him from down the hall as he turned to retrieve his notepad from her desk. She was standing in the doorway when he turned back around.

"Do you think you will be able to help her?" Her voice swept over him like velvet.

"I'm hoping, m'lady." He bowed and slipped past her to ascend the stairs two at a time. He could hear her father addressing her in Spanish as he closed the door to his room.

"Thought you'd never quit your talking and come up here," Captain McDougal said from Sean's leather-backed chair by the window.

"Damn, you scared the hell out of me, man. What are you doing in my room?" Sean scowled.

"Waiting for you."

"That's obvious. What for?"

"We need to have a little private talk, m'boy." McDougal fished a couple of cigars out of his vest pocket and passed one of them to Sean. "I didn't want to take a chance of anyone else hearing what we have to discuss."

"Now, what could we have to discuss that would be that important?" Sean struck a match and lit McDougal's cigar before lighting his own.

"You know that solicitor Mrs. Garcia has in San Francisco?"

"Mmhum, James Sattler. What about him?" Sean rolled up his shirt sleeves and began washing his hands and face.

"Well, it seems he's hired one of my crew members as an employee."

"Is that bad?"

"In this case, yes. Darrell Rodeen is one of the least trustworthy men I've ever had aboard the North Star. He's a poor gambler and a drunk to boot. He's always broke, but now, all of a sudden, he's flush with money and employed by Mrs. Garcia's solicitor."

"Perhaps Mr. Sattler is simply a bad judge of character. You can't get down on a man for that." Sean dried his face and tossed the towel over the foot of the bed.

"I only wish that were the case. Someone shoved this note under my door early yesterday in San Francisco." He pulled the crumpled piece of paper from his coat pocket and smoothed it against his leg. "It's from Salty Moran. I got suspicious and asked him to keep an eye on Rodeen. Three nights ago, Salty saw Rodeen hit a young Mexican on the head and toss him into the San Joaquin River." Sean stopped buttoning his collar to listen. "Salty dove into the river and rescued that young man from drowning. He is still in bad shape, but alive, and hiding out with a Mexican family not too awfully far from here."

"That's horrible, but it might not have anything at all to do with Mrs. Garcia's solicitor."

"One would think that." McDougal pulled a flask from his coat pocket and popped the cork. "Except that the young Mexican is the son of another one of Sattler's clients. It seems that this son was being a thorn in his side. He didn't trust Sattler and was trying to talk his parents into hiring another solicitor to take over their case. The trouble is, they've already given Sattler nearly every cent they have. Then, after talking to Bill Ralston, a banker I know quite well, I found out that Sattler talked those Mexicans into signing a power of attorney over to him concerning their property. That gives him the right to obtain loans against their rancho, which he already has. Those people are in hawk up to their eyebrows and don't even know it yet."

"That's a horrific story. I'll grant you that," Sean filled two small glasses from atop his dresser with the flask, but why are you telling me all this?"

"Because we have to do something."

"Why? I've never met those people you've been talking about." Sean tossed down his drink and began combing is hair.

"No, you damnable Irishman. I mean, in order to protect Mrs. Garcia." Captain McDougal scowled as Sean glanced over his shoulder and laughed.

"Protect Leonida? Do you honestly think she needs protecting, Captain? She's tougher than any ten of her vaqueros rolled together. Don't forget what happened in Dogtown."

"You still stewing about that? For the love of Queen Mary and the Scotts! No wonder the McDougals fought your clan for a hundred years. Your skulls are thicker than barnacles on Davy Jones' locker." Captain McDougal grew red in the face. "That was war, and she acted properly, as any commander would have. But this is a totally different type of battle. One with pens and papers, and men arguing their cases in a court of law. It just so happens, that solicitor she hired is as crooked as a dog's hind leg."

"So, what do you expect me to do?" Sean crossed his ankles and leaned against the dresser. "I didn't hire the man, and I can't fire him either. You should be telling her all this, not me."

"Yes, I suppose you're right. I just thought you would be concerned enough to want to help." McDougal jammed the cork back into the flask and shoved it inside his coat pocket.

"I'm sorry, Captain, but Leonida Garcia is a big girl. She let me know in no uncertain terms that she is able to handle her own affairs without any help from me. Besides, I wouldn't know what either one of us could do in the first place. This is something she will have to handle herself."

"Well, I can see this was a waste of time and good whiskey. See you later, Doctor. Hope you sleep well." He crossed the room to grab hold of the door handle before glaring back at Sean. "I, for the life of me, don't know how any red-blooded man could stand by and watch a woman like her being taken advantage of. But then, I don't know if an Irishman's blood is red."

"It's red, Captain. But we don't know that she's being taken advantage of yet, now do we? And yes, I will sleep good, once I get through examining my new patient down the hall."

McDougal slammed the door, and Sean turned back to the mirror to fix his tie. A soft rap on the door caused him to sigh. "Yes, come in."

"Doctor Kilkenney," Alice Carpenter poked her head into the room, "your patient is ready."

Chapter 15

"I'm afraid I have some bad news for you." Darrell Rodeen plopped himself in the chair and stretched his legs in front of James Sattler's desk. "It seems that the Ramos boy hit his head against something and fell overboard as the boat was pulling into Grayson."

"Did they search for the body?"

"Hell yeah, we all did. One guy even jumped overboard, but they never found hide nor hair of him. Never found the man that jumped overboard either. It's really too bad." Rodeen poked out his bottom lip and shook his head. "That stretch of river is full of snags and real treacherous. A man could get sucked under and never surface again. To make things worse, we were making the landing by night. We searched up and down both sides of the river the next morning for several miles, but they weren't to be found. It's sad, real sad."

"Yes, I'll have to notify Mr. and Mrs. Ramos of their son's accident. Poor people have had to face a lot of difficulty this past year, and now this tragedy. What about the other man who was lost? Does he have any family?" James crinkled his brow.

"No, not that anyone knows of." Rodeen shrugged. "I actually knew the man. He was a crew member aboard the North Star. Guess I should look up Captain McDougal and notify him. Maybe he knows a little more about the man than I do. He was kind of a loner, and never really close to anyone that I'm aware of."

"Yes, a real tragedy for both of them. Did anyone witness the accident?"

"No, I'm certain of that. I asked everyone aboard the next morning, and no one saw a thing. It seems they were all busy with the landing."

"Well, it's too bad things like this have to happen." James dipped his fountain pen and began writing in his checkbook. "Accidents like that seem to take a toll on a man emotionally. Here." He handed the check to Rodeen. "Careful, the ink's still wet. Take the next few days off and recuperate. I know where to reach you if there is an emergency."

~   ~   ~

"I don't know if you remember me, Mrs. Garcia, but I was one of the men who brought Irish out here when he got beat up in town that night." The large man stood at the front door twirling his hat in his hands. "Folks just call me 'Bear'."

"Perdon?" Leonida cocked her head to one side and grinned.

"'Bear.' Folks call me that, because I'm so big."

"Sí, I understand, and I remember you and your friends. You ate nearly everything in sight during your stay."

"Sorry, ma'am. Guess I do have a huge appetite." He stared at his boots.

"No, that's quite all right, señor. Your appetite actually pleased Maria. She likes cooking for a man who enjoys eating. I was amused at your referince to Señor Kilkenney as 'Irish'." Leonida smiled warmly.

"Well, that's what we used to call him when we come out to Californie together. None of us knew that he was a real-for-sure sawbones at that time."

"Pardon me for being so rude, Señor Bear. Won't you please come inside. I'll have Maria fix us some refreshments." She led the way to the dining room. "What is the nature of your visit to Rancho Manantial Escondido?"

"Well, I actually come to say goodbye."

"Que?" Leonida held up a finger as he started to answer and turned to Maria inside the kitchen door. "Maria? Could you bring some tea and something to eat for our guest, por favor?"

"Sí." Maria's face broke into a smile as she recognized the man standing beside her Doña. "Señor Bear." She rushed into the dining room and grabbed both of his hands. "It is good to see you again. Are you hungry? Maria will fix you some nice carne if you like."

"Mmmm." Bear glanced at Leonida, and she gave him a little nod. "That sounds mighty fine, ma'am. But only if it ain't too much trouble."

"For you, no trouble at all." She giggled and disappeared back into the kitchen.

"You have made her very happy, señor. Please, sit down and tell me." Leonida motioned toward the table. "You were saying you came to say goodbye?"

"Yes, ma'am." He held a chair for Leonida before seating himself. "You see, I got tired of all the hustle and noise of San Francisco and sold my business there. Too many folks in one place to suit me. I'm on my way to Monument Valley, Utah to build me a cattle ranch, kinda like yours."

"Sí, I agree with you. There are too many people and too much noise there for me also. That's why I like it here so much. I am able to go out in the evenings in the fresh air and watch the stars without worrying about some drunken man trying to molest me. Last time I was there, someone tried to grab me in broad daylight."

"No?" Bear shook his head. "What happened?"

"Juan jumped between us, but before he could do anything, two other men grabbed the man and pulled him away. I'm afraid they gave him a sound beating."

"Serves him right. Anyway, back to why I come. I knew Irish had come out here to see you, and I thought I'd just sorta take a little jog outta the way and say goodbye to everyone at one time, if it's okay with you, ma'am."

"Certainly." She turned in her chair and clapped her hands toward the open doorway. "Evangelina?" A young girl with large dark eyes suddenly appeared and gave a slight bow.

"Sí, Doña Leonida?"

"Find Señor Kilkenney and tell him he has a visitor."

"Sí, he is in Señorita Ruby's room." She bowed again and disappeared back through the door.

"Ruby? Not Ruby from The Rusty Rail?" Bear grinned.

"Sí, it is the same Ruby."

"What's she doing here?"

"She and another young lady named Aurie are here because someone murdered Ambrose Brice, and the judge in Columbia has asked Señor Hanky to investigate. It seems that Señora Carpenter is somehow involved also. All three women have confessed to killing the man, and Señor Hanky is having a hard time finding out who the real killer is. I hate to admit it," she gave a crooked grin, "but I hinted I could have killed him also, just to confuse things."

"You don't say? Now what in the world would you do that for?"

"Because Ambrose Brice was an evil man who molested young girls. They should be praising whoever killed him, instead of trying to hang them. Besides, I did try to kill him once, a long time ago in Dogtown." Leonida turned away at the sound of footsteps on the stairway.

"Yes, I heard about that, and wished a million times I'd a been there. That greasy little snake might not have gotten away," Bear said as Sean Kilkenney came into the room.

"Bear, it's good to see you, man." He clasped the big man around the shoulders in a hug.

"Good to see you too, sawbones." His squeeze caused Sean to grunt.

"What brought you all the way here. I know it wasn't Maria's cooking." Sean glanced toward the kitchen and laughed as the maid pronounced an oath his way.

"Oh, I wouldn't say that. She can whip up a mighty fine meal in her own right. Pull yerself up a chair and let's visit some."

"M'lady?" Sean turned toward Leonida.

"You may, if you wish, señor," Leonida said with a nod.

"My, pretty formal for a couple of friends, ain't it?" Bear's glance bounced back and forth between them.

"Sí, Señor Kilkenney and I have decided to treat each other with respect, in a formal way." Leonida kept her gaze locked on the big man seated toward her left.

"Well, I guess that's mighty fine, if that's what you want. But for my taste, I'd rather be on a familiar basis." Bear shrugged.

"It is what I want, and you, Señor Bear, have always treated me with respect. You refer to me as 'ma'am'."

"That's 'cause I was raised that way. I even used to call my ma that way when she was alive."

"And that shows a great amount of respect for your mother. I'm sure she appreciated it." Leonida placed a warm hand against Bear's arm and gave a squeeze. She caught Sean's scowl out of the corner of her eye and smiled. "Now, tell Señor Kilkenney the purpose of your visit. I'm afraid we have been very rude in interupting you."

"Oh, yeah." Bear turned toward Sean. "As I was telling Mrs. Garcia, I sold the restaurant in San Francisco and decided to go into the cattle business in Utah."

"Why? I thought you were doing a great business."

"It was good, but like I was saying when you come in, there's too many folks in one place to suit me. I was feeling kinda cooped up."

"But why Utah?"

"Ever been there?" Sean shook his head. "Well I have, and the part I'm going to, around Monument Valley, is one of the prettiest places on earth. Huge red cliffs and clear streams with water so cold it hurts your teeth. And sage so thick the smell makes you drunk. Snow in the winter and warm in the summer. Good place for cattle."

"It sounds wonderful," Leonida said.

"It is ma'am. And I'm going to stake me out a big hunk of it and build a cabin right in the middle, big enough to raise a passel of children."

"Oh? I didn't know you were married, señor." Leonida raised her eyebrows.

"I ain't, at least not yet. But I aim to be. Which brings me to another question." He studied Sean across the table. "I heard that young girl in the other room say you was in Ruby's room upstairs."

"Yes. She's sick," Sean said.

"Have you discovered what is wrong with her, Señor Kilkenney?" Leonida said as Maria set cups of steaming tea in front of them.

"Yes, I believe I have. It is a good case of lung fever."

"Lung fever?" Leonida said. "Is it dangerous?"

"It can be." He took a sip of tea. "But it's not something that you have to worry about catching yourself, if that's what you're referring to."

"Sí, that was one of the thoughts on my mind. We have all spent a lot of time with her these past few days. How sick is she?"

"She came close to dying." He returned his cup to the saucer with a tilt of his head. "She needs to stay warm, get plenty of fresh air and sunshine, and, for God's sake, eat some healthy food. Have you felt her ribs?"

"No, señor, I don't believe I have," Leonida chuckled.

"There's no meat on them. She's existed on a diet of tobacco and whiskey." Sean stared at the steaming plate Maria set in front of Bear. "Perhaps Maria could cook her some steaks and force her to eat them. They'll improve her teeth, if nothing else."

"Mmmm, very good, Maria," Bear said over a mouthful.

"See, you crazy gringo." Maria gave Sean a nod.

"Maria," Leonida took hold of the maid's arm, "Señor Kilkenney was just saying that Señorita Ruby is very sick and should eat a lot of carne. Could you please cook her some and take it to her room?"

"Sí, but she never eats the food I give her."

"Force her," Sean said.

"Fix her a plate like mine," Bear mumbled as he sawed at his steak with a knife. "I'll take it to her room and see she eats it." He paused to glance at Leonida. "With your permission, ma'am."

"Sí, if you wish, but why?"

"No offence, ma'am, but Ruby's the main reason I come back this way." He cocked his head to one side with a shrug.

~   ~   ~

Aurie Templeton allowed her fingers to trail through the water from where she sat on the edge of the fountain. Alice Carpenter and Paco were carrying on an animated conversation to her right, but she paid them no mind. She was watching Rosa and Tex as they played and teased each other in the shaded garden.

"She's so lucky."

"I'm sorry, what were you saying, honey?" Alice broke in the middle of a sentence to look at her.

"Rosa. She's so lucky. Married to a handsome man like Tex and going to have a baby."

"You'll get married and have a baby too, some day."

"No," she shook her head, "I'm not pretty like you or Rosa, and she's such a lady. Look at her." She motioned with her head.

"Well, I guess no one's ever told you the story about Rosa, have they?" Alice sat down and took Aurie's damp hand in hers. "Rosa used to work in The Rusty Rail same as you and Ruby."

"No." Aurie snapped her head up.

"Yes, but that was a little more than a year ago, before your time. Come to think of it, she wasn't much older than you are right now. The fact is, Ambrose claimed her father had sold her like a slave."

"Same as Mr. Semmens did to me." Aurie looked away.

"Yes, the same, but the sheriff we had then, Pod Randell, you heard about him, haven't you?" Aurie nodded. "Well, he got drunk one night and almost beat that poor girl to death. Tex was the one who brought her out here to Mrs. Garcia, and Doctor Kilkenney patched her up. Then, Mrs. Garcia taught her how to read and be a lady." Alice squeezed her hand and smiled. "I'm only telling you this to let you know you can be a lady, just like Rosa, if you really want to. You can get married and have children and a home too."

"No," she shook her head, "I'm still not pretty like she is."

"Señorita Aurie?" Paco said.

"Yes?" She shaded her eyes against the sun.

"I think you are a pretty lady now."

~   ~   ~

"I'm sorry, but I've got to get back to San Francisco." Salty Moran watched the young girl hovering over the figure lying in bed. He wouldn't have given a Tinker's damn for Manuel Ramos' chances of living when he pulled him from the river a week ago. He was lucky enough to find the boy's body caught on a half-submerged tree near the bank. Salty was struggling to drag him on shore when five or six vaqueros surrounded him.

"Hey, gringo." A good-looking young man with a thin mustache and a scar on one cheek pointed a gun at his head. "What you do to our friend here?"

"I'm trying to get him out of the river before he drowns. Give me a hand, will you?"

"Armando, pronto." He waved the gun and one of the men ran to grab hold of one of Manuel's arms.

"What happened to his head, gringo? You want me to believe the water did that?" He brought the pistol close to Salty's face.

"No, one of the men aboard the Golden Bell tried to murder him." He pointed toward the docking paddle boat. "He hit him on the head and threw him overboard."

"And you were trying to save him? Why, gringo?"

"Because I don't like seeing anyone hurt, especially a nice boy like Manuel. Now, would you quit pointing that thing at me?" He shoved the gun barrel aside. One of the other vaqueros grabbed for his shirt collar, but the leader waved him off.

"You like this boy? Why? He's Mexican."

"And I'm an Englishman, sailing under a Scottish Captain. What's that all mean? Nothing. Now, we've got to get this boy some help before he dies." Salty grabbed Manuel under the arms and began dragging him farther up the bank.

"I'm Mexican; do you like me, gringo?" The leader blocked his way.

"I might, if you would quit being such an ass, and help me save this boy's life." The leader chuckled and began giving rapid orders in Spanish. He draped an arm around Salty's shoulder as they escorted him through the thick brush toward the shanty town.

"You are muy hombre, gringo. I like you. I tell you what. Anything you want, you tell them Joaquin says it is okay, and they'll give it to you. Okay, hombre?"

"Joaquin?"

"Sí, maybe you have heard of me?" They stopped at the rear of a shabby cabin with a barking dog and two half-naked children in the yard.

"No, not unless you're claiming to be Joaquin Murrieta, and he's dead. They've got his head pickled in a jar of whiskey in San Francisco. I paid a dollar to see it," Salty said.

"Then they stole your money, hombre," he laughed.

"Who's head was I looking at?"

"Madra Dios, I'm supposed to know who's cabeza the gringos cut off? They paid Captain Love a lot of money por nada. You see me here, hombre. How can my head be in San Francisco? Besides, there are many Joaquin Murrietas. Every young vaquero who does not like what the Americanos are doing to our people want to be like me." A middle-aged woman came to the door and addressed them in Spanish.

"This is Sofia Mulgado. She doesn't speak much English, but her daughter does." Salty spied the young girl peeking at him through the door. "You will stay here until the boy is able to travel."

"But what if they come looking for us?" Salty shook his head. "I'd rather be farther away from the dock."

"And where would you go? No one will find you here, even if they look. Grayson is a large city, with many people. No one will even notice you."

Salty found those words to be true. After sending a note to Captain McDougal with one of Joaquin's men, he spent his first day at Sofia Mulgado's house hidden indoors. The following day, knowing the Golden Bell was no longer in port, and feeling braver, he ventured from the house to look around. No one, outside those interested in what money he might have in his pockets, gave him so much as a glance as he wandered the streets. One man tried selling him some whiskey and another opium. One overweight prostitute grabbed him by the wrist and tried dragging him into her tent. Deciding it wasn't the most pleasant city he had ever visited, Salty returned to the Mulgado's house and feasted on frijoles and corn tortillas. It was now eight o'clock in the morning, and time for him to be going.

"Wait, and I'll go with you." Manuel Ramos tried raising himself from the bed.

"No, you're not strong enough to travel yet." Salty shook his head. "You stay here a few more days. I'll be letting your family know you're still alive. Besides, it might be safer if Rodeen thinks you are dead, for the time being."

"But..." He propped himself up on his elbows.

"But nothing. I need to be letting Captain McDougal know what Rodeen and Sattler are up to. Yours is not the only ranch they're trying to get hold of. If they tried killing you, what's to keep them from trying to harm others? You stay here until I send for you."

"Gracias." Manuel fell back on the bed.

"You're welcome." He pulled his stocking cap down over his ears before placing two double eagles into the girl's hand.

"Here's forty dollars. It's all I've got. Take good care of him." He smiled and disappeared into the bustling crowd in the streets.

Chapter 16

"No, I don't quite have it all figured out yet. I'd like to ask the ladies a few questions before I let you know what I think for sure." Sean swirled the brandy in his glass while Judge Lloyd Hansen hovered in front of the chair he was lounging in. "Besides, Ruby won't be strong enough to go into town and stand trial for at least another week. Maybe two. You almost didn't have her to hang. You know that, don't you?"

"Dammit, boy, do you think I actually want to hang her? What's the matter with you?"

"Nothing, I'm sorry." Sean shook his head. "I'm just out of sorts, lately."

"Well, get back into 'sorts'. We're talking about the lives of three women here."

"Four women," Leonida corrected him as she passed the open door.

"All right, four women, and I want you to be certain when you give testimony. Do you understand me?"

"Yes, perfectly." Sean took a sip and set the glass on the end table. "It will still take Ruby approximately a week or more before she will be able to travel into town, and there is nothing I can do about that."

"Fine. How does three weeks sound? I have to hold court in Columbia come Monday, and one of the cases promises to be a lengthy one."

"That would be even better. In fact, it would not only give me time to finish my report, but tie up some loose ends in San Francisco."

"San Francisco? You're going back?" Loretta Stewart laid her book in her lap to stare at them. She had almost become a permanent fixture the past few days, perched in the window seat with a book from Leonida's library in her hand.

"Yes, I do have a business there, or at least I did before I came here. Now I don't know what I have, but there are some personal items that need to be taken care of fairly soon. You're welcome to return with me, if you choose."

"I don't know." Her eyes darted around the room. "I hadn't thought much about it." She shrugged. "Actually, I don't know what I was thinking. I can't stay here forever, can I?"

"Que, señorita? Why can't you stay longer?" Jose Flores stopped his searching through one of the desk drawers long enough to glance at her. "My daughter and I have enjoyed your company immensely."

"Well, I..."

"Do you have a position of employment waiting that is important? Aha." He held up a small leather-bound notebook with an eagle on the front and smiled.

"No, I'm afraid I was replaced two minutes after I left," Loretta giggled.

"Bueno, then you can stay as long as you want."

Leonida paused in her journey down the hall to fold her arms and lean in the doorway smiling. "By the way, Judge Hansen, what have you decided to do with those men who killed one of my vaqueros and tried to rob our mine?"

"I thought I'd hold their trial in Columbia while our doctor here is off doing whatever in San Francisco, if you don't mind. It would mean some of your men who were witnesses, like Vernon Blackstone and Tex, would be gone for a day or two."

"No, I think that is a very good idea. There has been too much sorrow around here as it is. And my papa is right, Señorita Stewart. We have enjoyed your visit and wish you to stay. Besides, we women need all the support we can muster to stand against the evil men who want to hang us." She nodded toward Sean and Judge Hansen.

"Now, just a minute, young lady," the judge started, but she cut him off with her laughter as she turned away. "Well, put me on the hog-train."

"Don't let it bother you too much, señor. She has been doing much the same to me since the day she was born." Jose grinned as he stuffed the notebook in his coat pocket. "So, Señorita Stewart, you will give us the pleasure of your company a while longer? I'm sure Señor Kilkenney won't mind you staying with us while he tends to business, will you señor?"

"No, not at all." Sean shook his head.

"Bueno, it is settled then. Come, I wish to show you something." Jose took her by the hand.

"Wait." She marked her page in the book with one of her laced gloves. "What is it?"

"One of the most beautiful sights you've ever seen, señorita. One of my daughter's mares just gave birth."

"Oh, really?"

"Sí, and the colt is black as the night, with white around each hoof." They disappeared through the door arm in arm.

"Well, she has certainly won the heart of everyone here," Judge Hansen said.

"Yes, she has." Sean tossed down the remaining brandy and rose to arch his back. "Guess I'd better get busy packing. The sooner I get moving, the better off I'll..." He was cut off by shouts coming from the stairwell.

"Put me down, you big idiot! I don't wanna go outside!" Both men stared as Ruby beat against Bear's chest with her fists as the huge man carried her toward the front door like a baby.

"Now, you just calm down, young lady, before I tan yer hide. Irish says you need to get some warm sunshine, and that's just what yer gonna do. It's cold up there in that room."

"I've got a ton of blankets and quilts to keep me warm. Put me down! I can walk."

"I ain't arguing with you none."

Maria giggled and held the door open.

"Doctor, tell him to leave me alone." She poked her head over his shoulder to yell.

"Nope, I'm not getting involved." Sean shook his head. "He's much too big to argue with."

~ ~ ~

"You shouldn't be paying her so much attention, Papa."

"Paying who so much attention?" Jose used his reading glasses to mark his page in The Conspiracy of Pontiac as he stared up at his daughter.

"Señorita Stewart."

"You interrupt my reading for that? I was at a very interesting part. I don't believe I've been showing her any more attention than I do Olga or Rosa or even Señorita Ruby." He slipped his glasses back on. "Besides, even if I were, what difference would it make?"

"You're old enough to be her father."

"Sí." He removed the glasses again to glare. "I'm also old enough to be your father, which I believe I am, and the tone you are addressing me in is not proper for a daughter to be using toward her father."

"I'm sorry, Papa. It's just that I'm afraid that you are somehow enamored with this young woman."

"I thought you liked her."

"I do."

"Then what is the problem with me also liking her?"

"Nothing, Papa, if that's all there is to it. But if you're starting to fall in love with her, do you have any idea how that will hurt Señora Carpenter? She happens to think a lot of you, Father."

"Sí, I have a vague idea how it would make her feel, if that were the case. But since I have already asked Señora Carpenter for her hand in marriage, I don't know how my treating Loretta Stewart the same as any other guest on this rancho could break her heart."

"You're engaged to be married?"

He nodded.

"To Señora Carpenter?"

"Sí, but that's only half true. She refuses to give me her answer until the trial in Dogtown is over. She's still claiming her guilt in the matter and is afraid of breaking my heart, as if it wouldn't break my heart to see her hang with or without an engagement or wedding."

"Why wasn't I told of this before now? Besides being your daughter, I am also the Doña."

"Because, my little niña, I just asked her not three hours ago while we were riding in the buggy. Besides, I don't see how confiding in you about my love-life could make any difference. You can't make up your own mind whether to give yourself to your doctor friend or not."

"Ah, that's not true." Leonida planted her hands on her hips and glared. Besides, he deserves having his heart broken just a little. He's the one who ran off and hurt me, don't forget."

"No, I haven't forgotten, and I seriously considered having him horsewhipped when he arrived with Señorita Stewart. But he has offered his apology a hundred times, not only to you, but to everyone on the rancho. He is not a warrior like me or Tex or Señor Hanky. I know what happened in Dogtown troubled you. It did everybody, but especially him, Niña. You are the daughter of a general and have my blood in your veins. You understand how things must be sometimes. On the other hand, he is a gentleman. A healer. I believe that is why you love him so much. You are going to have to accept him for what he is."

"He might be a doctor, Father, but he's also a fighter. You saw him when he fought those men in my room, and Judge Baines." Leondia shook her head.

"Sí, but why did he do those things? I'll tell you why. He did them for you, to protect the woman he loves. Listen to me, daughter." Jose shifted in his chair. "Right now, you're only making everyone, including yourself, miserable. If you love him, and I think you do, tell him. Life is too short, niña. You of all people, should know that. Something might happen to rob you of the chance. Besides," he picked up his book, "I'm tired of waiting for my grandchildren."

~   ~   ~

Leonida stopped at her bedroom door and held her stomach. It was churning the same way it did when she was five years old and had gotten into her mother's dried fruit. She ate until she was stuffed. Her mother refused to punish her, saying what lay ahead was going to be punishment enough, and indeed it was. But this had nothing to do with eating dried fruit. It was something far worse. She dabbed her eyes and quietly stepped into the hall, closing the door behind her. Her slippers glided easily across the carpet as she passed the room shared by Ruby and Aurie. No light shown from under the door, a sign that the girls were asleep. A crack of light found its way from Alice Carpenter's room as well as Loretta Stewart's. Both women had developed a habit of staying up half the night devouring the books in her library. The third door from hers was her objective, and it stood partially open, flooding the hallway with yellow lamplight.

She caught her breath and slowly pushed her way inside. The muscles in Sean Kilkenney's back and arms rippled through his undershirt as he folded a stack of shirts. He was humming an Irish ballad and had not heard her enter.

"So," she paused to clear her throat, "when may we expect your return?" Sean turned from his laundry to stare.

"In a week or so. I have to get back early enough to finish my report for Judge Hansen. But I do have at least one patient left in San Francisco I need to check on. I'm afraid I've been ignoring her."

"Her? Is she pretty?"

"Yes, m'lady, she is very pretty." He grabbed his carpetbag and began stuffing the shirts inside. "And talented. She happens to be a ballet dancer."

"I see." Leonida turned her attention to the painting of a mountain lake and adjusted the way it hung on the wall. "Do you love her?"

"Yes, m'lady, I'm afraid I do."

"Oh." She bit her lip as a tear welled up inside one of her eyes. "May I ask her name?"

"Yes, m'lady. It is Clara. Clara Baker. And she is ten years old."

"I see." She choked on her laughter and began searching for a handkerchief as she sniffled.

"Here, you may use one of mine." Sean held the white cloth at arm's length.

"Gracias." She blew her nose.

"Is there something you wanted in particular, m'lady?" He turned back to his packing.

"Will you stop calling me that?"

"I thought that's what you wanted." He glared over his shoulder. "Remember? By the fountain the other evening?"

"Sí, I remember well." She came closer and lowered her voice to a hoarse whisper. "But not once did I ask you to, to call me..." She waved a hand in the air.

"M'lady?"

"Sí, I did not ask that."

"No, but you did tell me to refer to you as Doña Leonida; did you not?"

"Sí, I did, but..."

"Well, *m'lady* is a term that has been used by gentlemen from Ireland and the British Isles for centuries and, unless I'm mistaken, it means much the same thing as your Spanish term *Doña* when referring to nobility."

"I know you are right," she lowered her gaze to the floor, "but I only said those things because I was angry. You will never know how much you hurt me, señor."

"I've got a good idea." He closed the bag and turned to face her.

"No," she shook her head, "and this is very hard for me to say." She held the handkerchief over her mouth as one of the tears spilled over. Sean reached for her, but she pulled away.

"Please, I have to say this. Just listen." She dabbed her eyes and blew her nose. "Your leaving hurt me almost as much as losing Rudolfo."

"Dear Christ, I had no idea."

"I know, but I loved you so very much, and tried very hard to hate you since then, but I can't. I still love you."

"I'm so sorry." He slipped his arms around her waist in a tentative hug.

"Oh." She threw her arms around his neck and crushed his lips against hers. "When will you ever learn how much I love you?" She kissed him again. "I want you to come back to me, Sean Kilkenney."

"I will." He drew her full body against his as he covered her mouth and cheeks with kisses. "I will never leave you again, no matter what."

"If that is the case señor, you may release my daughter so she can return to her own room." Jose Flores winked at them through the open doorway before ambling toward his own room humming a Mexican ballad.

"Buenas noches, mi amor." She kissed him once more before fleeing down the hall.

~   ~   ~

"I thought you didn't want to see me again." Clara Baker poked her pouty lip toward him.

"Oh, but m'lady, how could that possibly be?" Sean bowed deeply. "As I stated earlier, I was away on business that detained me much longer than I expected. But, I'm here now." He pulled up a foot stool and sat in front of the girl who was perched in a chair.

"Now, let's see that knee of yours. Does that hurt?"

"No."

"How about that?"

"Nope."

"Nothing seems to hurt at all?"

"Na-uh."

"Clara," Dorothy Baker scowled at her daughter, "use proper English. It is 'no sir'."

"That's what I said." Her mother only sighed.

"Well, let me see you walk around," Sean said with a grin. The girl bounced around the room like a rubber ball and finished by standing on the toes of her damaged leg and bowing with the other leg extended behind.

"Okay." Sean clapped. "I can see I spent countless hours worrying needlessly about you, m'lady. Are you still wearing the brace when you practice?"

"Only when we can force her to," Dorothy said, and even then we have to watch, or she'll slip it off when we're not looking."

"It makes my skin red, right here." She rubbed the sides of her knee.

"You might have to pad it with something soft." Sean glanced at Mrs. Baker.

"And it's stiff, and I have trouble dancing with it on." Clara gave one more twirl before sitting down.

"I know, but I still want you to wear it for a while longer, until we're sure your leg is completely mended. If it will make you feel any better, I think you can go back to dancing all you want."

"Really? Oh, I love you!" Clara jumped from her seat to hug him around the neck before bouncing around the room once more.

"Well," Sean grinned as he began collecting his bag and coat, "I'm a pretty lucky man. That is the second pretty lady that has told me the same thing the past few days."

"Oh really? And was the other lady any older than Clara?" Dorothy Baker grinned as she helped Sean on with his coat.

"Mmm yes, a might older. Twelve years older, to be exact."

"Ah, there might be a Mrs. Kilkenney in the near future then?"

"I'm doing my best to make sure that is the case, ma'am." He paused at the door to watch the young girl twirl her way around the living room. "Please let me know when her next dance recital is going to be held. I want to be there."

"It has been postponed until the later part of July, due to Clara's injury." She pulled a colorful flyer from a stack of paper and handed it to him. "They've turned it into a three-day event: Friday, Saturday and Sunday afternoon. You'd better write the dates on your calendar, Doctor." Dorothy opened the door. "What do we owe you? I don't think you like to do house calls for free do you?"

"No, but I'll be in town for a few days. I'll drop the bill off at your husband's office." He turned his attention to Clara as she came bounding to the front door.

"Are you leaving?"

"Yes, m'lady, I must be parting your company, but only for a while." He bowed graciously. "I shall return to watch you dance on stage. When you look at the audience, I will be easy to see. I'll be the one with a bunch of red roses, just for you."

~ ~ ~

"Just a minute." Walter P. Norton adjusted his wire-rimmed glasses and rummaged through an open file cabinet drawer. He gave every impression of being an accountant or banker, instead of being a top Pinkerton investigator. "Ah, yes, here it is." He returned to his desk with three separate folders. "I shouldn't be telling you this, Doctor, but you are far from being the only interested party in James Sattler. Two of these," he thumbed through the folders, "claim they are concerned about his taking advantage of the same party you mentioned, a Leonida Garcia."

"May I see those?" Sean got from his seat.

"No, I'm afraid not." He covered the folders with his arm. "Not without the permission of our other clients. I'm only telling you this because much of the information you've requested has already been collected. In other words, Doctor Kilkenney, your case was almost complete the moment you opened it."

"What is the possibility of combining the cases all into one? Wouldn't it be faster that way?"

"That's exactly what I intend to do, what we've actually been doing with the other two. But I still can't divulge the names of our other clients without their permission. What I will do though is approach them one by one and ask if they are interested in meeting with the other clients in my office. Who knows, perhaps one of you might know something that no one else is aware of that will help move this case along."

"Yes, that would be nice, since time is important in this instance." Sean rose to his feet. "Thank you for your time, Mr. Norton," he shook the agent's hand, "and see what you can do."

"Thank you, Doctor, but aren't you forgetting something?"

"Pardon?"

"The matter of our fee?" Walter Norton grinned.

"Oh, yes." Sean pulled a bank draft from his billfold. "I believe that should be adequate for the time being. I'll be spending most of my time at Mrs. Garcia's rancho, but I will be checking back with you every once in awhile. We can make any adjustments at that time."

"Yes, I believe a thousand dollars will be more than adequate," the agent laughed. "Have a good day, Doctor."

~   ~   ~

"I'm sorry, sir, but the man waiting by the door insists on seeing you. He says it's urgent." The waiter at The Comstock motioned toward the man in blue denims and striped shirt.

"Yes, I know him, Gerald. Show him to the table." Sean rose as Salty Moran was seated next to him.

"Mr. Moran, it's good to see you." Sean shook his hand. "Would you care for anything? I'm buying."

"No, I don't think..."

"Sure, you've got to help me. It's not every day you get to celebrate getting engaged, Gerald." Sean turned to the waiter. "Bring Mr. Moran the best steak in the house and bring another glass and bottle of wine."

"But, Doctor Kilkenney," Gerald lowered his voice and glanced around the busy dining room, "we do have a dress code."

"Yes, I'm aware of that. And I also have a strong code of friendship. I'm a very close friend of Francis Walker, and this man is a close friend of mine."

"Yes, sir. Although Mr. Walker no longer owns this establishment, he is well thought of. I'll see to Mr. Moran's needs right away."

"Wow, that's quite smooth, Doc. Who the hell's Francis Walker, anyway?" Salty grinned as his pale blue eyes darted around the fancy restaurant.

"Francis Allen Walker is Bear's real name."

"Na, you're trying to flimflam me, Doc. Really?"

"For real, Salty. But don't you dare tell him I spilled the beans, or he'll break both our necks." Sean paused as the waiter set a glass in front of Salty and filled it from the already opened wine bottle.

"Now, what's important enough for you to chase all over San Francisco looking for me? And, how did you know I was in here in the first place?"

"Well, you are harder to find than Black Beard's treasure, but I remembered you talking about coming here with Bear once, and how much you liked it. I just took a chance. Who I actually wanted to find was Captain McDougal. You got any idea where he might be hiding? I've looked all over the last forty acres of hell, and he's nowhere to be found."

"Sure, I just left him. He's out visiting at the Garcia rancho. Unless I'm mistaken, he's rather enamored with a very pretty female." Sean hoisted his glass in a toast.

"Captain McDougal? Naw," Salty shook his gray head, "the sea's his bride. We're supposed to be sailing before the end of the month."

"I'm telling you the truth, my good man. I've seen that look in men's eyes before, and have had it myself. Your Captain is in love. Of course, the young lady in question doesn't know it yet, but she will soon."

"Now, he's not the one we're celebrating the engagement to, is he?" Salty scratched the stubble on his chin.

"No, I'm afraid that happens to be me." Sean refilled both glasses. "I'm hopelessly in love, Salty, and the only way out is to marry the girl."

"Who might the lass be?"

"Leonida Garcia."

"Don't say?" Salty set the glass on the table and leaned close. "Then, perhaps you're the one I should be talking to. You see, the captain asked me to keep an eye on an old shipmate of ours, Darrell Rodeen. We spied him one night in The Silver Slipper tossing money around like he'd found the money tree. Well, seeing as he couldn't keep a copper in his pocket to save his own soul, the captain just naturally figures there's a rotten mackerel on board. Well, I follows him like the captain says, and it seems he's somehow tied up with that pirate your lady-friend has hired to represent her in court."

"James Sattler?"

"That's the one. I followed him to his office, and when he left, he was flush with money again. Then Rodeen takes a job aboard the Golden Bell, one of those paddle boats that forge the river? So, to keep an eye on him, I do the same. But as it turns out, the reason he's on that boat is because Manuel Ramos was working the same boat. His pa, Hector Ramos, owns a large spread east of Sacramento, and he's hired the same shark as your lady-friend to represent him.

"Now, here's where it gets really good." Salty paused to take a swallow of wine. "It seems Sattler's been bleeding these Mexicans for every copper they have, so the boy gets mad and tells him to go to blazes. Then, he takes that job aboard the Golden Bell to help support his family. Only Rodeen knocks him in the head and tosses him overboard just as we're pulling into Grayson."

"Yes, Captain McDougal mentioned something about that. Dirty bastard. Are you sure it was the same man Sattler hired?"

"I seen it with me own eyes. He bashed the lad's skull in and tossed him into the river. Only thing is, the boy didn't drown, 'cause I jumped in after him. I got him hid out with some Mexican friends until he can mend enough to go home. His folks know about it, but I told them to keep it quiet, seeing as they might try killing the boy again."

"But why would they want to kill him?"

"I ain't got that one figured out yet, Doc, but the way I see it, if they tried doing Manuel Ramos in, what's to keep them from trying to kill your lady-friend, if the same circumstances arrive?"

"Have you told the law about this?" Sean said.

"You know better than that, Doc. What law? Besides, I'm an old seaman, and James Sattler's a respected solicitor. Who do you think they would believe?"

"Okay, so here's what we're going to do." Sean pulled a business card from his billfold and handed it to Salty. "When we're finished eating, you go see this man, Walter Norton."

"A Pinkie, huh?" Salty studied the card.

"Yes, tell him I sent you. He's already looking into our shark for us. Tell him exactly what you've told me, and anything else you can think of. I've got to be heading back to Dogtown in the morning, and I'll see Captain McDougal. In the meantime, you be extra careful, Salty. They might be tossing you in the river next."

"Don't worry about me, Doc. They think I drowned trying to save that boy. I already checked." He hoisted his glass in a toast.

Chapter 17

"Damned skunk anyway. Pardon me, ma'am." Hanky glanced up as Leonida entered the kitchen.

"Sí, I will pardon you this time, señor, but what about your language in front of these ladies? You have a room full of women. Don't you need to ask their forgiveness also?"

"Yeah, I reckon you're right. Excuse the language, ladies." His eyes darted around the room.

"Now, tell me, señor lawman, what has upset you enough to profane a poor innocent animal inside my hacienda?"

"Huh? What are you talking about?" Hanky screwed up his face and stared at her.

"You were damning a skunk when I came into the room. I was wondering what crime the skunk could have committed to make you profane him."

"Oh, I was referring to Ambrose, not a real skunk."

"Really, then perhaps you should apologize to the skunks twice. Once for damning them without a reason, and once for aligning them with a human much worse than they are. Gracias." Leonida accepted the cup of tea from Maria. "May I join you?"

"Sure, most certainly." Hanky jumped to his feet to pull out a chair for her. Leonida smiled at the women around the table.

"My, but you are such a lucky man, Señor Hanky. I know many men who would envy you, being surrounded by such beautiful women. But I'm interrupting. Go on with your conversation."

"Well, I was just remarking that Ambrose was such a..." he rolled his eyes back and stared at the ceiling.

"Bastard?" Leonida calmly sipped her tea as Alice Carpenter gasped and Rosa giggled.

"You called it, sister." Ruby snickered as she lit a cigarillo. Loretta only grinned as she blew the steam from her cup.

"You took the words right out of my mouth, ma'am. Anyway, all he done all his life was cause folks like us grief. You'd think he coulda at least died properly. But no, he's gotta go get hisself kilt and cause us more grief."

"Sí, one would be inclined to agree with you. Which brings me to another question, señor. Since I am beginning to understand you when you speak, does that mean I am getting smarter, or am I digressing in my education?"

"I don't even know what you said." Hanky stopped in the middle of rolling a cigarette.

"No matter." She giggled and patted the lawman on the arm. "I was only teasing you, and I am actually looking for my papa. Has any one seen him?"

"Sí, señora," Maria said as she refilled several cups with hot water. "He took Señor McDougal and some of the men to the bunkhouse. They are planning a fiesta."

"A fiesta? Por que?" Leonida's eyes darted around the room.

"Who knows? Maybe they're going to celebrate my hanging." Ruby coughed, then smiled.

"No, señorita, I forbid you to talk that way!" Leonida glared.

"You can forbid it all you want, but that's exactly what's going to happen."

"No it isn't." Alice shook her head. "I've already told everyone that I killed Ambrose for abusing this young girl." She put an arm around Aurie, only to have her throw it off and jump to her feet.

"Stop it! Stop it! Why won't you please stop?"

"Sí, you are right, Chica." Leonida folded her in her arms. "No one is going to die because of that evil man. I have been praying in the chapel every day for all of you, and I know the Holy Father will send Saint Michael and his angels to protect everyone."

"Well, I wish I was as sure as you are, ma'am, but when it comes to court, the law's the law." Hanky struck a match and lit his cigarette.

"Sí, señor lawman, but it is not as powerful as Dios, and don't you forget that." She shook a finger in his face.

"No, ma'am, I won't. Besides, unless that Irish sawbones can come up with something, we may never know who done it anyway."

"Maybe everyone did." Rosa shrugged.

"What?" Hanky set the cup back on the table without taking a drink.

"I said, maybe everyone killed him. Everyone in town had reason enough to kill Ambrose. Me, Tex, Ruby, Doña Garcia and her papa. Everyone. What if, when the day comes, you told the judge that everyone killed him? What would he do then? Hang the whole town?"

"No, he'd more'n likely toss my carcass into jail." Hanky laughed. "It's not a bad idee at that. If Doc don't come up with something better, I just might use it. I'm shore proud that my boy chose to marry you. You're one fine lady." He studied her with pride.

"So, that shall be our defense." Leonida grinned and kissed the top of Aurie's head. "Either that, or convince them that Dios Himself struck that evil man down, like in the Bible."

"Say, that ain't bad either." Hanky nodded thoughtfully.

"Gracias, but I must go find my papa. You say they are in the bunkhouse?"

"Sí." Maria nodded.

"And no one knows what this fiesta is about?"

"You're kidding." Loretta grinned.

"No, señorita. Why would I jest about a fiesta?"

"Oh, I thought you of all people would know. Your father said it had to do with something he saw the other evening as he was going toward his bedroom." She studied Leonida over her cup of tea.

~   ~   ~

"But Papa, what makes you think we are going to get married?"

"Niña, you'd better be planning on marrying that man, or else you'll be in bigger trouble than you've ever been." Jose scrunched his eyebrows. "I taught my daughter better than to enter a man's bedroom unless they were already married. To each other, I might add. I'm sure there was no medical reason for the doctor to have his arms around you, with his lips pressed against yours. You'd better be planning on getting married."

"Sí, what ever you say."

"You do love him, don't you?"

"Sí, Papa, terribly so. Like I've never loved anyone or anything in my whole life. He's all I think about." She sat on the edge of the sofa with her hands in her lap.

"Then, you will be married."

"But he hasn't asked me to marry him yet. What if he doesn't?"

"He will." Jose turned toward the window and puffed vigorously on his cigar.

"I'm frightened, Papa. What if he changes his mind and leaves me like he did the last time?"

"He wouldn't dare. I will personally execute him if he does." He winked at her.

~   ~   ~

"'Tis a beautiful mackerel sky, isn't it?" Leonida turned from her spot on the veranda to see Captain McDougal smiling at her from the hall.

"It isn't polite to stare at women when they are inside their bedrooms, Captain." She grinned back.

"Please accept my apology, m'lady," he gave a short bow, "but your door was standing wide open, and it is such a lovely evening. Mind if I join you?"

"Please do." She turned back to watching the sunset as a cool breeze swept across her face and teased the ends of her hair. Loretta Stewart had perched herself on the edge of the fountain while Evangelina and Rosalina were demonstrating the Borrego to the rhythm of Pablo's guitar and several violins. She clapped her hands as the girls whirled this way and that.

"They will have her up and dancing with them in no time."

"She'll dance their legs off, if they're not careful. I've watched her on stage," he added after a glance from Leonida. "She's rather good, you know?"

"No, I didn't. What did you mean by a mackerel sky?"

"Oh," he turned from watching the scene below with a chuckle, "that's an old sailor's term. See how the clouds make a pronounced pattern across the sky?" He pointed. "That's similar to the markings on the back of a mackerel when you first pull it from the water. Dark green with darker bars or stripes."

"I see." She nodded. They turned their attention back to the patio as Loretta asked Pablo to change the key he was playing. She clung to the hem of her skirt and danced in the middle of the circle singing about a girl named Sweet Betsy From Pike. In a matter of seconds she had everyone, including the children, clapping and laughing, especially when Hanky decided to join her in the dance.

"You were right, Captain. She can dance and sing almost as beautifully as she looks."

"Yes."

She watched from the corner of her eye as he stared at the woman by the fountain.

"You love her very much, Captain?"

"Oh, about as much as you love that bloody Irish doctor of yours." He gave her a crooked grin.

"Madra Dios." Leonida shook her head. "I'm afraid there is no hope for either of us then."

"Perhaps, but I wouldn't want to change it. Would you?"

"No." She turned back to the scene below. "I don't think I could."

~   ~   ~

She was staring at the ceiling when she heard the clop-clop of hooves. Tossing back the covers, she scampered across the cold wood floor in her bare feet. This would be the fourth or fifth time she had made the journey this night, but she could not help herself. The downstairs clock bonged only once as she leaned over the railing for a better view of the corral. The familiar sight of the white mule caused her heart to leap into her throat. She watched as Sean removed his saddle and set the animal free inside the pen. He had left the carriage in San Francisco and ridden most of the night. Leonida smiled grimly, wanting to believe her amante was in a mad rush to fly into her arms, but to leave the carriage meant Loretta would either have to find another form of transportation, or be stranded at the rancho. Her love would never be that thoughtless. There must be another reason for the hurry. She had lain awake half the night praying for his safe return, and now that he was here, there was no reason to delay their greeting until morning when everyone would be clamoring about them.

Slipping a light summer robe over her nightgown, she skipped down the stairs two at a time, stopping only once to glance at the silent house before opening the front door. He was climbing the steps when she latched onto his neck.

"Ahhh!" he jumped backward and fell. "Jesus Christ! What are you trying to do, scare the hell out of me?" Sean stared up at her.

"Oh, I'm sorry." She covered her mouth and giggled. "I couldn't wait to see you. Did you hurt yourself?" She knelt beside him on the cool bricks.

"No, but you could have at least said something before leaping out of the dark at me."

"Sometimes, there isn't time for words, señor." Her hair seemed to cascade like water as she hovered close to his face. "Like now." She pinned him to the bricks with her mouth.

"Leonida," he broke free from her kiss, "what if your father see us like this?"

"Let him. He's already planning our wedding fiesta." She pressed him against the pavement with her body.

"Our wedding? I haven't even asked you to marry me, yet."

"Hush." She kissed him lightly. "You talk too much." She cradled his head in her hands and covered his mouth with hers.

Chapter 18

"Señor Kilkenney." Sean rolled over and covered his head with the pillow, but the pounding on the door refused to go away.

"Señor Kilkenney, are you awake?" He bolted upright as a pair of hands shook him.

"By damned, woman! Can't a man get any sleep around here?"

"Agh!" Evangelina Rodriguez jumped backwards and began speaking rapidly in Spanish.

"May the Irish gods have mercy on my soul. I've told you a hundred times, don't speak that jabber to me, because I can't understand a thing you're saying. Either speak where I can understand, or keep quiet!"

"Perdoname, señor, but Maria says hurry." She tied her apron in knots as she backed against the dresser.

"Ha, the witch can just forget it if she wants to poison me this early in the morning. What time is it anyway?" he squinted around the room.

"Morning, señor."

"Hell, don't I know that? It was morning when I went to bed. The time, the time." He pounded his palm with his index finger. "What does the clock say?"

"No comprendo, señor." She shook her head.

"Naw, you wouldn't understand, would you? Well, what does the witch want, anyway?" He glared as Evangelina remained frozen against the dresser. "Maria, dammit! What does she want?"

"Armando and Olga and Basilisa...many niños and niñas are sick. She say come. Hurry!"

"Oh, for Christ's sake." He tossed back the covers. The girl gave a gasp and covered her face at the sight of Sean's long-johns. "Well, you were the one who told me to get up." He pulled his pants on and grabbed his shirt. "What's the matter with them? They eat some of her cooking and wind up with a tummy-ache?"

"They have spots." She spun on her heel and made a dash toward the door.

"Spots?" He paused in the middle of buttoning his shirt. "What do you mean by spots?" He glanced toward the door. "Evangelina?" Sean poked his head into the hallway but she was gone.

He pulled on his boots, splashed water on his face and grabbed his bag. He was still in the process of buttoning his shirt as he descended the stairs. He was met by Maria as he entered the kitchen.

"What you mean, yelling at young niñas like that?" The angry woman waved her spatula like a sword as he backed against the wall. "I no like it when you make her cry."

"I'm sorry, but she kept pounding on my door, and then, she actually came inside and shook me awake."

"I send her to your room." She swung her weapon toward the stairs. Sean started to bolt away, but Maria swung the spatula back like an experienced swordsman.

"Christ, woman! Watch that thing."

"You yell at Maria, when I tell niñas to wake you. She is only twelve years old." She held up five fingers. "You don't yell at her, understand?"

"Yes, I'm sorry." Sean held both hands high in surrender as Hanky and General Flores snickered over their coffee.

"Gringo is loco in la cabeza." She slapped the side of her own head as she turned back to her stove. Sean glared at the men seated at the table before spying Evangelina cowering in the corner. He set his medical kit on the table and took one of the girl's hands.

"Evangelina? I'm sorry. I get a little cranky sometimes in the morning. Forgive me?"

"Sí."

"Are you sure? She nodded and Sean gave her a little hug. Maria had already placed a steaming mug of coffee by his medical kit when he turned back to the table. "Thanks." He took a sip.

"De nada." She shrugged.

"Got drug out of bed a little early, eh, Doc? Well, if that cat-fight didn't wake you up, that coffee's shore to. Bet I could shine my boots with it." Hanky grinned.

"What's the matter with Maria's coffee?" The maid glared at him.

"Now, don't get so riled up." Hanky held up a palm. "Nothing's wrong with yer coffee. I was just making conversation, that's all."

"Damn," Sean muttered after a second sip.

"Here." General Flores poured some of the contents from his flask into Sean's mug. "That'll take some of the bite off." He savored the next sip a few seconds longer before swallowing.

"Now, what is wrong with the children? Evangelina said something about spots, but I couldn't understand her that well. What kind of spots?"

"Looks to me like they kinda got themselves into an anthill, or stung by a passel of bees," Hanky said. "They's got these little red bumps all over themselves."

"Sí. And sometimes they are hot, like Maria's stove." The maid gave him a firm nod.

"Mmmm." Sean downed the contents of his mug in a couple of gulps and grabbed his bag. "Come on, Evangelina. Show me."

"Your breakfast." Maria set a plate piled high with beefsteak, rice and beans on the table.

"Save it for later." He could hear her mumbling something about a crazy gringo as he followed the house-girl out the door.

~   ~   ~

"Buenos dias, Doctor. How are you feeling this morning?" The soft voice behind him caused his heart to flutter.

"I am feeling very well, m'lady. How are you feeling?" Sean glanced from the sick child toward the woman standing in the doorway. The Segoviano cottage lay only sixty or seventy yards from the hacienda gate, and the Doña was sipping the cup of tea she had brought with her.

"Muy bien, gracias." She handed the cup to Elena Segoviano and crossed the room to squat beside Sean. "How is my little Olga?"

"Mmmm, not too well, I'm afraid."

"Oh, is it something serious?" Her green eyes darted from the child to Sean and back again.

"Oh, she will survive, as will the other children. It could be serious, though, but I'm afraid that it will pose more of a problem to the adults." He took a long minute to study her profile. "Tell me, my lovely lady, have you ever had Rubeola?"

"Perdon?" She stared at him. "I don't even know how to say what it is you said."

"No, I didn't think so. Your father probably hasn't had it either, nor most of the people living here." He grinned and shook his head.

"Sean, what is it?" She placed a hand on his arm. Armando and Elena Segoviano stared wide-eyed as the Doña drew within a few inches of Sean's face. "We're not going to get sick and die, are we?"

"No." He grinned. "Rubeola is a childhood disease that children usually get over in a matter of days, with no lasting effects. Olga will be fine, but it's you and the rest of the adults I'm worried about. You will feel sicker than the children, and swear you're going to die. And, there is the problem of who is going to take care of all the sick children when the adults themselves are ill?" He cocked his head to one side and grinned. "Looks like I've got my work cut out for me."

"Oh, I'm sorry we are bringing you all this trouble." He could hear Elena gasp as Leonida slipped an arm around Sean's waist and lay her head against his shoulder.

"Well, what's the verdict, Doc?" Leonida leaped to her feet at the sound of Hanky's voice. Sean cringed at General Flores' stern glare as he stared at them from over the lawman's shoulder.

"Measles."

"But, I thought you said it was..." Leonida crinkled her eyebrows.

"Rubeola?"

"Sí." She nodded.

"It is. It's just another name for the same disease."

"Oh."

"Leonida?" She turned at the sound of her father's voice.

"I have to go now." She squeezed Sean's arm and retrieved her cup from Elena's hand before disappearing out the door. He could hear a hushed, although somewhat heated conversation in Spanish taking place at the corner of the house as he closed his bag. Sean paused at the door and smiled at Evangelina.

"Tell them to make sure she drinks plenty of water." The girl stared at him with blank eyes.

"Agua." Hanky pointed inside his mouth, then pointed toward Olga.

"Ah." Evangelina nodded with a smile.

"And have them feed her soups...lots of soups, but nothing too heavy." He again received the blank stare.

"Let me handle this, Doc. You see 'bout some of those other kids," Hanky said. Sean could hear the ranger trying to explain his feeding directions to the Segoviano family in his home-made Spanish as he stepped out into the cool morning air. "Soupee. El Doctor says to feed the niña soupee."

"You say this could be dangerous for adults, Doctor?" General Flores stood tall and proud with his arm around Leonida's shoulder.

"Mmm, more uncomfortable than dangerous. Not that people haven't died from having rubeola, but they are usually extremely ill to begin with. With rubeola, you'll itch from head to foot, but not be able to scratch a thing. You'll also be feverish at the beginning, and sick to your stomach. To put it bluntly, you'll simply wish you were dead."

"Then, what are we to do to help stop the spread of this rubeola?" the General said.

"Not much you can do, except isolate the ill as much as possible. That means your people are going to have to cut down on their visiting one another until this thing goes away. I know how they like to bounce from house to house, but one sick child can spread the disease to two or three dozen homes, if we're not careful."

"How in the world did such a thing ever get here on this rancho?" Leonida shook her head.

"Oh, a million different ways. You're always having visitors wandering through here. One of them may have been carrying the disease."

"That family that arrived here last week," General Flores rolled his eyes skyward, "now what were their names? Miller. Joseph Emery Miller. I believe their youngest boy wasn't feeling too well, although he did climb out of the wagon and play with the children around the fountain."

"That's probably your answer then."

"So, what do we do in the meantime?" Leonida asked.

"Pass the word to keep the sick children inside and in bed. Make them drink a lot of water, and feed them soup, and pray that most of the adults are spared." Sean shrugged.

"Well, we best be getting back to the hacienda, Hija." General Flores took Leonida by the arm. Sean watched them walk a short distance away before running to catch up to their side.

"Excuse me, General, there is something I've been wanting to ask you, and I can't seem to find the proper time. So, I might as well ask it now, because I don't know how busy I'm going to be later."

"Sí, what is it, Doctor?"

"Well, I guess you know how I feel about your daughter."

"No, I don't know how you feel about Leonida." He stopped to stare at Sean. "Tell me, Doctor, just how do you feel about my little girl?"

"Well, I love her to pieces." Sean said with a shrug.

"Oh, I see." Jose nodded. "I guess that is why you wished to break her heart into a million pieces when you left, is that it? So you could have more little pieces of her to love?"

"No, no, that was damned stupid of me." Sean rubbed a hand across his face. "I was so mixed up at the time; I don't even know what I was thinking."

"Sí, I can understand that. Every man I have known has had that same feeling at least once, Doctor. But the difference between being a man of honor and a coward is, the man of honor will stand firm in the face of difficulty and see the battle to its end." He pointed toward the ground where they were standing. "While the coward will run like a frightened child. Now, you've acted bravely many times in the past, even saving my daughter's life on several occasions. Then you ran because of some internal conflict, when the battle was seemingly over with." Leonida kept her eyes glued toward the toes of her shoes as her father continued.

"You are about to ask for my little niña's hand in marriage. But living with another person is never easy, no matter how much you might love them. So you tell me, Doctor, what are you going to do in the future when things become confusing? Stay and fight like a brave man, or run like a coward?"

"I can only give you my word of honor as a Kilkenney. On my mother's grave, I will stay. I'll love and cherish Leonida more than my own life."

"That is all one can ask for. My daughter is all I have left, señor. Her mother and brothers are buried in Mexico. I give you my word of honor as General Jose Flores of Los Federales De Mexico, that should you ever abandon my daughter again, I will personally see to your execution."

"Papa!" Leonida gasped.

"No, it is a fair bargain." Sean nodded. "I would deserve being shot if I did something that stupid again."

"Then we understand each other. Now, you tell me, niña." He held Leonida at arm's length. "Do you wish to marry this man?"

"Sí, Papa, but I don't want you to ever shoot him." She shook her head. Jose laughed as he took her in a bear-hug.

"It is settled then, we shall announce your engagement at dinner tonight. I perceive that you have much work to do, Doctor, but do try to be on time for this important occasion."

"You couldn't keep me away with wild horses." He smiled at Leonida. The sound of metal-rimmed buggy wheels grinding against the hard-packed road caused them to turn.

"Rosa! Oh, damn, I forgot." He dropped his medical bag and ran toward the buggy waving both arms. "Stop! Wait right there!" Leonida bolted after him with her father at her heels. Sean was shaking his head and talking rapidly to Tex and Rosa when they caught up with him.

"How many other pregnant women are on the rancho?" he asked over his shoulder while Leonida tried to catch her breath.

"Several. There are Rosa and Angela. Guillermina and Oleta are also pregnant." She stared off into the distance while holding up a finger for each expectant mother. "Then, Teresa and Ramona...I really don't know. Why?"

"Because rubeola can be very dangerous for a pregnant woman. It can, and I don't want to frighten Rosa here needlessly, but it can hurt the baby."

"Just how do you mean that, Doc?" Tex chewed vigorously on the match stem stuck between his teeth.

"Well, not always, mind you. But sometimes when a pregnant woman is exposed to rubeola, her baby can be born deaf or blind, for one thing. Or, I've seen them have a weak heart."

"Santa Maria, Madré de Dios." Rosa crossed herself while Tex turned away to curse.

"Rosa spent most of yesterday with me at the hacienda. How is this going to affect her baby, Sean?" Leonida held him at arms length to stare into his face.

"I don't know. Maybe not at all. I would just recommend that we isolate all the pregnant women as much as possible until this sickness is over with." He looked at Rosa and shrugged. "I'm sorry. I really am."

"We know you are, and appreciate it, Doc. Be seein' ya." Tex clucked his tongue and turned the buggy around.

"Come, Doctor. Let's go drink some more of Maria's coffee and eat breakfast." Jose put an arm around Sean's shoulder. "Then we can busy ourselves with this isolation that you are recommending. You realize this will not be an easy thing," he said as the three of them walked arm in arm toward the hacienda. "The people here are very superstitious, especially the Indians. They may have our heads when we start taking the mothers from their children."

~   ~   ~

Sean and Hanky stumbled over each other trying to get through the door at the same time. "Hurry," Jose Flores yelled as he gave them a shove. The sound of a woman's screams coming from the patio had caused them to forget all about further discussions on the death of Ambrose Brice.

"Dagnabit!" Hanky said as he slammed into Paco rounding the corner of the building. Loretta Stewart stood frozen in the moonlight in front of the fierce Indian holding the lance.

"Ildefonso Baca," Sean said. "I might have known." Jose and Hanky broke into laughter as the Indian shrugged his shoulders.

"By the spirit of Davy Jones, what's going on here?" Captain McDougal bent over and clasped his side. He had sprinted all the way from the opposite side of the corrals.

"It seems Baca scared the hell out of Loretta here." Sean slipped an arm around the woman's shoulder.

"I'm sorry. I just turned, and he was standing there with that huge spear. I've heard so many stories. I didn't know he was a friend of yours." She collapsed against Sean with a shudder.

"What's wrong? What happened to her?" Leonida pushed her way through the crowd that had suddenly filled the patio.

"Aw, Miss Loretta just got a little scared because she bumped into Baca in the dark, that's all," Hanky said.

"Here." Sean eased Loretta toward McDougal with a wink. "Maybe you can calm her down a little. I need to be checking on some of the sick children."

"Sure." He slipped a huge arm around Loretta's shoulders. "Now, there's nothing to really be frightened of, m'lady. I've known Ildefonso for as long as I've been making trips up the river, and he's really a harmless fellow."

"Don't you believe a word of that," Sean said as the Captain eased her through the crowd. "Baca is anything but harmless. He tried to bash my brains out the first time I met him."

"Ah, I had forgotten about that incident. Perhaps that is why you act so strange at times." Jose gave them a nod and draped an arm around Baca's shoulder. Leonida smiled as the two aging warriors walked toward the kitchen door.

"He really does like you."

"Who? Your father?"

She nodded.

"I know. I like him too, but not as much as his daughter. I'm afraid I'm hopelessly in love with her." Sean took her hand. "Care for a moonlight stroll in the garden?"

"That would be nice, but I thought you needed to see the sick children."

"I already have, and I'll check on them again later tonight. I thought Captain McDougal would like an excuse to spend some time alone with Loretta."

"You noticed also?" She gave him a crooked grin.

"It's kind of hard not to."

"How serious do you think it is between them?"

"Well, right now it's kind of one-sided. On the Captain's side. I'm beginning to think Loretta's sort of leaning that way also. But I don't believe that either of them could ever love each other as much as I love the General's daughter."

"That is a good thing, señor, since you are about to marry her. I wouldn't think it would work any other way." She leaned her back against the oak tree as Sean slipped his hands around her neck to kiss her. "Ah." She held a finger between their lips. "We really shouldn't be showing such signs of affection in a public place."

"Really? And why not? Most everyone knows we are engaged to be married."

"Because, I'm the Doña, and I must keep up appearances."

"Hang your titles, anyway. How do you think you're going to look eight or nine months pregnant when we start having children?"

"Beautiful." She laughed.

"Yes, you will." His lips lingered long against her soft mouth. It was the sound of girlish giggles that caused her to pull away from his embrace.

"That's the second time you've done that to me." Sean glared as Paco and Aurie Templeton suddenly appeared.

"Sí," Paco shrugged, "but I cannot help it. The garden is so beautiful in the moonlight."

"Yeah, well enjoy yourselves." Sean slipped Leonida's arm inside his and turned back toward the hacienda.

"The second time?" she asked.

"Yes. Remember the first time you kissed me under that tree?"

"Sí."

"Well, that little devil was hiding right on the other side of that tree with Lupe Perez the whole time. That's how all the talk about you and me being in love got started in the first place."

"Really? I had no idea." She giggled. "That was a sad time. I miss Lupe and her grandfather." They paused at the steps oblivious of the men smoking in the patio. A small boy floated a wooden boat in the fountain, while a vaquero on one of the benches finished tuning his guitar and began to sing a ballad about lost love.

"Yes, I miss her too." Sean took both her hands and smiled.

"Not too much, I hope."

"Not as much as I'll miss you tonight." He gave her hands a quick pull, causing her to lean forward, and kissed her on the lips.

"Señor!" She jerked back to slap him, but he caught her arm in mid flight. Her face turned crimson at the hoots and whistles of the men as the guitar suddenly changed to a livelier tune.

"There is one thing you'll be learning real quick, being engaged to a Kilkenney, m'dear. I'm a red-blooded Irishman who's going to show affection to the woman I love anywhere and anyplace available. And it doesn't matter who's present. So, m'lady, you'd better get darned used to it." He gave her another kiss before releasing his hold.

"I really do have to check on the Segoviano children. I'll see you in the morning. Goodnight."

"Buenas noches," she said as he turned away. She waited until he had crossed the brick patio before adding "Mi amor," then scampered up the steps and into the house.

Chapter 19

"Well, that about does it." Hanky glared at Alice Carpenter across the breakfast table. "All four of you women are going to trial."

"But Señor Russell, you can't try all of them for killing one man." Jose laughed.

"Oh can't I? You just watch. The judge is hankerin' to get this wing-ding started, and I got me four women with four confessions. For all anyone knows, they coulda ganged up on the skinny bastard. Three of 'em coulda held him down while the other croaked him with his own butcher knife. Sorry, ma'am." He glanced at Alice.

"I can understand your frustration, Hanky, but why won't you listen to reason? I've told you the truth. These girls are only lying in an effort to protect me." Alice leaned against the table to plead her case.

"She's lying." Ruby paused to cough. "What reason would she have for killing Ambrose?"

"No, they're both telling lies." Aurie hit her fist against the table.

"Now, y'all hush!" Hanky snapped. "I've heard just about enough of this nonsense. I'm a taking all four of you to trial and that's that."

"You keep saying 'four women', Hanky. I only see three women. Who's the fourth?" Sean stared over the rim of his coffee cup.

"Mrs. Garcia."

"What? Oh, come on, now." Sean slammed his cup down, spilling some of its contents.

"You didn't take my niña's confession seriously, did you?" Jose laughed.

"Didn't say I did, but lying to an officer of the law's a crime all its own, and she's done that. If she's willing to muddle up the case I'm working on, then she's going to have to pay the price the same as anyone else around here, no matter how much me or anyone else might love her." He went back to sawing at the meat on his plate.

"Well, this is going to be quite a horse and pony show. Do you think Judge Hansen will allow you to bring all four women to trial?" Captain McDougal said. "Excuse me," he added as Sean and General Flores began grumbling to each other. "I'd like to hear Mr. Russell's answer to my question."

"I don't know if he will, but the way I see it, he ain't got much choice. He said I was to prosecute whoever done it, and I'm for letting all four get up on the stand and swear they're telling the truth. Then the jury can pick out the one they wanna hang. Maybe we'll get lucky and they'll hang all four." His glare caused Aurie to shift uncomfortably in her chair.

"Don't let him scare you none, honey. His growl is bigger than his bite." Ruby's laughter was cut short by a cough.

"Señor Russell, if you make my daughter stand trial for a crime she didn't commit, I'll..." Jose shook his head.

"You'll what, General?" Hanky laid his knife and fork in the plate.

"Have Maria feed you an old boot instead of burnt cow." Sean laughed.

"Hell, I think she's already done that. What is with this meat anyway, Maria?" Hanky turned to the maid.

"You bring sorrow to my Doña and these angels?" She put her hands on Aurie's shoulders. "Then you eat what I give you."

"What is it?" McDougal stared at Hanky's plate.

"You don't want to know." Sean shook his head.

"Looks as though you bought yourself a pocket full of trouble, señor." Jose grinned.

"That's all right." Hanky shoved his plate aside. "Y'all go ahead and have your fun, but unless I get the truth, I'm taking all four to trial, and it ain't gonna be so funny then. Another thing," he scooted away from the table, "if any one of you thinks I'm enjoying any of this, you're full of horse manure. I didn't want this job in the first place. It was your daughter who talked me into it." He pointed at General Flores. "Then she turns around and lies first chance she gets. Now, you and all these others can get your noses all out of joint if you want, but it ain't gonna make me no never mind, 'cause I'm gonna uphold the law. And the law says that a murder suspect is supposed to be locked up behind bars until the outcome of a fair trial, so," he put his hands on his hips to glare at the women, "y'all can just go pack yer bags, 'cause I'm taking every blessed one of you-uns to the pokey."

"What? You can't do that." Bear, who had just come into the room, jerked the cup Maria was trying to pour coffee into. "Oh, damn, I'm sorry," he said as she squealed and danced away from the scalding liquid, spilling even more.

"Ruby shouldn't be going anywhere. She's still sick," Sean said.

"That ain't my problem. Besides, we got a dead man that ain't gonna go anywhere forever, and it's highly likely someone sitting right here in this room kilt him. So, I'm locking up all four women until I get the truth. Now, you can stuff that into yer pipe and smoke it." He turned but stopped at the door to glare at General Flores. "Tell that daughter of yours she'd better be ready to leave in one hour."

"I don't believe that Mrs. Garcia is going to be going anywhere for a while." Loretta's voice drifted to the dining room door from the stairwell. She seemed to float down the last few rungs and into the room with the rustling of her skirts. "I just left her room, and she is feeling rather ill this morning."

"Por que? What is wrong with her?" General Flores scraped his chair against the floor as he jumped to his feet.

"I do believe that is Doctor Kilkenney's department. I only know she isn't feeling well."

"Dammit." Hanky stomped outside and slammed the door.

"I believe we have carried this ruse far enough," Alice Carpenter said. "He has every right to be angry. You girls should tell him the truth."

"Really? Then maybe you can tell me what the real truth is." Ruby grinned at her over her coffee.

~   ~   ~

"I haven't felt this sick since I was a little niña. I'm afraid I've gotten some horrible disease. I'm dying, Sean." Leonida rolled her head to one side. "Even my hair hurts."

"Mmm, it still looks beautiful if it does." Sean checked her pulse.

"What is it, Doctor." Jose hovered close to the bed.

"Give me a minute, for Christ's sake. I just got here."

"Go away, both of you. Just let me die. Oh, Dios." She draped her head over the side of the bed to vomit into a pan.

"Madra Maria, Madra de Dios." Maria crossed herself and mopped Leonida's face with a damp towel.

"Well, are you ready for the tragic news, m'dear?" Sean said after a few moments.

"Yes."

"I believe your are going to live long enough to become Mrs. Kilkenney and have lots of children." He kissed the fingers of the hand he was holding. "But in the next day or two, you are going to break out in hundreds of little red spots all over your body."

"Rubeola?" Jose said.

"I'm afraid so." Sean nodded. "And what about you, General? Have you had the disease yet?"

"I don't know."

"You haven't then, or you'd more than likely remember. I'm quarantining the entire hacienda until this thing is over. No one goes anywhere for any reason. Is that understood?"

"Sí." Maria nodded.

"Come now, Doctor, is it really that bad?" Jose crinkled his eyebrows.

"Yes it is. If this spreads among the Indians, it could be devastating. Their immune systems are not prepared to take on white men's diseases. I don't know just what damage something like rubeola might cause among the Yokuts or the Miwoks, but I have heard that a good dose of cholera left by miners coming to California has wiped out almost half the Comanche in Texas."

"Yes, I guess it is better to take precautions then. What do you wish us to do?" Jose sat on the edge of the bed and caressed Leonida's forehead.

"Just pass the word that no one is to leave their homes unless it is absolutely necessary. The cattle can take care of themselves for awhile. I don't want the Indians visiting the hacienda until we're positive this thing is over," Sean said.

"And when might that be?"

"I don't rightly know. It all depends on how many people have been infected and who are susceptible, like yourselves. It will just have to play itself out. And that's another thing I need to know."

"And what's that?" Jose said.

"Who has already had this darn thing and who hasn't. I might need some help, and I don't want to be asking anyone who might get sick to make the rounds with me." Sean smiled and leaned close to Leonida's ear. "Got to be going, Dear. Get some sleep."

~   ~   ~

The little man with stooped shoulders and gray hair hanging over his ears leaned heavily on his cane as he entered The Silver Slipper. He took his time finding just the right seat, and even longer sliding into the chair. Although his back was toward the table where Darrell Rodeen laughed and poured expensive Portuguese brandy for a couple of giggling dance hall girls, he could plainly see their reflection in the mirror above the bar.

"What can I get you?"

"I beg yer pardon, m'lady. Me hearin' isn't what it used to be." He squinted at the girl with bright red lips and bare shoulders.

"I said, what can I get you?" Her voice caused the men at the table to their right to snicker.

"I would like a bottle of your finest brandy, a block of cheese and some bread."

"Are you sure you're going to be able to pay for all that?" She lowered her voice and leaned closer to his gray head.

"Yes, I believe so, m'lady. Do you think this will be enough?" He dropped several gold coins into her palm.

"Mmmm, yes. I think that will more than take care of your order," she said, thumbing the shiny pieces. "Is there anything else I can get you?"

"Yes, m'lady." His feeble hand trembled as he pulled her close to whisper. "Keep a sharp eye on the bloke to me back. That's the one I've been telling you about. See what you can find out about him from yer two friends. He seems to have a loose mouth when he gets a little drink or two."

"Okay, but your hump is crooked." He could feel the hand on his back gently move the roll of towels to one side.

"Well, my, my." She straightened up and put a hand on her hip. "What a naughty boy you are. Are you sure you're up to doing such a thing?" The men at the next table laughed heartily.

"Hey, Sarah." One of them raised his voice above the music. "Better take it easy on the old man. His heart might stop when you take your clothes off."

"Yeah, says you." She swatted the air with her palm. "At least he's got the money to pay for what he's asking, which is more than you can say." She waited until they had ceased laughing before smiling at the man seated at the table.

"Is there anything else, dearie, before I get your brandy and cheese?"

"Yes." He motioned for her to come closer. "You're a doll, Sarah." He kissed her cheek. "I'll see you later in your room?"

"Oooo." She straightened up with wide eyes. "An all-nighter he says." She grinned at the men at the next table before kissing the old man on top of his head. Salty chuckled and watched the swishing of Sara's behind as she wove her way though the tables. Funny, he thought, he never knew how much he liked her before today. He'd have to take her away from all this someday.

~   ~   ~

Paco's lariat whistled as it sailed through the air to fall around the neck of the colt as it darted around the corral. "Alto, alto!" He pulled on the leather rope until the bucking colt's head was only inches from his chest. "Alto." He gently rubbed the animal's neck before slipping the noose over the colt's ears and swatting the animal on the rump.

"Gracias." He grinned as the colt snorted and galloped to the other side of the pen.

"That was wonderful." Aurie Templeton clapped her hands from her perch atop the corral fence. "I wish I could do something like that."

"Here." He held the coiled lariat toward her. "Come try."

"Oh, no, I could never do it." She shook her head.

"Sí." Paco grabbed her hand. "Come, Concho is gentle. He won't bite you."

"Is that the horse's name?"

"Sí, come try."

The dust poofed around Aurie's high-buttoned shoes to land on the hem of her gingham skirt as he led her to the center of the corral. The colt inched closer as Paco took his time showing her the proper way to hold the lariat and how much loop to have. He was close enough for Aurie to pet by the time the instructions were complete.

"Oh, he is so beautiful." She stared into the animal's hazel eyes.

"Sí." Paco rubbed the glossy brown coat. "Would you like to have him?"

"Have him? Yes, but I don't have any money, and I could never earn enough to own an animal like this." She hugged the horse's neck.

"You don't need any money." Paco grinned. "He is yours."

"But I could never ask Doña Leonida to just give him to me." Aurie shook her head.

"You don't know Doña Leonida very well. She would give you Concho and much more, if she thought you wanted him. But Concho doesn't belong to Doña Leonida. He is my horse, and I give him to you."

"You'll give him to me? Why?" She dropped the lariat in the dust to rub the animal with both hands.

"Because I love you, Aurie Templeton." Paco turned his back on her to check one of the colt's hooves. "I choose to give you Concho. But," he scooped the lariat from the dust, "we are forgetting our lesson."

"No," Aurie's thin blond hair whipped in the breeze as she shook her head, "I want you to repeat what you just told me."

"Que? I tell you Concho is your horse now. Come." He tried handing her the lariat, but she shoved it aside.

"Hang the lesson and quit beating around the bush. You know good and well what I'm talking about, Paco Morales. You just said you love me. Is that true?"

"Sí." He kept his eyes glued toward the dust at their feet and shrugged.

"Why won't you look at me then? Are my looks that bad? Or, do you have a wife and a bunch of children hidden away somewhere?"

"No, no." He shook his head. "It's just," he allowed his head to roll from side to side as he played with the lariat, "I only loved one woman before you, and she died. Bad things happened."

"Lupe Perez?"

"Sí."

"Angela told me about her and how she died. I'm sorry Paco; I really am." She covered one of his hands with hers. "If there was some way to take the pain away, I would."

"But you have, señorita. I don't have the hurt inside when I am watching you. This is hard for me to say." He paused to sigh deeply. "All I know is cattle and horses."

"No, you are doing well, Paco Morales. More than you think. I have been watching you, also. You are the kindest, most gentle man I have ever known."

"Oh, but señorita, you don't know me very well." He laughed. "I am a pistolero." He touched the gun on his hip. "I have done many bad things."

"Perhaps, but not to me. Angela also told me about some of those things, and how you and Juan did them to protect Doña Leonida and this rancho. I don't believe you're a bad person, Paco." She shook her head. "I know what's inside your heart, and I'm glad you love me. I feel safe when I'm around you. Promise you won't leave me." He stared at her for long minute. "Promise?"

"You don't have to ask, señorita. I don't have much to offer but a few horses and a saddle. I live there with the other vaqueros," he pointed toward the bunk house, "but I wish for you to marry me when this thing with Señor Brice is over."

"I'll marry you this instant, Paco Morales. You don't have to wait."

"I'm afraid he will." They both turned to see Josiah Russell perched atop his dung gelding watching them.

"Perdon, Señor Hanky. We did not hear you come," Paco said cheerfully. "Why must we wait to get married?"

"Because I've just been to see Judge Hansen, and he wants to start the trial just as soon as Mrs. Garcia is able to poke her head outside. Hopefully, Monday morning."

"Madra de Dios," Paco said as they watched the lawman walk his horse toward the watering trough.

Chapter 20

"That's very complimentary of you, Captain. Just how would you know if I sang like a nightingale or not?" Loretta clutched her white dress with blue ruffled trim in her hand as she danced gracefully from rock to rock across the stream.

"Because, my dear," Jonathan McDougal held her hand as she made the last dainty step to dry land, "I've heard you sing many times."

"Really? I don't believe that is possible. I can't remember singing anything since arriving here."

"Certainly you have." Pine needles and dried oak leaves crunched beneath their feet as they wove their way through the scrub oaks and sugar pines that lined the creek. Jonathan took Loretta's hand and slipped it into the crook of his arm. "I heard you just the other day, singing Barbara Allen as you hung your laundry. And let me tell you, it was certainly beautiful."

"Oh, you flatter me, Captain." Loretta giggled. "I don't even remember if I was in the right key or not."

"You were. I was also watching from the second-story veranda with Mrs. Garcia when you gave that little recital in front of the fountain, and I know you were only having fun, but believe me, my dear," he turned to face her, "outside of being able to run a tight ship, the one thing I do know is music. My parents wanted me to be a musician, so I studied the piano and violin as a child. Your voice is extraordinarily good. You are someone who has been trained in the classics. You're an opera singer, and too good to be singing in the likes of The Silver Slipper. Those bloody drunks wouldn't know good music if it jumped up and bit them on the nose."

The blood drained from Loretta's face as tears welled in her blue eyes.

"You know." She let her chin fall and turned away. "And just when I was starting to really like you. Who told you? Mrs. Garcia?"

"No, I had no idea that anyone on this ranch knew, except perhaps Doctor Kilkenney, and that bloody Irishman is so in love with Mrs. Garcia he can't see past his own nose." Jonathan placed his hands on her shoulders and leaned close to her ear.

"I've spent many an evening sitting in the back of that noisy, smelly place, just waiting for a chance to hear you sing. It was the highlight of my visits to San Francisco, up to now. Getting to know you these past two weeks has surpassed anything I could have wished for. I've found you to be a talented, cultured and well-rounded lady. With a very kind heart, I might add."

"Captain, you might not realize this, but singing wasn't the only thing I was required to do."

"Yes, I've known that also. There was a time or two I contemplated murder, watching you climb the stairs with some rabble. I have also wondered how you got yourself into such a fix, but I shall not ask. I know you were not raised that way."

"Come now, Captain." Loretta blew her nose before turning to face him with a weak smile. "It doesn't really matter how I got started being a whore, does it? The fact is, that's what I am. A twenty-dollar whore. That's what I get paid for...allowing men to paw me in bed. I guess that's what I'll be doing when I finally get back to San Francisco."

"The Devil you will." Jonathan grabbed her by the arms. "I won't allow it."

"I might remind you, Captain, you're not my father." She tried prying his fingers loose, but finally gave up. "And you don't own me. Besides, I'm rather expensive for one or two nighters." Jonathan released his grip to hold her face between his massive palms.

"Darling Loretta, listen closely. You are worth more than all the gold and silver these greedy bastards could ever dig out of the ground in ten lifetimes. And while I am old enough to be your father, I am offering you everything I am or will ever own. I listened to you sing, because I've loved you since the first time I laid eyes on you. How can I make you understand?"

"Why in the world didn't you tell me this in San Francisco? Why wait until now, after half the men in California have been to my room?"

"Forget all that." Jonathan scowled and swatted the air. "That's all in the past."

"I don't know that I can." She turned away. "There's been too many to forget. I dream about them at night and wake up feeling like I need to wash. But washing doesn't help. Nothing will."

"Loretta." He pulled her close to stare in her eyes. "I understand."

"No you don't. You can't." She shook her head violently.

"Let me at least try. I'll get Mrs. Garcia and Doctor Kilkenney to pray for you. Things seem to happen when they pray. I'll pray for you myself. But can't you at least let me try?"

"I really don't know..." She snapped her head around at the sound of crunching leaves. Sean Kilkenney was weaving his way toward them.

"There you are," he said between puffs on his pipe. "I've been looking all over for you."

"By damned, if the timing of the Irish isn't as bad as their ignorance," Jonathan growled.

"Oh, am I interrupting something?" His glance darted between the two of them. "I can leave and talk to you later."

"Yes, you are interrupting, and no, now that you're here, go ahead and speak your piece."

"Well, what I need is a huge favor from you. I will be tied up here for awhile, with this rubeola outbreak and the trial coming up."

"Have you heard any word on when that might be taking place?" Loretta asked.

"It might be as early as Monday, but I'm not sure. A lot of it depends on when Leonida, I mean Mrs. Garcia, is able to travel. Hanky is adamant that she is going to be placed on the stand with the others. Anyway, what I need is for someone to go to San Francisco and take care of some errands for me."

"That's a big request for even an Irishman. It must be important." Jonathan scowled.

"It is." Sean paused to relight his pipe, "and it must be kept as quiet as possible."

"Okay, let's at least hear it."

"I need for someone I can trust to meet with this man." He handed Jonathan a card. "He's a Pinkerton agent I've hired to check on James Sattler, Mrs. Garcia's solicitor. I believe he is cheating her."

"Walter Norton?" Jonathan laughed loudly. "By the memory of Blackbeard's ghost, you are the most stubborn, insolent man I've ever known."

"Why, what's wrong?" Sean scrunched his eyebrows.

"I came to you with the same suspicions, asking for help not three weeks ago, and you refused. So I went and hired the same Pinkerton to do exactly the same thing. And as you well know, I have one of my own men doing some snooping on his own. Could have saved yourself some money if you had listened to me in the first place." Jonathan waved the card in the air.

"Yes, but I was rather angry at the time. Mrs. Garcia and I had had a little misunderstanding, and I was not feeling too friendly toward her at the time. Will you help?"

"Yes, I will help, since it is for a good cause. I should be checking with the man myself, and seeing what, if anything, Salty Moran has discovered. But you know, don't you, that people are going to ask questions as to why I'm leaving with the trial being so close?"

"What if I go with you?" Loretta said.

"I beg your pardon?" Jonathan studied the woman at his side.

"I was suggesting that I go with you. I could tell everyone that you were nice enough to escort me back to San Francisco in order that I can collect some more clothing and take care of some personal matters. I don't like traveling alone. Besides, it isn't safe for a lady to travel without an escort, especially in a large city like San Francisco. If the doctor is a good enough actor, he might be able to convince everyone that Mrs. Garcia has, shall we say, some new complication from her illness that prevents her from traveling for a few more days. Perhaps this outbreak is a lot worse than he thought, and the whole rancho needs to be under a tight quarantine. That way, we'll be back in time for Hanky's horse and pony show." The men stared at each other for a long minute before Jonathan McDougal cleared his throat.

"Nothing would please me more than accompanying you to San Francisco." He took her hand and lightly kissed her fingers.

~   ~   ~

"So, what's yer plans, then? I mean after this whole thing is over?" Tex handed Hanky a cup of steaming coffee and took a seat beside him on the front porch of the cabin. The smell of fresh tortillas and fried pork with onions and peppers drifted though the open door.

"Hell if I know. Guess I'll be moseying back to Texas. Ain't nothing left for me here."

"You're dumber'n dirt with a head harder'n a clod." Tex sipped his coffee. "What the hell are Rosa and I? And what about your grandbaby? Don't none of us count for nothing?"

"I didn't mean it that way, and you know it. I love that girl inside more'n life itself. She's the best thing that could have ever happened to you."

"Well, you just said you was gonna go off and leave us. It's a long way to Texas, old man. And if you leave, we ain't gonna see you ever again. You know that just as sure as you're sitting there."

"Que? What are you men arguing about?" Rosa leaned in the doorway to wipe the perspiration from her brow.

"Oh, Papa here says he doesn't want to see his grandchild. He says he's going to go back to Texas after the trial." Tex scowled.

"I didn't say that. I just said I was going back to Texas where I belong, that's all."

"Por Que?" Rosa came off the steps to face the lawman. "What is in Texas that's not right here at our casa? You don't want my baby to have a grandfather or me to have a papa? Is that it?"

"No, you know better than that."

"You say you're going back to Texas and leaving us behind. What about your son? You think he doesn't need a papa? You think he doesn't love you?"

"I know he does. The same as I know you love me. All I was saying was that things aren't the same out at the ranch since I took this here star." He thumbed the badge pinned to his vest. "Folks aren't friendly toward me like they used to be."

"Oh, hell, Hanky. Quit feeling sorry for yourself." Tex tossed the remnants from his coffee cup in the yard. "You've been a lawman longer than most folks have been alive. And we both know that when you wear a badge, you're gonna have to make decisions that are going to make some folks angry. Them folks out at Mrs. Garcia's place are going to get over it, and so will you."

"Señor," Rosa knelt in front of Hanky and took one of his hands, "por favor, for me, be a grandfather to my baby."

"Hell, how do you say no to this girl, Tommy?" Hanky laughed and hugged Rosa's head against his chest.

"I don't, much. Well, now, would you look at who's showing up right at dinnertime?" Tex nodded toward the white mule and rider rounding the curve in the road.

"Can't say I rightly blame him after what Maria tried to feed me this morning," Hanky snorted.

"What brings you out here this time of day, Doc?" Tex met Sean in the middle of the yard as he dismounted the mule.

"Oh, nothing much. I was actually looking for your father, and took a chance that he might be here. I hope it's all right."

"You know better'n to ask a stupid question like that. You can come 'round here anytime you choose. Come on up and sit yer carcass on the porch while I turn yer jackass loose in the corral."

"Cathy's not a jackass. She's a nice gentle mule."

"Yeah, sez you. Go see the old man. That's what you come here for." Tex grabbed the reins and led the beast toward the corral. "Come on. You're as stubborn as that man what rides you."

"Doc? How's things out at the ranch?" Hanky glanced up from rolling a cigarette as Sean took a seat beside him.

"Busy; real busy."

"Señor Sean," Rosa poked her head through the door, "perdoname for not coming out to meet you, but I'm cooking right now."

"I know, and it smells delicious."

"I hope you are able to stay and eat with us."

"I wouldn't miss it for the world, Rosa."

"Ooo." She turned as something sizzled and dashed back toward the stove.

"Told Tommy that's why you come out here, to get something decent to eat." Hanky struck a match against his boot and held it to his cigarette.

"If you remember right, I've always been the one to complain about Maria's cooking, even when you thought it was good."

"Well, it didn't used to be half-bad, but I couldn't cut whatever that was this morning with a bucksaw. I just figured I'd better go somewheres else, or starve to death." He took a drag off his smoke and squinted at Sean. "What's on yer mind, boy?"

"Well, it's just that I don't believe that Mrs. Garcia is going to be able to travel come Monday morning. You should have a talk with Judge Hansen, and see if we can't postpone the trial awhile longer."

"Huh, how long we talking about?"

"I don't know. The fact is, this thing is spreading a lot faster than I thought. I'm afraid of what it might do to the Indians. You might have to postpone it for an entire month before we can start letting people come and go as they please."

"Don't know that Lloyd's gonna be too happy with that. He might just go on without her and drag her in when she's healed. What's wrong with her anyway? I thought she just had the measles."

"Rubeola, measles, yes," Sean nodded, "that's what she's got. But it's hit her harder than most, and she's a pretty sick girl. I don't think she should be moved for awhile. I've been saying, every time someone leaves this ranch, they take the chance of spreading the disease. Besides, with all this rubeola going around, I haven't had much time to complete my investigation."

"You haven't? Me and Tommy dug Ambrose up fer you and stood right there when you poked around on his rotting carcass. What more do you want?"

"Well, I need to question the women involved in the murder."

"Ya mean you haven't done that yet?" Hanky screwed up his face. "Hell, they've been right there the whole time. What's been holding you back, boy?"

"Like I said, I've been looking after sick families from early morning to late at night. Besides, if you'll listen to me, this ranch is supposed to be under quarantine. All this running around is only going to spread the disease."

"Yeah, well, I suppose yer right." Hanky tossed the butt in the yard as Tex returned from the corral. "I'll go have a talk with Lloyd tomorrie morning, but I ain't gonna promise you nothing. If he say's bring 'em in to trial, that's exactly what I'm gonna do, and when you get back there tonight, you pass the word around that if any of them yahoos try to stop me, I'm gonna shoot their leg off."

~　　~　　~

"Maria, I told you that no one was to see me in this condition," Leonida snapped at the maid, who stood holding the bedroom door partially open.

"But Doña Leonida, Paco says it's urgent." Maria glanced back over her shoulder as someone mumbled out in the hall.

"Who is there with him?"

"Señorita Aurie. They both wish to speak to you. It will make your heart happy, señora."

"Very well, let them in." Leonida pulled the blanket up as high as possible, hoping it would hide most of the red blotches covering her face.

"Gracias, mi Doña." Paco's spurs jingled as he entered the room. He stared at her a long minute before removing his sombrero. Aurie Templeton clung to him, partially hidden at his side.

"What is it you wish to see me about?" Her voice sounded muffled beneath the blanket.

"Señorita Aurie and I wish to be married."

"Oh?" She allowed the blanket to fall, then quickly grasped it back again. "That is wonderful news. When do you wish this wedding to take place?"

"Right away, ma'am," Aurie said as she hugged Paco's arm.

"I don't know if that would be wise, señorita." Leonida shook her head. "There would be no time to prepare a proper fiesta for such an event. Then, there is this sickness." She grinned and lowered the blanket from her face. "But most of all, what about the trial? Both of us are supposed to be there. Remember?"

"That is no importante, Doña Leonida. We do not wish such a big fiesta as Juan and Angela." Paco turned his palms upward and shrugged.

"But what about the trial, Paco? You should wait. What if something bad happens? What if the jury decides Señorita Aurie is the guilty one?"

"No," the vaquero jerked upright, "no, Doña Leonida, that will not happen."

"But, Paco..."

"No! They took Lupe from me. I will not allow them to take Aurie too. I will kill them." He backed toward the door. "I will kill them all."

"Paco, wait." Leonida tossed back the covers but he was gone.

"Go after him, señorita. Hurry, don't let him get away from you."

Chapter 21

"You must be Captain McDougal and Miss Stewart." Arthur Farnsworth bowed with a nod of his head. "The lady of the house is expecting you. Do come in." He stepped back, allowing them to enter the spacious house perched atop Rincon Hill. The massive brick structure was nestled among the mansions built by the town's most prosperous merchants. It reminded Loretta of one of the huge government buildings she had seen growing up in Boston.

"This way, please." His shiny black shoes seemed to glide silently across the tile floor as he led them toward a huge set of oak doors. The sound of someone playing Bach's cantata number 26 on a piano floated past the heavy doors and into the foyer. Farnsworth took hold of the brass handle with a gloved hand and smiled.

"Lady Clara is practicing at the moment. I'm sure you will excuse her attire."

"Yes, I'm sure we will," Captain McDougal said as Farnsworth opened the doors wide and bowed gracefully.

"Captain Jonathan McDougal and Miss Loretta Stewart to see Miss Clara." The young girl, dressed in white silk stockings and pink tutu with matching ballet shoes, stopped in the middle of a move to stand on one foot with both arms and the other leg raised high in the air and smiled. She had a shiny leather brace strapped to her right knee.

"Oh, do come in." The lady at the piano rose to greet them. "I am Dorothy Baker, Clara's mother. We received your note and are so pleased that friends of Doctor Kilkenney would drop by to visit. How is Doctor Kilkenney? We do miss him dearly."

"The doctor is doing well. He wanted to come, but there has been an outbreak of rubeola at the Garcia ranch and that's kept him rather busy," Jonathan said. "It seems that everyone, including Mrs. Garcia herself, has gotten ill."

"Oh, I'm so sorry. Well, do give him our best. He is such a darling man."

"So, this is the young lady I have been jealous about?" Loretta smiled at the girl who had finished her move without music and now stood grinning at her.

"Jealous? What in the world for?" Jonathan scratched his graying beard.

"Well, if you remember right, when we first met, I believed I was terribly in love with Doctor Kilkenney, and twice during that time, he slipped away to see some other woman named Clara. In fact," she took Clara by the hand, "he kept me waiting for over an hour the day we were supposed to leave to visit Mrs. Garcia. I was so jealous. I had no idea it was this beautiful creature here. He told me you were one of his patients, but I refused to believe him. You know how we women are. I thought he was just seeing another woman behind my back." Clara covered her mouth and giggled.

"Well, I can see where, if she were a little older, or if he was much younger, that might indeed have been a problem. In fact, if I were about twelve years old, I might have a bad case of puppy love myself. I'm very pleased to make your acquaintance, m'lady." The captain bowed gracefully.

"The feeling is mutual, Captain McDougal, Miss Loretta." Clara completed a perfect curtsey.

"Thank you, but it is 'Mrs.' now." Loretta gave Jonathan a crooked grin. "You see, between the time we sent word that we were coming, and now, I've become Mrs. Jonathan McDougal."

"Then, you're not going to marry Doctor Kilkenney?" Clara shook her head.

"No, I'm proud to say she's not. We Scotts know a good thing when we see it, and I got her to the altar first," Jonathan said.

"Good, because I want to marry him." Clara's eyes darted toward her mother as her face turned red.

"Oh, I see you were jealous of me also," Loretta nodded, "even though we had never met. Well, some men just don't have any sense at all do they? They go around breaking hearts without even realizing what they're doing."

"If it's any consolation, lass, the Irish bloke talks about you all the time," Jonathan said.

"Really?"

"Certainly, and he wanted to make sure you got this little gift. He asked me to deliver it to you personally." Jonathan pulled a small box tied with a pink ribbon from his pocket. "He says you're to be wearing it when he comes to see you perform on stage."

"Oh, my word," Dorothy said as her daughter pulled a small gold chain with a single pea-sized nugget from the tissue paper inside the box. "Does he have any idea what that is worth?"

"I'm sure he does, ma'am. The nugget," Jonathan pointed toward the necklace as Loretta fastened it around the girl's neck, "was taken from the bank of the Mokelumne River on Hidden Springs Ranch, where he is staying."

"Oh, it's beautiful." Clara watched her reflection in the glass as she danced in front of the grandfather clock. "Tell him I said thank you, thank you, thank you. And I hope you will come to watch me dance also."

"I wouldn't miss it for the world, m'lady," Jonathan said with a chuckle.

"Oh, I'm so sorry. I'm afraid I'm such a horrible host," Dorothy said. "Won't you please be seated? I'll have some tea brought in."

"Yes, but we can only be staying for a few more minutes, ma'am. We do have some important business to take care of."

"But you will stay just awhile longer, won't you?" Dorothy walked briskly toward the double doors. "I would like you to meet my husband. I believe I just heard him come in."

Loretta raised her eyebrows and smiled. "I was hoping I would get some time alone with my own husband before the day was through."

"You will, my dear." Jonathan patted her hand. She felt a cold chill sweep over her as Dorothy returned with a short, stocky man with a ruddy complexion.

"This is my husband, Samuel. Dear, I would like you to meet Captain McDougal and his wife, Loretta. They are friends of Doctor Kilkenney."

"Pleased to meet you Captain, Mrs. McDougal." The judge shook Jonathan's hand. Loretta smiled and nodded, but felt the chill increase as the judge took a second glance at her.

"We've just been admiring your daughter, Clara. She's such a sweet child. I can see why Doctor Kilkenney was so taken by her." Loretta's voice cracked, and she turned to cough into her hanky. "Please excuse me." She smiled and tried clearing her throat.

"Oh, I'm sorry, I forgot the tea." Dorothy disappeared through the door.

"Yes, we thought our little girl would never dance again, until Doctor Kilkenney got a chance to look at her. Do you realize I actually had to shanghai that man in order to get him to look at her? Always running here and running there." The judge shook his head. "I've never seen a man in such a hurry."

"I'm afraid he hasn't changed much." Jonathan chuckled. "He'll more than likely run right past the pearly gates when it comes time for him to go."

"Here we are." Dorothy returned with a uniformed maid at her heels carrying a tray. "I do hope you will forgive my forgetfulness."

"That's quite all right, Mrs. Baker. My throat is just a little scratchy. Probably from all the dust when we traveled."

"Cream and sugar, ma'am?" The maid handed Loretta a cup and saucer.

"No, thank you. Just a little lemon for me."

"I suppose you would like something a little more substantial than lemon in your tea, Captain?" Samuel Baker pulled a bottle of brandy from one of the cabinets along the wall.

"Yes, that does sound good."

"Now, tell me, where did you travel from, Mrs. McDougal?" The judge glanced at her as he poured some brandy in Jonathan's cup.

"From, let's see if I get this right," she stared at the ceiling, "Rancho Manantial Escondido."

"Where in the blazes is that?" Judge Baker set the bottle back on the shelf.

"It's near Dogtown, up Columbia way. Actually, it's closer to Angel's Camp than Columbia. And don't ask me to say its name in Spanish like Loretta did." Jonathan chuckled and raised his teacup in a toast to his wife.

I think it's rather beautiful," Loretta said. "It means Ranch Of The Hidden Springs, or Hidden Springs Ranch, whichever you prefer." She shrugged and sat on the piano bench beside Clara. "It belongs to a young widow named Leonida Garcia. That is where your doctor friend is at this very moment." She gave Dorothy a crooked grin and sipped her tea.

"Is she pretty?" Clara crinkled her eyebrows.

"Mrs. Garcia? Oh yes." Loretta nodded. "Very lovely, and nice, and rich and whatever you can imagine. Well, you get the idea." She leaned close to the girl's ear. "To tell the truth, I was rather jealous of her when we first met, because I was terribly taken with the doctor just like you. But I wound up loving her just the same, because you can't help liking her. Then, I met my husband, and he made it all better." She smiled at Jonathan. "I do believe he is the nicest man I've ever met."

"That is quite a compliment coming from a pretty lady, Captain." Judge Baker toasted him with the cup of tea. "To your health."

"The feeling is mutual, my dear." Jonathan toasted his wife.

"Garcia, Garcia." Judge Baker scowled and set the cup on the table. "Leonida Garcia. I'm presiding over her case. She claims to own some seventy-five square miles of property near the Mokelumne River, if I'm not mistaken."

"Indeed she does. It's a beautiful place too," Jonathan said.

"Yes, I'm sure it is. Too bad these people never took the time to educate themselves, or thought it was necessary to keep legal documents, like title deeds, in a safe place. I'm afraid she's going to wind up losing her ranch if she can't produce some proof that she actually owns it." He scowled as Loretta choked on her tea laughing.

"I'm sorry," she dabbed her lips with a napkin, "did you refer to Leonida Garcia is ignorant and uneducated?"

"Yes I did. Why?"

"She is far more educated than I am, and I attended finishing school in New England. The woman is well versed in at least four languages that I'm aware of." Loretta glanced at Clara and shook her head. "She really is too perfect."

"My wife is correct." Jonathan paused to set his cup and saucer on the table. "And she has a whole cabinet packed with legal documents and papers right inside her study. I'm required to give her a written receipt every time we trade goods or hides. I'll bet you any amount of money that she has kept every one of them inside that cabinet."

"I'll be damned." Samuel Baker sat in one of the over-stuffed chairs staring at the piano legs.

"What's wrong, dear?" Dorothy placed a hand on his arm.

"If what they've just told me is true, and I've no reason to believe they are lying..." He covered his mouth and shook his head.

"Sam?" Dorothy leaned close.

"I've just discovered that I've been lied to, and it makes me wonder how many other times someone's done the same thing. I've more than likely passed judgment cheating several families out of everything they own." He stared at Loretta with misty eyes. "I was about to do the same thing again. Now I've just got to think of what I can do about it. Thank you."

"You're welcome, but I don't know exactly what it is that I have done."

"You've shown me what I fool I am." He got out of his chair and stomped to the door to yell.

"Arthur? Get in here immediately."

"Yes, Master Baker?" The butler appeared as if he had been standing right outside the door. "What is it you wish?"

"I want you to go find Steven Jenkins, the court recorder, and tell him to cancel all plans for this evening. He is to get over here right now. Immediately." He finished scribbling on a piece of paper and shoved it at the butler.

"Yes, sir." Arthur glanced at the paper. "And what if he is not home, Master? What shall I do then?"

"Find him. Somebody at the courthouse, or one of his neighbors is bound to know where he is."

"Yes, sir." Arthur bowed and vanished as quickly as he had appeared.

"You had better inform the kitchen that we will be having guests for dinner." Judge Baker glanced toward his wife.

"Yes, dear." Dorothy paused at the door to smile at Loretta. "I believe we are having roast turkey and potatoes. I do hope you are fond of turkey."

"Well, yes, but..." She glanced at Jonathan.

"We thank you for the offer, but we must be going." Jonathan checked his watch against the grandfather clock.

"Nonsense. You're not leaving this house until I get the full story behind Leonida Garcia and that ranch of hers. I have the feeling a lot of people are being cheated out of their holdings in a court of law, and I really don't want to be a part of it, any more than I already have." He filled the empty teacup with brandy and stared at Jonathan.

"You have no idea how it makes me feel to suddenly realize that I've been so busy presiding over case after case, that I haven't really checked to see if what I'm being told is the truth or not. Many of the people coming into my courtroom can't speak English, so I've been just as guilty as everyone else in thinking they are ignorant. Maybe I've been the ignorant one." He took a sip of brandy from the cup and sat to stare at the silver tray and teapot.

"We're all ignorant, sir, until we become aware of the facts. But if we're lucky, we cease being ignorant and become educated in the matters set before us." Jonathan pulled a couple of cigars from his vest pocket and offered one to Judge Baker.

"Thank you." The judge pulled a box of matches from his pocket. Jonathan continued talking between puffs as the judge struck one of the matches and held it to his cigar.

"Leonida's story is a complicated one. Her parents were both of Spanish decent, while she and her two brothers were born in Mexico City. She was promised as a bride to Rudolfo Garcia when she was only fourteen, although I believe she was around twenty when they were finally married at the rancho, here in California. Her father, Jose Flores, is the only one of her immediate family still living, and he is staying with her right now."

"Rudolfo Garcia," Judge Baker mumbled as he lit his cigar. "He's the one Henry Baines had hung for shooting that man in the back?"

"Yes, but it was later proved, by Dr. Kilkenney, that it was a friend of Sheriff Randell that had actually committed the murder."

"He was nothing but a gunslinger posing as a sheriff. The same as Henry Baines posing as a judge. The both of them were nothing but criminals cloaking themselves with the law." Judge Baker puffed angrily on the cigar.

"Yes, I agree. Anyway," Jonathan paused to sip his tea, "it wasn't long after Leonida and Rudolfo were married that Judge Baines and Pod Randell concocted the plan to steal their land. They had some men attack and abuse Leonida, thinking it would cause Rudolfo to hunt them down and get himself killed in a gun battle, trying to defend her honor. It would have worked, except for Tex and Doctor Kilkenney pulling Rudolfo from the saloon the night he found them."

"Tex?"

"Yes, Tommy Burwell, an ex-Texas Ranger. Who, I might add, is a real gunfighter in his own right. He had befriended Rudolfo's brother, Carlo. As I said, it is rather complicated and involves a lot of people."

"We have all night. Go on." Judge Baker adjusted himself in his chair.

"But Jonathan and I were just married this afternoon. I was hoping to spend some time with my husband." Loretta gave him a crooked grin.

"Congratulations. I realize I might be ruining this one evening for you, but hopefully you will have a lifetime to make up for it. What we're discussing here concerns what is going to happen to another family for an entire lifetime. I'm sorry."

"Yes, I guess I was being a little selfish. It's just disappointing." Loretta shrugged. "Go on, dear."

"Well," Jonathan cleared his throat, "it seems that Judge Baines had thought Leonida would simply abandon the ranch and move back to Mexico. But she instead built an army of vaqueros and stayed right there. They tried all sorts of things to run her off, killing several people including the priest. But you already know what happened when she finally got angry enough to take her army into town."

"Yes, I am quite aware." Judge Baker refilled both teacups with brandy. "I suppose Judge Lloyd Hansen has all this listed in his report exonerating Mrs. Garcia?"

"Yes, he does. Mrs. Garcia has a copy of it in that cabinet Loretta mentioned."

"Good." Samuel Baker stuck out his bottom lip and nodded. "I hope she has more than one copy, because I'd like to have one for myself. I can always get one from Lloyd, if need be. I'd also like to see a copy of the deed to the ranch and anything else she might have."

"But, Leonida has already given all that to her solicitor. What is his name, dear?" Loretta glanced at Jonathan.

"Sattler, James Sattler."

"Dammit!" Judge Baker struck the arm of his chair. "Dammit, dammit, dammit! That silver-tongued devil has been inside my courtroom half a dozen times, claiming that the Garcias have absolutely no records of any kind. He's even told me she can barely speak English, let alone read or write. I'll bet you a year's wages against that ship of yours that he's already destroyed those records."

"I wouldn't take that bet," Jonathan said, shaking his head. "But we still might be able to come up with something." He pulled a card from his vest pocket. "Both Doctor Kilkenney and I have retained the services of this man to investigate Mr. Sattler. We were, shall we say, rather suspicious of his character."

"Mmm, I'm familiar with Walt." Judge Baker studied the card. "He's been with the Pinkertons for awhile. He's a good man. Has he found out anything yet?"

"I don't know. We were on our way to his office after we left here."

"It doesn't matter, I'll talk to him myself tomorrow. We'll all go. And if he has anything at all, I'll subpoena the records. I want to see what Mrs. Garcia has left inside her cabinet. If I can find anything at all that will substantiate my suspicions, Mr. Sattler had better hire a solicitor to defend himself inside my courtroom."

"She has them," Loretta said absently as she adjusted the laced ruffle on Clara's tutu.

"She has what, dear?" Jonathan said.

"Copies of everything you said." She paused to study the men staring at her. "Well, you don't suppose that she was crazy enough to give him the only copies she had, do you? She knew when this whole thing started that someone would be asking her to submit records, so she had Father Ramon, her priest, copy everything. She was showing me some of his work just the other day, and he's rather good, you know. It's hard to tell the original from a copy. She has all the originals tucked away in a neat little hiding place inside the church." Both men stared at each other a long minute before Jonathan broke into laughter.

"Damned women anyway. Here we are running around like spies trying to trap this man, when she already has all the proof we need right there all the time."

~   ~   ~

Loretta eased her body into the brass tub filled with warm, scented water. She could hear Jonathan humming an old Scottish ballad in the next room as she closed her eyes to relish the feeling. All the plans she had rehearsed inside her head for a quiet, romantic evening were for naught. The clock on the mantle of their suite inside the Kings Castle Hotel had just chimed eleven.

"Will there be anything else, ma'am?" The exhausted maid laid a stack of fresh towels on a stool beside the tub.

"No, Edith. You've been an angel. I'm just going to soak all the noise and busyness out of my body."

"Are you sure you don't want me to wash your back before I go?" She soaped the sponge.

"Not really." Loretta smiled and leaned her head back against the tub. "You must be as tired as I am. "Go get some rest. You deserve it."

"Thank you, ma'am." She handed Loretta the soapy sponge. "And congratulations. He seems like a fine gentleman. I wish you both a lifetime of happiness."

"Thank you, Edith."

Loretta closed her eyes and sank deeper into the tub as the door closed silently. The faces of all the men who had come to her room at The Silver Slipper suddenly appeared before her, laughing, wanting to press their sweaty bodies against hers and breathe their whisky breath in her face. They began squeezing her breasts and biting, hurting her. The drunken man with the belt was there laughing. She screamed and begged as he swung harder and harder, leaving scars across her back. *Oh, dear God, make them stop. Make them go away.* In just a few moments, she knew what would happen. She would go to her husband, but pull away as if his hands were made of fire. It had happened before. The men pawing at her frightened her. No matter how hard she tried, she could not become jaded like the other girls, thinking it was only a job. "Come on," Julia had told her, "it's like sweeping floors or washing dishes." But the man in the next room was certainly more than a customer, and she did want to please him. *God, don't make it happen again, not tonight.*

She dried her body and slipped into her most revealing nightgown, over which she put a silk dressing gown. Her hands trembled as she pulled the ribbon and shook her hair loose. Just a few strokes of the brush was all it needed to fall gently across her shoulders. A little dab of perfume behind each ear, one between the breasts, and another for each thigh should do it. She smiled into the mirror as she stepped into her slippers. She didn't look half-bad without makeup. In fact, she rather liked herself that way.

Jonathan raised his eyes from the book of poetry he was reading and removed his glasses as she came into the room.

"You were so quiet, I was afraid you might be asleep."

"Asleep? For you, my dear, I would stay awake an entire year." He lay the book and glasses on the end table and came to her.

"Jonathan?" Her body tensed as he placed his hands on her shoulders. "Please be gentle. I know you'll have trouble believing me, but I'm scared."

"Frightened? What of?" He held her against his chest.

"I don't know. Things. People."

"You don't ever have to be frightened of me," he mumbled as he repeatedly kissed the top of her head and temples. "I'll never hurt you. I promise." She froze as he tried leading her to the bed.

"That bad, huh?"

She nodded.

"Well, come then, and just sit here beside me." He sat on the edge of the bed and patted the spot beside him. "You don't even have to remove your robe, if you don't want."

"Oh, Jonathan," she fell on her knees and laid her head in his lap, "I'm so sorry. I want to make love to you, I really do. It's just that so many bad things happened. I just can't explain it right now."

"My dear," he lifted her chin to stare into her eyes, "unless I'm mistaken, we are making love right this moment. We've been making love ever since I asked you to marry me. If you are afraid of disappointing me when we have sex, I don't believe that is possible. But if that is something that is worrying you, we can wait. It's not that important to me. Come," he lifted her by her hands, "lay down beside me, and let's talk."

"Talk?"

"Sure, I want to find out everything I possible can about my wife."

"I don't think you really want to know everything about me." She lay her head against the pillow as Jonathan removed her slippers.

"You let me be the judge of that. I'll tell you when to stop." He began rubbing her tired feet and ankles.

"Oh, dear Lord in heaven. If you promise to do that every night, I'll slave for you the rest of my life."

"Mmm, I don't know that I want a slave. I could have bought one of those last time I was in India. You may continue being my wife. Now, tell me about yourself."

"What do you want to know?"

"Start with when you were born." He worked his way up to her calves. She tensed, thinking he might go higher, but he instead crawled up to lay beside her and started caressing her forehead with his fingers. He worked his way around her temples and cheeks as she talked. She soon found herself laughing and telling of the time she tried snitching a spoonful of her mother's chocolate cake batter and spilled the entire bowl down the front of her dress.

"I was so short, the bowl came tumbling off the table right on top of me. She wasn't even angry. She just stood there laughing, and said that was punishment enough."

"Your mother sounds like a wonderful person."

"She is. You'd love her. It's been so long since I've seen her."

"Then you shall, as part of our honeymoon. Now, roll over. I want to massage your shoulders. You've had a very trying day."

"Here." She jumped to her feet and pulled the tie on the robe and let it fall to the floor. "As long as you're going to pamper me, you might as well do a good job." She lay on her stomach with her hands under her chin. "Now, what were you saying about us visiting my mother? She lives in Boston, you understand. That is a long way for a visit, my dear."

"Ah, yes. But you forget I own my own ship, wife of mine." She could feel him pause as he pulled her hair away from her shoulders. He gently traced one of the scars across her shoulders to the edge of the low back of the nightgown.

"That was an entire lifetime ago, Jonathan." She felt a tear puddle in the corner of her eye. "Don't ask me about it right now, please?"

"All right." His voice was husky as he leaned close to kiss the mark. I can promise you, no one will ever hurt you again." She lowered her arms as he pulled the nightgown off her shoulders. His lips traced each and every scar as they cris-crossed her back.

"Where else are we going on our honeymoon?" She closed her eyes and sighed as his strong hands massaged her shoulders.

"I own a little piece of land in Edinburgh. I thought you might like to see it."

"Scotland?" She rolled to face him.

"Sure. My own mother lives there, as well as a couple of brothers and sisters. I thought I might gloat a little as I parade my fantastic, beautiful wife in front of them. You wouldn't mind, would you?"

"Mind? No, I don't think I would mind at all." She threw her arms around his neck. "I've always wanted to travel. That's what got me into all this trouble."

"What? Marrying me?" He pushed her away to frown.

"No, silly. You know. What I was doing in The Silver Slipper?"

"Oh, I thought that was some other girl, not my wife." He leaned on one elbow to study her. "Are you absolutely sure that wasn't someone else? Besides, I can't seem to recall ever being inside a place called The Silver Slipper."

"You really are the most wonderful man I have ever met." She pinned him against the pillow and kissed him long and deep. She caught her breath and tensed as he pulled the tie on her nightgown and slipped it completely off her shoulders. But instead of squeezing her breasts or hurting her, he took his time making love, slowly discovering every inch of his wife, and allowing her to discover him in return. He was slow and gentle when they moved together, allowing the passion to build. Then, when she was on the edge, he stopped to kiss and fondle her some more. She thought she would die when he paused to talk about what they would be doing tomorrow.

"Will you please shut up and make love to me?" She dug her nails into his back and covered his mouth with hers. It ended with an entire symphony exploding inside her head.

"Oh, God, I've never felt this way before." She buried her face into the crook of his shoulder. "I want to crawl inside of you."

"You already have, my dear. You already have." She fell asleep in his arms. The faces were gone. She awoke the next morning to find him sitting in a chair smiling at her.

"What? Am I that horrible looking?"

"No, just the opposite." He came to the bedside with a steaming cup of coffee. "You are that beautiful. I was just thinking how lucky I am."

"Really?" She took a sip. "I certainly feel the same about you. Sure you're not sorry you married me?"

"Never, my dear." He took the cup and set it on the night stand. "I'll spend the rest of my life loving you."

"Well, come in here and let me see." She tossed the blankets aside. It was better than she remembered, with the music inside her head lasting even longer.

Chapter 22

"Y'all stand. I'm declaring this here court in session. Judge Lloyd Hansen is gonna be presiding over these here proceedings. Judge?" Hanky nodded at the open-mouthed man staring back at him.

"Where is our bailiff, Mr. Jones?"

"Cary's home in bed with the runs, so, I decided to do his job fer him today."

"Well okay, I guess that will work. Everyone be seated." Lloyd waited until the snickering and scraping of chairs ceased before continuing. "Mr. Russell, will you please read the charges for us?" He waited a long minute before clearing his throat. "Josiah Russell, will you please read the charges?"

"Oh, yeah." Hanky scrambled to his feet as several men inside the crowded room chuckled. "Sorry, Judge." He cleared his own throat and squinted at the paper.

"Well, what this here paper says is that someone croaked Ambrose Brice, owner of this here saloon, and Ruby says she found his carcass next morning, right about there." He pointed toward the dark spot under Catherine Blackstone's feet, who instantly changed seats with her husband.

"Now, we don't rightly know who done it, 'cause we got four different women all claiming they was the ones who kilt him. Whoever done it croaked him by sticking this here knife in his gizzard." He waved the butcher knife at the jury.

"I'm a gonna be bringing all four women up here and let them tell their stories one at a time. It's gonna be up to y'all ta figure out which one really kilt that ol' skunk, whether it was Aurie Templeton," he pointed the knife at the women seated together, "or Ruby, or Mrs. Carpenter, or Mrs. Garcia, who ain't here, 'cause she's still broke out with all those red spots."

Lloyd stared at Hanky for a minute before turning to the jury. "I hope all of you understood what he was saying." He waited for heads to nod. "Well, let me put it this way. Was there anyone who did not understand the charges against these women?"

"They might have understood, but how do I put it on paper?" Suzanna Black, who was acting as the court recorder shook her head.

"Just write it the way it's supposed to be written, and if you come to a spot where nothing makes any sense, then stop us, and we'll try to figure out something you can put in the record."

"Well, all right then." She was still mumbling as she grabbed her pen and began scribbling.

"You may proceed, Mr. Russell. Call the first defendant to the stand."

"Oky-dokey. I'd like for Miss Aurie to come first, 'cause she's the one what's at the center of this whole nest of skunks. Well, come on." He motioned toward the girl when she didn't move.

"Me?" Aurie put a hand over her breast.

"Your name's Aurie, ain't it?" Hanky held out Woodrow Black's Bible as the girl shuffled forward.

"Put your right hand on this here Bible and swear that everything you say here today is nothing but the truth, so help you God." Her eyes darted from the Bible to Hanky's face and back again. "Well, go ahead. Put your hand on the Bible and swear you're gonna tell us the truth, even though you ain't done nothing but lie up to this point."

"Mr. Russell," Lloyd Hansen pounded his gavel, "we'll have no more of that inside this courtroom."

"Sorry, Your Honor." Hanky took a deep breath and smiled at the girl. "Ain't ya gonna tell us what really happened when Ambrose got hisself kilt?"

"Uh-huh."

"Well, then put yer hand on the Good Book." She slipped her right hand onto the leather cover. "Good. Now, are you gonna tell us the truth?" She nodded. "Okay, you can sit down." He waited until she had perched herself on a barstool next to the table where Judge Hansen was seated and adjusted her skirt for modesty.

"Now, most of us know who you are, but just so's we get it right, tell us your full Christian name."

"Aurie Loraine Templeton."

"That's a pretty name." Hanky propped one foot on a chair and smiled at her.

"Thanks."

"You're welcome. How old are you, Aurie?"

"Thirteen."

"Could you tell us how come you wound up staying at a place like this and working fer a hydrophobied skunk like Ambrose Brice in the first place?"

"Mr. Semmens sold me to Mr. Brice."

"Now, I know all about Mr. Semmens, 'cause you done told me. But just so's the rest of the folks inside the courtroom can also know, why don't you just tell us the whole story?"

"We were trying to cross the Mojave desert when we ran out of water. We were at the rear of the line, and the oxen pulling our wagon began to give out. They kept going slower and slower, until we couldn't even see the rest of the wagons. Pretty soon, one of the oxen jut gave out and died. We were stranded out there with nothing."

"And no one came back to give you any help?" Hanky glanced up from the cigarette he was rolling.

"No, there wasn't much they could have done anyway. Nobody had any water. They were almost as bad off as we were."

"Then what happened?"

"We sat there for days. I really don't know how long. Pa wandered off looking for water, and we never saw him again. Then Mama died. We buried her in the sand and piled some rocks on top of her grave."

"You said we buried your mother. Who else was with you, Aurie?" Hanky sat in the chair in front of the girl and leaned forward smoking his cigarette.

"My brother, William, and my sister, Catherine."

"And where are they now?"

"They both died. I buried them beside Mama." She stared at the wall as though she were looking across the great Mojave.

"Were they older or younger than you, Aurie?"

"Both younger. William was ten, but Catherine was only three."

"What kept you alive?"

"I don't know. After William died, I was too weak to really bury him, so I just piled a bunch of rocks on top of him. Then I laid down inside the wagon, thinking I was going to die also. I woke up later inside Mr. Semmens' wagon. His wife was feeding me water with a spoon, while her husband and son were rummaging through our wagon to see if he could find anything he thought was worth keeping."

"Were they nice to you?"

"His wife was, but their boy Marvil, was a lot older than me and he kept trying to catch me alone. He'd grab me and try doing things like Mr. Brice wanted me to do."

"And what did you do?"

"I fought him. I even scratched his face once, and I guess that made him and his father both mad, because the next thing I knew, they were complaining that I was eating too much food and drinking too much water. They said I wasn't earning my keep, and they were going to get rid of me first chance they got. But they didn't do that, because we passed through several towns before we got here to Dogtown. That's when Mr. Semmens came in here and started drinking. The next thing I knew, he was shoving me toward Mr. Brice, saying he'd sold me. His wife started yelling, but he only hit her. Last time I saw her, she was crying and looking back at me from the wagon."

"That's when Ambrose took over." Hanky crushed his cigarette under the toe of his boot. "Mind telling us exactly what it was Ambrose wanted you to do?"

Aurie's mouth dropped open as she gripped the edge of the stool and glanced around the room.

"Well, come on. We've gotta know, if we're gonna believe a little girl like you got mad enough to croak him. What was it he wanted you to do?"

"It was... it was nasty things."

"Nasty things? Like what?" She only stared at him. "Did he want you to take your clothes off?"

"Yes. And when I wouldn't do it, he would hit me and tear them off himself," she said as tears spilled down both cheeks.

"Stop it! Stop it, you beast!" Alice Carpenter jumped to her feet. "Leave that poor girl alone. She's suffered enough."

"Order." Lloyd Hansen pounded the gavel. "Either you restrain yourself, madam, or I'll have you removed from the courtroom. Now," he turned to Hanky, "are you sure we have to hear all this, Mr. Russell? Everyone here knows what type of a person the deceased was."

"Well, yeah. I was just trying to show everyone what was going on, so's they would know why this young'un wanted to cut his heart out."

"All right, you may proceed, but try to keep your questions as decent as possible. There are women present."

"Yes, sir." Hanky sat staring at the girl for a long minute.

"Let's just say for the record that Ambrose wanted to touch you, and have you touch him in ways that only people who are married to each other should do. Is that correct?"

"Yes."

"And when you refused to do those things, he beat you?"

"Yes." Hanky waited for the murmuring inside the room to cease before asking the next question.

"What happened the night you killed him?"

"He came into my room."

"And which one would that be?"

"Right over there." She pointed at one of the small wooden doors at the back of the room.

"Okay, he came into your room. Then what happened?"

"He did some of those things to me, then came back out here to drink. Ruby was here and they started arguing. She kept saying that he should leave me alone, but he only got mad and threw a chair at her. She ran into her room and locked the door. That's when I ran out here and grabbed the knife."

"And where was the knife when you grabbed it?"

"On the bar beside a loaf of bread."

"Then what happened?"

"He laughed at me and said I was stupid and didn't have the guts to use it. Then he started coming toward me and said he was going to beat the hell out of me if I didn't put it down. So I got real scared and stabbed him."

"And what happened after you stabbed him?"

"He staggered backwards and fell right over there." She pointed toward the bloodstain on the floor. "Then Ruby came out of her room and said not to worry about it, because she would take care of everything. She said it wouldn't matter if you hung her for killing Mr. Brice, because she was sick and going to die anyway."

"So you're saying that she didn't kill him; you're the one who stabbed him. Is that right?"

"Uh-huh."

"You're such a liar, Aurie," Ruby said. "I'm the one who killed the bastard."

"Order." Lloyd pounded the gavel several times. "You'll have your turn tomorrow, young lady. In the meantime, you will refrain from using profanity or making comments, the same as Mrs. Carpenter. Is that clear?" He waited for her nod. "Now, Mr. Russell, is there anything else you would like to ask this young lady?"

"No, sir. I think we've just about covered everything we need to today."

"You may step down, young lady." Lloyd nodded toward Aurie. Hanky escorted her to a seat next to Ruby as the judge continued giving instructions to the jury. It was then he spied Paco leaning in the doorway, glaring at him.

~   ~   ~

"I'm not in the habit of consorting with prostitutes." The well-dressed man glared as the scantily-clad girl approached his table.

"Well, excuse me. I just thought that you might need a little company." She flipped her chestnut hair over a bare shoulder with a shake of her head.

"I'm afraid I can't excuse you. There's no excuse for being a whore." He rolled his top lip back to reveal a perfect set of teeth.

"I guess not. The same as there's no excuse for being a bastard." She turned away as he laughed.

"Hey, wait a minute. You've got spunk. Sit down. I kind of like you. What's your name?"

"Francie." She slipped into the chair next to him. "What's yours?"

"It doesn't really matter, does it? Let's just say I'm someone who likes women with spunk." He filled two glasses and slid one of them toward her. "I like to play exciting games. How about you?"

Chapter 23

"Don't you have a last name?" Judge Baker removed his glasses to study the large black man. Jonathan and Loretta were seated in the back of Judge Samuel Baker's courtroom waiting for James Sattler to present Leonida's case.

"No, sir," he shook his head, "not one given to me since being brung to these United States. They just calls me Frank."

"I see." The judge slipped his glasses back on to scan the papers before him. "Tell me in your own words, Mr. Calloway," he glanced at the neatly dressed white man standing to Frank's left, "why did you have Frank arrested and dragged into my courtroom?"

"He's a runaway, a fugitive. I believe those papers will prove that I bought and paid for this man five years ago in Georgia. He's been the property of my plantation ever since. I brought him with me to San Francisco on business. Evidently he's been listening to some ridiculous talk of California being a free state, and now he's gotten the idea that he can just run off and do whatever he wants, so I had him arrested. I believe that by the time we're through here today, he'll know his proper place in society."

"Mmmm, I can agree with you there Mr. Calloway," Judge Baker folded his hands and leaned forward, "but not in the way you were thinking. California is and has always been a free state. You knew that when you chose to bring Mr. Frank here, did you not? Now, I can't help what the laws are in Georgia concerning slavery, but I am sworn to uphold the laws of the State of California, and seeing as California is indeed a free state, I am giving Frank his freedom." He slammed the gavel.

"Wait, you can't do that. He's my property, and I have my rights," Calloway said with a raised voice.

"Yes, and so does Frank. Now, get out of my courtroom, and if you ever try something like this again, I'll have you thrown into prison for participating in illegal traffic of human flesh."

"Does that mean I no longer has to do what this man says?" Frank said.

"Yes, sir. You're a free man." Judge Baker stepped from behind his podium to shake his hand. "Now, go out of here, and make this a better country."

"I thank you, sir. I thanks you a whole lot."

"Next case."

"The State of California versus Leonida Garcia." James Sattler approached the bench with a stack of paper which he placed on a table in the front of the courtroom.

"Mrs. Garcia was unable to make today's hearing, Your Honor. I will have to conduct business on her behalf in her absence."

"Well, I'm indeed sorry to hear that, counselor. Perhaps you should inform Mrs. Garcia that without proof that her land was indeed given to her late husband's family by Governor Pico, then she will loose it."

"I already have, Your Honor, but it doesn't seem to make any difference. In fact, I have trouble believing she understands the gravity of the situation, although I have explained it on numerous occasions."

"That man's going to go to hell for all the lies he's telling," Loretta whispered.

"Shhhh." Jonathan held a finger to his lips. "I want to hear this."

"As I stated the last time you were in this courtroom, counselor, I would like to talk to her personally. Is there any particular reason she isn't here?" Judge Baker rolled the gavel over and over in his fingers.

"I don't honestly know, Your Honor. I informed her of the date when she was in my office two weeks ago, but she must have forgotten." Sattler shrugged.

"I will tell you what, then. You make sure that she is here...let's see," he scanned the calendar in front of him, "the next open date is August the 15th. Try your best to have her here, counselor. I'll rule on her case after talking to her."

"August the 15th? But, Your Honor, that's almost three months away." Sattler dropped his folder on the table with a thud.

"Yes? Is there a problem with that date?"

"Just that I was hoping to have her case wrapped up before then. I do have a heavy caseload."

"As heavy as your caseload might be, Mr. Sattler, I can damn well guarantee you it is nothing compared to mine. I doubt that anyone inside this courtroom can help it if you did not do your job well enough to bring Mrs. Garcia's case to closure. The hearing is set for August 15." He slammed the gavel down with a loud crack.

"Now, is there anything else, counselor?"

"No, I don't believe there is, Your Honor." Sattler collected his folder from the table. "Thank you for your time."

"You're welcome, counselor. Have a good day." He smacked the gavel once more. "Next case, please."

Loretta turned away as the red-faced solicitor passed on his way out of the courtroom.

"There was no need to worry, my dear. He was so angry he wouldn't have seen you if you were standing in the middle of the isle waving a flag," Jonathan snickered.

"I didn't want to take the chance."

"I know." He crinkled his eyebrows as a young woman made her way to the front.

"Roxanna Coxin, is it?" Judge Baker glanced up from the papers in his hand.

"Yes."

"It says you're charged with indecent exposure. You removed all your clothing in the middle of Dupont street? Why?"

"I was intoxicated, Your Honor. You see I had been out to dinner with some friends, and we started..."

"Intoxication is no excuse for that type of behavior, young lady. Ten days hard labor." He smacked the gavel.

"We'll wait a few more minutes," Jonathan shook his head with a chuckle, "then we'll go talk to this Pinkerton man. I would also like to see what Salty has found out about Rodeen before we meet with Judge Baker this afternoon."

"Yes." Loretta nodded with a frown. "When do I get to be alone with my husband again? When we get back to the hotel around midnight?"

"Don't worry," he said as he squeezed her hand. "I have that all planned too."

~   ~   ~

"Tell me the truth, Doctor. How dangerous is this disease to our babies?" Angela sat on the steps beside Sean and wrapped her arms around her knees to stare at him. Juan and Angela had moved in with Tex and Rosa to isolate themselves until the ravages of the rubeola plague were over.

"It's hard to tell." Sean shrugged and beat the ashes from his pipe against the steps. "I've seen pregnant women get ill and have perfectly healthy babies. But I've known some pretty reputable doctors who claim that rubeola can cause deafness or weak hearts in infants, or a number of other things. Now, whether those babies would have had those defects anyway is hard to tell. I would just rather not take the chance with you and Rosa. You're both too important to me. I wouldn't worry too much about it right now, if I were you." He squeezed her hand.

"Gracias." She smiled. "You are importante to us also. How is Doña Leonida doing?"

"Oh, she's doing just fine. She is well beyond the sick stage right now. She just doesn't want anyone to see her with those little scabs covering her face and arms. On the other hand, she is also about ready to scratch the wallpaper from her bedroom walls." Sean chuckled. "She hates being cooped up. The fact that I came here first, before going to give her my version of what happened in court today, means that I am in big trouble. You and Rosa had better say some prayers for me. In fact," he rose to his feet, "I'd better be going."

"Yer not sticking around for some of Rosa's vittles?" Tex leaned out the open door.

"No, I'd really love to, since I'll be eating Maria's burnt cow at the hacienda. But as I was just telling Angela, Leonida will more than likely give me what for when I show up as it is."

"You're leaving?" Rosa came to the door with a pouty look on her face.

"Yes, but I'll be back tomorrow to see how Tex Junior is doing." He leaned over and kissed her forehead.

"Hey, Pard, none of that, now." Tex grinned as he slipped an arm around his wife.

"Huh, what are you going to do when I help deliver that baby? I suppose you'll threaten me with that gun of yours?"

"No, ya just got to do it with yer eyes closed, that's all."

"Oh, with my eyes closed is all. We'll just see about that. I'll bet you'll be begging for me to do some sort of miracle the first time Rosa gives a little whimper."

"Don't you worry, Señor Kilkenney," Angela slipped an arm around Sean's waist, "if he gets in your way, I'll have Juan tie him to a post inside the barn."

"Like hell you will." Tex put a hand on his hip to glance at the silent vaquero rolling a cigarette. "You wouldn't try doing some dirty, low-down trick like that, now would you, pard?"

"Who can tell, señor." He shrugged. "A man can only do what his woman wants him to do at a time like this. It would be much better for us to go to the barn and drink tequila when the time comes."

"Now, that sounds like a much better plan. Hell, yeah, that's what we'll do." He slapped Juan on the shoulder.

"That's about right. You two will be drinking, and I'll be doing all the work," Sean said.

"Perdoname, señor." Angela put an arm around Rosa. "Who will be doing all the work? I think you will be the one watching, while Rosa is working."

~ ~ ~

"Evening m'lady." Sara Miller jumped, and came close to dropping the globe to the lamp she was lighting.

"Ouch!" She let go of the match as it burnt her fingers, and stomped the flame out on the floor. "How'd you get in here, Salty? You scared the hell out of me, sitting in the dark like that."

"Oh, my. Such language coming from a lady." He slipped his arms around her waist from the back, as she placed the globe into position and adjusted the flame.

"I'm no lady." She pushed his hands away and glared. "I'm nothing right now, but an angry whore who wants to know who let you in my room."

"I did."

"Like hell. I keep that door locked to keep bastards like you from slipping in here some night and slitting my throat."

"Sara, it's me you're talking to." Salty held out his palms. "I've never hurt you before, and I'm bloody well not going to start now."

"I know, I know," she turned to fill two glasses with brandy, "but it scares the hell out of me to know that someone can get inside my room with the door locked. Here." She shoved one of the glasses toward him. "Now, who let you in? I've got to know."

222

"I did, just like I told you. I know you leave that window open most of the time, so I just shimmied up the drainpipe, and came right on in."

"Dammit." Her hand shook as she set the brandy glass on the table.

"Hey, I'm sorry I scared you so bad." He reached for her, but she pulled away.

"No, it's all right, really. I'm glad I found out about it now, instead of waking some night with some bastard leaning over my bed. I'll just have to start sleeping with the window locked, is all."

"You're shaking like a leaf." Salty grabbed and held her close. "What's got you so keyed up anyway?"

"You didn't hear about Francie?"

"No, what about Francie? Last time I saw her, she was with Lorna at Darrell Rodeen's table. That was about a week ago. Why?"

"Well, John Gullings, the boy who cleans up around the bar?"

Salty nodded.

"He found Francie out back in a pile of trash. She was all cut up into small pieces." Sara buried her face against his chest as she sobbed. "She was only fifteen years old."

"Damn. Oh damn." He pulled her to the edge of the bed and sat rocking her in his arms. "Do they know who did it?"

"Hell no. What do you think? She was just another whore, like the rest of us. There's more where she came from." They sat silently for awhile, until she quit crying.

"I'm sorry; I had no idea. When did this happen?"

"About five or six days ago. Right about the time you last saw her." She pulled the hanky out of his shirt pocket and blew her nose. "Say, where in the hell have you been, anyway?" She pushed back to stare at him.

"I was well-seen at a Mexican rancho near Sacramento. I had nothing to do with Francie's death."

"Oh, I didn't mean it like that, and you know it." She laid her head against his chest. "Doing something like that would be the farthest thing from your mind. I was just wondering why you weren't around to see me? You're only in San Francisco for about three, maybe four weeks at a time. Then you're gone again for another three or four months. Sometimes longer."

"Yes, I know and I've decided that I don't like it much anymore." He kissed the top of her head.

"Who are you kidding, Salty Moran? You've got saltwater in your veins, instead of blood. You'll never give up the sea." Sara laughed as she retrieved their glasses of brandy from the table.

"Maybe not entirely. I have been considering settling down somewhere and piloting a small fishing boat. There are a hundred places right here, from Oregon to Mexico, where a man could make a fair living for his family doing just that. Then, I'd have the best of two lives. I'd still have the ocean during the day, and a nice warm house, loving wife and children by night. I might even get me a dog to lay in front of the fireplace and wag his tail."

"Ho, I can just see Salty Moran doing that." She patted his chest with a laugh. "It sounds like a nice dream. Where are you going to find a woman who'll do all the housework, take care of your children and dog, raise the garden, and put up with your coming home smelling like fish every night?"

"Well, I was hoping I had already found her."

"Really?" She climbed out of his lap and downed her brandy in one gulp. "That's not too nice, Salty."

"What isn't?"

"Holding me on your lap when you've got another woman waiting for you somewhere. But, I've had men do worse. I've had them climb into bed with me, then go home and climb right into bed with their wives."

"I don't have any other woman, Sara. The woman I'm hoping to make my wife is you." She stared at him a minute before laughing.

"All right, the joke is over, Salty. Finish your brandy and get the hell out. Only leave by the door this time, and not the drainpipe, because I'm keeping the window locked from now on."

"Okay, Sara." He stood and tossed back the brandy. "But I wasn't kidding. I know I haven't been much of anything to you, but I suppose that was because I always thought more of you than the other girls. I was seriously thinking we might do exactly what I was saying." He paused as he grabbed hold of the doorknob. "I guess I was just being sentimental. Captain McDougal and Loretta got married day before yesterday. I was hoping I might do the same." He shrugged and gave the knob a twist.

"Close the door."

"I was just leaving."

"I said, get back in here and close the door." She waited until the door was shut before continuing. "Your Captain McDougal married Loretta Stewart? I thought she left here with that doctor. What's his name? Something funny like McKinney."

"Kilkenney."

"Yeah, that's it. Didn't she leave with him?"

"That I can't swear to, but I just saw her with the captain this afternoon, and they are sure married. And as happy as a couple of seagulls with a gullet full of mackerel." He took both her hands in his.

"Sara Miller, I'm only a poor sailor. But I don't drink more than the average bloke, and I don't believe in throwing one's hard earned money away at the gambling table. And you've seen my habits with women. I haven't much to offer you in the way of comforts, but I've saved enough money to buy a pretty good fishing boat and put a roof over your head. If that would be enough for you, I'd be honored to make you my wife."

Sara tilted her head back and laughed before bursting into tears, then laughed some more.

"Dear God, you don't have anything to offer me? Look around you, Salty." She waved an arm in the air. "Everything I've got is in this room. I don't have anything to give you."

"I didn't ask you to give me anything. All I want is you."

"You don't understand." She sat in a chair by the table and kissed his hand repeatedly. "I can't even give you that. I gave a little of myself every time someone grabbed or pinched my bottom as I waited on tables, or when I hiked my skirt on stage, or a million other things. They took a little of my soul every time they came into this room. I don't exist, Salty. There isn't any Sara Miller left to give. What you see here is an empty shell that doesn't feel or even care anymore."

"That's a damned lie," he said as he knelt at her feet. "Why, just a moment ago, you were crying your eyes out over Francie. Don't tell me you can't feel."

"Don't make more out of that than what it was. It was just one whore crying over another whore."

"We're all whores in one way or another, Sara. We give little parts of ourselves to others, hoping we're going to get something in return. You," he shrugged, "happened to give yourself right here. I gave myself to the sea. Maybe if these two whores get together, we can make something beautiful."

"You'd do that, wouldn't you? You'd really marry me? Knowing what I am?"

"In a heartbeat, if you'll have me."

"Say when, Salty Moran. It'll only take me a second to pack my bags. I'll even live aboard that ship of yours, if that's what you really want."

"Just as soon as I find out what it is that Captain McDougal wants to know. It shouldn't take but a few more days. A week or two at the most. Then I will be coming to get you, Sara Miller. I can promise you that on my mother's honor." He got to his feet and walked to the door.

"You say that Darrell Rodeen was the last person you saw Fancie with before she died?"

"Yes, why?"

"Just curious, that's all. What about Lorna? She was with them. She didn't see her go off with anyone else, or anything like that?"

"No, Francie was with that same man when Lorna left with another customer."

"Did she have anything to say about Rodeen?"

"Nothing, except he was an awful braggart, who threw money around like he had a rich uncle. What are you thinking, Salty? Are you saying that man killed Francie?"

"I don't know what I'm thinking. Just don't go near him if he comes in here again. Love you, Darling." He tossed her a kiss and opened the door.

"Salty?"

"Hum?" He paused.

"Do you have to go? I mean, it is getting sort of late, and I don't have to go back to work."

Salty cocked his head to one side and raised his eyebrows before closing and locking the door. "Pour some more brandy, m'dear, while I lock the window. Never can tell, some bloke might just shimmy up the drain pipe to spy on us."

Chapter 24

"I take it Mr. Jones is still under the weather?" Judge Hansen studied Hanky over the rim of his glasses.

"Yes, sir."

"Very well, you may proceed."

"Put yer right hand on this holy book and swear that you ain't gonna tell us no more tall tales. I don't wanna hear nothing but the truth coming out of yer mouth, young lady."

"All right." Ruby laid her hand on the Bible and raised the left high in the air. "I swear that I'm going to tell you the truth, so help me God."

"Fine, you can sit yerself down." Hanky laid the Bible aside. "Now, seeing as most everyone only knows you as 'Ruby', maybe you can tell us your real name."

"Ruby." Hanky glared at the pretty redhead as Judge Hansen pounded the gavel at the laughing audience.

"Order. The spectators in the courtroom will please refrain from laughing. Young lady," he turned to Ruby, "please state for us your full name, for the record."

"Sure, Ruby Fay Lang."

"You may proceed with the examination, Mr. Russell," Judge Hansen nodded.

"All right. Ruby, you done told me that you kilt Ambrose your own self. But that story was so full of buggers and hanks..."

"I beg your pardon," Judge Hansen interrupted as the room roared with laughter. "What did you say?"

"I said her story was full of buggers and hanks."

"I thought that was what you said. What in the world...I'm sorry. I don't even know what you meant."

"Well, you know what a bugger is, don't you?"

"Yes, Mr. Russell, I'm well aware of what a bugger is. What is a hank?"

"A loop in a rope. A twist, or turn. A knot, fer Christ's sake. She's lying." He pointed at Ruby.

"Why didn't you just say you didn't believe her story?"

"I was trying to when you interrupted me."

"Very well, then. Go on with your questioning." Judge Hansen sat back and folded his hands.

"Okay, Ruby..."

"Excuse me, Your Honor." Susanna Black squinted at the judge. "I didn't catch all that about buggers and hanks. Do I really have to put that into the record?"

"No. You may skip that part if you choose."

"Thank you."

"You may proceed, Mr. Russell."

"Thanks." Hanky glared at the woman scribbling at the table. "Ruby?"

"Yes, I'm still here."

"So you are. Go ahead and tell everyone here exactly how you done it, and don't leave anything out, okay?"

"Okie-dokie, sheriff." She folded her hands in her lap. "It happened pretty much like Aurie described, except for who did the killing. That old sonofabitch had been..." She stopped at the pounding of the gavel.

"I've already warned you once about using profanity in this courtroom, young lady. If you do that again, I'll hold you in contempt and fine you five dollars for every offence. Do you understand me?"

"Yes sir."

"All right, you may continue."

"Well," she paused to cough. "Ambrose had been...well, I don't know a nice way to say it, but he'd been raping Aurie repeatedly inside that room." She pointed. "That was his way of showing us girls how he wanted us to treat the customers. He did it to me and Rosa and everyone who's ever worked here. I told him to leave her alone, because she was just a kid. But he told me to," she glanced at the judge, "let's just say he said some bad things to me."

"And where did this happen? Inside Aurie's room?" Hanky said.

"No, he'd come out here for a drink. That was another one of his little tricks. He could do whatever he wanted, but the girls never got a break during his little training exercises. Anyway, we started arguing, and he threw a chair at me, so I went off to my room and locked the door."

"Which one is your room?"

"That one over there, on the other side of the bar." She pointed again.

"Okay, then what happened?" Hanky propped one of his boots in a chair and leaned an elbow on his knee.

"When I heard Aurie start crying and begging again, I got real mad and decided someone had to do something. So, I came out here and grabbed the butcher knife from the bar."

"Why'd you choose the knife."

"Because I didn't have a gun." Hanky had to wait while Judge Hansen pounded the gavel at the laughing crowd once again.

"That's a fair answer. Except seeing as there's a scatter-gun under the bar, why didn't you use that?"

"Because I was mad and didn't think of it. Besides, I didn't want to kill him. I just wanted him to leave her alone."

"Fair enough. Go on, tell us what happened next after you grabbed the knife."

"I went into Aurie's room and told him to leave her alone. He grabbed at me, so I stabbed at him with the knife."

"Did you cut him?"

"No, but he got real mad, and started calling me all sorts of names. He tried to choke me, but I broke free and ran out here. He followed, saying he was going to kill me. That's when I stabbed him."

"Why'd you wait until morning to go find Woodrow? Why didn't you go right then, right after you stabbed him?

Then you lied, saying you just happened to find him lying there, trying to make us think someone else had killed him. Why, Ruby?"

"Because I was scared. You don't know what it's like, being the town whore. Who's going to believe you when you are telling the truth? Just like now. Everyone here knows what a bastard Ambrose was..."

"Five dollars for contempt of court." Judge Hansen pounded the gavel. "I warned you, young lady."

"That's fine, 'cause he was, and every mother's son knows what he was, and how he was treating Aurie. But not one of you lifted a finger to help, and when someone does do something, you put them on trial for murder. Well, that's okay because I did it, and I feel good about doing it too. 'Cause it saved Aurie and a dozen other girls like her from becoming like me."

"Order." Judge Hansen rapped the gavel as the courtroom erupted with cheers. Some women like Susanna Black and Alice Carpenter were crying while several men were calling for Ruby's release.

"Order, I say. Or I'll clear the courtroom." Lloyd Hansen turned to glare at Ruby as the crowd finally silenced themselves.

"Miss Lang, you will kindly restrict your comments to the questions asked, or I'll fine you another twenty dollars for contempt. Do you understand me?"

"Sure, but what are you going to fine me for? Telling the truth?"

"Twenty dollars for contempt." He whacked the gavel.

"Oh, go pound your nose for all I care. You're going to hang me anyway."

"Forty dollars, and one more comment like that, I'll have you removed from the courtroom."

"Go ahead, see if I care."

"Sixty dollars!" He came out of his seat with another whack of the gavel to point at Hanky. "Sheriff Russell, remove this defendant from the courtroom and lock her in the jail until she can show some respect."

"That might be a long time, Your Honor."

"Do you want to be held in contempt also?"

"No sir." Hanky shook his head.

"Then do as you're told. I don't care if she has to sit inside that cell for the next twenty years. She is going to learn some respect for the law."

"Twenty years my ass," Ruby laughed. "You're only going to keep me there until I hang and you know it."

"That's enough." Hansen pounded the gavel.

"Besides, why should anyone respect the law? It was the law around here who killed all those Mexicans and let Ambrose get away with what he was doing."

"One hundred dollars!" He almost threw the gavel at her. "And if you don't get her out of here right now, I'm fining you right along with her." He pointed at Hanky.

"Yes, sir. Come on, Ruby." He took the girl by the arm. "Boy, you shore done it now." They were stopped by a huge man pushing his way to the front of the courtroom.

"And who might you be?" Judge Hansen barked as the man approached the table where Susanna Black was seated.

"Folks 'round here just call me Bear."

"Well, state your business."

"I come to pay Miss Ruby's fines." He pulled a leather wallet from his coat pocket. "I think they come to one hundred and twenty-five dollars, if I calculate right."

"Mrs. Black?" Lloyd stared at Susanna.

"Yes, I believe he is right. The first five dollars was for..."

"I don't care to know all the details, just take his money." He glanced over at Hanky while Susanna counted the money. "Well, what are you standing there for? Carry out your orders."

"Come on Ruby. Let's go before he decides to hang us both right now." Hanky pulled her down the isle.

"You ain't hanging that girl." Bear glared at Lloyd.

"I beg your pardon? Do you want me to hold you in contempt of court also?"

"No, it's just that she didn't kill that man, and you ain't gonna hang her for it."

"It just so happens she says she did kill him. Now, do you know something that could shed some light on this case? Were you here, or do you happen to know who really did kill Mr. Brice?"

"No, but I know Ruby didn't do it."

The judge buried his face in both hands as the courtroom broke into chuckles. "Just go away. I don't want to hear anymore. Court's adjourned for the rest of the day." He cracked the gavel once more.

Bear pushed his way to the door where he turned and raised his voice. "You ain't gonna hang her."

"Dear God, why didn't you just give me a simple bank robbery or stage hold up?" Lloyd collected the papers in front of him before quickly turning toward the jury.

"Hold it! I don't want any of you discussing any of this case with anyone, do you understand me? And you two," he pointed at Aurie and Alice Carpenter, "are still under arrest. Don't go wandering off anywhere until Sheriff Russell returns. Understand?"

"Yes, Your Honor," Alice said, and returned to her animated conversation with General Flores.

~   ~   ~

The old man hunched over a bottle in the corner of the bar eyed the loud man at the table in the center of the room. He had three giggling, scantily clad women clinging to his every movement as he bragged and tossed money around like he owned the San Francisco Mint.

"He's starting early today," Sara Miller mumbled as she cleared several empty glasses from Salty's table.

"Yeah, he must have something to celebrate. I'm going to slip out in a minute and see if I can't find out what exactly it is."

"Okay, but you be careful, Salty Moran. I don't want to be a widow before I have a chance to become a bride. By the way," she paused as she turned away, "your hump looks better today."

"Thanks."

He waited a few more minutes before grabbing the bottle and staggering out the door. He quickly blended with the foot traffic flowing along Market Street. It took most of an hour before he climbed the stairs to the third floor of the Sea Gull Hotel to Darrell Rodeen's room. He took one quick glance around to make sure no one was watching before pulling a ring filled with keys from his coat pocket. It was the tenth key that let him inside. "A common skeleton key. Not very secure, Darrell me lad." He pushed the door open.

"Eeeww." He shook his head at the messy room. No sailor worth his salt would have ever allowed his cabin to get this cluttered. He kicked an empty bottle as he tried lighting the lamp. Flies buzzed around a half-eaten steak on the small table.

"Okay, Salty. You're here, now what?"

The drawers held nothing of interest, and neither did the sea chest at the foot of the bed. He was about to give up when he noticed a piece of colorful cloth peering from the back of the wardrobe. Gripping the edge with his fingers, he gave a grunt and the heavy piece of furniture slid away from the wall.

"Bless me soul. Salty, you've found Black Beard's treasure." He removed the expensive blue jacket and white silk shirt from the nail driven into the back of the cabinet. They were both splattered with blood stains. He stared a long minute at the knife taped to the wardrobe before pulling it loose. It had a thin six inch blade that was razor sharp and folded inside the bone handle. It snapped open with a flick of the wrist. The knife also had dried blood on the white handle.

He rolled the knife inside the shirt and jacket before sliding the wardrobe back into place and blowing out the light. He had just cracked open the door when he heard Darrell's loud voice mingled with a girl's laughter coming down the hall.

Chapter 25

Leonida sat in the back of the courtroom with a black veil covering her spotted face. Alice Carpenter had just been sworn in and Hanky was scanning the tiny note pad he had used when questioning the women.

"You said you were at home when you heard Aurie Templeton crying and begging for help. Is that right?"

"Yes, Mr. Russell, that is correct."

"You mean to tell me, that a feller can hear a girl her size crying all they way from that room over there," he pointed, "to your bedroom way across there?"

"Yes they can, but I wasn't in my bedroom, Mr. Russell. I happened to be in my kitchen fixing myself some tea, as I'm sure you have written in your notes. The walls in this saloon have a lot of cracks in them and you'd be surprised at what a person can hear, especially coming from the backrooms. Some of them only have canvas walls. Ike and I used to try sleeping with our windows closed even in the summertime, but we still heard more than we cared to. I could give you names of some of the men who frequented the backrooms and the girls they were seeing, if you'd care."

"No, I don't think that will be necessary," Hanky said as a few men in the audience coughed, while others chuckled. "Why don't you just tell us in your own words what happened the night Ambrose got hisself kilt?"

"All right." She adjusted herself in the chair. "As I told you before, I closed the store early, because there were no customers."

"What time was that?"

"Around 3:30 p.m."

"Okay, go on." Hanky pulled up a chair and sat in front of Alice, crossing his legs. "Business was bad, huh?"

"Well, it hasn't been good for quite awhile. You know yourself that there are only about half the people in town that there were a year ago, and more are moving every day. The biggest account I have is the people from the Three Mile Mine, and I hear Mr. Black is considering shutting it down also. Anyway, to get back to what we were talking about, I closed the store around 3:30 and decided to have an early dinner so I could finish the book I had borrowed from Mrs. Garcia."

"Which book is that?"

"The Taming Of The Shrew, by Shakespeare. I've had it for almost a month."

"What did you have for dinner?"

"Mr. Russell, this is all very interesting, but is this line of questioning ever going to get around to the subject of Mr. Brice's death?" Judge Hansen scowled.

"Yes sSir. I was just trying to establish that this here lady had no intention of killing that snake anymore'n anyone else in town."

"That would be fine, if you were her defense attorney, but you're not. You're trying to make some sort of sense out of this murder, even if it convicts Mrs. Carpenter. Now, the reason she's here is because she's already confessed to killing the man. So, please allow her to tell us how she went about killing him."

"Okie-dokie." Hanky grinned at Alice. "Seems he's got a burr under his saddle this morning, so you'd best get on with it. I'll just sit here and listen."

"To answer your question, I had chicken and dumplings for dinner. It's easy to make a nice meal when the store isn't busy. I had just sat down to eat, when I first heard Aurie crying for help. I had to stop and pray that God would send someone to help that poor girl. I would have taken her into my house to live the day that man brought her to Dogtown..."

"Mr. Semmens?"

"Yes, but Mr. Brice had offered him money, so he gave her to him. When I heard about Mr. Semmens selling that poor child, I actually went to Ambrose and offered to take her in. I even offered to pay him more than he'd given Mr. Semmens, but he just laughed at me and told me to get out of his saloon."

"Okay, you were sitting at your table with chicken and dumplings and praying for God to send someone. What happened next?" Hanky pulled out the makings and began rolling a cigarette.

"Nothing. That child just kept crying, and every once in a while, I could hear Ambrose yell and hit her. I couldn't eat. I just put the chicken back into the pot and got down on my knees with my Bible. It was more than I could bear. I'm sure there must have been at least a dozen or more strong men who heard her crying. I still don't understand why no one bothered to help her. It must have been hours, because when I next looked, it was starting to get dark."

"What time was it when you heard the argument between Ambrose and Ruby?"

"I can't really remember. It was already dark by that time. It might have been around 8:30."

"Could you hear what they were saying?"

"Not everything, but she was definitely telling him to leave Aurie alone. They called each other some bad names. I heard Ambrose yell, then there was a loud crash. It must have been Ruby who slammed the door because I heard Ambrose laughing. It wasn't but a few more minutes when that child started crying and begging again. That was when I decided that no one else was going to help, so it was up to me."

"Then what happened? What did you do next?" Hanky struck a match on the bottom of the chair and lit his cigarette.

"I laid my Bible on the table and went out the rear door. I had every intention of simply taking that child away from him and locking her inside the store to keep her safe.

Then I thought that maybe I'd go find you, or your son, to help straighten the situation out. But things just didn't turn out that way."

"What made you decide to use the knife? Why didn't you grab the shotgun from behind the bar and blow his head off?" Hanky scowled at the jury as a couple of men chuckled.

"Like Ruby, I had no intention of killing him, Hanky. I just wanted to take Aurie away and get her out of there. The truth is, I got inside that saloon, and realized that there was no way he was simply going to let me walk away with her. He was a mean man. I had seen the results of some of the beatings he had given Ruby and the other girls that used to be here. I knew that he would simply beat me also and throw me out of the saloon. I started to go back and get Ike's pistol, but I saw that butcher knife lying on the bar, so I grabbed it instead. I thought it might frighten him enough to let me get Aurie away."

"Madra de Dios." Leonida shook her head as she watched Alice twist and knot the handkerchief in her hands. She glanced at her father seated next to her. His own hands were balled into tight fists. *Have mercy, Holy Father. She is a good woman.*

"Okay, you got the knife in your hands. Now, I want you to tell us what happened when you entered the room where that skunk was torturing that young'un.

"Mr. Russell," Judge Hansen leaned over the table and glared, "would you please refrain from referring to the deceased in such derogatory terms?"

"Yes sir. Whatever that means."

"Quit calling Ambrose Brice names."

"What I was saying wasn't half as bad as what I was thinking. But I'll stop, if it's bothering you."

"Thank you."

"Now, back to what we was discussing." Hanky took a drag off his smoke and plucked a bit of tobacco off his tongue. "What happened when you entered that room over there?"

"He had her pinned on the bed and was..." her voice broke.

"Take yer time."

"He got up from the bed, saying he told me to never enter his saloon again. I said that I had told him to leave Aurie alone. That's when he came at me, and I held the knife up and he cut his hand as he grabbed for me." Her eyes glazed over as she held the handkerchief like a weapon. "I told him to step aside and let Aurie pass, but he said he was going to beat the hell out of me instead. He grabbed my throat. Oh God!" She buried her face in her hands.

Hanky took his time crushing the cigarette under the toe of his boot before kneeling beside Alice's chair and slipping an arm around the woman.

"Wanna take a break?"

"No," she shook her head, "I'd rather get it over."

"Okay, he's trying to choke you. What'd you do next?"

"I tried to get away. I backed out of the door into this room, but he kept right after me, his hands around my throat. I couldn't breathe. Then I fell across one of the chairs and he landed on top of me. That's when he got up with the knife sticking in his chest. He told me that I killed him. Then he fell right over there and died." She stared at the spot.

"Is that when Ruby and Aurie came out of their rooms?"

Alice nodded.

"What happened then? Is that when y'all cooked up this cock'n-bull story about Aurie and Ruby killing him?" Alice kept staring at the dark spot on the floor and shook her head.

"I don't know. I just sat there."

"Ya done good." Hanky hugged her and got to his feet. "I think I'm done asking her questions, Your Honor. Unless there's something else you wanna ask her yerself."

"No!" General Flores leaped to his feet.

"Papa." Leonida grabbed at his coat sleeve.

"This is all a mistake. She couldn't have killed that man. She couldn't kill anyone."

"Now, General," Hanky stepped away from Alice as the judge pounded his gavel, "we both know that she kilt two of them skunks during that fracas here in town awhile back herself."

"Silencio!" He kicked the chair in front of him as people scattered.

"Papa, no!" Leonida tugged on his arm.

"Remove that man from the courtroom," Judge Hansen yelled.

"She didn't kill him. I will deal with you later." General Flores pointed a finger at Hanky as Bear and Woodrow Black drug him toward the door.

"Court's dismissed for the day." Judge Hansen rapped the gavel.

"Well, looks like you got the whole State of Californie mad at you, old man," Tex sniggered and slapped Hanky on the back. "What's yer next move? Gonna get the rest of the country to join 'em in hating yer guts?"

"Why don't you go home and take care of your pregnant wife?"

"Señor Russell," Leonida stepped in front of him, blocking his way out the door, "you don't really think Señora Carpenter killed that man, do you?"

"It ain't up to me, ma'am, but you're next."

"Me?"

"Yeah, you. You said you kilt him too, so I'm gonna put your carcass up on the stand same as them other women, and let you tell your story."

"Me? But..." He brushed on past her and disappeared out the door.

~   ~   ~

"Come on, breathe as deep as you can." Sean held the stethoscope to Ruby's back. She was hunched over in a chair in the dining room while the angry voices of Jose Flores and Paco drifted from the front porch, where they argued with Hanky over the trial.

"I can't. It makes me cough."

"That's exactly what I want you to do." He listened intently to the rattling inside her chest as she inhaled. He tossed the stethoscope back into the medical kit as she bent over coughing.

"Oh, damn that hurts."

"Good."

"What?" She stared at him through watery eyes.

"I said, good."

"What do you mean good? This really hurts. You can go to hell." She took a drag off her cigarillo and coughed again.

"I said good, because you're still alive, and as long as your lungs hurt, they are doing their best to heal themselves. But you're certainly not giving them much of a chance."

"Yeah? Well, I'd like to know what else I can do? I've been laying around for several weeks now doing nothing. *Stay covered with warm blankets. Drink your broth. Get plenty of warm sunshine*," she said in a nasal tone and wagged her head.

"You can stop filling your lungs with these." Sean grabbed the cigarillo from her fingers and tossed it into the fireplace.

"Hey, I just lit that!"

"Good. Now I don't want to see you lighting another." He grabbed her handbag and tossed it to Bear. "See if she's got any more and take them away from her."

"Hey, give me that." Ruby tried to snatch the bag, but Bear simply held it out of reach.

"Now, listen to Irish, young lady. He knows best."

"Like hell he does. I'll bet he keeps on smoking that stinking ol' pipe of his."

"Probably, but I'm not the one who's got lung fever. You've got to give your lungs time to heal themselves."

"I've been trying. Besides, I don't know what difference it makes. They'll more than likely hang me in a week or so anyway."

"Will you please stop with the talk of hanging? No one's going to hang you."

"Doc's right. You was in court today. Who's gonna believe you done it after listening to Mrs. Carpenter?" Bear handed her the handbag minus the tiny cigars.

"I wish all three of you would stop that talk." Leonida stood in the open doorway holding a cup of tea. "Señora Carpenter is in the kitchen having tea, and is able to hear every word you are saying."

"Oh, I'm sorry, Ma'am." Bear hung his head.

"I was talking about myself, not her. It was these stupid men who were making it sound like," she paused to cough, "well, you know."

"I know, señorita," Leonida said, cutting her off. "But the whole subject of who is going to be hanged, and who isn't, is ridiculous."

"And it might interest you to know that I agree with you one hundred percent." Sean smiled as he snapped the medical kit closed.

"Que?"

"About the whole trial being ridiculous." He glanced around at the staring faces. "I don't mean to sound crude, especially since Hanky and the judge are only doing their jobs, but I don't believe that anyone inside that courtroom this morning will get hung."

"And why is that?" Alice Carpenter joined Leonida's side. Her hand shook as she took a sip from the cup in her hand.

"Oh, I'm just guessing, but I don't believe we've found Ambrose's killer yet." He grinned and touched the end of Ruby's nose with his finger. "And if you don't start taking better care of yourself, I'm going to have Bear turn you over his knee and paddle your backside."

"Now, I know for certain Maria's right," Ruby said after Sean had left the room.

"How's that?" Bear stared at her.

"Sean Kilkenney is loonier than a bedbug."

~   ~   ~

"Maria?" Leonida's shoes whispered across the upstairs carpet toward the stairwell. "Maria?" she raised her voice.

"Why is it every time you want someone, they always disappear?" She bounced down the steps to the landing, where she paused to glance around. "Maria?" The house was silent.

"As Señor Hanky would say, *this is enough to make a preacher cuss*." She allowed the door to bang shut behind her as she bounded down the front steps toward the fountain. "Maria? Evangelina? Papa? Anyone? Where are you?" She stared at the empty patio. There were no children or dogs running and playing.

"What is going on around here?" Her heart beat faster as she rounded the corner of the house toward the chapel. "Someone is going to have a lot of explaining to do when I find"... She came to a sudden stop at the sight of the mourners in the graveyard. A black crow gave a mournful cry as he fluttered his wings in the oak tree shading an open grave.

Leonida bolted upright in bed with beads of sweat forming on her forehead. She spent the rest of the night sitting in her chair by the window.

Chapter 26

Salty Moran clutched the knife tightly as he lay on his back watching the bedsprings inches from his face wiggle and jerk. He didn't know the whore's name, but he had seen her a time or two talking with Lorna inside The Silver Slipper. Whoever she was, she didn't seem to be bothered with the filthy condition of Darrell Rodeen's room. He rolled his head to one side as the springs came close to smashing his nose. The girl giggled and Darrell moaned as the springs became suddenly quiet. Salty gritted his teeth as a roach crawled up his left cheek and paused to wiggle his antenna.

"You're not bad, Honey," the girl said as she crawled out of bed. Salty could have grabbed her bare ankle from where he lay with the roach tickling his cheek.

"Neither are you, Diamond. Say, what's your real name, anyway?"

"Diamond's all you need to know for now. It describes what men find under my clothes, just like you did. Right?"

"Yeah, sure," Rodeen chuckled. The girl shook out her underwear before slipping them on.

"You're a messy housekeeper, Darrell. Don't you ever pick anything up?"

"No, I don't. I figure I only sleep here, so why bother?"

"You weren't sleeping a few minutes ago, were you?"

"No. Hey, what's the hurry? Come on back to bed."

"I can't." Salty saw her hand as she picked one of her shoes from the cluttered floor. "They're gonna be angry as it is. None of us girls are supposed to leave the place alone since Francie got herself killed."

"You weren't alone. You were with me." Darrell's bare feet hit the floor on the other side of the bed.

"That's not what I mean. We're supposed to have two or three other girls with us, and we're never supposed to leave with a customer. Say..." She sat on the edge of the bed and bent over to tie one of her shoes. Salty could see her brown hair through the roach's antenna as it brushed the floor. "You don't happen to know anything about who killed her, do you? Lorna said the three of you spent quite a bit of time together that afternoon."

"Why? Are you afraid of me?"

"No, I wouldn't be here if I was. I've been with you several times before, and you've never hurt me. You don't plan on doing it now, do you?"

"You kidding? You're my Diamond." He could hear them kissing as they came together.

"No kidding, Darrell, I've got to be getting back."

"Okay, I've got some things to take care of myself." Salty counted to twenty after Darrell closed and locked the door to make sure they were gone.

"You miserable bastard." He swept the roach from his cheek and smashed it with an empty bottle he found lying under the bed. "Dammit!" He rolled out from under the bed, brushing and shaking his clothes. He could feel his skin crawl as another roach ran across the base of the wall.

"Filthy whore will sleep anywhere. Probably has fleas and no telling what else."

Salty cracked open the door to see several men congregated at the end of the hall. He pulled the door closed and locked it from the inside. Checking the window, he found the alley empty. Stuffing the knife and bloody shirt inside his own, he crawled out the window and latched onto the brick ledge with his fingers. It took three swipes with his left hand to close the double-sash window. Now, it was a matter of inching his way past three other apartments before reaching the drainpipe at the corner of the building.

"Captain McDougal is going to have to get him someone else to do his work. Cockroaches crawling on your face. Whores trying to smash your nose with bedsprings. Now a ledge loaded with bird shit. I don't care what kind of trouble that Mexican's having."

A couple of cats fighting in the trash below caused him to glance down. The three stories suddenly turned into a mile.

"Dammit!" He moved toward the drainpipe faster, "Nothing's worth this."

~   ~   ~

"No, I'm not concerned with evicting the Ramos family at the moment. I've already gotten that taken care of." James Sattler grinned and leaned back in his chair. "Besides, the company taking possession of their property can handle that small problem."

"And when will that happen?" Darrell glanced up from the cigar he was lighting.

"Right after we get Judge Baker's final ruling, my boy. Always, first things first. If you take one step at a time, everything in it's proper order, things will always turn out as they're supposed to. It was too bad to hear about the Ramos boy drowning. Real tragedy." James grinned and shook his head. "Besides, it would look a little better if we give them a little time to grieve over the loss of their son before taking their land away, now wouldn't it?"

"Yeah, I suppose so," Darrell snickered. "When's the judge gonna give his decision, anyway?"

"Soon, I hope. He was supposed to make a ruling on the Ramos case next Tuesday, but I hear he caught some sort of caduseus condition and had to cancel his court dates the past few days."

"Well, it's easy to get gut ache and the runs in San Francisco if you eat at the wrong place. That is, if you don't wash it down with enough alcohol." Darrell hoisted his glass of rum in a salute.

"That could be, but the judge lives in a fancy house with live-in servants and a full-time cook," James said.

"Hell, I'd fire the sons a bitches then," Darrell said with a laugh.

"He may have, but things will happen in their own good time. In the meantime, there is one little thing I want you to do for me." James shifted some papers on his desk. "Ah yes, here it is." He pulled a crude map from under a pile of papers. "I'd like for you to take a little trip out to the Garcia rancho. It's near a place called Dogtown, not too far from Jamestown and Columbia."

"Yeah, I've been there before."

"You have? Oh, yes, I forgot. Your Captain McDougal is close friends with the woman." He paused and grinned. "That might be a good excuse for your showing up. You're looking for the Captain, and hoped you'd find him there."

"That'd work, but what am I really there for?"

"You're trying to find out where she is getting all her money. Every time I put the squeeze on her, she'll squeak and squawk like she doesn't have a penny, but in a couple of days she always seems to come up with a wad of money that would choke a horse."

"What's wrong with that? Just keep squeezing her."

"Well, you can only charge someone so much for anything you do, and I've just about crossed that line with Mrs. Garcia. Besides, her land skirts the Mother Lode, and I've got a big mining company interested in her property. There's a nasty little rumor making its way around the mining towns that there's a lot of gold hidden under all that cow shit."

"Maybe she's got her own mine, and that's where she's getting all the money. Mexicans were pulling gold out of the ground long before we got here." Darrell took another sip of rum.

"You're not the only one who's thought of that. Rumor has it that she's got herself a dredging project worth a million operating right along the river. And that's exactly why I want you out there. Spend a couple of days nosing around. See what you can come up with."

"Okay, but what if I do find out she's got her own gold mine, and there's no way you can squeeze her out. What then? Want her to have some sort of accident?"

"No, no." James laughed. "Judge Baines and Pod Randell already tried that and got themselves killed for their efforts. We'll just take what we can get and move on. That's why I'm smarter than Judge Baines and Pod Randell. You have to know when you've drawn a bad hand, and when to fold. Both of them kept betting on a dead man's hand, when the lady had already drawn four Aces."

"Yeah, that makes sense." Darrell turned the map over and studied it for a second. "I'll need some money."

"I'm afraid the account is almost dry." James pulled the checkbook from the drawer. "That's why I need you to find out if we've drawn a bad hand with her or not. How about forty dollars? That's about all I can afford at the moment."

"It'll have to do then, won't it?"

"You've been going through a lot of money lately," James said as he dipped his pen in the inkwell.

"Well, whores are expensive, Jimmy. Almost as expensive as a card game." He grinned as James handed him the check.

~   ~   ~

"That is horrible." Loretta's ashen cheeks were streaked with tears. "I can't believe anyone would do something like that. Oh, God." She turned away from the bloody shirt and knife lying on the table to bury her face against her husband's chest.

"Yes, it is ghastly, isn't it?" Judge Baker scratched his chin. "You're sure this is the knife used for killing," he glanced at Salty, "what did you say her name was?"

"Francie. I believe it was actually Francine Jordan, but you'd have to ask one of the other girls to make sure."

"You're sure about the knife, though?"

"Well, about as sure as I can be. He was the last man she was seen with that night. Then she turns up dead. I found this hid behind the wardrobe in his room. What more evidence could we need?" Salty flapped his arms in the air and let them drop to his sides.

"I know that I'm sounding like the devil's advocate, but I'm a judge, and I know what someone like Jim Sattler would do with that evidence in court. First of all, your Darrell Rodeen is employed by Mr. Sattler himself, so whether we like it or not, that makes him a respectable citizen of this city. Second, Miss Jordan, if that is her real name, was simply another prostitute working at one of our many nightclubs."

"Simply a prostitute?" Loretta flashed her moist eyes at him. "She was a human, regardless of what you might think."

"Yes, and I agree with you. I'm simply telling everyone here in this room what will happen if we have Mr. Rodeen arrested and go to trial with this evidence. There are no witnesses who actually saw him kill her, and there is no way we can prove that knife as the weapon. I wish to God that there was some way we could prove the blood on this shirt is actually hers, but we can't." He grabbed the shirt and let it fall back to the table.

"So, we turn our backs and let him go?" Captain McDougal stroked Loretta's hair as she leaned her head back against his chest.

"No, I didn't say that. What we do is, keep a close eye on him. He will slip up and make another mistake sooner or later, then we nail him. When we go to court, we will not only have this shirt and knife, but we'll have enough evidence to nail both him and James Sattler to the wall." Judge Baker filled several glasses with brandy and handed one to Loretta. "Here, drink this. It'll make you feel better."

"What if he decides to kill another girl?" Salty said.

"We'll just have to take that chance for now, and hope he doesn't. In the meantime, you could possibly warn the girls at The Silver Slipper to beware of being alone with him."

"They've already been made aware. When I was inside his room snooping around, I had to hide under the bed because he brought a girl called Diamond into the room." Salty glanced as Loretta snapped her head around at the mention of her former co-worker. "She said that none of them were supposed to leave The Silver Slipper alone. But it didn't seem to stop her."

"You hid under the bed?" McDougal snickered. "What were they doing the whole time?"

"What do you think they were doing, you ol' barnacle?"

"Honey." Loretta frowned and swatted her husband on the arm as he laughed.

"Well, maybe you can ask this Diamond some questions. Perhaps she, or one of the other girls might know something that will be helpful." Judge Baker said.

"Already working on that, Sir."

"Good. Now, I perceive it's almost time for dinner," the judge said, glancing at his watch. "I hope you can stay and dine with us, Mr. Moran."

"I'd be happy to, Your Honor."

"Good. Captain, perhaps you can show Mr. Moran where he might freshen up a bit. I'd like to have a few words with your wife in private, if I may."

"Yes, I'd be happy to," he said as Loretta grabbed hold of his arm. Her damp eyes were wide as he kissed her cheek. "It will be okay. I'll see you in a minute."

"M'lady." Salty gave a quick bow before following the captain out the door.

"He's strange." Loretta shook her head.

"Oh, I don't know. I've found that most people are strange, if you really pause to study them." Judge Baker closed the door and pulled a large envelope from the desk drawer, before sliding a chair close to where she was sitting. He smiled a long minute before clearing his throat.

"I've been wanting to give you a wedding present, but I couldn't decide what a lady married to a sea captain might want. But I believe you would rather have this than a bag of gold." He handed her the envelope.

"What is it?" She lay the envelope in her lap to peek inside.

"It's your records."

"My what?"

"Your court records. I had the files expunged. As far as the court is concerned, Loretta Stewart has never been in trouble with the law."

"You've known all along, haven't you?" Loretta's hands shook as she pulled the papers from the envelope.

"It wasn't too hard to figure out. I just want you to know that your secret is safe with me, Mrs. McDougal."

Her bottom lip trembled as she lowered her head to scan the pages. "When did you recognize me? The first or second time I was in here?"

"No, I see a lot of people in court, but there aren't too many beautiful women in San Francisco named Loretta, so your case stuck in my mind more than others. But I actually wasn't positive until just a moment ago, when you were so upset over Francie's death. Now," he raised a palm when her head shot upward. "I believe your reaction was the proper one. I wish everyone would become just as angry whenever something like this happened. Perhaps if the criminals who do those things knew no one was going to tolerate such deeds, they would think again before they did them. But that's not what I wanted to talk about."

"I know." She lowered her head. "I'm sorry. I'll quit coming here with my husband. I hope you will find some way of explaining to your daughter that won't make her feel hatred for me."

"What in the world are you talking about?"

"About my being who I am, and coming here. Singing and dancing with Clara and drinking tea with your wife. Look," she snapped as he started to chuckle, "I know whores aren't welcome inside the homes of fine upright citizens, so I'm willing to leave peaceably and not cause any more trouble."

"Just relax." He put a hand on her shoulder as she started to rise. "I said your secret was safe with me, didn't I?"

"Okay, what is it you want, then?"

"Want?"

"Yes, when men say that sort of thing, it means they want something. If it is for me to be unfaithful to my husband, you can forget it."

"Now, you have offended me, Mrs. McDougal." He rose to refill two of the brandy glasses. "Dorothy and I have been married almost fifteen years, and I have never, nor will I ever touch another woman. I love my wife very much."

"I'm sorry."

"Apology accepted." He handed her one of the glasses. "I only wanted you to know you can relax in my presence. I've noticed how you stiffen every time I come into the room where you and Clara are having fun at the piano, or having tea with my wife. On the other hand, you are extremely cultured and educated. I have no idea how you got involved in working at The Silver Slipper, but I don't believe you ever intended to get mixed up in that lifestyle."

"I didn't."

"Good. I also don't believe what you used to do for a living is a disease that can possibly be passed onto my family. And even if it were, I have a feeling, after watching you these past few weeks, that you have been cured."

"What are you saying, then? I don't understand what it is you want from me?"

"Want? I don't want anything from you, my dear. What I have been trying to say is, that I happen to like you and I'm extremely happy that you were able to marry someone like Captain McDougal. He is a fine gentleman and will make you a wonderful husband, as I'm sure you will make him a wonderful wife."

"This is too, too... I don't know what to say." Loretta shook her head as her voice choked.

"You've said it." He smiled gently. "Oh, by the way, I had that drunk who was convicted of the robbery released from prison. Now, come on. Wipe your eyes and let's go to dinner before Mr. Moran and that husband of yours eats everything on the table."

"Okay." She laughed and stuffed the envelope inside her handbag. "He does have a rather healthy appetite."

"You know, Mrs. McDougal, you do have a beautiful singing voice." He opened the door and took her by the arm. He continued talking as they crossed the massive entryway toward the dining room. "That husband of yours should think about allowing you to sing in the theater."

"Oh, I don't think so, Your Honor." Loretta shook her head. "It's ideas like that, that got me involved in my former profession."

"Mmmm, I see." They paused at the dining room door. "We shall discuss it at a later time, but I suggest that for the time being we find our places while there is still something left to put on our plates."

Chapter 27

"Time to close the bar, Ruby," Hanky said as Judge Hansen pushed his way through the swinging doors. "Court's about to get started."

"Okay, drink up boys." She jammed the cork back into the bottle. "This might be the last time you get served by Ruby Lang. They might be hanging me tomorrow."

"Like hell they will." The man with dirty coveralls and a red beard glared at the lawman. "Ain't none of us gonna stand for it."

"Come on." Hanky reached across the bar and took her by the arm. Cary Jones banged the table with his claw hammer and cleared his throat.

"All rise. Court is now in session. The Honorable Judge Lloyd Hansen presiding, on the first day of June, 1852."

"You may be seated," Lloyd Hansen said as he took his chair behind the card table at the rear of the bar. "You may call your next confessed killer to the stand, Sheriff."

"Yes Sir. I'd like fer Mrs. Garcia to come forward." He waited until Leonida had reached the witness stand before grabbing the Bible from Cary Jones' hand.

"But, that's my job, Hanky."

"Not today, it ain't. Sit yerself down." Cary grumbled as he took his seat.

"Put yer right hand on the Good Book, Ma'am." Hanky held the well-worn Bible in front of her. "Now, do you swear to Almighty God, that you ain't gonna say nothing inside this here courtroom that ain't the truth?"

"Are you asking me to swear that I'll tell you the truth, Señor Russell?"

"That's what I said in plain English, ain't it?"

"Order, order!" Judge Hansen pounded the gavel. "Just say 'I do', Mrs. Garcia, and let's get this over with."

"Bueno, Your Honor. I do, Señor Russell."

"Okie-dokey, that's all I wanted. You can sit yerself down." He handed the Bible to Suzanna Black and pulled an empty chair close to where Leonida was seated at the front of the courtroom.

"Suppose you tell us who you are, and where you're living, Ma'am."

"My full name is Doña Leonida Margarita Flores Garcia, and I live at Rancho Manantial Escondido. Is there anything wrong, Señor?" she said as he raised his eyebrows and nodded.

"No. That's the first time I knew what your full handle was. It's right purdy."

"Gracias."

"You're quite welcome. Now, you consider yourself to be a religious woman, don't you, Ma'am?"

"Sí, I suppose I do. I pray every day, and try to be. Why?"

"Well, I was just wondering. You know, I see you inside that church you got out on the ranch praying and reading that Bible of yours, sometimes twice a day. Now, I've read the Bible some, not as much as I should, I'll admit. But it seems to me, that I read somewhere that it says lying is a sin. Is that right?"

"Sí, you are correct, Señor."

"Mmm, I thought so. Now, I supposed that'd take in hinting that something was true, when it really wasn't, wouldn't it?"

"I don't understand, Señor."

"Sure you do. Like when you started hinting that you was the one who kilt Ambrose Brice. You told me in so many words that you got up in the middle of the night and rode that black of yourn' into town, came right into this very saloon, and stuck him in the gizzard with his own butcher knife, then went back home and went to bed. Now, didn't you?"

"Señor," Leonida giggled, "all I said was it was a possibility."

"But you knew I was in the middle of investigatin', and your purpose of saying what you did was to muddy up the waters. Now, ain't that right?"

"I don't understand what you're saying." Leonid slowly shook her head.

"Come on now, Mrs. Garcia." Hanky grinned toward the jury. "I know fer a fact that you can read and scribble words better'n anyone in this here courtroom. I heard you say once that you can speak four different languages. Are you trying to tell me you don't understand what I'm saying now?"

"Sí. Could you speak a little slower?"

"Okie-dokie, I'll make it real simple." He got from his chair and leaned close to stare her in the eyes. "I'm only going to ask this once, so I want you to listen real close. I want you to think real hard before you answer, 'cause you done laid your hand on the Good Book and swore to God you was gonna tell the truth, and I don't think He'd like it none if you was to lie. Ready?"

She nodded.

"Did you murder Ambrose Brice?"

"No." Leonida dropped her gaze to her lap and shook her head. "No, I did not."

"Fine." Hanky stepped back to stare at Judge Hansen. "I think I'm through with her."

"Well done, Mr. Russell. You were in total control. Well done. You may be seated. I want to talk to Mrs. Garcia myself. In fact," he raised his voice, "I'd like to address the whole courtroom for a moment. It seems that nearly everyone inside this building has taken the opinion that Mr. Brice deserved killing, and that whoever did it should receive some sort of award. A great many of you have the mistaken opinion that lying during an investigation, or while on the witness stand, or making threats to the law officer, who is simply doing his sworn duty, is perfectly okay. Well, I can't change the way you feel inside, but the rest is going to change immediately. I'm holding Mrs. Garcia in contempt of court." Leonida snapped her head up to stare.

"These are very serious charges, Ma'am. While you never actually lied here on the stand today, you did lie to Mr. Russell during an investigation. And you did your best at every turn to make his job harder, right down to wasting the time of everyone inside this courtroom today. Now, I could make it easy and sentence and fine you today, but I'm not. Since you chose to make things difficult for us, I'm going to make them difficult for you also.

"You're to show up in this courtroom every day during this trial. You're to be seated up front with the defendants," he pointed the gavel at Ruby, "instead of in the rear with your father. Do you have any questions?"

"Sí. What if I am required to be in court in San Francisco? As you are aware, they are conducting hearings concerning the ownership of our rancho."

"You should have thought of that before you decided to make a mockery of our murder trial." He slammed the gavel. "And at least two of you three women," he swung the gavel toward Aurie, Ruby and Alice, "are lying. And may God help you, because you've not only lied to Mr. Russell, but you've lied to the entire court under oath. Now, we're going to get to the bottom of this and find out who really killed Ambrose Brice. But I'll tell you right here and now, the two who are lying will more than likely wish they could trade places with the killer. Because I won't tolerate any more lying in my courtroom. I'm going to throw the entire weight of this court behind sentencing you for perjury." He slammed the gavel with a loud crack.

"Now, I realize that it's a whole week away, but court's dismissed until nine o'clock Monday morning. I have a couple of trials to conduct in Columbia. Simple things like a stage holdup, for one." He glared at the women as he gathered his papers.

~   ~   ~

Rodeen slid the map across the desk and leaned back in his chair with a sigh. "I went out there like you said."

"And, did you find out where the mine is located?" Sattler glanced up from fumbling for a bottle and glasses in his bottom drawer.

"Nope. But I did find out that the whole ranch is under quarantine. Seems they've got some sort of measles outbreak or something. Anyway, I was met with a welcoming party about five miles or so inside the ranch, and they didn't act too friendly. They were quite rude, actually." Darrell leaned across the desk to accept the glass of whisky and held it upward in a toast. "Told me not to come back."

"Well, that calls for a change of plans." James returned the toast. "It'll make it a little more interesting. Give us a greater challenge."

~   ~   ~

Leonida's skirts swished with the clicking of her boots as she paced the tiny room at the rear of the chapel.

"Sit, my child. Your tea is getting cold." Father Ramon grinned.

"How can I, Father? He, he called me a liar in front of everyone inside that filthy cantina." Her hand shook as she pointed in the direction of Dogtown. "I don't know when I've been so insulted or angry."

"But you did lie, didn't you?"

"Que?" She placed her hands on her hips to glare. "Not you too, Father? Not once did I actually say I had killed that man. I don't believe that anyone knows who killed him. The murderer is probably hundreds of miles from here right this moment. How could anyone even think such a thing?"

"Because you said so, my child, and you are Doña Leonida. People on this rancho are supposed to be able to believe their Doña, aren't they?" They stared at each other a long minute before Leonida sat in the empty chair and propped her elbows against the table with her chin in her hands.

"I was only trying to prove a point, Father."

"And what was that point?" Father Ramon smiled and sipped his tea.

"That it didn't have to be Señoritas Aurie or Ruby. Any number of people would have had more than enough reason to kill Ambrose Brice. He was an evil man, Father. It made me angry when that old ranger started accusing Señora Carpenter of the murder. The questions he was asking in court made it sound like she was guilty. She is a very close friend of mine, and my father likes her very much."

"Sí, I understand he does. She is not Catholic, is she?"

"No, but what difference does that make? She's still my friend and my papa still loves her. Can't a Catholic love a Protestant?" Leonida crinkled her eyebrows.

"Sí," he nodded, "but it sometimes causes problems when they marry, unless one of them is willing to give up their church. And in my position, I am always praying it will be the Protestant who changes. Let me ask you something, my child." He reached across the table to take one of her hands. "Was it not Señora Carpenter who stood inside the courtroom and said she had killed that man? In fact, didn't all three women volunteer that information?"

"Sí."

"Then, why are you angry with Señor Russell?"

"Because he believed them. Now they are having to go through the humiliation of being accused publicly and go through a court trial. You saw how he treated me today. Acting as though I was going to lie to him right there inside the courtroom."

"Ah," he nodded and released her hand, "the Doña's pride has been hurt."

"Perdon? I think not. You are mistaken, Father. I am angry because of that Texas gringo's insistence that we all go to trial. You've seen the way he has been treating us. There is no way that my pride has been hurt."

"Sí, I've seen the way Señor Russell has been treating you, and I think he has been a perfect gentleman, considering the circumstances."

"Que? I did not think my priest was blind."

"Oh, I see more than you think, my young peacock."

"Peacock?" She gritted her teeth and scooted away from the table.

"Sí." He nodded and motioned with his hand as she leaped to her feet. "Now sit down. I command you as your priest. I have something to say, that I should have said long ago." He quietly sipped his tea until she had seated herself.

"Look at yourself, mi Doña. Back rigid like a board, jaw clamped tight in anger. You remind me of one of Francisco's peacocks strutting about. Proud, showing your beautiful feathers for everyone to admire. And you have every reason to be proud, on the surface. Dios has given you beauty that surpasses any woman on this rancho, including Señorita Loretta, who is like a flower herself. You are educated far more than most men I know, and are very wealthy. Every time some disaster threatens to destroy you, Dios blesses you even more. You have beauty, wealth and power on your side, Doña. These are good things, if used properly. But they have made you like the peacock, who thinks he is more beautiful than all other birds. The only problem is, it is his pretty plumes which make him an easy target for the predators who wish him harm."

"Those are horrible things to hear coming from my priest." Leonida's voice was a hoarse whisper.

"Sí, but I only say them because you needed to hear what has happened to you, my child."

"I can't believe what you're saying is actually true." She shook her head. "I pray each day. I try to be what Dios wants me to be. I'm at every Mass." She pounded the table with her finger. "You know that, Father."

"Sí, you are a very religious woman, my dear, but even your religion has made you proud."

"Ah, now I know you are mad. There is no way one's religion could cause them to become prideful, if they really love God."

"No? Why then, did our Lord cleanse the temple? Answer me that, my peacock. Were not the scribes, priests and even the money changers religious people? I'll have you know that not many Catholics worship Dios as religiously as they did. Yet our Lord threw them all out of the temple. Why?"

"I don't know, Father." Leonida shook her head. "But they were not like me."

"Sí, but they were very much like you. They were in positions of leadership and people trusted them. But they became puffed up in their own pride, instead of being proud of Him." He pointed upward toward the ceiling. "Then, they started making their own rules, saying it was lawful to do this, and not that. People had to purchase their sacrifices at the temple, instead of bringing one from home. They were ordering the people to do things Dios had not intended, and setting themselves up to be like Dios himself.

"You see, my child," he leaned across the table to stare into her green eyes, "that is the great lie el Diablo would like us to believe. He told the woman in the garden if she ate the forbidden fruit she would become like Dios, knowing right from wrong. In reality, he was telling her she could make up her own rules, and that was exactly what she did. The fruit? What did the fruit mean?" He frowned and turned his palms upward. "The fruit itself meant nothing. It was the act of disobedience that cost her and her husband. And we have been doing the same thing ever since. Making our own rules to live by."

"That is a fine story, Father, but what does it have to do with me? I ask you that?" Leonida turned her head toward the blank wall.

"Everything. Because you knew what was the truthful and right thing to do from the beginning. If you had told Señor Russell that you did not know anything about that man's death when this whole thing started, you would not be in trouble right this minute. Instead, you chose to tell a half-truth, which is nothing less than a whole lie. Now look at you. You're all puffed up and angry at that man for something you did. This is not right."

Leonida stared at the wall a long minute before slowly nodding her golden head. "Sí, you are right, Father. I am sinful. I have this anger inside and I don't know what to do about it."

"The next time you are in the chapel, try telling our Lord about it. Tell Him exactly how you feel." Father Ramon laughed as she snapped her head around. "You won't shock Him, my child. Dios already knows what goes on inside your heart. Ask Him to forgive you and help you to change. I will pray with you."

"Then what?"

"Que? You shall go around like a good Catholic and make amends to everyone you have offended."

"Everyone?"

"Sí, everyone, including Señores Russell and Kilkenney."

"Señor Kilkenney? What have I done that I should apologize to him for? I allowed him to return after he ran away and hurt me. Then he returned with another woman, I was angry, yes. But I eventually gave in and told him that I still love him. In fact, as you well know, I've agreed to marry him. Where is there any wrong in that?"

"Nothing, unless you are willing to start your marriage on a half-truth."

"I don't understand what you are saying." She shook her head and turned back toward the wall with folded arms.

"In all that you said, I never heard you once mention that you have forgiven him for hurting you."

"Ha!" She snapped her head back around. "He is the one that left and should be apologizing to me. I've done nothing to be sorry for."

"Oh, but he did apologize many times, my niña, but you have refused to accept his apology and that is wrong."

"What are you talking about?"

"You are still bitter and untrusting of the man you have agreed to marry. I'm afraid I cannot perform your ceremony unless you have a change of heart."

"Not marry us?"

"Sí. I can only imagine what would happen the first time he did something to upset you. You'd start dragging up the past, accusing him of things he thought were forgotten. No," he shook his head, "it would not work, mi Doña. You'd only drive him away."

"Hay, I come in here expressing my anger toward what happened in that, that cantina, and my own priest turns it around making me out to be evil."

"I did not say you are evil, my child."

"You said I was prideful, angry and bitter, and that I'm lying to the man I am going to marry. Then," she pointed a finger at him across the table, "you say you are not going to marry us unless I have a change of heart. Now you tell me, Father Ramon, if that is not saying I'm an evil person, I'd like to know what you are saying."

"It is true I said those things, but only to get you to open your heart. You are bitter, Niña."

"Perhaps. But it was wrong for him to accept my love and trust, then leave, wasn't it? He hurt me deeply, Padré. I don't know if I can forgive him."

"But you must. This is what Dios wants of his children. I'm not saying you have to marry him, but you do have to forgive. And you have to forgive Señor Hanky also. The man is only doing his job. The job you encouraged him to do."

"Oh, caramba." She buried her face in her hands.

"And just to show you how wrong a person can be in their thinking, I should tell you this." He got up to retrieve the kettle of hot water. "Someone besides Dios knows who killed Señor Brice."

"Que? Do you know, Father?"

"Sí." He nodded as he refilled both cups.

"Who? Tell me, Father."

"I am not at liberty to say. I've sworn my silence. You will find out soon enough, child. Perhaps Monday we will all know."

Chapter 28

"Blue blazes and thunder. At this point there's not much I can do." Judge Samuel Baker combed his fingers through his graying hair. He gave the stack of papers in front of him a shove. "I've studied everything from a dozen different angles, but I can't find a loophole anywhere. They've signed away power of attorney on the entire ranch to that crook, and he in turn sold it to that company from the east who wants to develop it. They own it all. He's even got receipts proving he spent every cent of the proceeds on legal costs."

"So, you are telling me that my family has been cheated out of everything they own, and there is nothing you can do about it?" Manuel Ramos leaned across the desk. "That isn't possible. You are a judge. There has to be something!" He waved off the protest of his parents as they tried pulling him back to his seat.

"I'm afraid not, at least for the moment. You and your parents both agree that it is your father's mark on every one of these papers." He grabbed a stack of them and let them fall back to the desk.

"Yes, but what did he get in return? That Mr. Sattler was supposed to defend us in court and all we got was nothing. He won our case, si," he nodded his head violently, "but now we find we have won nothing. Somebody else owns the land that was rightfully ours to begin with. He didn't even say thank you for stealing us blind."

"Yes, I'm afraid that is about the size of it." Judge Baker shook his head as the young man began to curse in Spanish.

"But what if we can prove fraud on Sattler's part? Won't that make a difference?" Captain McDougal looked up from lighting his pipe.

"It might. But the key question is, can we prove it? Right at the moment, this case looks water-tight. The man certainly knows how to cross all his t's and dot his i's, I'll give him that."

"Well, you tell your parents not to give up hope, son. I still have my man working on your behalf." McDougal smiled before shaking the flame from his match and tossing it in the ashtray.

"Señor Moran? The one who saved my life that night?"

"Yes, and he's mighty interested in helping you folks."

"And that is another thing." Manuel turned back to Judge Baker. "You say this Darrell Rodeen is working for Señor Sattler, and he is the one who tried to kill me? Doesn't the fact that he has a killer working for him prove something? Why hasn't something been done about that man?"

"Well, to answer your first question, the only thing we can prove at the moment is that he's a bad judge of character. He'd simply say that he didn't know anything about Rodeen's attempted murder, and we'd be right back where we started from. As to why we haven't had Rodeen arrested, we all thought it best to have Mr. Moran and a couple of others tail him and see if he doesn't, in fact, do something that might incriminate Jim Sattler. Maybe, if we can really nail him with something big, then we can see about getting your land back. But, it'll be tough sailing no matter which way we go about it."

"Sí, but now my parents and I find it difficult knowing which Americano to trust." He turned to address his parents in Spanish. "We will be going now. You will let us know if you find a way of helping us get our land back and putting those men in prison?"

"Absolutely." Judge Baker stood to his feet and shook their hands. "And you stay out of sight for the time being.

You're supposed to be dead, remember?" He waited until they had closed the door before pounding the desk with his fist.

"I think the thing that makes me the angriest is that these people lost their land inside my courtroom. Why, why, why couldn't I see what was happening?"

"Like you said, Sattler is as slippery as wet moss." McDougal beat the ashes from his pipe. "But we will catch him. No one is so smart that they can get away with stealing forever."

"Let's hope so." The judge looked up as his wife entered the study with Loretta and his daughter.

"What is the matter, Dear?" Dorothy said as she paused in the middle of the room to stare at him.

"Nothing really. Well, that's not true, everything's wrong." He leaned across the desk to comb his fingers through his hair again. "I had to turn those people away with no real hope of getting their land back."

"Why? They had no idea of what was happening to them. The parents don't even speak English. They were trusting their solicitor to make the right decisions for them."

"Yes, but they gave him power of attorney, and he's built such a case, I don't know. Unless we can prove that James Sattler is a corrupt man, we will have trouble recovering a dog or a cat from that ranch those people call home."

"Perhaps I can help," Loretta said as she sat on the edge of the sofa next to her husband.

"And how is that, young lady?"

"Well, let's just say that in my former profession as an entertainer, I had a rather close relationship with James Sattler. Not only did he defend me in your courtroom, but I could tell you some things about him that wouldn't set too well."

"Really?" Judge Baker glanced at his wife who was staring at her new friend open-mouthed. "And what might that be?"

"I would rather not say, unless it is absolutely necessary. It, uh, might not look too good for my husband," she shrugged, "or anyone else I happen to care about."

"Can't you at least give me some sort of hint?" He leaned forward.

"Don't worry about Clara or me turning our backs on you, Dear." Dorothy Baker laid a hand on Loretta's shoulder. "If there is something you can say to help those poor people, you had better go ahead and tell my husband. It won't go any further than this room."

"Oh, but I'm afraid it will have to." Loretta's hand shook as she opened her handbag and removed a laced handkerchief. "You see, I would have to take the stand in court to testify against him, and some things would come out about my past that I would rather keep hidden." She glanced around at the staring faces before taking a deep breath.

"Okay, I didn't really have the money for Jim defending me in court, so we made a deal. I was supposed to keep an eye on the customers who came into The Silver Slipper and mark the ones who were flush with large sums of money. Then, I was to get them good and drunk and take them up to one of the rooms upstairs. He even gave me a little bottle of pills I could slip into their drinks that would speed the process up. I liked using the pills," she lowered her head to study the hanky in her fingers, "because the men would simply pass out the minute they got inside the room and I could leave. They never seemed to remember anything," she glanced at the judge and shook her head, "not even the money."

"So, what happened after you got them inside the room?" Judge Baker said as he filled a glass with brandy.

"Jim would slip inside and relieve them of their money."

"Ha, we got him." Judge Baker slammed the bottle down on the desk.

"I don't understand." Dorothy shook her head. "Why would a successful solicitor like James Sattler resort to stealing? He makes plenty of money."

"Because he has a horrible gambling problem. He loses everything he makes and then some. I even heard once that some men he owed money to were threatening to break both his legs. Dear God, I feel so dirty." She sniffled as her chin dropped to her chest. Jonathan slipped an arm around her shoulders and pulled her close.

"Well done, my dear." The judge handed the glass of brandy to Loretta. "What you've just told us is enough to lock his black soul up for a long time. But," he paused in the middle of filling several glasses, "we won't use you on the stand unless we absolutely have to. Mr. Moran seems to be very thorough. He may come up with something yet. But, by damned, we've got him one way or the other." He handed his wife and Jonathan McDougal each a glass of brandy before holding up his own in a salute.

"Here's to the end of James Sattler."

"Amen," Jonathan said and smiled at his wife before tilting his glass.

~   ~   ~

"Hey." Loretta opened her eyes as the door creaked open. "I'm in the middle of taking a bath."

"Really?" Jonathan folded his arms and leaned in the doorway to stare. "You've been in here an awful long time. I was beginning to think you might have drowned."

"Would you please close the door? I feel a draft." She folded her arms across her breasts.

"Um-um." He shook his head. "I have all the windows closed with a roaring fire in the fireplace. It's warmer in the bedroom than it is in here."

"Well, I'd like some privacy."

"Why? I've seen you naked before. Remember? I'm your husband." He came toward the tub.

270

"Jonathan, please!" She lowered her head and scrunched in a modest ball inside the tub.

"Loretta McDougal," he said, taking the sponge and washing her back. "I like the sound of that name. In fact, I like it so much, that I take out our marriage certificate every once in a while just to see it printed in ink."

"You do?"

"You can bet your last pence on it."

"Jonathan?"

"Mmmm?"

"Do you still love me? Even after what I said this afternoon?" She shifted to see his answer, but quickly turned back around to cover her breasts.

"You're trying to be funny, aren't you?"

"No, I really have to know. You're the kindest, most gentlest man I've ever known, and I don't want to lose you." He dropped the sponge to scoop one arm under her knees and lift her from the tub.

"Jonathan? What are you doing?"

He answered by covering her mouth with his.

"Put me down. You're getting your shirt all wet."

"Hang the shirt. It'll dry." He kissed her again.

"Stop it. You're dripping water all over the floor," she said as he headed toward the bedroom.

"It'll dry also. And would you quit covering yourself?" He laid her across the bed and pinned both of her hands on either side of her head. "I like to look at you."

"Now, the blankets are all wet."

"There are more inside the closet." He licked some droplets from one of her breasts.

"Jonathan?" Her voice became husky as he worked is way to the other breast. "You never answered my question. Do you still love me?"

"More than ever. It took courage to do what you did." He kissed her mouth lightly and worked his way down one cheek to her ear. "I not only love you, I adore and respect you more than you could ever know."

"Oh, God." She clamped both her arms and legs around him in a tight squeeze. "I don't know what I've ever done to deserve you."

"The feeling is mutual, my dear." He rolled on his side and ran a hand along one of the legs wrapped tightly around his waist. "Now, I want you to release me, but just long enough for me to get these wet clothes off. Then, I want you to get in the same position and see if we can't sleep that way all night."

"Really?" She straddled him and began unbuttoning his damp shirt. "I'll bet you can't hold still that long."

~   ~   ~

"Got some change to help out a poor bloke?"

"Hell no." James Sattler pushed his way past the hunch-backed, gray-headed man with an outstretched hand. "Go take a bath and get a job."

"Yes, sir. And I hope you have a good day, sir." Sattler paused to scowl over his shoulder before climbing into the shiny black carriage waiting at the curb.

"Yes, sir, a good day. Because I plan on having myself an even better one," Salty said as the carriage disappeared over the hill. He removed the large key ring from his coat pocket as he climbed the stairs. "Yes, sir, a real fine day."

"Let's see, not that one, or that one." He began humming as he tried the keys one by one. He had completed the first stanza of Blow The Man Down before the lock opened with a loud click. One quick glance around and he slipped inside, re-locking the door. He tied a piece of red twine around the right key as a reference before returning the ring to his pocket.

"My, my, Mr. James Sattler, but you are one messy bloke," he said staring at the paper strewn office. "How's a fellow like me supposed to find what he needs in this bilge?"

He lit the lantern and began thumbing through the papers on the desk, being careful to leave the piles exactly as he had found them. Next came the stacks on the floor, then the desk drawers. The locking file cabinets proved to be more of a challenge, but a quick twist of a lock pick got him past that hurdle.

"Garcia, Garcia." He thumbed through the folders. "Ah, here you go, Salty me lad. Leonida Garcia." He laid the file on the desk. He had almost finished scanning the pages when he heard footsteps coming down the hall. He quickly shoved the file cabinet closed and blew out the light. Then, tucking the Garcia file inside his jacket, he took refuge inside the coat closet as someone began turning a key inside the lock. Salty peered through the crack in the partially open door as Darrell Rodeen stepped inside. Dammit. He gritted his teeth as Rodeen began removing his coat.

Chapter 29

"Señor Kilkenney." Sean glanced up from removing a splinter from Olga Segoviano's foot. Leonida's black boots poking under the hem of her brown riding skirt clicked against the bricks as she crossed the patio to where Olga was seated on the fountain's edge.

"Just a second, I've just about got it." He turned back to the task at hand.

"Ow!" Olga cried as he gave the piece of wood a jerk.

"Aye, I know it hurts, darling, but it had to come out. If we had left it in there, it might have made you sick. Now we wouldn't want that, would we?"

She shook her dark head.

"But, you can show this new white bandage off to all your friends," he said, wrapping the tiny foot. "And, I'll bet this will make it feel all better." He fished a peppermint stick from his bag. "Now, run along and have fun." He chuckled as he watched her share her candy with several friends, all taking turns licking the tasty treat.

"How long do you think that bandage will stay clean, let alone on her foot?" Leonida giggled.

"About as long as that candy lasts. Then she'll be off to new adventures." He snapped his bag closed and straightened to face the woman standing before him. Her black veil had been replaced by a brown flat-brimmed hat that hung loosely against her shoulders by the drawstring, allowing her golden hair to dance in the breeze. The white blouse tucked inside her brown skirt hung open at the neck, revealed white skin that had been hidden by years of tradition. Her open short-cropped vest failed to hide the shapely breast pushing against the cloth. The belt pulled snug around her small waist only amplified the vision.

"You're staring a me." She took a step backward and giggled. "What is wrong?"

"Wrong? Nothing." He began fumbling with the latch on his medical kit.

"Then why were you staring?"

"I was just thinking how beautiful you are."

"Oh, gracias. You like my new riding clothes, then?" She held out her arms and danced in a circle.

"Yes, they are fine. But you would probably look just as beautiful in rags."

"Again, I thank you. That is possibly the nicest compliment you have ever given me." She grinned.

"Well, I ought to be offended, since I have told you that I'm hopelessly in love with you. I was under the impression that might have been the greatest compliment."

"Sí," she nodded, "I stand corrected. That was a much bigger compliment. But I'm glad you like my new clothes anyway. My father doesn't think much of them. In fact," she shook her head, "he doesn't like them at all. I can't repeat the things he said just a moment ago when he saw me."

"Oh?" He took her by the arm and began to stroll leisurely toward the courtyard gate. "I was thinking of taking a little walk. Do you mind?"

"No, I would love it." She clasped her free hand over his forearm, causing her shoulder to rub against him. Dry oak leaves crunched under their feet as they followed the gurgling creek away from the hacienda.

"What did he find wrong with them?" Sean said after a long moment.

"Who?"

"Your father."

"Oh, you mean my clothes." She paused to face him. "He says the blouse is too revealing, and that the neck should be up here," she pulled her collar tight, "like my other clothes. He says the skirt is too short. It shows my ankles and that is immodest. I told him no one can see my legs, because they are covered with leather boots, but he wouldn't listen. What do you think, Señor?" She turned around much slower this time. "Am I really being immodest dressed like this?"

"I think you are entirely fantastic."

"Gracias, but since you said I would look good in rags, I don't know if I should believe you or not."

"Well, you are, and I would have a hard time believing that I was the only man in the world who thought so. I've seen other men sneaking a look at you every now and then."

"Sí, that is what my father said. He thinks if I dress like this, men will think unholy thoughts about me."

"He's entirely correct," Sean snickered. "I've been guilty of that myself a time or two, but I've always prayed and asked forgiveness afterwards," he added quickly as her mouth dropped open. "That was before you even had those clothes."

"Madra mia, I guess that is something men do, isn't it?" She turned away as her cheeks flushed.

"Yes, but it is a good thing. How would Tex or Juan and their wives, or even your parents have gotten together if men didn't feel that way about the women they love?"

"Bueno, since you put it that way, I will accept it as a compliment."

"It was meant to be."

"But, I saw my father staring at Señorita Loretta when she was here. Does that mean he is in love with her too, Señor?" She gave him a crooked grin.

"No." Sean chuckled. "I think in your father's case it was more than likely pure lust. He probably had a whole lot more repenting to do in church than I did. On the other hand, she is pretty, and you have to take in the fact that her clothes show a wee bit more of her than yours do of you."

"Sí, I told my father that, but it only made him angrier. He said I am Doña Leonida, and a Catholic, and that I should not dress like a gringo pagan. That made me angry, and I'm afraid we traded words. I told him that Señorita Loretta was not that kind of lady, and he should apologize to her when she returns. I also told him that I did not believe that she is immodest in the way she dresses. Do you agree, Señor Sean?" Her green eyes sparkled as she stared up at him.

"What miss Stewart wore the whole time she was here, was entirely modest, by modern standards. The main difference lies in the neckline." He took hold of her collar with his fingers. "Your culture has taught you to keep your neck covered for modesty's sake. So did ours, until lately. Now the women in our larger cities, such as San Francisco, are dressing more like the ladies in England. Believe me," he grinned, "Loretta dresses modest, compared to what I've seen. The ladies there wear their neckline much lower, even in their pretty evening gowns. It is, shall we say, pretty enticing to the men."

"Bueno," she nodded, "I knew I was right. Oh, that reminds me of why I wanted to see you." She pulled a crumpled envelope from her skirt pocket. "I received a letter from Señor McDougal. Here, you may read it, if you wish. Part of it is written to you anyway."

"It's about time. They've been gone more than a month now." Sean laid his medical kit in the leaves and opened the envelope.

My Dear Leonida Garcia,   *29 May, 1852*

I am writing to let you know we are doing well, but the business we must attend to is going to take awhile longer. I've had the pleasure of seeing Judge Samuel Baker and his family on several occasions, and he agrees that your case has not been handled well by your solicitor, James Sattler. He asked me to advise you not to give him any more money until he has conducted a proper investigation into the matter.

From what I can detect, it may well be that the man is involved in defrauding several other landowners besides yourself. I now have one of my trusted men, Salty Moran, working on the case also. I believe you will remember him.

He was at your wedding to Rudolfo, and also at Juan and Angela's wedding. He is the short wiry man with graying hair and friendly smile.

Also, tell that Irish horse-doctor that Loretta is as lovely as always, and I have been keeping an eye on her. Or perhaps, it is she that has been keeping an eye on me. I also ran into another good friend of his. A certain Clara Baker. I will offer my apology in advance for saying so, my dear, but this young lady will give even you a run for charm and beauty. I don't know how that bloody Irishman does it, but young Clara has a terrible case for him. She has asked me a million times how he is doing and when he will be returning to San Francisco. You can tell the blasted Irishman I said he isn't worth her affection.

Well, I guess I should close this rambling chicken-scratch for now. I will be writing to keep you informed of matters, and will fill you in completely when we return.

Sincerely yours in Christ's name,

Captain Jonathan McDougal

Sean laughed as he folded the letter and returned it to its envelope.

"So, Señor, I've had my suspicions about Señorita Stewart all along. But just who is this, this muy buena chica? This one who has the terrible case for you? Am I supposed to be jealous?" Leonida's smile faded as Sean laughed.

"No, but you are, aren't you?"

"What makes you say that? It is nada to me how many lovers you've had." She turned her back on him. "You will do nothing but break her heart anyway. Just like you broke Señorita Stewart's and mine."

"For your information, M'Lady, the muy buena chica in question is the same ten year old ballet dancer I told you about."

"Oh."

"But as for my breaking Loretta's heart?" Sean chuckled as he shook his head.

"Sí, the woman is terribly in love with you. Don't tell me you didn't know that."

"Well, I knew she liked me a little, but in love with me?" He put his hands on her shoulders but she jerked away to glare at him.

"Are you really that stupido, Señor? Or, do you really like playing games with the feelings of the women who love you?"

"I would have to say that I'm stupid, then." He took hold of her shoulders and held on this time as she tried to pull away. "If I had any brains, I would have never left you in the first place. I aim to make that up to you any way I can. But as far as Loretta, we were never more than friends in the first place, as far as I was concerned. And I find it hard to believe that you haven't noticed the chemistry between her and Captain McDougal."

"Que? Señorita Stewart and Señor McDougal? Sí, I knew he was in love with her, but her with him? He is old enough to be her father." She crinkled her eyebrows at him.

"Yes, and your father is a wee bit older than Mrs. Carpenter, also, and that hasn't stopped them."

"That is different."

"How so? Because he is your father?"

"Sí, and Señora Carpenter is a friend of mine, and we have both lost our husbands."

"I thought Loretta was your friend also."

"She is, but the situation between my father and Señora Carpenter is entirely different from you and, and Señorita Stewart."

"But we were not discussing me and Loretta, my dear Doña. We were discussing her and Captain McDougal, were we not?"

"Sí." Her green eyes darted away from him. "I'm...you have me confused."

"About my feelings for her? Or, my feelings for you?"

"Neither." He grabbed hold of her arm as she jerked away.

"Oh, no you don't. You're not going to get away so easy this time, M'lady."

"You let go of me. You're hurting my arm." She tried pushing him away, but he pulled her close and kissed her roughly, almost crushing her lips. She gave him a resounding slap as he released his grip on her. "Don't you ever do that again."

The words had no more escaped her mouth when he grabbed her again in a bear-hug. His lips kissed her cheeks, eyebrows and ear as they sought to find her lips on the struggling, darting face.

"You let me go, you...cerdo. I'll scream."

"Go ahead. Call me whatever you want, my dear," Sean stopped to stare into her angry face, "but you are going to listen to me this time. I've apologized enough for hurting you, and I've told you that you are going to have to drive me off your property, because I'll not leave you again. And I'll be damned if I'm going to spend the rest of my life trying to explain my relationship with Loretta Stewart, or any other woman I might be friends with. I can't help what you think her feelings are toward me. That is how it is. Do you understand me?"

"You are right about one thing, Señor. You will never leave Rancho Manantial Escondido, because I am going to have Ildefonso Baca kill you the first chance I get."

"Really?"

"You may believe that before anything else, Señor."

"Good. Then it won't matter if I kiss you some more." He covered her mouth with his.

"Don't! Quit. I order... Please..." The struggling eased with each kiss until she slipped her arms around his neck with a strange whimper. Her kisses came quick and heavy as she sought his mouth, cheeks and neck. He eased her to the leaves and returned the kisses.

"God, you have no idea how much I love you," he said, brushing her hair away from one cheek. "You're all I think about. I lay awake at night with this big empty spot inside. The only thing that makes it better is to hold you close."

Her lips sought his as she wrapped both arms around his neck and pulled him down on top of her.

"Leonida?" The voice came from the gate, mingled with the sound of barking dogs.

"Papa!" She bolted upright.

"Leonida!" It was followed this time by the sound of vaqueros speaking in Spanish.

"I must go."

"Wait." He grabbed for her arm, but she pulled away.

"He must not find us here together like this. It is not right. There is no carabina."

"Hang the chaperon."

"No, I must go." The leaves crunched under her boots as she jogged·up the hill.

"That's fine, M'lady, don't listen to the man who loves you." He chuckled. "Let's see how you explain the leaves and grass stuck to your hair."

~   ~   ~

"Señor Sean." Angela breathed heavily as she ran into the bedroom without knocking.

"It's a good thing I wasn't getting dressed, young lady."

"Your door was open, Señor." She held her breast and heaved. "Come quickly."

"Why, what's wrong?" He slipped his jacked on and grabbed for his bag.

"Rosa, it is her time."

"Okay." He closed the door and slipped an arm around the breathless girl. "You didn't run all the way up the stairs to tell me, did you?"

"Sí." She nodded.

"You'd better stop that type of foolishness, or it might be your time before it's time. Maria," he yelled as they reached the bottom of the stairs.

"I already tell her, and she and Doña Leonida have gone."

"Mmmm." He paused to stare as they reached the door. Manuel, the stableboy, already had a saddle on Cathy and was leading her to the front door where Juan's bay nervously pawned the bricks.

"You didn't ride that horse all the way from Rosa's house, did you?"

"Sí." She put one foot in the stirrup and pulled herself into the saddle. "Juan and I go to see how she is doing and find her having pains in her belly. Hurry."

"But you shouldn't do things like that. You're pregnant yourself. Get down from there."

"There is no time. Come, Rosa needs you." She turned the bay and galloped past the fountain.

"Damned crazy people anyway." He hung his medical kit from the pommel and stepped into the saddle. "What do they need a doctor for anyway?" He dug his heels into Cathy's flanks and the mule darted after the bay with a snort.

It only took Cathy a minute to warm up to the race before she began to lengthen her stride. Sean held onto his derby as the ground beneath the mule's pounding hooves became a blur. He soon caught up with and passed Angela as the small cabin owned by Tex and Rosa came into view.

"Holy Irish Saints in Heaven." He pulled the snorting mule to a halt in the yard. "It looks like Sunday Mass at St. Michael's." There were horses lining the front porch, while others roamed free, nibbling grass where they could find it. Several children chased a barking dog around a carreta, causing the ox to bellow and stagger backwards.

"Come." Angela dismounted and grabbed his arm. She said something to one of the boys in Spanish as they elbowed their way past the people lounging on the porch. The lad ran to tend to their mounts.

"Señor Sean." Maria grabbed his other arm to pull him past Juan and the expectant father crowded at the bedside. "See? I tell you he would come." She smiled at Rosa. Sean removed his coat and hat and sat on the edge of the bed to hold her hand.

"What the hell's going on around here? It looks like a bloody circus out there." He shook his head at Leonida.

"Sí, but Rosa and her husband are very popular on the rancho. Everyone wants to celebrate the birth of their son."

"How is she, Doc?" Tex leaned over his shoulder.

"Well, from the looks of things, I'd say she is about to give you that son you've been bragging about the past eight or nine months."

"Yeah, but how is she?"

Sean glanced at Rosa and they both started laughing.

"She is doing fine. Juan? Why don't you take this worried chap out on the porch with the other men and give him something to calm is nerves?"

"Sí, Señor Sean." He grabbed Tex by the arm. "Come, I think Paco has some tequila."

"You'll let me know if anything happens, won't you?" Tex struggled against Juan's grip.

"Believe me, you will be the first to know, outside of Rosa, that is." He waited until the men had left before starting his examination. He stopped as Tex poked his head back through the door.

"You need someone to heat up some water or anything?"

"What for? You don't plan on boiling your baby, do you? Go on and get out of here, man, so this young lady can finish creating a new life." He glanced up at Leonida who stood smiling in the corner.

"Is there any way we can stop his bloody interruptions?"

"I'll think of something, even if I have to have Paco tie him to a post."

"Now, how are we doing, young lady?" He turned his attention back to Rosa as Leonida left the room.

"Ow, it hurts, Señor Sean." She crinkled her brow as another pain gripped her.

"Aye, but it will be worth it, lass. Once you hold that little one to your breast, you'll soon forget all about the pain."

~   ~   ~

The baby was taking its time coming into its new world, so Leonida decided to join those gathered on the porch. Several of the women had set up temporary kitchens on the front lawn and were preparing a feast while others were still arriving. Pedro Manzo was turning the crank as a side of beef roasted over a fire. Ramon Segoviano expertly backed a carreta into the yard loaded with several kegs of wine and brandy. Others were busy tuning their instruments. Rosa's child was going to be welcomed into the world with a grand fiesta. Leonida felt a strong arm around her shoulders as her father leaned to kiss her cheek.

"Ah, but it is a happy time, Niña. There is nothing that causes the heart to sing like the birth of a new son or daughter."

"Sí." She hugged him with both arms. "Were you this happy when I was born?"

"Oh, you don't know the half of it. For one thing, my friends and brothers were all gathered in the next room toasting your arrival before you had actually come. As you know, you have eight uncles, and that is not counting my friends. I'm afraid to admit it, but by the time you came into this world, I was about ready to leave it, at least for awhile. But when I held you in my hands," he turned both palms upward and slowly shook his head, "I knew I was holding

284

the most beautiful child in the whole world. You were a gift from Dios. I sat on the bed with you in my hands and cried."

"Oh Papa, I love you." She buried her face against his chest.

"The only thing that could make me happier would be for you and that gringo doctor to decide to quit fighting and get married so I can hold my grandsons the same way."

"I have already told him that I will marry him, Papa. But, he's got a lot of changing to do before that can ever happen." She gave him a crooked frown.

"What about you, Niña? Don't you have to change too?"

"Que? You just said I'm perfect." Her laughter was cut short by the crying of a baby from inside the house. She only stared at her father for a second before bolting toward the door. Maria stood blocking the bedroom door. The sound of hurried footsteps sounded like cattle as people crowded behind her.

"Uno momento, Doña, Señor Kilnenney is making sure Rosa is okay."

"What's wrong Maria?" Tex pushed through the crowd to bump into Leonida.

"Nothing is wrong, Señor Tex. The doctor is just cleaning them up."

"Okay, Maria." The maid smiled at the sound of Sean's voice and held up one finger.

"Just Doña Leonida and Señor Tex first. The other's will have to wait."

Leonida stepped through the door as her father voiced his complaint about being kept outside. Sean was handing the angry child to its smiling mother as Tex rushed to the opposite side of the bed.

"How you doing, Honey?" He leaned to kiss Rosa on the forehead before glancing up at Sean. "Let me have a look at my boy, Doc."

"I hate to be the bearer of bad news, my friend," Sean chuckled, "but your son is actually a girl."

"No, really?"

"Yes, a beautiful girl, just like her mother. And," he leaned over to kiss the tiny head, "I'm taking the pleasure of being the first man to kiss you, M'lady."

"She is beautiful." Leonida leaned over Sean's shoulder to stare at the tiny face. "Thank you, Doctor. Thank you very much."

"You're welcome, but I didn't do much. I just watched while Rosa did all the work. And you did extremely well, young lady." He leaned to give Rosa a peck on the cheek.

"Hey, now. That's enough of kissing my women," Tex scowled.

"I'll check on you later." He winked at Rosa. Leonida followed him through the door as her father and Hanky took their places. He stretched and arched his back before accepting the cup of coffee offered by Angela. She waited until he had answered their questions before taking a seat beside him on the steps.

"I want to thank you for being a friend to my people. I know you don't have to stay here and do these things. You could be making a lot of money in San Francisco."

"Again, you're welcome, but I'm here because I want to be. And I think you know why, don't you?" He eyed her over the rim as he took a sip of coffee.

"Sí, my father says we should stop arguing and get married." Sean almost choked on the coffee and had to wipe his lips on his sleeve before setting the cup on the steps.

"No kidding?"

"Sí, he says he wants to hold his grandchildren in his hands, like Señor Hanky is doing right now. What do you think? Is this possible?" He stared at her a long minute before laughing.

"Well, yeah, it's very possible. That's why I asked you to marry me. I believe I've received your father's blessing...sort of. It's what I've always wanted."

"I did not think this was such a funny matter, Señor. I was trying to be serious."

"I didn't mean to laugh, you just took me by surprise. I mean, what's gotten into you? I've never heard you talk this way before."

"Nothing has gotten into me. You asked me once to marry you, and I said yes. But we always wind up arguing, so I asked if it was possible. But you are laughing at me as though you find the subject humorous."

"Oh, come on now," she pulled away as he reached for her hand, "quit being silly."

"I am not silly." She leaped to her feet. "This is exactly what I was trying to explain to my father. We can't have a decent conversation without one of us getting angry. Have a good day, Señor, and thank you again." She could hear him mumbling something about a bloody-hard-headed woman as she walked away.

Chapter 30

Salty Moran eased deeper inside the closet as his hand found the knife strapped to his belt. He slowly exhaled as Darrell Rodeen tossed the jacket across one of the chairs and struck a match.

"Oh, dammit." He almost dropped the hot globe from the lamp. He stuck the scorched fingers inside his mouth as he lit the wick, then replaced the globe and adjusted the flame. "Idiot musta just left." He checked his watch. "That means he was late for his poker game." He took his time pouring himself a drink and making himself at ease in James Sattler's chair. He propped his feet on top of the desk and hoisted his glass. "Here's to you, Jimmy boy. Hope you lose your ass." He downed the drink and closed his eyes.

It seemed an eternity before the man's chin began to droop and the sound of his snoring drifted toward the closet. Salty eased the door open. He had only taken two steps toward the main office door and freedom when it swung open and the huge frame of James Sattler loomed before him.

"What the hell..." James' words were cut short as Salty snatched the brass spittoon from the floor and swung it in an arch that ended on the large man's head. He fell back through the doorway with a whimper of pain.Salty then leaped toward the desk, swinging the spittoon as Darrell jerked upright from his sleep. The brass gave a dull ring and the sleepy man pitched over backward as the strange weapon smashed against his nose. Salty bolted through the door, pausing long enough to kick Sattler in the groin as he struggled to his feet. He could hear the man groaning as he descended the stairs to the street in three or four bounds. The fresh air felt cold and inviting as he wove his way through the crowded street. The fog had begun rolling in and that would make his escape even easier. He would have to find a new disguise. Sattler had seen the old hunchbacked beggar as he swung the spittoon. He pulled his jacket tighter, causing the file to press against his chest. "It'd better be worth it," he mumbled. "That was a lot of work, if there's nothing inside worth seeing.

~   ~   ~

"Christ almighty." Sattler staggered to lean one hand against the desk as the other clutched his crotch. "What the hell's going on here?"

"Damned if I know." Darrell crawled to his feet as blood dripped through the fingers covering his nose. "I was asleep in your chair. Who the hell hit me?"

"Watch it," Sattler said as several drops of blood landed on the desk. "Get a towel, or something." He waved a hand toward the counter holding a pitcher of water and a bowl. "Oh, damn, that hurts." He slid to the floor.

"Who was it?" Darrell repeated as he held the damp towel to his face.

"I don't know. Some deformed beggar that had asked me for money earlier on the street. What was he doing in here anyway?"

"Hell if I know. Something to steal, more'n likely." Darrell tilted his head backward in an effort to stop the bleeding. "Musta snuck in here while I was dozing."

"We'd better look around and see if anything is missing." Sattler struggled to his feet with a groan. "I guess we'd also better start locking the doors behind us after business hours. Damned town is filling up with nothing but thieves and cutthroats." He glanced up from checking the desk drawers as Darrell started laughing. "What's so funny?"

"What the hell do you think we are?" Darrell plopped into one of the chairs and laughed harder.

~   ~   ~

"Interesting, very interesting." Walter Norton thumbed through the file marked Garcia, Leonida. "I don't actually see anything out of the ordinary, but I'm no judge or lawyer either. You'd better have Judge Baker take a look at this. He might be able to find something that we can't."

"That's where I'm headed after I leave here," Salty said.

"What are you going to tell him when he asks how you happened to get hold of this file? Breaking and entering is against the law, you know."

Salty looked up from a pan of black dye where he had been tinting his gray hair. "I'll tell him I bought it off a hunched-backed tramp. I don't know... The poor bloke more than likely stole it, thinking he could make enough to buy a bottle of rum. So I gave him five dollars."

"Buying stolen property isn't exactly legal either." The Pinkerton glanced at him over the rim of his glasses.

"Yeah, I know. But I just figured the judge might want to see to it that Sattler gets the file back in tact, seeing as he just happens to be the one presiding over Mrs. Garcia's case."

"You're good. Very good." Walter Norton went back to scanning the file. "By the way, you missed a spot on the back of your neck. There is a big blob of gray saying look at me, look at me."

~   ~   ~

"I'm very sorry. I hope you will forgive me." Loretta came back to the parlor holding her handkerchief to her lips. She had suddenly felt nauseated and had to excuse herself in the middle of having tea with Dorothy Baker and several of her friends. Even now, the toasted bread sticks with butter and jam seemed to swim on the plate in front of her. "I don't know what's come over me. These past few mornings, I have simply felt awful." She closed her eyes and took a deep breath.

"Mmmm, and how long did you say you and Captain McDougal have been married, my Dear?" Helen Phillips, a heavy-set woman with graying hair adjusted her glasses.

"Two months, almost to the day."

"Yes...," she drawled and smiled at the others. "What do you think, Dorothy?"

"It might be a little early to speculate, but that is a possibility." Dorothy raised her eyebrows.

"What is? What are you talking about?" Loretta glanced around at the smiling faces.

"Helen thinks you might be pregnant." Dorothy smiled.

"Pregnant? No, I couldn't," she laughed then stared wide-eyed, "could I?"

"Things like that do happen, especially when we're young and newly wedded." Helen adjusted her glasses a second time. "It happened to me five times, so I think I have a little experience in the matter."

"What's the matter, Dear? Don't you want to have children?" Charlene Johnson placed a hand on her arm.

"Oh, well yes, several. I just never thought it could happen so soon. I took it for granted it would happen in a year or so, not right now."

"Well, you might not be, so I wouldn't worry too much about it." Dorothy grinned. "You could very well be fighting some mild sickness, for all we know."

"How long has it been since your time of the month has occurred?" Helen asked before crunching another bite of toast dripping with butter and jam. The sight caused Loretta to close her eyes.

"Ah, just before Jonathan and I were married. But I've always been irregular, so I didn't think much about it."

"Mmmm, drink some more tea with lemon, Dear. It will help settle your stomach," Helen said between crunches.

"No, thank you. I'll just sit here awhile, if you don't mind. Are you sure?" She added, "I'd hate to tell Jonathan, and then have it not be true. He does love children so."

"I'll tell you what you do." Dorothy leaned forward and smiled. "You keep it a secret for another month or so, and by then you will know if it's true or not. In the mean time, we girls will be planning the biggest party you ever saw."

"Thank you," Loretta said as they chattered about what they would do at the party. *Just don't have any toast dripping with butter*, she closed her eyes as Helen took another bite.

~   ~   ~

"Where in the world is she?" Michelle LeVoe paced back and forth in front of the stage. Lucile Hocking, the piano player, was a half an hour late for practice and the clock was still ticking. The dancers had already finished their warm up and were beginning to wander around the stage aimlessly.

"Okay, okay." She clapped her hands. "We will run through the routine without the music. Perhaps Mrs. Hocking will arrive later and can pick up where we are."

"Oh, man, that's hard," one of the girls complained.

"Why don't you ask my momma or Mrs. McDougal to play for us?" Clara said.

"Oh, no." Dorothy Baker shook her head. "Loretta is a much better player than I am."

"Mrs. McDougal?" Michelle glanced at Loretta seated on the front row next to Dorothy. "Would you mind?"

"Oh, they're just bragging a little. I can't really play that well." She grinned and shook her head.

"Mmm-humm, she plays for me all the time when I practice at home," Clara said. Michelle stared at the primly dressed woman for a long minute before clearing her throat.

"Mrs. McDougal, Clara and her mother both disagree with you. Besides, it would just be until Lucile arrives. Think of the children. You wouldn't want them to waste a whole practice, would you?"

"Go on." Dorothy gave her a shove on the arm. "You're the piano player. I was never that good. I simply plunk on the keys."

"Quit acting silly. You play the piano wonderfully." Loretta patted her on the arm.

"Not as good as you. Now, go play for the girls. At least until Lucile arrives."

"Okay, but don't expect too much. I'm a little rusty." Loretta gave a crooked grin as she got up from her seat. She seated herself at the piano and removed her gloves.

"Are you familiar with Bach?"

"A little."

"Good. We'll start with this section right here." Michelle pointed to the sheet music. "Cantata number 26, the opening chorus."

"All right," she stared at the sheet music, "I think I can do this. Clara and I have gone through this piece at her house." It only took a moment before her fingers were flowing up and down the keys. She glanced up to see Clara hovering at the edge of the stage with a huge grin.

"Wonderful, my dear. Why didn't you tell me you could play earlier?" Michelle patted her on the shoulders. "Okay, everyone," she clapped her hands toward the girls on stage, "we are going to go over the part everyone had trouble with yesterday. Places everyone, places."

"Excuse me. I wasn't here yesterday. What am I supposed to be playing?" Loretta shrugged.

"Oh, I'm sorry. Cantata number 208, Was Mir Behagt, the soprano aria." She waited until all the dancers had scampered to their positions before raising both arms and nodding at Loretta like a true conductor.

She had lied. She was very familiar with the opera, having held the part of lead soprano several years before coming to California. Her fingers seemed to take on a mind of their own as her eyes scanned the notes. She began humming the words at first, and then singing them softly. She forgot herself by the time they were halfway through the piece. She was once again eighteen years old and on center stage at the opera house in Long Island as the orchestra played. The full skirts of her costume rustled as she stepped forward to sing her part. Her entire soul and being filled with the words as they flowed from her tongue. Then it was over, and she was staring at the silent stage as Michelle LeVoe and the dancers stared back.

"Oh, my gosh, I'm sorry." One hand covered her mouth as the other grabbed for her gloves. The piano stool crashed to the floor as she darted toward the exit.

"Wait, somebody stop that woman," Michelle yelled. An old man with gray hair and matching stubble suddenly appeared, blocking her way.

"Excuse me." Loretta tried going to the right, but the arm holding the mop bucket stopped her. "Please let me by." He held up the wet mop as she tried the left.

"I'm sorry, but Mrs. LeVoe is calling."

"Please." She glanced over her shoulder, then covered her face as Michelle LeVoe and Clara Baker scampered down the aisle toward them.

"Thank you, Paul, for stopping this angel," Michelle said, placing both hands on her shoulders. "Come my dear, we must talk."

"No." Loretta kept her face covered as she shook her head.

"No? Why not? We must talk. Come." She tugged on her arm.

"No, I'm afraid there's nothing to discuss." She straightened her back, took a deep breath and smiled. "I have no idea what came over me, but I'm sorry for spoiling your rehearsal. I'd rather not go back there and face those children right this moment. I know Clara will forgive me, but facing the others might be a little embarrassing."

"Spoil our rehearsal, and embarrassing? Do you have any idea what she is talking about, Clara?"

"No." She shook her head. They were suddenly surrounded by the rest of the dancers, urging them back toward the stage.

"My dear, you should have seen them dance while you were singing. They were angels celebrating the heavenly music from above. You must sing for us. I will not take no for an answer."

"No, I'm afraid I can't. It would be taking away from Clara and the rest of the children. They've worked so hard. I simply couldn't do that to them. Besides, I'd have to ask my husband first, and we're supposed to be leaving San Francisco any day now, and you really don't know anything about me. I get terrible stage fright. I simply can't." The excuses kept coming even after they had seated her next to Dorothy on the front row.

"Are you finished my dear?" Michelle smiled.

"You haven't listened to a word I said, have you?"

"Absolutely not. You may take your place at the piano anytime you wish. Places everyone," she clapped, "places."

Chapter 31

Bear could hear her coming long before she reached the spot where he was sitting on the creek bank. "Catch anything, Francis?"

"Na, don't guess they're hungry. Sit yerself down, Ma'am." He brushed the leaves off one of the rocks with his huge hand. "And just call me Bear, ifin' ya don't mind."

"Okay, Bear." Ruby perched herself on the rock and wrapped both arms around her knees. She stared at the gurgling stream a long minute before smiling. "But I kinda like Francis myself. I think it's cute."

"Ya do?"

"Yeah, I do." She smiled and turned back to watching the water.

"Thanks. I like Ruby Fay, too. I think its purdy and suits you real good."

"Really?"

"Yeah. I hope you don't mind me saying so, Ma'am, but you're just about the purdiest woman I've ever seen."

"No, I don't mind." She laughed. "But I think you've been out in the sun too long. There's a lot of prettier women than me right here on this ranch. Take Mrs. Garcia, for instance. Then there's Rosa and Angela. And don't forget Loretta Stewart. She's awful pretty."

"Well, I ain't for running none of those women down when it comes to looks, 'cause just like you said, they're sure enough purdy. But your looks suit me just fine. I've always liked red hair and freckles, and you got 'em both. Whether you know it or not, the good Lord made you just about as perfect as He could."

"Boy, for such a big guy, you're sure romantic, aren't you, Francis?"

"I'm sorry, Ma'am," he turned back to his fishing, "I shouldn't a been saying such things."

"No, I didn't mean it like that." Ruby laid a hand on his arm. "What I meant was, it's unusual for a big strong man like you to be saying such pretty things to a girl. I liked hearing them, it's just that," she shrugged, "I don't deserve it."

"Oh, no, don't say that, Ruby Fay." He shook his head. "What you didn't deserve was being stuck in that hell-hole in Dogtown and being treated the way you were. Ain't no one deserving of that kind of treatment, especially someone as nice as you. You got a good heart. I know that." He finished with a nod.

"Well, I'm afraid if I've got any heart left, it's as hard as this rock I'm sitting on." She patted the chunk of granite. "Let's don't forget I'm a whore. If you lined up all the men who's seen me, they'd probably make a line completely around this rancho."

"Now, you're not making any sense at all, if you don't mind me saying so." He laid the cane pole between them and shifted to take hold her hand. "It's a mighty big ranch Mrs. Garcia has here, and it'd take a whole lot of men to do what you just said. Besides that, you used to be a whore, but you ain't no more, because it's been more'n a month since that saloon's been closed for anything more than holding court. The way I see it, your being a whore is kind of like your cough. You used to have it, but it's mostly gone now. In another week or so, you'll completely forget you ever had it."

"Oh, I think my past is a little worse than that." She tried pulling her hand away, but he held it tight. "There was a time I used to pray it would go away like a bad cold or something, but it never did. I used to lie awake at night, because when I closed my eyes, I could see them coming. A huge line of men, all leering and laughing, putting their hands all over my body until it didn't matter any more. I just stopped feeling. Then I stopped praying. I don't believe I have much of a heart anymore." She gave him a crooked smile and shrugged.

"Don't you think the Lord heard none of your prayers?"

"Hell no," she laughed, "or I wouldn't of been stuck in that back room."

"You ain't stuck there now, are you? Ambrose has done been sent to his grave, and you got about a million folks right here on this ranch who love you to pieces. And I've done pledged to look after you the rest of my born days. If that ain't answering your prayers, I don't know what is, Ruby Fay." She stared at him until her eyes began to moisten.

"Well, if he was going to answer my prayers, he coulda acted a little quicker. That brings me to another question. Why are you treating me so damned nice? What did I ever do to you that makes you think you've got to be my keeper? I don't recall ever going to bed with you."

"You didn't." He shook his head. "I'd a never done nothing like that to you, Ruby Fay. I wanted to take you out of that place from the first time I laid eyes on you. I know'd back then, when I first come to Dogtown, that you didn't belong there, and I would of, but I didn't have no money or no way of taking care of you. After I went off to Sacramento, the Lord blessed me with some good luck, and I've got me a little something now. I've got plans of building me a ranch similar to this one in Utah or Arizonie. The only reason I come back this way was to see if you wouldn't go with me. You wouldn't have to marry me right away, if you didn't want to. You could have your own room and everything. And if you didn't want to marry me a'tall, you wouldn't be beholdin' to. You could stay there and be my friend, or just mosey down the road. But at least you'd be shed of Dogtown, 'cause you don't deserve to be treated that way."

"You could probably get a dozen girls to go with you, and all of them would marry you in a heartbeat. Why me?"

"Well, like I was saying..." His gaze seemed to drift everyplace but Ruby's face.

"Francis, look at me. Are you trying to say you love me?"

"I guess I am, Ma'am."

"Why don't you just say it, then?"

"Cause it's kinda hard. You're so gosh-darned purdy and I'm..."

"The nicest man in the world." She hugged and kissed his hand. "I'd love to go with you to build your ranch, but I can't. I'm on trial for killing Ambrose, remember? I'm sorry for hurting you, Francis, but I just can't go. They might hang me real soon."

"Oh, quit talking foolishness. You didn't kill Ambrose and everyone knows it."

"What makes you so sure of that? Hanky and the judge believe I did."

"Naw, they ain't stupid, and neither am I. In the first place, you're kinda like me, Ruby Fay. You like things laid out real simple-like. You could have killed him anytime you wanted during the past two years, and yet you didn't. And if you was gonna kill him, you wouldn't have used that knife. Just like Hanky says, anyone could tell that you was scared of him, 'cause he used to slap you around some. So, you wouldn't of gotten close enough to use the knife, because he might have taken it away and hurt you. Naw, if you was gonna kill Ambrose, you woulda done it like me. You woulda taken that scattergun out from under the bar and blowed him into next year. That's what you would have done."

"Well," Ruby said after a long minute. "I guess I can't argue with you. You seem to have it all figured out inside that head of yours. You don't believe I'm guilty at all, do you?"

"Nope, not a'tall." He shook his head.

"But what if I am?"

"You ain't, 'cause me and Hanky got together with Irish, and we all have got an idee who done it, and it ain't you."

"No, I don't believe that." She shook her head slowly.

"It's the truth. Why would I lie to you, Ruby Fay? The thing is, you know who done it too."

"Well, even if what you say is true, don't forget I'm still the town whore. You'll have a hard time making that jury of Mormons believe I'm anything but guilty. They'll more than likely hang me no matter what you, or Hanky, or Dr. Kilkenney says."

"I'll admit they're pretty much for upholding the law, but there ain't no way I'm gonna let them hang you, especially fer something you didn't do."

"Yeah, I'm well aware of that," she nodded, "but I don't know how you're going to stop it." They sat silently for a long minute watching the trout swim lazily past the worm on Bear's hook in the clear stream.

"Well, if they don't hang me, still wanna take me to Utah when this is all over? You know I don't really love you like you want. I don't know if I can ever love anyone that way."

"Ruby Fay, I'd take you to China if you wanted to go." He turned to squeeze her in a bear-hug.

"Hey, you got one," she squealed as the pole suddenly leaped from the rock and into the stream.

"Great God Almighty." He splashed through the water.

"Hurry!" She clapped and giggled as the huge man chased after the darting pole.

~   ~   ~

"I can't do that, and you know it." Loretta jerked the dressing gown from the hanger and flung it across the bed.

"Why not? I think it would be a perfect chance for you to show your talents to this city." Jonathan smiled as he filled two glasses with brandy.

"Huh, San Francisco has seen more than enough of Loretta Stewart's talents. No, thank you."

"Perhaps, if that is how you think of yourself," he handed her one of the glasses, "but I don't recall as they've seen the talents of Loretta McDougal yet. Have they?"

"Why are you so intent on me getting up in front of a bunch of people to sing?"

"Because, I love you and I love to hear you sing. You have a lovely voice, my dear." He toasted her before taking a sip from the glass.

"I'll sing for you anytime and any place. Just not in front of a bunch of people at that opera house."

"And why not?"

"Because, as if you haven't figured this out yet," she sat on the edge of the bed rolling the brandy glass between her palms, "too many people know about me here. It wouldn't take long for them to realize that the woman on stage with those lovely dancers is one of the whores from The Silver Slipper."

"Now, you've offended me." He set the glass on the table and stared at her for a long minute. "Look at me. Come on, take a good look. Do I look like the type of person who would allow his wife to prostitute herself?"

"No, but you knew I was a whore when you married me. Remember? I tried to talk you out of it."

"No, as I recall, you were staying at Leonida's rancho when I asked you to marry me. I had no reason to believe you were in the process of prostituting yourself there amongst the vaqueros."

"You, my dear husband, are so full of horseshit it isn't funny. You told me yourself, that you used to go sit in the back of The Silver Slipper and listen to me sing. You've known all along that I used to work there and what I was required to do." Loretta wiped her nose with the back of her hand and took a gulp of brandy.

"Yes, and the key words are used to. You used to work there, but you don't anymore. You're my wife, and I love and respect you more than you'll ever know. Perhaps with God's help, someday you'll learn to do the same." The knock at the door brought a moan from Loretta. "By the way," he paused with his hand on the doorknob, "horseshit is not a proper term for a lady to use."

"I hate to be bothering you, Captain, but Judge Baker would like to see you and Lady McDougal both first thing in the morning, if possible." The small man with dark hair, glasses, three-piece suit and brown derby leaned casually against his cane.

"I believe that's possible. Come on in, Salty." Jonathan opened the door wider. "Care for a drink?"

"Ah, yeah, thanks." His smile fell. "Is it that noticeable, I mean that you can recognize me right away?"

"Mmmm, I don't know." Jonathan handed him the glass. "I did, but I don't know how many other people will."

"How about you, M'lady? Do you think Jim Sattler or Darrell Rodeen will know who I am if they see me?" Loretta frowned as she studied the change of costume.

"Probably not. Not at first anyway. It's your voice. You sound like a sailor. Try changing your accent to say, more New England or proper English. And why do you keep referring to me as Lady McDougal or M'lady?"

"I'm sorry, M'lady, but it wouldn't be fitting for me to speak of you any other way." Salty shook his head.

"Why?" her eyes darted to Jonathan and back again.

"Because you're married to the captain here."

"Yes, and that makes me the captain's wife. But Lady McDougal or M'lady sounds rather formal, don't you think?" Loretta snickered and took another sip of brandy.

"Yes, as well it should be, for a Baroness."

"A what?" She choked on the brandy and had to cover her mouth to cough.

"I take it this pirate never told you about his being a Lord. He was knighted for bravery before sailing off to make a second fortune here in America."

"No, he only told me his family owns a small cottage in Scotland, where his mother and brother are presently staying." She stared at Jonathan who calmly sipped his brandy.

"Well, maybe I should tell you something about this husband of yours. He comes from a long line of nobility. His father happens to be a Baron and that small cottage happens to be a castle. So, that makes you a future Baroness, M'lady." Salty raised his glass and bowed.

"It's only a small castle and doesn't amount to very much." Jonathan gave her a crooked grin.

"A small castle with a lot of land and servants, if you don't mind my saying so. Sort of like Mrs. Garcia's place in a different sort of way." Salty tossed down the rest of his drink and handed the empty glass to Jonathan. "But, to answer your question, M'lady. You married a Lord, and that makes you a Lady. Now, if you'll excuse me, Lady McDougal, I'll bid you and your husband a good night." He bowed gracefully and backed toward the door.

"The judge says nine o'clock will be fine, Captain."

"Tell him we will both be there, Salty. Good evening."

Loretta stared at the door long after the little man had gone.

"Still feel like a whore, my dear?" Jonathan freshened her glass of brandy.

"No. I don't know how I feel. Is what he said true? Are you a Baron, and does that make me a Baroness?"

"I'm afraid so." He chuckled and took a seat at the table. "Future speaking, that is. My father's the actual Baron. I'm just a simple Lord."

"Why didn't you tell me?"

"Why? Would it have made any difference?"

"Maybe. I don't know if I would have had the courage to marry a Lord."

"Exactly." He hoisted his glass in a salute. "Besides, I've never taken much stock in names or titles. They're all sort of stuffy, don't you think?"

"But Jonathan, don't you see what you've done?" She knelt at his knees. "I don't want to disgrace your family. What are they going to think when they find out who you married."

"Great Queen of Scots." He burst out laughing. "My darling wife, do you think the fame of Loretta Stewart and The Silver Slipper has actually reached the shores of Scotland? I have my doubts that it has reached beyond the outskirts of San Francisco. Think of what you're saying, my love. Absolutely no one knew about you, outside of me and that Irish doctor, when you were at Leonida's ranch. Am I right?"

"Not entirely. Rosa suspected what I was the first time we met. She claims one whore can tell another whore simply by the way they act. I just don't want to disgrace you, Jonathan." She laid her head in his lap.

"Well, what are we going to do about it then? Do you want a divorce?"

"Heavens, no." She snapped her head upward.

"Okay, I wouldn't have given you one in the first place. So, I recommend that you forget about the past, and start thinking of yourself as my wife. Is it a deal?"

"I love you so much." She threw her arms around his neck and covered his face with kisses. The dressing gown never quite made it to her body and was tossed carelessly to the floor. She slept peacefully, tangled in the sheets with her long limbs wrapped around her husband's body.

Chapter 32

"I still think it is the stupidest idea that either of you have ever had." Loretta paused her pacing to glare at the two people seated on the sofa. They had conspired against her and now had her cornered inside her own apartment, trying their best to talk her into singing during Clara's dance recital.

"But, Lady McDougal, all I ask for is one little song. The rest of the program will consist of the children dancing." Michelle LeVoe leaned forward to plead with her.

"Bach's Cantata number 209 is not a little song by any stretch of the imagination. Besides, the performance is only two weeks away and there is no way I could be ready by that time."

"You're ready now. The way you sang during the practice was perfect. Besides, I'm not asking you to sing the whole cantata. Just one little part." She turned toward Jonathan. "You're her husband. You tell her."

"Michelle's right, my dear. You sing like an absolute angel."

"How would you know? You were not even at the practice. Besides, even if I did choose to sing, it would be like stealing from the children who've worked so hard. How would they feel, seeing me get up there on stage with the audience staring at me, instead of watching them?"

"You wouldn't have to be on stage with them. In fact, I can see it in my mind right this minute." Michelle stared at the ceiling and moved her palms as if she were smoothing a rumpled picture. "The children would be on center stage dancing like the angels they are, and you would be standing lower," her eyes dropped toward the rug, "standing just above the orchestra pit. Your voice would blend with the violins to stir the hearts of the audience."

"You are so full of it," Loretta snickered and shook her head. "Every eye in the audience would instantly turn toward me the minute I opened my mouth and you know it. Besides, look at me, both of you." She bent forward and pointed toward her lips. "I am not going to sing. Got that?"

"Yes, Dear," Jonathan said as Michelle nodded. That was ten o'clock Saturday morning. Loretta decided to celebrate her victory with a day of shopping. After a light breakfast of dry toast with her morning tea, she took time making sure her hair was piled on top of her head just right. She topped it off with a green hat to match her green and cream color dress and powdered her nose and neckline. Then, grabbing her handbag in one hand, and Jonathan's arm with the other, she headed toward the lobby where they were met by the entire dance troupe.

"Thank God you're here." The man behind the counter scampered to greet them. "I was just going to send for you. They refuse to leave without seeing you, Mrs. McDougal."

"Did you know about this?" She glared at Jonathan who simply shrugged and tilted his head to one side.

"Loretta, pleeeeease sing for us." Clara Baker grabbed hold of her hand. She was instantly engulfed by pleading children. She spied Clara's parents near the door with Michelle LeVoe, grinning.

"You are going to pay for this, Jonathan McDougal. Mark my words - you are going to pay dearly," she hissed through clenched teeth.

"Yes, Dear."

~   ~   ~

The notes from the violin section filled the room as Michelle LeVoe smiled and blew her a kiss from behind the curtain. After only two weeks of practice, Loretta stepped forward. She could see Clara Baker and several other dancers from the corner of her eye as they seemed to drift across the stage. The conductor gave her a short nod, letting her know her part was only two beats away. She picked it up perfectly, projecting her clear soprano voice over the orchestra and toward the audience. The theater was packed.

The ballet would have been well attended to begin with, mostly with parents and friends of the performers and those genuinely interested in the finer arts. But Michelle had seen to it that hundreds of fliers had been printed and distributed the past two days, stating that a special appearance would be made by the beautiful Baroness from Scotland. The appearance of a new woman anywhere in California would have caused a disturbance, where the male population was more than ten times the female, and San Francisco was no exception. Every seat was taken, with men lining the back of the theater and sitting in the aisles. She was convinced that few of the rough-clad men knew the first thing about the ballet, and cared less for the musical score. She also had little doubt that even fewer understood the words she was singing in German. But they were there, all hoping to get a glimpse of The Baroness.

It was fear of that glimpse that had caused her to balk at the chance to sing in the first place. She would have jumped at the chance if her audience had been in Denver or San Diego or Los Angeles. But far too many people had seen her in San Francisco and knew her. She could handle being called a whore, because that was exactly what she was, at least, until she met Jonathan. But she simply could not stand disgracing such a fine man. Then there was Clara and the other children she had become fond of. The thought of having some of the patrons of The Silver Slipper whistle, hoot and holler while she was singing caused her stomach to knot even now. That was why she had insisted on having her hair tinted red and wearing a costume that included a feathered mask to cover her eyes. Evidently it had worked, for there was nothing but standing applause when she had finished and stepped back to perform a perfect bow.

"You were magnificent, my child." Michelle grabbed her hands and kissed both cheeks. "Go." She motioned toward the stage. "Your audience is calling for you. Take another bow." The cheers erupted louder as she stepped from behind the curtain. She bowed once to the crowd and then graciously toward the dancers before retreating behind the curtain a second time.

"Oh, my God," she fell against Jonathan's chest, "I don't know when I've been more frightened."

"It didn't show. You were absolutely wonderful." He removed her mask to kiss her forehead. "Bach would have been proud."

They watched the rest of the ballet from the box reserved for Judge Baker and his wife. It wasn't until they were leaving the theater with Clara that they were accosted by a smiling James Sattler in front of the crowded building.

"Well, well, here she is at last. Perhaps you'd do the honor of introducing me to this lovely creature, Judge. She sings like an angel, and looks even better."

"Certainly." Samuel Baker removed his hat. "Baroness, this is James Sattler, one of our more famous solicitors in San Francisco. Jim," he nodded toward the grinning lawyer, "I'd like for you to meet Lady McDougal, of Edinburgh."

"A Baroness, eh?" He chuckled. "I'll say one thing darling, you almost had me fooled, but, just for old times' sake, I'm pleased to meet you." James took her hand and bowed with a grin.

"Sheka!" Loretta turned an angry glare toward Jonathan. "Céard siade seo amadán bagairt?"

"I'm afraid my wife doesn't understand western customs too well, Mr. Sattler. I hope you will forgive her, but she is rather offended that you would address her in such a familiar fashion, especially when she has never seen you before."

"I, I'm sorry. She looks so much like someone I used to know, that I..." James stepped back to stare. "If she isn't Loretta Stewart, the resemblance is remarkable."

"B'eg me baile, a chrói, bh' me brùth aige."

"Ban-diùc a chrói." Jonathan laughed and patted her gloved hand. "You must excuse us, but we do have to make an appearance at the cast party."

"Certainly. Pleased to meet you both." James doffed his hat with a slight bow.

"Boiteag." Loretta glared at James one last time before walking briskly toward the carriage. Several people crowded close to have her and Clara sign their programs as Jonathan held the door for them. She glanced up several times to see James Sattler staring back as she scribbled away.

"I'm glad I happened to see you, Mr. Sattler." Judge Baker stepped in front of James. "I was going to send for you in the morning, and this will save me the trouble."

"Ah yes, what is it?" James turned his attention toward the judge.

"Well, it seems that there have been some questions raised in a couple of the land grant cases you are representing."

"Such as?"

"Such as, you told the court that Mrs. Garcia is uneducated and cannot read or write. You also said that she doesn't have any documentation as to the ownership of her property."

"And?" Sattler scowled. "I believe I went all through that with you at least two or three times. What seems to be the problem?"

"The problem is, that I've found evidence to the contrary. The woman is not only educated, but she has documents concerning her ownership of that ranch coming out her ears."

"That can't be possible. Who told you that?" Sattler glanced toward Loretta who kept signing programs as though she hadn't heard their conversation.

"Never mind who told me. Just be in my office at nine o'clock tomorrow morning and bring the files with you." Judge Baker turned to leave, but paused to stare at the pale man. "Oh, and bring the Ramos file also. I'd like to go over that one with you too."

"Why? I thought we'd closed the Ramos case."

"Yes, we did, but I'd like to see it again, if you please." Samuel Baker took his wife's arm and escorted her to the opposite side of the carriage where he opened the door. Loretta waved and blew a kiss to the crowd before climbing inside.

"What were you saying to that man, Loretta?" Clara scooted close to her side as the carriage started forward with a jerk. "I didn't understand."

"Never mind, honey." She squeezed the girl's hand and stared out the window.

"She was speaking Gaelic, my dear. That's the language they speak in Scotland and Ireland where Doctor Kilkenney and I come from." Jonathan shifted to smile at her.

"Un-huh, I understood that part. I was just wondering what she said, because she looked mad enough to punch him."

"Clara!" Dorothy frowned.

"You're right. I was almost that angry." Loretta giggled. "In fact, that's exactly what I said. I was afraid if my husband didn't get me away from there, I was going to pound him real good." She nuzzled Clara's nose with her own. "He's not a very nice man."

"Mmmm, you could say that. Outside of making a reference to horse fertilizer, and calling him a maggot, that's a pretty accurate translation."

"Jonathan." Loretta elbowed him in the ribs as Judge Baker laughed. "I'm sorry, and I do hope you will excuse my husband's poor manners."

"That's quite all right, my dear." Dorothy covered her lips with a gloved hand and giggled. "I have often thought similar things about certain people myself."

"Oh, by the way, Clara," Jonathan reached behind the seat to retrieve a bundle of roses, "these are for you. They arrived with this telegram while you were dancing your heart out on stage."

"Really? Who are they from?"

"I don't know. Open the telegram and see." He grinned.

"Doctor Kilkenney!" She held the telegram to her breast and beamed. "He says he's sorry he couldn't be here tonight," she continued to scan the telegram, "but he wants us to come and visit him where he's staying on the ranch."

"Hmmm, that might make Doña Garcia jealous. Having such a pretty girl like you vying for his attention." Jonathan tweaked her nose. "By the way, I don't know exactly what it was you said to that man, Sam, but I'd say that he's scared to death," Jonathan said as the carriage stopped to allow several people to cross Montgomery Street.

"He'd better be," Judge Baker scowled, "because I'm through being made a fool of. He just might spend the next several winters inside a federal prison, if I can prove what I think has been going on. What I want you to do is find your man Salty. I'm issuing a warrant for Mr. Rodeen's arrest, and I want to see the look on his face when Salty Moran and Manuel Ramos walk through the door."

Chapter 33

"Do you know who you are talking to?" James Sattler glared defiantly across the table at Samuel Baker.

"Yes Sir, I most certainly do. I believe it is you who have failed to understand who you are addressing in such a tone. I am a Federal judge, and you are a solicitor, if I am not mistaken."

"Yes, and I'm the best damned lawyer in San Francisco. I've won more cases in court than anyone else, and I've made a lot of influential friends. I would be cautious about pushing this issue if I were you."

"That sounds like a threat to me, Mr. Sattler." Samuel grinned as he began stacking the papers in front of him.

"No, it's not a threat. It is a statement of fact. My friends will take offence at your implication that I have been less than honest. I'll have you know that I have done nothing but present my clients' cases with the utmost honesty and integrity. There's nothing I've done inside the courtroom that could be construed as dishonest. In fact," he pounded the table with his index finger, "there's never been anything I have ever done, inside or outside the courtroom, that could be considered as anything but completely honest."

"Well, I must admit that's quite a statement." Samuel raised his eyebrows and grinned. "While I'm not about to question your conduct in your private life at this point, I am questioning your conduct inside my courtroom." He grabbed one of the files and held it in the air. "Either you were lying when you said the Garcia woman couldn't read or understand English, or you haven't taken the time to get to know your client very well. In either case, that makes you a poor solicitor, and disqualifies you from her case. That is my opinion, and it will stand unless you can prove to me otherwise. I'm ordering you to turn over all documents on this, and all of your cases, so I can review them. I'm also suspending you from all court activities until we can get a ruling on your conduct by a panel of judges. You will be lucky if you get by with a simple fine and a suspended license. I'm thinking seriously of having you pay restitution to the families you've cheated."

"You can't do that. I have friends who are judges themselves. I'll talk to them. I'll ruin you if you pursue this."

"I've already discussed the matter with most of them, and they've said they will be willing to sit on the panel to review your conduct. In fact, it was your friend, Judge Carlson, who brought into question the fact that you postponed several hearings inside my courtroom, stating that Doña Garcia could not be present, when in fact," he shuffled through the stack of papers to retrieve a hotel register, "we have records showing that she was here in San Francisco on those dates."

"I had no idea she was here, if that's even true."

"You'd better be careful." Samuel pointed a finger across the table. "You're awfully close to calling me a liar. Most of these were records collected by The Pinkerton Agency, and you're welcome to call them a bunch of liars in court if you wish. They've also collected a list of witnesses that are willing to swear under oath that Mrs. Garcia told them she was here to appear inside my courtroom on those dates, and yet, my own court calendar shows you appearing on the proceeding dates, informing me that she was unavailable to make her appearances. Now, somebody is lying, and I aim to find out who. Then, there's the little fact that you said she had no records of ownership, when in fact, they were right here in this file." He shoved the folder across the table.

"How'd you get that? That's my property."

"Not any more. It is now the property of the court. That's not all." He folded his hands to glare at the angry man across the table. "I have a sworn statement from a Loretta Stewart, who you represented, that says you perjured yourself inside my courtroom. She is willing to stand up in court and say that you knew she was guilty of theft, and yet you proceeded to incriminate an innocent man and send him to prison. In return, you blackmailed her into helping you steal thousands of dollars from drunken patrons at The Silver Slipper where she was employed as a singer."

"So, that was her I saw last night in front of the theater." James snorted. "Well, I've got news for you, judge. She wasn't just a singer, she's nothing but a common whore. Now, who are they going to believe if you bring that information to a trial? Me, or a whore?"

"She's well aware that her former profession will come out, and that a lot of people will think less of her. She's also aware that she could be facing a prison sentence herself, but in spite of that, she is still willing to take the stand and tell the truth. There's also the matter of some large unpaid gambling debts belonging to you. I think you'd better do some soul-searching, Mr. Sattler. You might also think about having one of your friends represent you in court."

"Am I under arrest?"

You may consider yourself so, after you turn over your records to Mr. Jenkins, the court deputy. There will be another officer with him to whom you can surrender."

"Is that all?" James hissed through clenched teeth.

"Yes, you may go now, but I will repeat my order. You're to turn over all records to Mr. Jenkins. I've already informed him of my intentions, and you will find them waiting for you in the lobby."

~   ~   ~

"Go away, I'm sleeping." Darrell Rodeen glanced at the door through a haze and rolled over, nudging Diamond's nude body.

"Who is it?" Diamond pulled several strands of hair away with her fingers to stare at him.

"Hell if I know." The knocking at the door grew louder. "I said, go away." He jerked his head to one side and yelled, but the pounding persisted.

"Mr. Rodeen? Mr. Rodeen, this is the San Francisco Police Department. Please open the door. We need to talk to you."

"The police? What do they want?" Diamond bolted upright, clutching the sheet to her breast.

"To disturb my sleep." He rolled out of bed and grabbed his pants from the floor.

"Mr. Rodeen, please open this door."

"I said, hold your horses. I'm coming." He buttoned the pants, leaving his belt unbuckled and unlatched the door. "Whadda ya want?" He cracked open the door, which was instantly pushed open, driving him backward. Two uniformed officers entered as he staggered toward the bed.

"Are you Darrell Rodeen?" the larger of the two asked as the other closed the door.

"Yeah, what's this all about?"

"I'm afraid we have a warrant for your arrest. Please finish dressing and accompany us to the police station."

"Arrest? For what?"

"For murder. Please finish dressing. It will all be explained when we get to the station."

"Murder? Darrell?" Diamond stared wide-eyed.

"You too, Ma'am." The second man stepped forward. "We'd like for you to come with us and answer a few questions, if you don't mind. We'll turn our backs while you get dressed."

~   ~   ~

"I believe that is everything." James Sattler stood beside the empty file cabinets while Robert Jenkins taped the pasteboard boxes shut and labeled them.

"Are you sure there isn't something you've overlooked?" Walter Norton glanced around the room. The fact that a Pinkerton agent had not only accompanied them, but seemed to know the inside of his office as well as he did, raked across Sattler's nerves like a file.

"You seem to have been in here snooping around quite a bit of the time. Suppose you tell me. Do you see anything we might have missed?"

"I just thought you might like to include the envelope taped to the bottom of the desk." The blood drained from Sattler's face.

"How'd you know about that?"

"Never mind how I knew." Walter shrugged. "Would you like for me to retrieve it?"

"Suit yourself, you son of a bitch." He turned his back.

Walter laughed as he ripped the envelope loose and passed it to Robert Jenkins' waiting hand. "I believe the judge will find those interesting. They are additional i.o.u's and demands for money from his gambling partners."

"Think there's anything else he's hiding?" Robert glanced around.

"Not unless it would be the maps and legal documents taped to the back of the file cabinet." He grinned at James, who was visibly sweating. "I'd say Mr. Sattler is a strange mix of characters. On one hand, he certainly isn't above breaking the law to get what he wants. On the other, he can't seem to bring himself to actually destroy documents, even though they might incriminate him. He simply hides them here and there. Isn't that right, Mr. Sattler? The trouble is, the places he chooses to hide them in are the exact spots most investigators would think of looking."

"Go to hell."

"No, I don't think hell's the proper place for a Baptist. You can go if you choose, but I've already made my choice to go to the other place. Oh," he turned toward Robert Jenkins, "I would advise that you give this place a thorough going over once you have more time. Turn every drawer and take a look at the bottom. Look under the rug, any place where he might have stuck something. Salty Moran and I didn't have much time to see everything the night we were here." He could see James' jaw working from the corner of his eye.

"I'll make sure I do that. Thanks a lot." He rose from labeling the last box. "Ready, Mr. Sattler?"

"In a minute. I'd like to use the toilet first, if I may. It's right behind that door. You can watch, if you don't believe me."

"No, that won't be necessary," Robert Jenkins said. "Go right ahead. Just make it snappy."

"Yes, Sir. Whatever you say." He saluted.

"Doesn't think much of himself, does he?" Jenkins snickered as the door to the bathroom closed.

"Yes, he's an arrogant one all right. It's been my experience that a lot of them act that way out of anger at being caught. They don't want to take credit for their own bad behavior, so they start blaming someone else. It usually winds up being someone like you and me."

"He'll probably forget about us, and start blaming Judge Baker before this is all over."

"Hey, hurry up in there," Jenkins yelled at the door. They glanced at each other when there was no answer.

"Dammit." Jenkins pounded on the door. "Sattler? Open this door."

"Stand back." Walter Norton took one huge stride and kicked the door near the handle. It flew open with a bang as pieces of the latch rattled against the opposite wall.

"Jesus." Jenkins rushed to the open window in time to see Sattler reach the ground by using the rope tied around a drain pipe. "Who in the hell keeps a rope in the bathroom?"

"He does." Walter dashed for the front door. It was no use. The alley was deserted by the time they rounded the corner.

"Don't blame yourself." Walter held his side gasping for air. "I would have never thought of a rope inside a bathroom either. It's up to the police to catch him now."

~   ~   ~

"Hey, you're supposed to be dead. Both of you." Darrell laughed as Manuel Ramos and Salty Moran entered the room. Loretta shifted uncomfortably in her chair inside the Judges' chamber and reached for her husband's hand.

"Well, that's not exactly the response I expected, but it'll do." Samuel Baker nodded. "I take it you not only knew about their supposed untimely demise, but had something to do with it?"

"Not ol' Salty there. He jumped overboard entirely on his own. But I'd sure as hell like to know how he got out of the swift current in the middle of the night with all those snags along the bank."

"It wasn't easy, I'll tell you that. Especially pulling this boy's dead weight against the current," Salty said.

"You admit to trying to murder the Ramos boy then?" Judge Baker squinted at him.

"Well, I wouldn't quite put it that way, Your Honor. It was more like a business deal. He was in the way of Sattler closing the contract on all that property they claimed to own. He wanted him removed and paid me to do it. Salty wasn't even supposed to be there."

"A business deal? How could you possibly look at murdering someone as a business deal?" Loretta shook her head.

"Easy. It's just a job like any other. Besides, it wasn't as though I was disposing of anyone important. He's just another Mexican."

"Hold on son." Jonathan grabbed Manuel by the collar as he bolted from his chair. "Let the law take care of him."

"Let me go and I'll kill him right now." Manuel jerked against Jonathan's grip, only to have the captain lift him off the floor and drop him into one of the chairs.

"You're not big enough," Darrell said with a smirk.

"He doesn't have to be. I am." Samuel Baker got from his chair to face him. "Inside my court, it has never made any difference the color of a man's skin, or the accent on his tongue. You are being charged with the attempted murder of Manuel Ramos, and as far as I'm concerned, you have just made a full confession in front of these witnesses." He waved a hand toward the McDougals and the court recorder who was busy scribbling on his notepad. You are also being charged with the murders of Francine Jordan and Lorna Woods."

"What?" Rodeen threw his head back and laughed.

"Well, I must admit that is the first time I've had that reaction to a charge of murder," Samuel said after Rodeen had finally composed himself. "Is there any particular reason you thought that was humorous?"

"Hell yeah. You don't actually think I was the one who killed those girls, do you?"

"Mr. Moran found this jacket, bloody shirt and knife fastened to the back of your wardrobe." Samuel pulled the items from a pasteboard box and dumped them on top of the table.

"That isn't nice, Salty." Darrell grinned and shook his head. "Snooping around an old shipmate's room like that. I'm sorry to inform you that those things don't actually belong to me. Take a look at the handkerchief stuffed in the inside pocket." Samuel fished around inside both interior pockets and came up with a white handkerchief.

"This one?"

"Yeah." Darrell nodded. "Take a look at the initials. J. S., right?"

"Yes." Samuel glanced toward the staring faces in the room. "What are you trying to tell us?"

"I'm saying those things don't belong to me. They're Jim Sattler's."

"He's right." Loretta's face paled as she nodded her agreement. "James is so full of himself, he had all his handkerchiefs monogrammed."

"I told you. I didn't kill those two girls. Ask anyone. Hell, ask Diamond. She's right in the next room. I liked Francie and Lorna. They were good whores. Why would I want to kill them? That jacket and shirt belongs to James Sattler. So does the knife. He was wearing them the night he killed Francie. I was hanging onto them because I kind of figured it was like an insurance policy, if you know what I mean. Yeah, I did bop the Mexican boy in the head and toss him overboard, because Sattler paid me to. But I didn't kill any whores. Sattler did. He gets a charge outta hearing women beg and cry for mercy. He's the sick one, not me."

"You're both sick." Samuel Baker tossed the knife on the table and ran a trembling hand across his face. "May God have mercy on us all."

"Why, what's wrong, Judge? We've got them both, don't we?" Jonathan chuckled.

"No we don't." He lowered his gaze to the floor and shook his head. "I got word not a half an hour ago that James Sattler slipped out of a third story window and got away. I'm afraid," he took a deep breath and smiled weakly, "that we've allowed a killer to slip through our fingers. Now that he's carrying a huge grudge, no telling what he might do."

Chapter 34

"I don't understand why you won't let me tell them we're married. Are you ashamed to admit you married an old salty-dog like me?" Jonathan licked and sealed the envelope addressed to Doña Leonida.

"You're joking, aren't you?" Loretta paused brushing her hair.

"Well, you've never given me a reason for your secrecy." He leaned against the desk to study her.

"It was going to be my little surprise," she sat on the bed and wrapped her arms around her knees. "I actually had thought we would be returning to the ranch in a matter of days, or weeks at the most. Then," she shrugged, "it's been close to three months now, and I'm embarrassed for not telling them sooner. Does that makes sense?"

"Yes, it makes perfect sense. But, my dear," he kissed the fingers wrapped tightly around the brush, "I write about you in my letters all the time, saying how well you are doing and how lovely you are. I have a suspicion that they might think we have been living together without being married."

"Na, you don't think..." She shook her head. "Well, Sean might because he knows about... Oh, my word. What are Mrs. Garcia and her father going to think of me? Or you?"

"Huh, don't worry about me. I'm a sailor, remember? But it might have been better to tell them in the first letter, instead of waiting until now. I still haven't." He waved the envelope in front of her nose.

"You could tear that one up and write another."

"No, it wouldn't make much difference anyway. We stand a good chance of beating this letter to their ranch. We'll make a large banner to drape across our carriage saying, Loretta and Jonathan were married on the 19th of May, 1852. That should solve the mystery."

"It might, except very few people on the ranch know how to read." She giggled. "Jonathan?"

"Yes?"

"Do you really know how much I love you?"

"How much?"

"I don't know if it's possible to tell you."

"Hey," he said as tears welled up in her eyes, "I'll be satisfied if it's only half as much as I love you." She threw her arms around his neck and crushed his lips against hers.

"I'll die if you ever stop loving me."

"Impossible." He held her face between his palms and kissed her nose. "But how are you going to feel when I'm old and can't get around too good? You'll still be young and beautiful. Will you be sorry you settled for me then, Lady McDougal?"

"Oh, don't even joke that way." She leaned her head in his lap. "You're my very life. I feel so much a part of you that I want to crawl right inside of you."

He caressed her silky hair. "I'm glad you can't. If you were inside of me, I might not be able to admire your beauty. I love just watching you walk across the floor. You simply amaze me. Every small part of every little thing you do. But come on." He lifted her head to kiss her once more. "I have to mail this letter, and we have to start thinking of what we are going to take. We've accumulated quite a few things these past few months, and we'll have to store what we aren't taking to the ranch."

"All right, my husband. But first things first." She stood and began unbuttoning the silk dressing gown.

"Certainly, M'lady." He tossed the letter on the desk. "How could I have forgotten?"

~   ~   ~

"She's quite a lady, isn't she?" Sean smiled at the tiny face.

"Yes, but not so loud. You'll wake her," Leonida whispered.

"I didn't think I was that loud." His whisper matched hers.

"It doesn't take much to wake a baby. Besides, I just got her to sleep."

"You've been tending her a lot lately. Where is her mother?"

"Her mother is getting some much needed rest, and I had to fight to get to watch her. I actually had to use my status as Doña to take her from Angela. You don't know how difficult it is to hold her with all these people around." Leonida smiled at bundle in her lap.

"Yes I do." Sean scooted his chair closer. "I haven't held Martha Russell since I delivered her. Every time I see her, she's being rocked by you or Maria or Evangelina, or one of a million women on this rancho."

"Why, Doctor Kilkenney. Do I detect a hint of jealousy in your tone?" Her green eyes sparkled as she grinned.

"Well, yeah." He nodded. "She's just as much mine as anyone else's. I brought her into the world. Yet, everyone else is hogging her. She won't even know me when she gets old enough to talk."

"Here," she placed the baby in his lap, "I'll share."

"Thank you." He grinned. "Look." His eyes darted toward Leonida and back again as the tiny lips made a sucking motion in her sleep. "She's simply marvelous."

"Yes, and so are you."

"Huh?" His head snapped her way.

"I said that you are marvelous."

"I don't know what would make you say something like that."

"Because, Señor Kilkenney, it is true. You are such a mix of characters, it's hard to predict what you are going to do from one minute to the next. You dash from one end of the rancho to the other, seeing to the needs of others, while you allow your own needs to go unattended. Yet, you'll complain about the smallest of things."

"Such as?"

"Such as the way Maria cooks."

"M'lady," Sean gave her a crooked grin, "burning a beautiful beefsteak isn't a small matter. One of these days, I am going to teach her how to cook."

"Perhaps you should. She respects you. You know that, don't you?"

"So I have been told. Hey." He crinkled his eyebrows. "I've never asked, but how many of these do you want?"

"How many of what?"

"These. Babies." He nodded toward Martha.

"I've always thought five or six." Leonida shrugged. "We Mexicans believe in having large families. That is, if I ever get married again."

"What do you mean if ? We're going to get married here right soon."

"Really? I'm happy to hear that, Señor, since as you have never asked."

"What?" His sudden shift caused the baby to stir.

"Shhhh, quit being such a man."

"What do you mean I've never asked? I've told you a hundred times that I want to marry you."

"Sí, you have told me, but you've never asked, have you?"

"I most certainly have. I not only asked you, but I asked your father's permission the day of the rubeola outbreak."

"So you did. But a lady always wishes to be asked in the proper way, Señor, even if men do not care for such things." She cocked an eyebrow and turned toward the fountain.

"Okay." He cleared his throat. "Leonida, I would get down on my knees, but I can't because I'm holding a baby. But I do love you, and I would like to ask for your hand in marriage."

"Bueno." She nodded. "That is an improvement, but if that's all there is, I would still have to say no."

"No?" He caught himself as Martha jerked with a whimper. "What do you mean no," he added in a hoarse whisper.

"You haven't followed proper procedures." She looked incredulous. "You're from Ireland, Señor. Don't tell me you have forgotten the proper steps that must be followed."

"I left Ireland when I was a child, M'lady. I had never asked anyone to marry me at that time. Besides, we are in California, a whole ocean and continent away from Ireland. What difference does it make how things are done in the old country?"

"Sí, we are an ocean away, but the fact remains that you are Irish and I am Spanish. We are both educated and cultured in the old ways. These poor people we have come to live amongst have never had the privileges we've had. I know how you've struggled to become a doctor, and I commend you. My family has struggled also, during the years of war. But it is up to us to set an example and teach others how things should be, if we are to become civilized."

"Okay, refresh my memory. What is the proper way to ask a Spanish lady to marry me?"

"You must first ask my father for permission." She stared in the distance.

"Sounds reasonable. I'll ask him this afternoon. Then will you marry me?"

"No."

"Wha..."

"Because you still haven't asked in the proper way. You must first ask his permission to ask me. Then you must come and ask me if I will marry you. Then, if I say yes, you may return and tell my father. Then, he will give his consent and announce our upcoming wedding to everyone else."

"Huh, that is some of the biggest blarney I've ever heard. The way I remember it happening was, the man would ask the girl's father and he would say yes or no. The girl didn't have much to say in the matter one way or the other."

"Sí, that's the way it is done in my country also, except for one thing. I am the *Doña*, and that makes things different." She shifted to study him. "Señor, I know what I am asking might sound silly, but if I am worth marrying at all, isn't it worth just a little trouble to earn that privilege?"

"Just answer me this one thing, Doña Leonida Margarita Flores Garcia. Both of us are as stubborn as my mule, Cathy. What in the world are our children going to be like?"

~   ~   ~

James Sattler wiped the perspiration from his brow and straightened his collar. He glanced around before entering the bank to draw most of his money from both his savings and checking accounts. "Yes, I'm going to be away for awhile on business," he told the questioning teller. "I'll be needing most of this before I can close the deal."

"I'm sure we can arrange a loan, if that might help, Mr. Sattler."

"No, that won't be necessary, John." He chuckled. "I just didn't want to be caught short. You have no idea how embarrassing it is to take a client out to dinner and a night on the town, then not have enough money to pay the bill."

"I can imagine." He nodded with a smile. "Here is your money." He counted the bills. "Have a good trip."

His next stop was The Silver Slipper. He had been waiting to repay this debt since sliding down the rope into the alleyway. The man at the bar informed him that Sara Miller was in her room at the end of the hall at the top of the stairs. He rapped on the door three times with his knuckles and waited.

"Yeah, who is it?"

"Got an important message for Salty Moran."

"Salty isn't here." The door remained closed. He waited a minute before knocking again.

"Miss Miller?"

"I said Salty isn't here. Go away."

"I'm sorry, but this message isn't for Salty Moran. It's from Salty Moran. He says it's urgent." He hit her the instant the door flew open, knocking her to the floor. The stunned girl struggled to sit upright as he closed and locked the door.

"Sorry, I lied," he said with a laugh. "The message is from me to Salty. You can give it to him when he returns." He kicked her in the face as she scrambled across the floor on all fours. "The little son of a bitch should have minded his own business."

Her scream was cut short by another kick as he pulled the knife from his coat pocket.

~   ~   ~

"I'm not going to allow you to go free, but I will promise you that things will go a lot easier on you if you help us find James Sattler." Judge Baker studied the man who was lying on the cot inside the cell smoking a cigarette.

"Well, Judge, seeing as I'm in here, and he's out there, I don't see how in the hell I'm supposed to help you."

"What you say may be true, Mr. Rodeen, but you know the man's habits better than anyone else. I believe you have an idea where he might be heading next."

"Maybe." Darrell blew a smoke ring in the air.

"We just buried another girl from The Silver Slipper this afternoon. I won't bother you with the details of what she looked like after he had finished with her. Doesn't that mean anything at all to you? What if it had been that girl you are so fond of? What's her name, Diamond? Wouldn't that bother you at all?"

"Sure it would, Judge." He sat up to crush the butt in the ashtray. "And it feels like saltwater in a wound knowing he butchered Sara Miller. She was a good whore, same as the others. But seeing as I stand to be hung for trying to kill that Mexican boy, I'd kind of like to know what I'm going to get out of helping you find Sattler."

"The satisfaction of knowing you've done the right thing, for starters."

"Shit." Darrell laughed and flopped back onto the cot.

"How does not hanging sound?" Darrell sat back up. "I'm not going to promise you anything specific, but I will guarantee that you will not hang, if you can tell us anything that might help catch him."

"Okay, for starters, the fact that he killed Sara tells us he's out for revenge. He somehow feels that he's been robbed, and he's going to get back at everyone he thinks had something to do with his losing whatever he felt he had. You know," he laughed and lit another cigarette, "he actually thought he was going to become a judge someday, just like you."

"Well, let's hope people like him never get into positions of power. What else can you tell me?"

"Well, like I was saying. He's out to get even. Just create a list of people that had anything to do with your catching onto his fleecing these Mexicans. Loretta might be a good starting point." He nodded thoughtfully. "And that man she married. Keep an eye on them, because he'll pop up sooner or later wanting to cut their throats.

"Then, there's that Pinkerton agent. Tell him to watch his backside. Then, there's always you, Judge. Think about putting a couple of guards inside your own house. You see," Darrell grinned, "Jim Sattler doesn't think like you or me. If we get angry, we go after the person we feel gave us the raw deal. But when he killed Sara Miller, that was his way of getting back at Salty Moran. He knew how Salty felt about her, and he wants him to have to live with his pain for awhile. Now, back at you, he'll simply go after your wife and daughter." He chuckled as Samuel Baker's face paled.

"Is there anything else?"

"No, just make a list and start warning people to watch their backs, and put a guard next to your wife and kid."

"Thank you, Mr. Rodeen. You have been a great help."

"Don't forget when I stand inside your courtroom."

"I won't, Mr. Rodeen. I promise you, I won't."

~   ~   ~

Walter Norton exited the carriage and climbed the steps to his office two at a time. He had just enough time to clean up the few things on his desk and pick up a handful of roses at the vendor on the street corner before meeting his wife for dinner. The present, he thought as he stuck the key in the lock. He must not forget the present he had left in the top right-hand drawer of the desk. It was her birthday. Yet she was the one who was about to give him the greatest present he'd ever had. She was eight months pregnant with their first child. The lock snapped open as he caught his breath with a searing pain in his lower back.

"How does it feel knowing you're going to die, Mr. Pinkerton Agent?" Sattler wiggled the knife and laughed as Walter cried out in pain.

Chapter 35

"It's like trying to catch the devil himself." Samuel's hand trembled as he passed the glass of brandy to Jonathan. "I sent an officer to warn Walter Norton and he found the poor man lying dead on the steps of his office. The keys were still in the door."

"Oh, dear God," Loretta sobbed.

"That's why I called all of you here. I have every reason to believe that what Mr. Rodeen told me this afternoon was true. The only difference being that James Sattler seems to be one step ahead of us. That is why you see that uniformed officer in the other room. I want to keep my family as safe as possible until this thing is over. I would advise all of you," he glanced at Salty Moran sitting stoop-shouldered in a chair, "to do the same."

"Well, I hope you don't mind me saying so, Your Honor. I hope he does come to visit me." Salty's voice was a coarse whisper.

"I understand. What about you, Jonathan? You've got Loretta to think about."

"We were thinking of returning to visit Mrs. Garcia for awhile."

"Now might be a good time for that visit." Samuel rolled his unlit cigar back and forth in his fingers as he stared into space.

"How are we ever going to catch that man, if everybody goes into hiding?" Dorothy Baker glanced around the room. "I mean, we're the only ones who seem to know what he's going to do next."

"That'll be up to the police, Dear. I've already informed them of what Darrell Rodeen said, and they are busy combing this city from top to bottom." Samuel frowned as Salty chuckled.

"Begging your pardon, Your Honor, but a man could lose a shipload of monkeys in San Francisco and not find them. I I'll just hang around The Silver Slipper and make myself known. Maybe he'll get brave enough to come visit."

"You might be right about the monkeys," Samuel said. "but if Mr. Rodeen is correct, you might sit inside that saloon a lifetime before you see Sattler."

"Why's that?"

"Because, according to Rodeen, Sattler is the type of man who wants his victims to suffer long and hard. That's the reason he killed Sara Miller, so you would carry the pain of her loss for a lifetime. He warned me to post that guard to protect my wife and child, because it was his opinion that Sattler would come after them to get back at me. I believe he might go after Jonathan next, to get at Loretta."

"Well, that might make things easier then." Salty grinned. "Pass the word around that we've all headed back to the Garcia place. It might be good for you to come along for a visit too. That way, when he does decide to come after the captain, I'll be hiding in the shadows, waiting."

"That's not a bad idea, Sam," Jonathan said. "Mrs. Garcia has close to a hundred vaqueros and Indians working her place. Knowing some of them the way I do, I kind of like the idea of having them around at a time like this."

"I believe I might do that." Samuel set his brandy glass on the table. "I have a case I must preside over the next few days, but I'll send Dorothy and Clara with you, and join you in a few days."

"No, I don't want to leave you, Sam." Dorothy grabbed his arm. "That man might come when I'm gone, and hurt you."

"No need to worry, Dear." He leaned to kiss her forehead. "I'll keep Arthur and that policeman right beside me twenty-four hours a day. Absolutely nothing is going to happen to me. It's you and Clara I'm worried about."

~   ~   ~

"Sí, you may ask my daughter to marry you, Doctor." Jose nodded. "In fact," he paused to savor the aroma of the freshly lit cigar before continuing, "I've already given you permission to marry her. I wish you would marry her this afternoon." He raised his eyebrows and grinned. "That would give her someone else to argue with. The trick will be for you two to quit arguing long enough for Father Ramon to complete the ceremony."

"I got me twenty dollars that says they get hitched." Tex held the gold coin in the air.

"Ah, but Señor," Paco grinned, "I agree with the general. They fight all the time. They are like two gatos trying to make love."

"Caramba, you know nothing." Juan frowned. "It is because they are in love that they argue."

"Sí, but when they are angry, they won't speak to each other. How can they get married when they act that way? I take the bet." Paco nodded.

"Ha, you are a fool. Angela and I fight all the time and we are married. I take the bet against you." Juan pulled a coin from his pocket.

"Hey, you two. It's my future happiness you're talking about." Sean glared at them.

"Por que, Señor." Jose shrugged. "Let them make their bets and go ask Leonida. I wish you well."

Sean left the room with the intention of joining Leonida who busy playing a game of tag with several children around the fountain's edge. The sound of the general's voice drifting through the open window caused him to cringe.

"I myself will wager that they do get married, but not before having at least one more disagreement to drive them apart. The real question is, how long will it be before my first grandchild is born?"

"Huh, that's an easy one. Nine months to the day," Tex's easy drawl reached his ears. Sean shook his head as he reached the brick patio in one huge bound.

"They'd bet on their mother's soul, given the chance."

~   ~   ~

"Where have you been? Everybody's been worried sick, believing something happened to you." Arthur Farnsworth scowled as Salty stepped in out of the early morning fog and removed his stocking cap. The smell of rum and tobacco was almost overpowering.

"No need for you to worry, mate. I've been keeping myself busy spreading the word that everyone inside this house is taking a little vacation to the Garcia place."

"Indeed. Well, you'd better come on into the washroom and get presentable. Everyone have been seated for breakfast. You may inform them of your actions when you join them."

"Yeah, they'll be interested ta know that I even included you and the judge on this trip. I told everyone I could think of, so's that devil Sattler's sure to find out." He paused to stare at Loretta standing in the dining room doorway. "M'lady." He nodded as Farnsworth ushered him onward.

"Hey, Artie, me mate," he mumbled as the butler helped him with the smelly sweater. "Did ya ever see my girl Sara Walker a'fore she died?"

"No Sir, I'm afraid I never had the chance."

"Ah, too bad. I'll swear on Davie Jones' grave she was just as pretty in her own way as Lady McDougal."

"That is saying quite a lot, Sir." Farnsworth filled a basin with water and handed Salty a washrag and soap.

"It's true. Every last word." He ignored the washrag and splashed water with both hands. "She was about as nice as any woman can be."

"I'm quite certain she was, Sir, and I do offer my sincere regret as to what has taken place. Not only to her, but everyone," he said as Salty dried himself.

"Yeah, but when James Sattler decides to follow us out to Mrs. Garcia's place, I got me a little present to give him." He handed Arthur the towel. "Bought it special for him last night from a Portuguese sailor at the pier." He brushed back his hair and reached inside his boot to retrieve a knife.

"Since Sattler likes knives so much, I thought I'd give him a real good one." He grinned as he slipped the gleaming ten-inch blade from its sheath.

~   ~   ~

James Sattler took a deep breath and grinned as he watched Dorothy and Clara climb into the carriage behind Jonathan and Loretta. Salty Moran was the last to enter. Judge Baker leaned inside to give his wife and daughter a kiss before Arthur Farnsworth closed the door. A shake of the reins and cluck of the driver's tongue, and the carriage bolted forward, leaving the judge and butler standing in front of the Victorian residence in the fog.

James eyed the armed policeman standing behind them from his vantage point across the street. It would be hard getting close enough to the judge to use the knife, but no matter. He didn't actually want him to suffer physically as the Pinkerton agent had. In fact, had James known Walter Norton was married, things would have gone differently for the man. No, he shook his head. He wanted Judge Baker to suffer long and hard for causing him to lose his position and stature in this city. He turned to stroll lazily down the fog shrouded street.

The drunken sailor had passed the word from one rum joint to another along the waterfront, and on into the city. The judge was so frightened at what had happened that he was shipping his entire family off for safety. Their going to the Garcia rancho was a stroke of luck. Sattler had been on the ranch several times and had a fair idea of its layout. He also owed Doña Garcia a little something for all the trouble she had caused him. Her arrogant attitude raked across his soul. There wasn't any Mexican superior to a white man, especially one that was as educated and refined as he was. He'd see her begging for mercy before this was over, and, it wouldn't take much to get back at Loretta, either. His paces quickened as he turned on Clay Street toward the harbor.

The little whore was some actress; he'd give her credit for that. But the fact was, she was still a whore and would be rotting inside some a cell if it wasn't for him. He was the one who thought of pinning the theft on that drunk, as well as concocting the plan for fleecing those rich bastards that came to her room. Her looks had always attracted the ones with big bankrolls. He gave her credit for that also, but turning on him like she was some righteous choir member was uncalled for. She owed him double, and he might get her and that husband of hers both for good measure.

He paused to take a deep breath. The Garcia rancho was crawling with vaqueros and Indians, so it would take some work, but he already had a plan working inside his head. All he needed was a few men, and he knew just where to find them. Just dangle a little gold in front of them, and they'd be more than willing to do anything he wanted. James didn't have much left, but Leonida Garcia did. Everyone knew she had hundreds of thousands of cattle on her property, but only a handful knew she actually had a gold mine, and Jim had an idea she kept most of the gold right inside her house.

~   ~   ~

"Hey, Irish." Sean glanced up from hoeing the garden as Bear rounded the corner of the hacienda. "Me and Ruby was just wonder'n when you and Mrs. Garcia was getting hitched. Got any idee?"

"Well, real soon, I hope. We haven't set any date yet. Why?"

"'Cause," he turned to spit, "I got Ruby talked into going with me when this horse'n pony show's over with in Dogtown, but it's a fer piece to Utah. I gotta get myself up there and build us a cabin and truck in a whole lot of supplies before it snows. I'd like to stay around and see you two tie the knot, but if yer gonna stay like ya are for awhile, I'll just have ta mosey on down the trail. Know what I mean?"

"Yes, I believe I do. I'll let her know and try to pin her down to a date real soon."

"Well, ya needn't make it sound like Ruby and me's trying ta push her into marrying you iffin she don't wanna get hitched. We was just wondering, that's all." He slapped Sean on the arm and grinned before turning away.

"No, I understand. I won't make it sound that way. I'll let you know just as soon as I find out myself." Sean rubbed his arm.

~   ~   ~

"But, Señor, these things take time." Leonida fluttered her eyelids and turned away. Sean could easily see Ildefonso Baca standing statue-like in the shadows under the oak tree from where they sat at the fountain's edge. The moon had just appeared over the tops of the trees to cast its soft glow across the wooden boat dancing in the water just behind them.

"Why do I get the distinct feeling that I am somehow being flimflammed again?"

"Que?" Leonida's head snapped around as her jaw clamped shut.

"I said that I get the feeling that you are somehow leading me on. All I asked for was a date as to when we are getting married. People are asking me, Leonida, and I feel like an idiot not being able to answer them."

"Well, I am sorry if you feel that way, but I'm sure there must be some other reason other than my not being able to give you a day, like Monday or Tuesday."

"Oh, so we're back to throwing insults again, are we?" Sean stood and put his hands on his hips. "I didn't ask you here this evening to argue, Doña Leonida, or to be insulted. All I asked for was a date. I asked your father's permission, like you wanted, and he said yes. Then I asked you right proper-like and you said yes. Now, people are asking me when, so they can make plans. Is that too hard to understand?"

"Now, you are the one being insulting." Leonida's green eyes flashed in the moonlight. "I understand very well what you are saying, but I've done nothing that should make you feel like you're tonto in la cabeza. If you feel that way, that is your own doing. I've had nothing to do with it." She gritted her teeth as he rolled his eyes.

"Really? Well then give me a date and I won't feel that way."

"I can't." She leaped to her feet and turned her back on him. "I'm sorry, but these things take time."

"Time for what?" Sean's voice cracked. "By the powers of heaven, I can't figure out what's so difficult. Bear and Ruby are getting married right after the trial."

"Sí," Leonida spun on her heel to glare, "but Señorita Ruby is not the Doña, is she?"

"Oh, your title. I suppose that changes everything."

"Sí, it does happen to change everything. The other landowners would feel insulted if I did not invite them. Their ranchos are located across California all the way to the Mexico border. I have already sent four of my best vaqueros on some of our fastest horses requesting their presence at our wedding. I have set the tentative date as August the fourth, but that could change, depending on when we hear from the others. I am sorry, Señor, if things on this rancho move on a different timetable than you are used to. Have you forgotten, muy poco tiempo?" She turned to stare off into the distance.

"No, I haven't forgotten. I only wish you would have told me this in the first place." He placed his hands on her shoulders.

"I had originally wanted us to get married earlier, but it didn't seem to work with the trial and everything. It was to be sort of a surprise. July 4 is your Independence Day, isn't it? I thought it would be fitting to take your independence away on that day." She shrugged. "It was a silly little joke of mine."

"No, it isn't silly at all. I like it." He smiled. "And I'm sorry I got irritated. I guess I need to trust you more."

"Sí, perhaps we both should." She turned to face him. "Sean, I love you so much, but you frighten me."

"Frighten you? Why?"

"Because you left me once, and I have these dreams," she stared at the bricks and shook her head, "that you and I are married, and I'm so happy. Then I turn and you are gone. Everyone is gone. I'm all alone and frightened. Then, in my dream last night, I ran to find you, and I stumbled and fell inside the grave yard. There, in front of me is an open grave beside Rudolfo and Carlo's graves. I'm so afraid to look in it, Sean, because I'm frightened that I will find you there." She grabbed hold of his vest with both hands.

"Promise me," she gritted her teeth and shook him, "promise you will never leave me, no matter what."

"I give you my word." He tried taking her in his arms but she shook him again.

"No, you don't understand. I need to know. I have to know that you won't leave...that you won't even die before I do. Promise me that and make it come true."

"Dear Mother of Christ," he slipped both arms around her, "I'm sorry that I did this to you. I promise that I will be with you always. I will never let you go again, ever." He held her tightly until she quit shaking.

"I'm afraid you will have to, for awhile anyway." She sniffed.

"I'll have to what?"

"Let me go. My father would be angry if you insisted on holding me all through the night."

"Is it time to go inside already?"

"I'm afraid so," She gave him a crooked smile, "but, I shall be looking forward to you doing the same for many years to come, Señor. I have your word that you will not die before I do. Is that correct?"

"On my mother's honor." He lifted his right hand.

"Bueno." She gave him a quick kiss on the lips. "You'd better not break your promise, or I'll have Baca shoot you if you die before me." She kissed him again and ran toward the house.

Chapter 36

"All right, now y'all have heared these three women tell their stories." Josiah Russell paced in front of the jury. "All three of them claims to have croaked Ambrose, but we know that ain't likely, seeing as there was only one knife and he only got poked with it once. Try as I might, I couldn't get none of 'em to change their stories. The only one I could get to change her tune was Mrs. Garcia right here in this courtroom, and I never counted her in the mix in the first place. But these other three," he pointed toward Aurie, Ruby and Alice with a sweeping motion, "are sticking by their word. Now, at least two of 'em are lying through their teeth. I ain't convinced in the least that all three ain't telling a whopper."

"What are you saying, Mr. Russell? That there might be an entirely different person who is guilty of murdering Mr. Brice?" Lloyd Hansen leaned forward and furrowed his brow.

"Yeah, reckon I am." The judge groaned and rubbed a hand across his face.

"Proceed."

"Well, I ain't for taking up much more of this court's time, so, I'm gonna call Doctor Kilkenney to the stand. Y'all know how the court asked him to look into things, so I'm gonna ask him to tell you in his own words what he found. Doc?" Josiah took a seat next to Aurie while Sean made his way to the front.

"Do you swear to tell the truth and nothing but the truth, so help you God?" Cary Jones held the Bible as Sean took the oath.

"Yes I do."

"You may proceed, Doctor." Judge Hansen rapped the gavel, cutting the swearing-in short. "We all know who you are and where you are staying." Cary scowled as Sean cleared his throat.

"The process I used in my investigation is known as ballistics. It is the study of the dynamics of projectiles, or, to put it into simple terms, how an object travels from one point," he held a fountain pen between his fingers and floated it in a high arch through the air, "to the other." We normally think of it in terms of firing a gun or cannon, but it can include the study of other weapons such as a bow and arrow, or spear, or catapult, or, as in this instance," he grabbed the butcher knife from the table, "a knife."

"The question is, who propelled the knife, and how did it strike, killing Ambrose Brice? Now, as a matter of ballistics, it would depend on how the knife was held or thrown, and who did the holding or throwing. We have determined by testimony, that it would have been impossible for the knife to have been thrown. That is, unless the murderer took the time to drive the weapon all the way through the body to the handle after he or she had thrown it, and that is highly unlikely. So, we determine that the knife was being held in someone's hand at the time of the murder.

"The next questions are: Who was holding the knife, and how did they strike him? That takes in the next aspect of my investigation, calling on the angle and force of the blow. Let me demonstrate." He scanned the audience and motioned for Tex to come forward.

"Now let's say for demonstration purposes, that I was going to stab Mr. Burwell with this knife. If I held the knife like an inexperienced knife-fighter, as I would assume these women are, I would hold the knife as so, with the blade pointing downward from my hand. That would cause me to drive the blade in a downward motion, as so." He moved his hand across his shoulder in a slow arch. "The blade would then be driven into the body in a downward angle, as you can see. But, if I held the knife as most experienced knife-fighters do, I would hold the knife as so," he turned the knife over in his hand, "with the blade sticking upward, my stabbing motion would cause the knife to enter the body at an entirely different angle."

"This is all very interesting, Doctor, but where is it taking us?" Judge Hansen said.

"To our killer, Your Honor. If you will just give me a few more minutes, I believe I can prove beyond a shadow of a doubt who killed Ambrose Brice."

Judge Hansen rapped the gavel as a mumble rolled through the courtroom. "You may proceed."

"Thank you, Your Honor, and thank you, Mr. Burwell; you may be seated. I would first like to call Aurie Templeton forward. I would also like to call Paco Morales to the stand." He waited until he had them both positioned a few feet apart in front of the jury before continuing.

"After measuring Mr. Brice inside his coffin, I have determined that Mr. Morales and Mr. Brice are almost the exact same height, and that is why I have asked him to come forward. Now, Miss Templeton," he handed her the butcher knife, "I want you to show us how you stabbed Ambrose Brice the night of the murder." She gasped as her eyes darted from the knife to Paco and back again.

"It's okay, I don't really want you to attack Mr. Morales. I only want you to show us how you held the knife and struck at him."

"I can't remember."

"Just try your best. It's okay." He nodded and waited until she had finished her demonstration. Thank you, you may be seated, but I want Paco to stay.

"As we can determine from Miss Templeton's actions just now, she held the knife as an inexperienced fighter, and struck Mr. Brice about here, near the collar bone," he pointed toward Paco's chest, "driving the blade downward toward the left lung and perhaps the heart. Now, I would like to call Miss Ruby Lang forward and have her give us the same demonstration." It only took Ruby a matter of seconds to grab the knife and pretend to stab Paco and hand it back.

"Thank you, Miss Lang, he said as she sat down. "As we can see, Miss Lang held the knife much the same way. The only difference being, she is somewhat taller than Aurie, causing the angle of her blade to differ. It would have been driven almost directly downward, through the neck, cutting the windpipe, right lung, and catching the heart. Now, I would like Mrs. Carpenter to come forward."

"I can't remember. I was so frightened." She trembled as she took the knife.

"Don't worry. Just do your best."

"I believe I was holding the knife like this. But I only pointed it at him." She gripped the handle with the blade poking upward and held it next to her breast. "I didn't want to hurt him. I only wanted to frighten him. He was drunk."

"Thank you." He removed the knife from her hand. "You may sit down for the time being." He waited until Alice had taken her seat before continuing. Ruby was leaning forward in her chair with a scowl, glaring at him.

"As we can see, Mrs. Carpenter's knife would have entered Mr. Morales' chest at this angle, and traveled into the left lung and perhaps the heart. Upon examining Mr. Brice's body, we found the path of the knife to have been almost exactly the same, except for two very important differences. Mr. Morales' wound would have been here," he pointed with the tip of the knife, "several inches lower than Mr. Brice's, which was here.

"Now that can be accounted for by the excitement of the struggle, or several other things that might have occurred that evening. Perhaps Mrs. Carpenter has forgotten exactly how high she held the knife."

"Are you telling us, Doctor, that Alice Carpenter is the one that killed Ambrose Brice?" Judge Hansen crinkled his brow and scratched the stubble on his chin.

"On the surface, it would seem that way, Your Honor."

"No, he's lying. She couldn't a done it. She's too nice a lady." Ruby jumped to her feet.

"Sheriff, get that woman out of here and lock her in the jail." Lloyd pounded the gavel.

"Begging your pardon, Your Honor, but I would like her to hear what I have to say next, because her testimony could be important to the case."

"All right, if you say it's important. But," he pointed the gavel at the angry girl, "I'll tell you right now in front of God and this jury, one more outburst from you, young lady, and you'll spend an entire year locked inside that little cell. Do you understand me?"

"But..." Josiah cut her off by shoving her downward in the chair as Lloyd raised the gavel in anger.

"All right, Doctor you may proceed." He said after a Ruby quited herself.

"Thank you. The one question that has not been answered is, is Alice Carpenter strong enough to drive this blade completely through a man's chest, up to the knife handle? While she is a fine looking woman, I don't believe she is capable of generating that much strength in her forearms and wrists. I would have a harder time believing that she would be capable of standing over the man, once he was wounded, and pushing the knife completely through his body. On that, I agree with Miss Lang. Alice Carpenter is too nice a woman to commit such a ghastly deed. No, something else happened that evening that caused Ambrose Brice to die."

"Well, get to it man, before we all die of old age," Lloyd Hansen said, then rapped his gavel to stop the laughter.

"Yes, Your Honor. You may be excused Paco. Thank you. I'd like for Mrs. Carpenter to return to the stand." He handed her the butcher knife as she came forward.

"Now, you and I are going to play a little game. I'm going to be Ambrose, and you've just come into the room to stop me from molesting Miss Tempelton. Go ahead and point the knife at me. Go on. You won't hurt me, I promise." He waited.

"Now, I'm not paying much attention to you," he turned away, "because I'm busy molesting Miss Templeton. What are you going to say to get my attention?"

"I don't know exactly. I believe I said, leave that girl alone."

"That's close enough. Now, what am I supposed to do, if I'm Ambrose?"

"He, he said some bad things, then turned and attacked me. He said he was going to kill me."

"How? How did he try to kill you, Mrs. Carpenter?" Sean yelled.

"He tried to choke me." She screamed as Sean turned quickly and grabbed for her throat.

"What the hell?" Josiah grabbed for his gun as he came out of his chair. The entire courtroom was standing as Lloyd pounded the gavel.

"Order! Order!" He waited until they had retaken their seats. "Now, can you explain what in the devil you are doing, Doctor?"

"Certainly. As you could see from my demonstration, when Mrs. Carpenter got frightened she shoved the blade against my chest." He pointed toward the small tear caused by the knife point on his white shirt, where a red stain had begun to appear around the cut. "But it was not in order to stab me. It was more like trying to push me away, to keep me from choking her. I believe that was exactly what happened the night Ambrose Brice died." Again the courtroom broke into low rumbles.

"I'll ask you again. Are you saying Alice Carpenter is the one who murdered Mr. Brice?"

"No, just the opposite, Your Honor. I'm saying that Alice is the one who entered that room with the intention of helping Miss Templeton," he pointed toward the closed door, "and she did grab this butcher knife off the bar and held it exactly as she has shown us here today. But she did not kill Mr. Brice."

"Then who in God's name did the killing?" Lloyd Hansen turned red in the face.

"Mr. Brice himself did the killing."

"Oh, for Christ's sake." The judge buried his face in his hands.

"You see, Your Honor, it was like this. Come on." Sean turned to Alice. "Hold the knife against me just like you were a moment ago. According to your own testimony, you said that when Ambrose attacked you, you backed out of Miss Templeton's room into this room. Is that correct?"

"Yes."

"Were you still holding the knife against his chest?"

"He was choking me."

"Then you tripped over a chair and fell to the floor. Is that correct?"

"Yes, right over there." She pointed toward the dark stain on the floor.

"Would you mind lying on the floor right now, Mrs. Carpenter?" She gave him a blank stare.

"Go on. Lay on the floor, just as though you had tripped over a chair."

"Well, I don't know exactly how I was laying. I just fell. It happened so fast." She took her time positioning herself and modestly brushing her skirt. The room was filled with the scraping of chairs as those in the back stood for a better look.

"If you were going backward and tripped over the chair, you would have most certainly landed on your back. You were still holding the knife against Mr. Brice's chest, as he was still trying to choke you. Isn't that right?"

"Yes, I guess so." She pointed the blade upward.

"So, you see, Your Honor, if I happened to be Ambrose Brice the night of the attack, I would most certainly be in a terrible predicament. Here I am, with my hands around this lovely lady's throat, and we're moving rather rapidly across the room, when she suddenly falls, still holding the knife against my chest for protection. Now, Mrs. Carpenter, I want you to hold very still." Sean placed his hands on the floor to hover above the sharp blade.

"As you can see, there is not much room for error. I am able to hold myself above the blade, simply because I am sober and have no intention of harming the lady on the floor. But if I were intoxicated, and we had been moving rather rapidly in the dark, I'm afraid that I would have fallen against the knife, and the force of my weight would have certainly driven it through my body, right to the handle." Sean rolled to one side and helped Alice to her feet.

"Now, allow me to ask you one last question, Mrs. Carpenter. Did you notice any tender spot or bruising on your own body following the attack?"

"Yes, I had a rather nasty bruise right here." She pointed to a spot just below her right breast.

"That was caused by the handle of the knife when Ambrose fell." Sean turned to face the judge. "I don't know what the gentlemen of the jury will say, Your Honor, but I believe Ambrose Brice, in his drunken fury to choke the life out of Mrs. Carpenter, fell against the knife and killed himself."

"Are there any further questions or testimony, Marshal?"

"Nope, I don't think so." Hanky shook his head.

"Then court's adjourned until eight o'clock in the morning." Lloyd Hansen smacked the gavel. "At that time I will charge the jury and hopefully, we'll get a verdict and bring this case to a close."

Alice suddenly broke into huge sobs and buried her face against Sean's chest. "Shhhh, it's almost over with." He held her close and caressed the back of her head. He could see Leonida standing just a few feet away, staring at them as people began pushing and crowding closer.

Chapter 37

Sean glanced up from where he was seated on the bricks at the fountain's edge. The clicking of her boots against the brick patio contrasted sharply to the soft strumming of Pablo's guitar coming from the bunk house. A dog barked outside the gate and the oak leaves rustled in the evening breeze.

"May I sit with you for awhile?" She slipped the veil from her head and combed her hair free with her fingers.

"Sure." Sean brushed several leaves from the bricks with his palm. She perched herself primly on the spot and took a deep breath.

"It is a nice evening, isn't it?"

"Yes, fitting end to the day." He struck a match and lit his pipe. She took another deep breath and fumbled with the edge of the veil for a moment.

"That was a wonderful thing you did inside the courtroom today."

"Thank you, but anybody could have done it, given the chance."

"I think you're wrong, Señor. You made us all see how that evil man caused his own end. Up to that moment, even I had believed that Señora Carpenter had killed him. She is a kind and generous woman, and I was afraid for her."

"You are a kind and generous woman yourself, Leonida." He grinned as she glanced at him from the corner of her eye. "But the truth was there all the time. All it needed was for someone to pry it out of hiding. The truth is always there, if you look hard enough."

"Sí." She studied him with moist eyes. "And what is the truth you see now, Doctor?"

"Well, let me see." He laid his pipe on the bricks and shifted to take her hand. "What I see is a beautiful woman that has been hurt a million different ways by a million different people, and didn't deserve any of it."

"Are you certain, Señor?" She crinkled her eyebrows. "A million is an awfully large number."

"Yes, I suppose that was a slight exaggeration, but I know that she was abandoned by someone who loves her deeply, and didn't deserve being treated that way."

"Are you sure she didn't deserve being abandoned?"

"Positive."

"Then how will she ever get over this horribly empty feeling that is inside her?" She leaned closer with her lips slightly parted.

"I don't know. I guess the doctor will have to investigate. It may take some time."

"There is plenty of time on Rancho Manantial Escondido. Our motto is muy poco tiempo, remember?" Her lips were close enough for him to feel her breath.

"Yes, but a good doctor always takes his time to investigate every possible avenue. What made you decide that he should take up this case? Is this woman who's been hurt a friend of yours?"

"Yes, a very close compañera. She saw you in the courtroom today and asked me to talk to you. She thought you were simply wonderful, especially the way you comforted Señora Carpenter after the truth was discovered. She would like you to do the same for her."

"Mmmm, that might take some doing. Is she absolutely sure?" Sean's fingers trembled as they found a strand of her hair. "It could get expensive."

"It is no importante. She owns a gold mine and would pay the cost. How expensive are we talking, Doctor?" Her cheek and nose caressed his forehead.

"It will cost everything she has, especially her heart and soul."

"Her soul? What about Jesus Cristo? Shouldn't He have something to say in the matter?"

"Yes, I suppose He should keep the part that belongs to Him, but I would require the rest." He ran his lips across one cheek to her earlobe.

"She is a hard business woman, Señor Kilkenney. If she gives you everything, even her heart and soul, how will she know you will complete your end of the bargain?"

"I will give her my own heart and soul to hold as collateral. Will that help?"

"Sí." Her breath became uneven as Sean caressed her cheek with his palm.

"Are you frightened?"

"Terribly so. But I think you should start your investigation as soon as possible."

"Yes, I agree." He was shocked as she threw her arms around his neck and crushed his lips against hers. Her mouth seemed to find every square inch as she covered his face and neck with kisses. Then, just as quickly as she started, she jumped to her feet and brushed the wrinkles from her skirt.

"I love you Sean Killkenney. I believe I have since the night you stopped me in the corral with Rudolfo's pistol." She sniffed and wiped the corner of her eye with the back of her knuckles. "At least I believed you cared enough for me to stop me from getting myself killed. That is why I have been so angry with you for leaving. You have my heart and soul, Señor. Please treat them kindly." She spun on her heel and ran toward the house.

Sean stared long after the door had closed, then chuckled. What had taken place in the corral seemed so long ago he had pushed it to the back of his mind. He tilted the pipe in his fingers and grinned. She had made it sound so matter-of-fact. He had gone outside to smoke that evening also, but the assault he had received after taking the gun away made him wonder if she would not have killed Henry

Baines. He was certainly glad that Carlo, Rudolfo's brother had come to his rescue.

He he relit the pipe and released a cloud of aromatic smoke. His recollection of that night differed from hers. It scared the hell out of him. He had decided to let her get herself killed the next time she chose to do something stupid, but he hadn't done that either. It was as though God had moved her into his life. He had been there every time Leonida Garcia had needed protection from Henry Baines and Pod Randell, and the times she was close enough for him to feel her body pressed against his and smell her hair had driven him insane. She had somehow crept through his pores captivated him to the point of distraction. He couldn't even forget her in busy San Francisco.

"Well, by the Irish gods, Sean Kilkenney, now that you've got her, what in the hell are you going to do with her?" He laughed and blew another cloud into the air.

~   ~   ~

"Whadda ya think is gonna happen in court tomorrow?" Tex handed one of the steaming cups of coffee to Hanky and took a seat beside him on the front steps of the cabin. Rosa's soft humming drifted from the kitchen through the open doorway as she fed the baby.

"Well, I imagine the jury's gonna say that Ambrose kilt hisself." Hanky took a sip and used his bottom lip to clear several droplets from his moustache. "By the way, I never said thanks to you and Rosa for naming that baby Martha, after your mother. She would have liked that."

"Yeah, well we kinda figured she deserved more than being buried and forgotten on the Texas Panhandle." They both sipped coffee in silence as Chico, Rosa's mongrel dog, sniffed his way around the woodpile.

"Doc did a fine job convincing everyone that Ambrose did it for hisself, didn't he?"

"Mmm-huh." Hanky nodded.

"Think it really happened that way?" Tex set his cup aside and pulled the makings from his shirt pocket and began rolling a cigarette.

"Yeah, pretty much. I don't see how else it coulda happened. Like Bear says, Ruby woulda have blowed him all to hell with that scattergun. If it would have been left to Aurie, she would still be in that back room getting beat and poked by that bastard. Nope, I figure it was just like Doc says. Only thing that bothers me is his saying Ambrose didn't suffer none. I'd a like to seen that knife cut his gizzard out and let him bleed to death real slow."

"Well, I thought about going back into town a time or two myself and blowing his leg off after that little fracas with Pod Randell, but I had Rosa to think about, so I just kinda kept putting it off." Tex handed the cigarette to Hanky and started rolling another.

"Na, ya did right. A married man ain't got no business going around shooting people no matter what kind of skunks they are."

"I weren't married at the time."

"The hell you weren't. Ya got hitched within a couple of weeks after Henry Baines got his neck stretched." Hanky struck a match and held it to Tex's cigarette first, then lit his own.

"Yeah, but I coulda taken care of Ambrose before me and Rosa got married."

"Uh-huh." Hanky nodded. "That woulda been a nice wedding present. Hey, let's me and you get hitched this afternoon, honey. I just blowed Ambrose Brice all to hell, and he's lying in the middle of Dogtown bleeding to death."

"Ya forget who we're talking about. After the way he treated her, Rosa woulda done the Mexican Hat Dance on top of his head."

"Huh, ya got me there." Hanky snickered. They smoked in silence as the setting sun began to cast a red glow across the cloud-scattered sky.

"Whadda ya think's gonna happen to them women? Judge Hansen gonna go easy on 'em for lying?" Tex said.

"Hell, I don't know. Kind of depends of which side of the bed he wakes up on tomorrow. He's pretty much for going by the book, but he's got a tender spot, if you can find it. Aurie's about the same age as his own daughter, so he's gonna naturally look at her different. Woodrow said Susanna, is gonna fix the judge an extra special breakfast and give him a talking before he even gets out of the house."

"What are you gonna say if he calls on you to testify?"

"Me? Nothing." Hanky crushed the butt under the toe of his boot. "It don't make me no never-mind what he does to them women. I ain't gonna be around here long enough to worry none anyway."

"You ain't? Where in the hell do you plan on going, Old Man?"

"Don't know." Hanky got up to stretch his back. "Back to Texas like I said. Just as soon as the gavel falls."

Tex watched his father in silence as the old ranger limped toward the corral. A sniff caused him to glance over his shoulder at the door. Rosa was standing in the doorway holding their baby. A tear slowly mapped its way down one cheek as she stared toward the corral. He turned his attention back toward his father who was feeding his horse a handful of grain. *You're doing it again, ain't you? First, you leave me to be raised by the Burwell's after Ma died, and now you're running away from your granddaughter.*

~   ~   ~

"Sean? Sean?" Leonida scanned the empty kitchen. "Where in the world is he?" she mumbled. He had only gone to the kitchen to fetch her a fresh cup of tea. The teapot was whistling as steam shot from its spout, but her husband was no where to be found.

"Maria?" she called as she stepped into the hall, but there was no answer. "Caramba." She set the teapot aside and went to the patio. It was deserted also, but voices were coming from the rear of the chapel. "What in the world?" Her boots clicked against the bricks as she rounded the corner of the church to find the cemetery packed full of mourners.

"Maria," she tugged on the weeping maid's arm, "why are we having a funeral and no one has told me? Who died? Who's funeral is it?" The maid stared past her, weeping.

"Juan? Paco?" She dashed from one vaquero to the next. "Angela? Will someone please tell me who's funeral this is?" She stumbled and fell at the edge of the open grave. "It's empty," she said, staring down at the open pit.

"It certainly is. We have been waiting for you, because it happens to be your funeral." She jerked up to see several men standing on the opposite side of the grave. She could see Sean as she scrambled to her feet. He stood silently at the edge of the crowd with his arms around two small children, a boy and a girl. She somehow knew the children were hers. "Welcome to hell, Doña Leonida."

"No, please don't." She shook her head as the man pointed a gun and fired. She was immediately engulfed in flames.

"Agh!" Leonida bolted upright in bed. She spent the rest of the night wrapped in her blanket sitting in her chair by the window, waiting for the sun to rise.

Chapter 38

Leonida had to use both hands to steady the cup in order to sip her tea. She glanced from time to time at Father Ramon who sat quietly studying her from across the table. A rooster flapped his wings on top of the hitching post outside the window and proceeded to crow. The sound caused her to shift and glance at the sun peeking over the top of the hills through the open door. She took another sip of tea and pulled her housecoat tightly against the early morning chill.

"I'm sorry about insisting the door stay open, Doña. But if one of our people happened to see you leaving this early dressed like that, they might get the wrong impression." Sparks leaped up the chimney as the priest tossed another log into the fireplace. Sitting in the dark wrapped in the blanket had given her little comfort, and after what seemed like endless hours of prayer inside the chapel, she found herself knocking on Father Ramon's door, seeking answers.

"Esta bien, Padré, I understand. I'm sorry for disturbing your sleep. I shall go now." She spilled some tea trying to sit the cup on the table. "Oh, I'm sorry."

"Nonsense, you stay seated. I'll clean it up. It's only a small spill anyway. You ought to see the messes that Julio Romos leaves when he comes to visit. He likes warm goat's milk with chocolate. Now that's a sticky mess to clean."

"He is a good boy." She smiled.

"Sí, but that is not what you have come here to discuss. You say you've been having the same dream for months?"

"Sí. It started shortly after Señor Kilkenney left for San Francisco. But at first, it was different. I was simply looking for him. I never said anything, because I believed they came because I loved and missed him so much."

"That is probably the case," he said and nodded thoughtfully.

"But then it began to change. I kept seeing the graveyard and the empty grave, only I didn't know it was empty. I would stumble and fall right at its edge, but I always woke before I had a chance to look inside. I was always alone. But a few weeks ago, maybe a month...I don't know...I started seeing people. A few at first. Señors Hanky and Tex. I would ask them questions, but they never spoke to me. They only smiled and talked with each other. Then came Paco and Juan and many other vaqueros, but they acted the same way." She paused to rub the dark circles under her eyes with her fingers.

"Tonight was the worse of all. Seeing everyone, including you, gathered inside the cemetery, waiting for me to die. I shall never sleep again. I know that's true." She shook her head. "I'll never be able to close my eyes. Not ever."

"Nonsense, you'll eventually get so tired it would be impossible for you to stay awake if you tried. Let me ask you a question. You say Señor Sean was there with two children?"

"Sí, a small niño and a smaller niña."

"And you've never seen them before?"

"No, never." She shook her head.

"But you said that you knew in this dream they were yours." Father Ramon rested his head in his palms to stare.

"Sí, but..."

"Ah, ah." He waved his index finger in the air. "You are in such a hurry that you are forgetting something. They were your children, my Doña. So, if your dream is correct, and I am not saying it is, you must be going to live long enough to get married and have children. Am I not correct?" She nodded.

"Good, at least we can agree on that point. Now the second point, and I feel this one is more important than the first. It is your dream." He pointed at her. "Am I correct in that assumption also?"

"Sí, but..."

"Ah, ah." He waved the finger again. "Let me talk and you listen."

"Perdon."

"Accepted. Since it is your dream, you have complete control over it. This I believe from my own experience. As a child, I was plagued with a bad dream much the same as you are. My dream wasn't the same dream you're having, but mine was always the same dream about wolves trying to catch me and tear me to pieces. I think it was because those beasts were plentiful near the small village where I grew up in Mexico. I remember one time racing toward the house in fear, because a pack of them came near the bean field where my father and I were working. They were hungry and wanting to eat the mule my father was using. We had no gun with which to frighten them, but my dog, Jose, fought them fiercely. The fight didn't last very long, but it gave us time to get the mule to safety. I found Jose's body later, all torn into little pieces."

"Oh, how awful," Leonida cried.

"Sí, and I shall always be grateful that Dios gave that small creature such a huge heart. But I think that is why the dreams came. In my dreams the wolves would chase me up a tree, snapping and snarling, trying their best to tear me to pieces like Jose. I would wake my mother crying." He paused to take a sip of tea.

"This went on for years, until one day after spending time in prayer, it came to me like a bolt of lightning. The dream was mine. It was given to me perhaps by God to test me, or maybe a devil, who knows? But it was my dream. I could do with it as I chose. So, that night when I went to bed, I lay in the dark thinking of each and every detail of that dream. I lived it from the beginning to the end. When I came to the part where the beasts had me pinned up in the tree, I gave it another ending.

"I chose for my weapon my father's machete. The huge knife suddenly appeared in my hand, and I dropped from the branches right into the middle of the pack of wolves. You should have seen me in my dream. I swung the machete and two wolves were instantly headless. I turned this way and that, swinging my weapon." The priest waved his arm in the air. "I was so fast none of the beasts had a chance. The last one ran yelping like a wounded coyote. I waved my weapon in the air with a cry of victory. The dream never bothered me again."

"That's simply wonderful," Leonida giggled, "but do you actually think it will work with my dream?"

"Why not?" He grinned. "It is your dream. Give it a different ending. Look, child," Father Ramon leaned across the table to hold her hand, "you say you don't know who the men were in your dream?"

"No, I couldn't see their faces, but I believe they were Judge Baines and Pod Randell who had come back for revenge. The one who spoke," she paused thoughtfully, "he used correct English, like an educated man. Judge Baines' English wasn't good, but much better than Señores Hanky and Tex."

"It seems odd that Mexicans should be discussing the use of poor English by Americanos." Father Ramon chuckled. "Let's assume that the men in your dream were Judge Baines and Pod Randell. They were evil men, and now they are dead. That is fact number one. The only person I know of that has ever come back from the grave is Jesus Cristo, and I don't believe He is going to shoot or send one of His own to Hades. So, the next time they come to you in your dream, tell them they are not real, because they are dead. Tell them to go away and leave you alone, because you are God's child and you plan on living a long happy life. Sí?"

"Thank you, Father. I knew you were a gift from God the first time I talked to you." She kissed his hand. "Now, I must go, before someone does see me." Leonida rose from the table with a guilty grin. "Bendiciones de Dios."

"God bless you too, my child. I'll see you later for Mass," he called to her after she had stepped into the cool morning air.

Chapter 39

"Will the jury please rise?" All eyes inside the courtroom turned toward the group of coverall-clad miners as they rose to their feet. Judge Lloyd Hansen allowed his gaze to drift over each and every one of them before continuing.

"You're charged with bringing back a verdict in this case, strange as it may seem. You've heard the testimony of each of these women, and what Doctor Kilkenney had to say. Now, it's up to you to decide which one is telling the truth. This is a serious matter, concerning not only the life of the deceased, but the lives of these women as well. A guilty verdict will change the lives of everyone involved, but the truth is what matters the most.

"I'm also charging you to bring back a verdict of guilty or not guilty on each of these women, concerning their conduct inside this courtroom. I'm charging Aurie Templeton with perjury, for lying to this court concerning the death of Ambrose Brice. The same goes for Ruby Lang, but I'm adding contempt of court to her charges, and I'm charging Doña Leonida with obstruction of justice. Only Mrs. Carpenter acted properly, so I'm not adding any charges to her case.

"Now, you have the charges, so I'm dismissing you. You will deliberate in the back storeroom, which we've cleaned for your convenience. You'll find a table, plenty of paper, and pencils and coffee. We tried to think of everything, but if we've missed something, you may ask Sheriff Russell. He will be standing guard to make sure no one bothers you. You may be dismissed." He brought the gavel down and turned to the courtroom. "Court's adjourned until further notice."

Tex escorted the four women to Alice Carpenter's apartment at the rear of the store to wait. The water inside the teapot had not yet begun to boil when Paco banged on the rear door.

"Señor Hanky says to come quickly. The jury has made up their minds."

"Tell him we'll be right there." Tex set his lips into a fine line and stared at the women. "Well, ladies, it's time to pay the fiddler. Better rustle."

"That didn't take long," Ruby snickered. "Wonder who they're gonna hang?"

"You quit talking like that, Ruby Fay," Aurie said. "It's like Father Ramon says. You have to believe that God is going to work things out for the best."

"Yeah, well he could have had some mountain lion come and eat that old buzzard years ago, and none of this would have happened in the first place."

The building was packed, and it took time to weave their way past those standing in the aisle to reach the front of the courtroom. They had no more taken their seats, when Judge Hansen entered, and Cary Jones began beating his clawhammer against the table.

"All rise. Court's now in session. The Honorable Judge Lloyd Hansen presiding."

"You may be seated." Judge Hansen scowled at Cary before turning toward the Jury. "Have you reached a decision on all charges?"

"Yes, Your Honor, we have." Woodrow Black rose from his seat.

"Mr. Jones, would you please get me a copy of the jury's decisions?" Lloyd took his time reading the handwritten verdict before handing it back to Cary. "Please see that Mrs. Black receives this, so she can file it with the records. Will the defendants rise?"

Aurie Templeton started whimpering as she stood, and Alice held the girl in her arms and caressed her head.

"You may proceed, Mr. Black."

"In the charge of murder, we find all four women innocent, Your Honor. We ruled in favor of Doc Kilkenney's testimony, that Ambrose killed himself."

"Fine." A cheer rose from the audience, and he had to wait for Aurie to compose herself as she burst into open weeping. "Will the spectators please refrain from celebrating until these proceedings have been completed? What about the other charges, Mr. Black?"

"We find Aurie Templeton guilty of one count of perjury."

"Oh my God, I don't believe this." Ruby shook her head with a smirk.

"Quiet, or I'll add to your charges, young lady." Lloyd smacked the gavel.

We find Ruby Fay Lang guilty of one count of perjury and two counts of contempt of court."

"Aw, come on now." Bear stood to his feet.

"Quiet, or I'll have you removed from the courtroom. That goes for everyone. One more outburst, and I'll clear the building." Lloyd rapped the gavel several times. "Okay, you may proceed."

"There were no charges brought against Mrs. Carpenter, but we did find Doña Leonida Garcia guilty of one count of obstruction of justice."

"Is that all?"

"Yes, Your Honor."

"You may be seated." He nodded toward the jury. "Will all four women please come forward?" He took his time studying each face before clearing his throat.

"I don't know if you realize it or not, but each and every one of these charges is serious, containing a fine and possible prison sentence. Is that clear? Do you understand what I'm saying?" All four women nodded.

"First of all, I'd like to thank Mrs. Carpenter for being as truthful and forthright as she could possibly be under difficult circumstances. As usual, justice did win out. Our system isn't perfect, but it is a whole lot better than most places you can find in this world. Try as hard as we might, we do make mistakes, but each and every one of us here this morning can thank God we did arrive at what I feel is not only reasonable, but the truth. You may be seated, Mrs. Carpenter." He waited until Alice had taken her seat before glaring at Aurie.

"Miss Templeton, I know your story and understand that you've been mistreated terribly. I can understand why you thought it was necessary to lie in order to protect Mrs. Carpenter. She's a fine lady, but that is no excuse for lying to Sheriff Russell and the court. I thank God for the way things turned out, because in another time or courtroom, you might have gotten yourself hung. Now, you tell me, would that have been right?"

"No Sir, but it wouldn't have been right for her to die trying to help me either." Aurie sniffed.

"No, it wouldn't. But she's not going to die, now is she?"

"No Sir."

"Good. Now, for perjuring yourself in this courtroom, I'm fining you twenty-five dollars, but, I'm going to pay your fine myself, in hopes you have learned your lesson." He rapped the gavel. "You may sit down." He waited until Aurie had seated herself beside Alice before glaring at Ruby.

"Miss Lang, you've caused me more trouble than the last gang of cut-throats I had hanged in Columbia. I had almost made up my mind to leave you locked inside that jail, except there aren't any bars to hold you inside the cell. Now, just like Aurie, I understand you've had a hard life, and I understand why you lied. But you are also rude and obnoxious. You came a whole lot closer to getting yourself hanged than Miss Templeton did."

"Thank you." Ruby smiled.

"What did you say?"

"I said, thank you. That was my objective. Mrs. Carpenter is the only real friend I've had in this town, and I'd die a million times for her." Judge Hansen shook his head.

"You are one strange girl, Ruby Lang. I can only hope and pray that your life will take a better turn from now on. I'm fining you seventy-five dollars for your conduct inside this courtroom which, I'm sure, that large gentleman in the back will pay for you. Will you promise me you are going to try your best to find another profession than the one you've been involved in?"

"I already have. I'm going to Utah and raise cattle and horses."

"You are?"

"Yes Sir, I am." Lloyd glanced toward Bear who nodded.

"Fine. I wish you well. You may be seated." He smacked the gavel.

"Mrs. Garcia?" He folded his hands to study her.

"Sí?"

"I don't know when I have been so disappointed in anyone in my whole life. You are a leader, and people look up to you and follow your example. Like the others, I know what a rough time you've had. I agreed with the way you handled yourself during the terror Henry Baines and Pod Randell brought against you. I would have expected you, of all people, to have conducted yourself in a proper manner in this case also. What do you have to say for yourself?"

"Señor Hansen," she held her palms upward and shook her head, "I was only trying to protect my friend. I only wanted to prove that anyone could have killed that man. I never actually lied."

"And, you never actually told the truth, did you?"

"No, but I didn't lie."

"If you never actually told the truth, then you most certainly lied. You of all people should know that. A half-truth is as good as a whole lie. What kind of an example did you set for your people? Those who look up to you and follow your example? How many Rubys and Auries are going to be tempted to lie when they are in a difficult situation? You have a lot of children on your ranch, and all of them look up to you. I find your actions repugnant, and I'm fining you two-hundred dollars. Twice as much as both previous fines put together, because your actions were twice as bad as these young girls. You are a refined and highly educated woman that knew better. That's not all." He took a sip of water.

"I know you're a religious woman, and that's good. I happen to be religious myself. So, I'm ordering you, as part of your punishment, to spend one hour each morning for the next month praying and asking God to instill inside you the importance of telling the truth. If we ever start accepting half-truths and lies as being the truth, then God help this country. Do you understand your punishment, young lady?"

"Sí, and may I say I am terribly sorry."

"I hope you are." He smacked the gavel one last time and grinned. "This case is closed. Court's dismissed."

~ ~ ~

The cool night air blew gently against her cheeks as Leonida walked slowly past the tack house and followed the corral fence. Rudolfo's black Arabian snorted and trotted toward her as she stopped beside the barrel of grain.

"Sí, you've been a good boy." She scooped a handful and held it while the horse's soft lips took it from her palm. The sound of violins and guitars mingled with laughter and singing drifted from the patio where the party was beginning. It would soon become a full-blown fiesta. No sooner had they returned to the rancho, than Bear and Ruby had Father Ramon marry them in the middle of the courtyard. That had been the start. Now the Indians had several beeves and goats roasting over bonfires while women were cooking tortillas and spicy sauces. She smiled and wiped her palms against the hem of her skirt as several young maidens dressed in colorful costumes giggled and dashed past the corral toward the music. Woodrow Black guided his wagon around the bunkhouse toward a vacant area where a line of wagons from town were already parked. He had Judge Lloyd Hansen with him, who tipped his hat and said "good evening" as they passed. The judge then helped the children from the wagon as Woodrow held out his hands for Susanna.

"There you are. I've been looking all over for you." She turned as he appeared from the direction of the chapel.

"Hola, Señor Kilkenney. I did not see you coming."

"Small wonder. It's getting dark." He offered his arm. "Care for some company? Or, am I intruding on your privacy?"

"Sí, I would like your company, and no, you're not intruding at all." She smiled. "I wanted to be alone while I was thinking."

"I don't blame you. It's been a busy day, and Judge Hansen was tough on you in court today."

"Not as tough as he should have been. He was correct. I've had time to think, and I know now what I did was misleading. Niñas like Olga and Evangelina look to me for guidance. I hope they will forgive me." She shook her head.

"My, you *have* been in deep thought," Sean chuckled, "but, I wouldn't worry about losing their respect. You might not be perfect, but you're pretty close in their eyes."

"What about your eyes, Señor? How far have I fallen in your sight?" Sean slowly allowed his gaze to take her in from head to toe, and back again.

"Well, I don't know. I don't see much change, but I'd have to put my arms around you to find out for sure."

"Why is that?"

"It's a scientific fact that a person starts losing body mass before they shrink in height."

"Que? I don't understand." She put one hand on her hip to stare back. "You wouldn't be telling me one of Señor Hanky's stories, are you?"

"Absolutely not. When a person is ill, they start losing weight. Body mass. We don't have any scales, so I'll need to put my arms around you to find out."

"What about my guests? Shouldn't I welcome them first?"

"I don't know if we should wait that long. A person losing body mass might be in serious trouble. Besides," he pulled her close, "there will be plenty of time to welcome them later. This fiesta might go on for several days."

"Sí, you're right, but what about my papa? What if he sees us?" She leaned against his chest.

"The last time I saw your father, he was conducting the same examination on Mrs. Carpenter."

"Oh." She could hear his heart pounding as she slipped her arms around his waist. "So tell me, what do you think, Doctor? "Have I lost stature?"

"Not an ounce, my Dear. Not an ounce."

She tilted her head back as his lips sought hers.

Chapter 40

"I don't see how you are in any bargaining position, Jim," Ken Edwards grinned, "especially seeing as you owe me a wheelbarrow full of money. What I normally do if someone welches on his debts is have Frank here start breaking bones." The huge bearded man seated at the bar laughed and cracked his knuckles.

"Yes, I'm aware of that. But if he proceeds to break my bones, then I won't be able to pay you, will I?"

"I'm not so sure he's going to pay you anyway, Ken," the man with a thin moustache and black hat said with a snigger. Black Jack was all James had ever heard anyone call him. "The word's out over town that he's been cuttin' whores with a knife and stealing money from the Mexicans he's supposed to be helping in court. Every lawman in the state's after his hide."

"That right? Maybe I'd have better success collecting the money he owes by turning him over to the law." Ken pulled the cigar from his lips to spit on the floor.

"Maybe you could," Jim nodded, "but you'd never get as much as if you sent a couple of your boys with me."

"Just where is all the money you're talking about?" Ken said as he calmly shuffled a deck of cards.

"At a ranch near Angel's Camp."

"Really. Why didn't you just ride up there, collect all this money and come in here and pay your debts?" Ken slammed the cards on the table.

"Because, like Black Jack says, I've gotten myself in a jam, and," he shrugged, "once I leave San Francisco, I don't plan on coming back. So I thought if you sent a couple of your men along, they could collect what I owe and bring it back."

"The hell you say." Ken leaned back in his chair to chuckle. "Sounds like a big pile of manure to me. What do you guys think?"

"I think you're right, Boss. Want me to bust him up a little?" Frank climbed off his barstool.

"Not just yet." Ken held up a hand. "Give me a couple of minutes. Come on, Jim," he nodded, "tell me something interesting before Frank breaks both your hands."

"I'm not lying. Okay, so I wasn't exactly thinking of returning your money when I came in here. In a way I was, but not really."

"Then what were you thinking?"

"To be blunt, I need your help getting the money."

"This is getting better all the time." Ken grinned at Black Jack. "Now, why would a big fancy lawyer who dresses like you need my help collecting from someone who owes him money?"

"Because she's got a lot of men working on her ranch that don't exactly like me."

"This wouldn't be that ranch that sits closer to Dogtown than Angel's Camp, would it? The one owned by that woman who took a army of Messkins and Injuns into Dogtown and hung that Judge last year?" Black Jack slowly paced around the table to stand behind Ken.

"Well, yes, but why's that a problem?"

"Hell, you just got through admitting she's got an army that hangs judges, and she doesn't like you." Ken wiped the corner of his eye with a knuckle as he laughed.

"Yes, but it's really no problem. Listen," he leaned forward, "she's got a real honest-to-god gold mine right on her property. They're pulling a lot of material out of the ground. I'm as sure of it as I've ever been of anything in my entire life. Nearly every time she paid me, it was in gold. Not paper or coin - gold. She keeps it right there inside her house. Can you believe it? No bank or vault. Just right there in the house."

"What about a safe?" Black Jack struck a match to light his cigarette.

"I've never seen one. The last time she paid me, she pulled the sack right out of the desk drawer."

"She could have known you were coming," Ken said.

"She did, but even if there is a safe, it wouldn't matter. We can still get the gold."

"You seem sure of yourself." Ken leaned on his elbows to stare. "What makes you think it's going to be as simple as you make it sound?"

"Because I'll take care of that problem. I know the woman, and I know what will make her turn over the gold without anyone getting hurt."

"That brings me back to my first question, and you'd better give me a good answer, because I'm starting to get impatient. If it's so easy, why do you need us?"

"Just for backup. Just in case something goes wrong. But nothing will, I'm sure of it."

"You'd better be. Because if you're not, I'll guarantee that you'll die slowly and painfully." Ken tapped the cards with his index finger. "I don't like the idea of trying to rob a bunch of Mexicans on a ranch the size of a small state. If anything did go wrong, it would take a hell of a long time just getting out of there. And I'll tell you right now, the only reason I'm even considering this stupid idea is because you owe me close to fifteen thousand, which in turn, makes me pretty stupid. But I'm a gambling man, so I'll tell you what," he tapped the cards one more time and leaned back, "we'll cut for the fifteen thousand. You win, we'll ride with you and help steal the Mexican's gold. You lose, I sit here and get fifteen thousand in pleasure watching Frank bust you up, one bone at a time. Go on," he nodded, "you first."

James' hand trembled as he cut the deck and turned his card face up.

"Ooooh, five of clubs, Jim. That ain't too good." Frank cracked his knuckles again.

Ken cut the deck and turned the card face up without looking. It was a two of diamonds. "Okay Jimmy-boy. We'll ride with you. Simply because I like living on the edge of a cliff. It's more exciting that way. But if you're the slightest bit wrong about any of this, those Mexicans are really going to enjoy seeing just how many bones Frank can break before a man dies."

~   ~   ~

Leonida set her cup aside with a giggle as Tex shuffled into the kitchen. His eyes were bloodshot and his blond hair stood every which-a-way.

"Oh, God bless you." He grabbed the mug of black coffee from Maria's hand and took a sip. Last night's fiesta had not actually ceased. A handful of celebrators had watched the sun rise before finding a spot to lie down. No sooner had they quieted, when others crawled out of their wagons or tents and began preparing for the day's festivities. Rosa had taken her baby to one of the upstairs bedrooms around ten-thirty. Leonida had no idea when Tex had finally decided to join them. She had retreated inside around midnight herself, while he and Sean were conducting arm-wrestling contests near the fountain.

"You'd better sit down, Señor, before you pass out."

"Yeah, thanks." He pulled a chair away from the table. "Where's your pappy and the rest of the folks?"

"They are still asleep. The way you were carrying on last night, I'm surprised you're awake this early."

"Don't know that I am." He grinned. "The only reason I'm up a'tall is, Martha woke me up crying. Rosa's up there feeding her now. They'll probably be down in a minute."

"She's a beautiful niña," Maria said, refilling both cups. "She looks like her mother."

"You can say that again. Got her mama's temper too. Neither of them liked it too much when I come to bed last night."

"You were rather noisy, Señor. You woke me up just finding your way down the hall. What were you doing?" Leonida crinkled her brow.

"Trying to get one foot in front of the other, mostly. They didn't work too good. Still don't know that they do even now." He glanced toward his feet. "At least I got my boots on the right feet."

"Who won the contest?" she asked over the rim of her cup.

"Which one?"

"The arm-wrestling."

"Don't rightly know. It was a toss-up between Bear and Vernon Blackstone. Me and Doc had it made until they got involved. Hell, either one of 'em could pick up this house. Anyway, I got the bright idee that I could get shed of Bear by reminding him it was his wedding night. So, I told him he'd better get upstairs to Ruby afore someone else decided to keep her company. That's when he tossed me into the fountain. Well, I decided to wander upstairs after that." Leonida spilled her coffee laughing, and Maria scampered across the room to retrieve a towel.

"And what about Señor Sean," Maria paused with the towel, "did he get a bath too?"

"Don't know that either. Last I seen of him, he was about to get his arm torn off by Vernon Blackstone. That Irishman's plenty strong, but Vernon's little finger's bigger around than his whole arm." Their attention was drawn toward the patio by the sound of horses.

"It's Señor Hanky," Maria said, peeking out the window. "He has two horses, and the one is packed with a lot of things."

"Oh, damn him." Tex scooted away from the table.

"Why, what's wrong?" Leonida got to her feet as Tex jerked open the door.

"Hey, looks like y'all had yerselves a wing-ding last night," Hanky said, stepping over Paco to reach the door. The vaquero and several others lay sleeping in different positions, making travel in and out of the hacienda difficult.

"Yeah, shoulda been here. What's the grip on yer hoss fer?"

"Aw, you know me, Tex. I can't stay put in one place too long. I kinda get the itch to see new places once't in a while. Hey," he said turning his attention toward Maria, "ya can't spare a mug of coffee for a poor traveling man, can you?"

"Sí." She nodded slowly. "Come inside."

"Where do you plan on going, Señor Hanky?" Leonida took his arm and led him through the door.

"Don't rightly know. First, I thought I'd go back to Texas, but then I hear the country's mighty purdy up Oregon way. So, I was thinking I might mosey up there for a look-see."

"You might wish to spend the winter here first. Some of the Indians say it gets cold in Oregon during the winter months." She held onto his hand as she turned to face him.

"Na, I'll be all right. I've slept in the snow 'afore, and it ain't never kilt me yet." He grinned as Maria handed him the cup. "Much obliged."

"De nada." Maria shrugged and turned her back. Leonida felt a lump form in her throat as the maid blew her nose and hurried from the room with a sob.

"What's got her goat?" Hanky said as he took a sip.

"You don't know?"

"Uh-uh." Hanky shook his head.

"Perhaps you'd better tell him, Señor Tex." Leonida pulled two chairs from the table and sat down.

"Na, it'd be no use." Tex frowned. "Ya ain't gonna changed his mind none. He's onrier'n Doc's mule."

"Well, I can't rightly argue with you none on that, but what's got you folks so het up anyways? Y'all knowed I was gonna be heading out just as soon as we got the Ambrose Brice deal settled."

"Not all of us, Señor." Leonida shook her head. "At least I didn't. You have been staying at Rancho Manantial Escondido for more than a year, and I was under the impression you liked living here."

"Well, I do. Y'all are fine folks."

"Then why are you leaving? We have all grown to love you. Maria certainly has. That is why she runs from the room crying. She thought you were in love with her. We think of you as part of our family, and it will break our hearts if you leave now." Leonida shifted in the chair at the slamming of a door. Rosa descended the stairs two at a time mumbling in Spanish with Maria at her heels.

"Here." She shoved the crying baby toward Hanky.

"Huh?" The ranger rose to his feet.

"Put down the cup and hold your granddaughter."

"Well, okie-dokie. I was planning on doing that anyways..." He had no sooner taken the baby in both arms when Rosa kicked him soundly in the shin. "Ow, damn!" Her heavy soled boot gave a thud as she kicked the other leg. "Oh, geez, stop it!" He tried backing away as she kicked at him a third time. She finished by giving him a resounding slap across the cheek.

"You will not cheat my daughter out of having a grandfather. Do you understand me?" She backed him into the corner with a finger pointed in his face. "I never had a grandfather to tell me stories while I sat on his lap, and I will not allow you to rob Martha. You will be a grandfather to her. Do you understand me?"

"Yes, Ma'am." She turned as if to leave, but spun back to poke the finger in his face a second time.

"You will not leave this rancho unless Tex and I go with you. Is that understood?"

He nodded obediently.

"Bueno." She paused beside the chair where her husband sat grinning. "You may unpack his horse when you finish your coffee."

"Yes, Ma'am." He nodded as she left the room.

"Oh, good God. Will someone please take this baby whilst I sit down?" Hanky hobbled toward the table.

"Bueno." Leonida took Martha in her arms and started cooing.

"Damned woman liked to broke my bum leg." Hanky plopped into the chair and started rubbing both shins.

"Better do what she says, or she's liable to blow yer leg clean off," Tex snickered.

"Yes, looks like you're going to have your grandfather after all," Leonida said to Martha as she wove her way through the sleepy crowd that had gathered in the hallway. She paused in front of Sean and smiled, allowing her gaze to fall from his face to the baby in her arms and back again. She climbed the stairs and paused to smile at him once more before disappearing into one of the bedrooms.

Chapter 41

"Oh, my, it's absolutely heaven." Dorothy Baker's head rotated from side to side as the buggy neared the hacienda.

"Look, Mama!" Clara leaped to her feet and pointed.

"Careful, Clara. Sit down." Dorothy tugged at her daughter's skirt.

"But look at all the horses. There are millions of them."

"If you think there are a lot of horses, just wait until you see the cattle." Jonathan McDougal leaned close to the girl. "There has to be a hundred times more cattle than horses."

"Really? Do you think they will let me ride one of the horses?" She bounced back to her feet.

"They'll have you on one faster than you can blink. Everyone, including children a lot smaller than you, rides a horse."

"Oh, look, look." She pointed toward a dark-skinned man with long-flowing hair, breaking a horse as they passed the corral. The fence was surrounded by cheering vaqueros as the beast snorted and bucked its way around the arena.

"Is that man an Indian?" Dorothy turned toward Loretta who was straining to see the spectacle.

"Yes, I believe that is Ildefonso Baca. Hanky said he's Chemehuevi." She glanced at Dorothy and back to the corral. "They are a branch of the Paiutes from Arizona. Most of the Indians you will see are either Miwoks or Yokuts. Oh, here he comes right now."

"The Indian?" Dorothy twisted in her seat to see as the buggy ground to a halt by the stables.

"No, Hanky. The tall Texan with the limp. He's got Paco and Juan with him." Loretta accepted her husband's hand as she stepped from the carriage. Salty jumped down from where he had been seated next to the driver and began unloading the bags.

"Well, now, how's the purdiest woman in the whole world?" Hanky lifted Loretta from her feet in a hug and kissed her cheek.

"Hey, easy how you handle my wife, you crazy horse-wrangler." Jonathan grinned.

"Wife? Don't tell me ya done got hitched?" He stepped back to stare.

"Yes, I happen to be Mrs. Jonathan McDougal." Loretta pulled the glove from her left hand to reveal a diamond ring.

"Well, put me on the hog-train. Can you believe that, Paco? A young purdy filly like her marrying an ornery sea-dog like him?"

"No, Señor. She is so young, and Señor McDougal is like Pedro, the mule."

"Hey." Jonathan removed his hat as the vaquero scooted behind Hanky laughing.

"Well, congratulations to ya both." He shook Jonathan's hand and kissed Loretta once more. "But I see ya brung us a couple more purdy ladies. Maybe ya can tell me who these fine folks are 'afore everyone steals them." Hanky removed his hat to help Dorothy and Clara from the carriage. They were already surrounded by curious onlookers, with more coming.

"This is Dorothy Baker, Judge Samuel Baker's wife, and her daughter, Clara," Jonathan said. "I talked about them in the letters I wrote to Mrs. Garcia."

"Pleased to meet you, Ma'am." Hanky bowed. "I'm Josiah Russell, but most folks just call me Hanky. My two pards here are Paco and Juan."

"Buenos dias." The vaqueros removed their sombreros with deep bows.

"We are happy to meet you also." Dorothy curtsied.

"It'll take ya a year to meet most of the other folks crawling 'round this here ranch, but ya do need to meet this feller," he said as General Flores made his way toward them. He was decked in black riding breeches with silver conchos and a matching vest.

"This here's General Jose Flores. He's Leonida's father and sort of runs things around here." Hanky stepped back as Jose offered Dorothy his hand.

"I'm afraid our Texas friend forgot to tell me who you are, Señora."

"I am Dorothy Baker, and this is my daughter, Clara," Dorothy said with a curtsey.

"General." Clara performed a perfect stage bow, almost touching the dust with her nose.

"Señorita, I'm charmed." Jose gave a gallant bow of his own. "I'm sorry my daughter isn't here to greet you, but she has chosen this afternoon to go riding. I'm sure she will have returned by the time you have freshened yourselves from your journey."

"Is Doctor Kilkenney here?" Clara asked.

"Sí, señorita, but I'm afraid he, like my daughter, has chosen this afternoon to be away from the hacienda. Would you be the Señortia Baker he has been talking about?" Jose stooped to stare her in the face. "He did not tell us you were so beautiful."

"Yes...I guess I am. Thank you. Did he go riding with your daughter?"

"No, he has gone fishing at the creek. Come inside and I shall send someone to bring him to you."

"Okay, but can I see the horses first?"

"Sí, you may see all the horses you wish. These vaqueros will show you," Jose said. "We will be inside the hacienda when you are finished." The girl grabbed Hanky by the hand and started tugging him toward the corral.

"Can I ride one?"

"Clara." Dorothy started after her, but Jose took her arm and chuckled.

"No need to worry, Señora. They will look after your daughter. No harm will come to her. Come, I will have Maria fix us some tea."

"Do you have any idea where Sean actually is?" Loretta asked as they crossed the brick patio.

"Sí, where we built the small dam. I will send one of the boys for him now if it is important."

"No, don't bother. I'll go," she paused to glance at Jonathan, "if it's all right with my husband."

"Que? Did you say husband?"

"Yes, it is okay with me, Dear, but hurry back." Jonathan kissed her forehead. She paused to recognize several children who had run up to greet her as Jonathan explained about the wedding.

The tiny heels of her shoes made walking on the soft earth difficult as crossed the meadow. She hiked the hem of her skirt in order to take larger steps. *I know I don't deserve it, but I love him so much. Please, God let me have his baby.*

~   ~   ~

"There you are." Sean turned at the voice behind him.

"Well, by the Irish gods, when did you get back?" He dropped his fishing pole and grabbed her in a welcoming hug. "You don't know how good it is to see you." He held her at arms length to stare her up and down. "Has that Scotsman treated you right? You look ravishing."

"Oh, he treated me more than right. You'll never guess."

"You're married."

"How'd you know? Did he tell you in his letters?"

"No, but I noticed the way you two were looking at each other before you left. Let me see the ring." He grabbed her left hand. "Ah, at least he's not a cheapskate."

"No, he's the exact opposite. I'm the one who has to keep him from buying me things." Loretta giggled.

"Don't discourage him. The bloke can afford every cent he spends on you and more."

"Oh, and before I forget," she placed a hand against his arm, "we brought Clara and her mother with us."

"Really?"

"Mmhmm. She's a darling child."

"Well, give me a second or two to grab my tackle, and we'll join the others."

"Wait a minute." She grabbed his arm. "I wanted to see you alone before we were surrounded by people and can't talk. I need to thank you, Sean, for everything you've done. For treating me like a lady, when you knew very well what I am, was..." She shrugged. "Most of all I need to tell you how very, very happy I am."

"I'm glad. You deserve it." He held her by the shoulders and smiled.

"But there's something else," she said as he turned away. "I need to ask you a favor."

"Yes, what is it?"

"I need to find out if I'm pregnant or not."

"Pregnant? Hey, that's wonderful. Does Jonathan know?"

"No, I wanted to make sure before I told him. One of the girls I worked with at The Silver Slipper told me that women who, who work in that profession, sometimes have trouble getting pregnant. I saw a doctor in San Francisco, but all he'd say was it's too early to tell. Sean, I know Jonathan wants children so badly. I don't want to get his hopes up and then disappoint him. Can you understand?"

"Perfectly. Well, hmmmm. What your friend told you is sometimes true. They can catch something or have an injury, but I can say for certain that the exact opposite is also true. There are many a bastard child who's mother is employed in that very old profession." He grinned. "We can do our best to find out what your situation is, but not here in the open. We'll have to find a secluded spot at the hacienda, maybe tomorrow morning? You can say you're not feeling well, and I'll give you an examination in your room. How's that sound?"

"That's easy enough. I'm sick and throwing up most mornings lately."

"That's a good sign. How long since your time of the month?"

"Past three months now."

"Have you ever had any diseases that you know of?" She shook her head.

"Well, I'd say from the sound of things, you are going to be a mother in a matter of months," he nodded, "but we'll make sure in the morning."

"Oh, God, I'm so happy." She threw her arms around his neck.

"So am I. Hey," he leaned back to study the smiling face, "I haven't got to kiss the bride yet."

"Well, have at it mister." Sean placed his lips against hers a few short seconds before hugging her once more. That was when they heard the stifled cry. He jerked away to find Leonida standing beside her horse under one of the oak trees.

"Hey, look who's back." Sean held onto Loretta's hand as he started toward her.

"No." Leonida gave her head a quick shake.

"No what?"

She raised the riding crop as he drew closer.

"Hey, wait now. What's wrong?"

"Wrong?" Leonida pointed the crop at him first, then Loretta. "Oh, Dios." She shook her head violently. "How could you?"

"Oh, you don't actually think that Loretta and I are..."

"How could you?" She mounted in one flying leap.

"Leonida wait. Let me explain."

"Dejame sola, gringo cerdo." She gave the reins a yank and turned the beast as Sean made a lunge toward her arm.

She dug her heels into its flanks, and the animal darted away, causing him to fall face first.

"Leonida," he yelled, but she had already crossed the creek below the dam and was speeding toward the river.

"You stay here. It will be better if I go after her." Loretta untied his mule and hiked her skirts enough to climb onto the saddle. "Sorry, I didn't mean to cause a scene."

Sean watched as Loretta galloped after the fleeing Doña.

"Damned women. Who needs them anyway." He kicked a large rock at his feet. "Oh, Christ!" He hopped on one foot before finding a spot to sit down. "Dammit, Sean Kilkenney. Now you're stupid on two counts."

Chapter 42

Sean's mule bolted across the stream, soaking Loretta's back with icy water, then immediately stretched her long legs into a ground-eating stride. She forgot trying to guide the animal and clung desperately to the saddle-horn. Tears streaked her face as wind and dust whipped at her eyes. Leonida was in plain view by the time she cleared her vision. Loretta could see her blond hair flowing in a stream as the woman turned in the saddle to glance back at her. She whipped the black horse with the riding crop, but the mule only increased her pace to match the horse she was gaining on. The mule's breathing became a loud rasping noise, and Loretta tugged on the reins, thinking the animal might kill herself trying to catch the black horse, but the mule seemed to increase her pace. Leonida turned into a draw and Loretta hung on for dear life as the mule followed.

The mule suddenly stopped with both sides heaving for air. It took a second for Loretta to clear her eyes enough to see Doña Leonida turn her lathered horse to the left in a circle, then back to the right. She had ridden into a tiny boxed canyon with no exit. She finally turned her horse to face Loretta with an angry glare

"Dejame sola." She caused the horse to prance back and forth in front of the mule.

"I have no idea what you said, but if you will just listen..." Loretta started but Leonida cut her off by raising the crop in the air.

"Silencio, or I will whip you good. You, you..."

"Hey, now," Loretta dismounted, "I don't care what you think of me, but I absolutely will not allow you to hit me with that thing. Now, get off that horse and listen." The angry woman slid from the saddle and stepped away from the horse, tapping the riding crop against her gloved hand.

"Uh-uh," Loretta shook her head, "you get rid of that thing first." Leonida tossed the crop at the horse's feet and stood with both hands on her hips. "Good." Loretta stepped closer only to receive a resounding slap across the cheek.

"Ah," she gasped before returning the favor. Leonida grabbed her cheek in disbelief for a quick second before doubling her fist and knocking Loretta to the ground.

"You bitch!" Loretta wiped blood from bruised lips. She came from the ground swinging wildly. She was certain her blows did no real harm as Leonida stumbled in her retreat and fell to the ground. Loretta pounced on top of her only to discover she had hold of an angry cat that squirmed this way and that, hitting, scratching and biting.

"Knock it off. Stop it! Oh, Christ." They rolled across the ground. She couldn't free herself, although she tried several times to kick Leonida away. Her long skirts kept tangling around her legs, while Leonida's riding skirt and light vest seemed to give her all the freedom she needed. It was after receiving several kicks in the shins and several more blows to the face, that she finally caught hold of Leonida's long hair.

"Ow," Leonida cried as she jerked her head backwards. "Let go!"

"Not a chance, sister." Loretta pulled harder as Leonida's fingernails came close to raking her face. "Knock it off, or I'll make you the first bald Doña in history."

She grabbed hold of Leonida's wrist with her free hand and shoved it upwards while tugging hard on the hair. Leonida screamed and kicked, but her movement allowed Loretta to roll her on her side, where she pinned her to the ground with a shoulder as she continued tugging on the hair.

"I will kill you." Leonida clawed at the ground with her free hand. "I am going to scratch your eyes out. You and

Sean Kilkenney both. Ahhh," she screamed as Loretta tugged harder on her hair.

"You'll be as bald as my Uncle George if you keep this up." Loretta swung a leg over the squirming body. "Now, shut up and listen." The sound of a man's laughter caused her to snap her head upward. She quickly counted eight men leering back.

"Oh, Christ Almighty." She let go of Leonida's hair and rolled to a sitting position. Leonida came up muttering something in Spanish, and Loretta braced herself for another attack, but the woman stopped upon hearing a man's voice.

"I don't know exactly what she said, but I'll bet it wasn't exactly lady-like."

"James Sattler." Loretta struggled to her feet. "You and your friends keep popping up in the strangest places. What in the world are you doing way out here?"

"Oh, I just missed your company, Loretta. Hell, you two didn't need to stop on our account. We were having fun watching. Go on and finish whatever you were trying to settle."

"Yeah, I ain't seen a good cat-fight in a long time," one of the men sniggered.

"It is finished, Señores." Leonida started brushing the dust from her skirt.

"Oh, darn," Loretta stared at the piece of cloth hanging from her waistband, "I just bought this dress."

"I believe Señorita Stewart just asked you a question. What are you doing on my property?" Leonida snatched the riding crop from the ground.

"Is this your property?" A husky man in a black vest and hat glanced around. "I thought we were on your property twenty miles or so back that way." He pointed west.

"We were. It's all her property, Ken," James snickered. "Seventy-five square miles of it. But to answer your question, Doña Leonida, I actually did come here looking for Loretta or her husband."

"Husband?" Leonida cocked her head to glance at the woman standing a few feet away.

"You didn't know she and that sea captain got married in San Francisco?"

"No, I didn't."

"That's what I was trying to tell you when you slapped me." Loretta rubbed at a scrape on her elbow. "Now that you've found me, what do you want, Jim?"

"Well, I've been thinking." The men seemed to drift into a huge circle around the two women as he stepped closer. "Seeing as you helped create that mess back in San Francisco, you might want to make things right. Perhaps you could help persuade Doña Leonida here to increase her payments to my law firm."

"Fat chance."

"I take it the lady doesn't like you much." Ken chuckled.

"What is this man talking about?" Leonida glanced at Loretta before taking a step toward Sattler. "I've already given you more than enough money to represent my case in court. I'll not give you one peso more until I see results."

"You aren't going to see any results, Leonida. He's not taking your case or any other to court." Loretta casually moved closer to Leonida. "He's running from the law, and if they catch him, they're going to hang him."

"Por que? What is this woman saying?"

"Ah yes, I'm afraid it is somewhat true, Doña Leonida. That's why I had to come all the way out here to bother you for another payment on your account. I'm ashamed to admit that I desperately need the money to relocate to a different area."

You didn't listen to me earlier, Señor. I said I'm not giving you anymore money until I see some results in court." Leonida began tapping the crop against her gloved hand.

"No, I'm afraid you're the one who doesn't understand. I'll give you results. Unless you want to see Lady McDougal die a slow painful death, you will give us a nice sizeable payment of, let's say, everything you have." Jim cocked his head to one side and grinned.

"You wouldn't dare." Leonida took a step backward. "They will hang you if you hurt this woman."

"Hell, you just got through beating the stuffing out of her yourself, and didn't I just hear you threaten to kill her for pulling your hair?" The man who spoke was tall and thin with a tiny moustache and dressed in black.

"Yes, you heard and saw her right, but Doña Leonida thinks she can make up her own rules, Jack." Jim began to pace slowly in a circle around the women. "She thinks it's all right for her to ride into town and kill sheriffs and hang judges. Isn't that right, Doña?"

"I was justified in what I did. Your own courts said so."

"What about you, Jim? Is it okay for you to steal money from helpless drunks and go around town cutting girls to pieces?" Loretta no more than got the words out before she received a backhanded blow that spun her off her feet. She was trying to lift herself when she felt Leonida's hands on her shoulders.

"You bruto. Don't you ever do that again."

"What would you do about it if I did?" He laughed. "Actually, I don't have to touch her at all. Frank, could you please give these women a little sample of what might happen if they don't cooperate?"

"Yeah, be glad to." The huge man cracked his knuckles before grabbing Loretta's left arm. He gave it a twist that caused her to scream.

"Leave her alone." Leonida charged the man with her riding crop only to receive a blow that knocked her backwards.

"No, wait. Don't break anything just yet. We need her well enough to travel," Jim said.

"Oh, God!" Loretta rolled on her back crying as she held her arm.

"Well, what will it be, Doña? Are you going to cooperate? Or do we watch Frank break Lady McDougal's bones, one at a time?"

"You...you devil." Leonida scooted to Loretta's side and held her head in her lap. "Sí, I will give you anything you want. Just leave this woman alone."

"See, I told you it would work, Ken." Sattler grinned at his partner. "I'll tell you what, Doña Leonida, you two just sit here and rest awhile. We'll leave Frank to keep you company while we get our horses. Then we're all going to take a nice ride down to your hacienda so you can make your donation."

~   ~   ~

Broken Tooth eased the tension and lowered his bow. His arrow had been pointed at the large man who had hit Doña Leonida. Had he touched her one more time, he would have certainly died, but the man now stood watching, as the Doña comforted the woman he had hurt. The other men had gone to the horses that were tied in a clump of trees outside the draw. Broken Tooth and Dark Skies had been following the white men from the moment they entered Rancho Manantial Escondido. The men had spent the night near the dead cougar's den and moved out early this morning, going slowly. They stayed in the shadow of the trees, following the river. Only men who plan on doing evil would act in such a way.

They were now returning with the horses. Dark Skies had gone to get Ildefonso Baca and the others. There were too many for Broken Tooth to fight by himself, so he would follow. There would be no need to mark the trail, because they were leaving one that his woman, Barking Dog, could find. Broken Tooth would simply stay out of sight and wait for the others. That is, unless one of the men chose to hurt Doña Leonida. Then he would fight and and if need be, die.

~   ~   ~

Sean stomped the dried mud from his boots and leaned his fishing pole against the side of the railing on the front porch.

"Hey, amigo. Why are you walking? What happened to your mule?" Armando Segoviano and several vaqueros had followed him through the gate laughing.

"I loaned it to a beautiful lady, which is something you blokes would never have thought to do. The lady would have had to walk, while you rode. Am I right?"

"Ah, but Señor," Armando held out his palms and shook his head, "I would have held the beautiful señorita in my arms while we both rode the mule."

"Bah!" Sean shooed at them and turned away.

"Catch anything?" Hanky drawled through a cloud of pipe smoke.

"Just a lot of hell. Loretta came and told me that she had married that Scottish pirate while they were in San Francisco. I was giving the bride a hug and kiss when Leonida suddenly appeared as if by magic. You would have thought I'd declared war or insulted the Queen by the way she was acting."

"Sean!" a mid-sized blur dashed out the door to bury herself against his chest and latch both arms around his waist.

"Clara? Is this my Clara?" He pried himself free enough to scoop her in his arms.

"Yeah, it's me." She smiled and hugged his neck. "You still love me?"

"Yes, Princess, I certainly do love you. When did you get here?"

"We rode with Captain McDougal and Loretta," Dorothy said from the doorway. "My husband had to stay and take care of a few things in court. He will be along in a couple of days. It's good to see you again, Doctor."

"It's time to get down now, Clara. Let Doctor Kilkenney rest now."

"Aw."

"It's okay." Sean grinned, and hugged the girl tighter. "I really did miss her. Both of you."

"What was it you said about kissing my wife and catching hell?" Jonathan eased through the door to eye him.

"Ah, yes. I was congratulating the bride with a hug and kiss...just a short one, mind you, when your daughter," he scowled at Jose Flores leaning inside the doorway, "simply appeared out of nowhere."

"She has a habit of doing that. You should have known better by now." Jose blew a huge cloud of cigar smoke in the air. "So, tell me. Was she angry?"

"Angry? I don't think anger would describe what she was feeling. She threatened me with her riding crop and called me a couple of names before riding that black devil she calls a horse as fast as it would go toward the river."

"The river? Mmmm, that's not a good place for her to be by herself. Why didn't you go after her?"

"I started to, but Loretta...Mrs. McDougal," he corrected himself, "said it would be better if she explained everything first. She took my mule. That's why I was walking. I expect they'll be coming back any minute now."

"If they don't kill one another first," Hanky drawled as he beat the ashes from his pipe.

"Now why in the world would that happen? She was just going to explain to Leonida what was going on." Sean scowled.

"'Cause, you numbskull, the girl yer fixin' ta marry saw you squeezing and kissin' the woman who's doing the explaining. You said yerself that she was hotter'n a hornet in July. I'll bet you a month's wages she either says something, or takes a whallop at Loretta before she can even get a word out. They've probably already scratched one another's eyes out, and are wandering around somewheres blind."

"Ah, don't listen to him, Darling." Sean grinned at Clara. "He's just a crazy Texan."

"Crazy, am I?" He pulled a couple of gold coins from his pocket and slammed them on top of the railing. "That's forty U.S. dollars saying at least one of 'em comes in all buggered up. Whadda ya say, General?"

"No, I'm sorry, Señor. I'd be foolish to take that wager. I know my daughter's temper. But," he glanced toward Sean and sighed, "I would be willing to wager my last peso that she has once again canceled the wedding. Unless someone with a little more sense comes along, I shall never see my grandchildren."

"And you had bloody-well hope that my wife isn't returned to me all torn up, you crazy Irishman," Jonathan growled, "or I'll have Salty hang your hide in the sun to dry."

"Ah, you're all nuttier than Aunt Martha's fruitcake." He sat Clara on the porch. "They will both come riding though that gate any minute now, laughing and joking about this whole incident. Especially after she explains that she's pregnant. Just you see."

"Pregnant? My daughter had better not be pregnant, or I'll see to your execution this afternoon." General Flores' cigar smoke stung Sean's eyes as he came closer.

"Not Leonida, you numbskull. Loretta."

"Pregnant?" Jonathan scrunched his eyebrows.

"Bueno," General Flores nodded, "but I hope you're right, doctor. If you were going to hug and kiss Señora McDougal for any reason, you should have done it publicly in front of everybody, especially Leonida. My daughter more than likely feels betrayed."

"Did you say pregnant?" Jonathan grabbed Sean's arm.

"Yeah."

"The General's right." Hanky nodded as he scooped the money back into his pocket. "Yer back where you started from, Doc. Too bad ya ain't got no pills to cure that streak of stupid you have toward women." He swatted Sean on the arm and ambled off toward the corral.

"I'm sorry," Dorothy giggled, "but they are right. I know I would be fit to be tied if I happened to see Samuel kissing another woman. If there's anything I can do..."

"Oh, forget it." Sean plopped in one of the leather-slung chairs. "If she's angry, she's angry. She'll just have to get over it."

"If she doesn't want to marry you, Sean, I will." Clara pulled a chair next to his. "You'll just have to wait a few years, that's all."

"I'll tell you what, Princess. If things don't straighten up around here, I just might take you up on that offer."

"You said Loretta's going to have a baby?" Jonathan grabbed him by the shirt collar.

"Yes, you're going to be a father." Sean swatted his hand away. "I'll never know why it takes the Scots so long to understand plain English."

~   ~   ~

Baca arrived with two dozen vaqueros and watched silently one of the men helped Loretta onto the mule. Her left arm hung limp at her side. The men formed a line as they moved forward, following the river southward. Doña Leonida and Loretta rode side by side in the middle. Baca quickly motioned to one group of Indians with his right arm, then to another with his left. The men disappeared as if the earth itself had taken them in. The first group rode silently, keeping the women's captors between them and the river. The second group followed the captors, their unshod horses moving silently in the soft earth.

Baca placed a hand on Broken Tooth's shoulder, and the Yokut mounted his pony in one leap and rode away. Baca joined the first group of Indians. They would not attack unless one of the men touched the Doña. If that happened, none of the men would live, and Baca himself would kill the one who hurt her. He had sworn an oath of honor over her husband's grave to keep her safe.

Chapter 43

Sean stood on the porch staring at the gate. The heavy wooden doors had been pushed wide and left open, as they were on most days, revealing rolling hills dotted with scrub oak and pine. Cattle and horses alike wandered free, eating the rich grass. He checked his watch for the third time. It was three forty-five. He shoved the watch back into his pocket and surveyed the sky. The sun was past the halfway point and starting its decent in the western sky. It was time to start worrying. The women should have been back an hour ago. The aroma of spicy food began to drift through the kitchen window as Maria started preparations for the evening meal. Three laughing boys chased a dog across the patio, followed by a much smaller giggling girl. He walked to the edge of the fountain to stare past the gate. Several vaqueros on horseback were lazily drifting toward the stables. One of the men began to twirl his lariat while they laughed and talked. Maybe Hanky's right, and they are stumbling around blind. He glanced at his pocket watch once again. The hands seemed to be moving faster than normal. Leonida and Loretta had been gone nearly two hours now.

He shoved the watch back into his pocket and headed for the stables with the intention of saddling a horse, when a lanky Indian galloped his lathered pony into the courtyard and started beating on the bell with his war club. Sean stopped in the middle of the patio to stare and was almost knocked to the ground as General Flores and Hanky burst past him. They were followed closely by Captain McDougal and Maria. He calmly pushed his way through the gathering crowd to listen as the brave slid from his pony to face

General Flores. Sean could only catch a word here and there of the brave's mix of Spanish and Yokut, but he understood enough to know Leonida and Loretta were being held captive by eight white men, and one of the men had already hurt one of the women.

"Dammit." He turned toward the house as the general began barking orders.

"Know what that Injun said out there?" Hank caught up and matched him stride for stride.

"Enough. I'll get my medical kit and guns and meet you at the corral in less than a minute." He bounded up the stairs two at a time. He quickly loaded the .58 caliber Couttys and stuffed them into his belt before grabbing an extra bag of shot and his medical kit. General Flores was giving orders to the women and children as he bounced back down the stairs.

"Sean?" Clara grabbed hold of his hand.

"I'll be okay. Everything will be fine. You do exactly what your mamma says. I'm going to go and make sure Mrs. Garcia and Loretta are okay. We'll all be back in a jiffy and go riding tomorrow morning. Okay?" He leaned to kiss her forehead.

"Okay."

Hanky had two horses saddled and waiting by the time he reached the corral.

"Better rustle, boy. There ain't gonna be no bad guys fer us to catch if we lolly-gag much longer."

"I'm ready." He hung the medical kit on the pommel and pulled himself into the saddle.

"That Yokut's gone to fetch Tommy. He'll meet up with us at the river with Juan and Paco. They're out punching steers near the Blackstone place."

"Dammit, I shouldn't have let them go."

"Hey, don't go blaming yerself fer things a woman does. They are funny critters, son, and they'll do most anything they want, regardless of what a man says. Besides, didn't you say Mrs. Garcia run off madder'n a wet hen? I doubt you could've stopped her if ya tried."

"No, but I could have stopped Loretta."

"Yeah, but then the woman yer fixin' ta marry would've been out there all by herself. Is that what ya want?" Hanky pulled a plug of tobacco out of his shirt pocket and took a bite. "Chew?" He offered the plug to Sean.

"No, thanks."

"It'll settle yer nerves, boy." He shoved the plug back into his pocket. "Well, get ready to ride. Here comes the general, and he's fit to be tied."

~   ~   ~

"How is your arm?" Leonida pulled her horse close to Loretta.

"I've gotten some of the feeling back. Now it just hurts like the dickens. I think he might have broken something."

"Are you and Captain McDougal really married like that man says?"

"Yes, almost four months now. We got married the instant we arrived in San Francisco." Loretta forced a weak smile.

"Why didn't you tell me in any of your letters?"

"I wanted it to be a surprise. I honestly thought we were going to be returning much sooner than we did."

"I wish you had. It wouldn't have been such a shock to see you kissing Doctor Kilkenney. I don't believe that..."

"Come on now," Loretta started to laugh but grimaced and grabbed her arm instead, "you would have gotten just as angry if you saw Maria kissing him. Right?"

"Maria? I would be furious."

"Exactly. I was the one in the wrong here. I shouldn't have gone looking for him in the first place. I'm a guest here, and Sean Kilkenney is your future husband. But I will always think of Sean as my special friend. I wanted to tell him privately about getting married and how wonderfully happy I am. He was so excited that he grabbed and kissed me. That is what really happened, but I don't blame you for getting angry. As I think about it, if I had happened upon you kissing my husband," she shook her head, "I don't know what I would have done. It wouldn't have been pretty, I'll tell you that much."

"I'm sorry I caused you all this pain, Señora."

"You didn't cause me any pain, Leonida. He did." She nodded toward the front of the line. "I've known Jim Sattler longer than I'd like to admit. He's an evil man. You can believe that he means everything he said, and more."

"He doesn't actually think he's going to get away with robbing the rancho, does he? I have almost a hundred vaqueros, counting the Indians."

"It wouldn't matter if you had Lincoln's army living here. He thinks he can, and that's good enough for him. He plans on keeping you as hostage, so your father and the other men will stay back while he gets away."

"Sí, I can see him trying that. It might work for awhile, until Tex or his father shoots him with that big gun. What about you? If they have what they want in me, why don't they let you go?"

"Me? I was one of the reasons he had to leave San Francisco." Loretta gave a weak smile. "Jim Sattler plans on killing me the first chance he gets."

They rode in silence as Leonida allowed the events of the day to roll around inside her head. Her feelings toward the woman sitting atop Sean's white mule were almost as volatile as they were toward Sean. She had felt crushed the moment she first laid eyes on Loretta, climbing out of Sean's buggy. Like everyone else, she had mistakenly thought Sean had returned to parade his pretty wife in front of her. But neither Sean nor Loretta were the type of person who would do something that distasteful. Leonida smiled and shook her head as she remembered how quickly her hurt feelings had turned to anger the moment she discovered the truth. She glanced toward Loretta as the woman moaned. She was holding onto her arm with her head tilted back and eyes shut.

"Señora, are you all right? Is there anything I can do?"

"Ah, yeah. You can get me a hot cup of tea with a little brandy." She opened her eyes and grinned. Her pale complexion was whiter than normal.

"You are sure?" She waited until Loretta nodded her head. "Bueno, you looked as though you were going to pass out." They rode awhile longer before Leonida turned her horse aside toward a pile of rocks and brush.

"Hey, what the hell do you think you're doing?" the huge man growled.

"I need to stop."

"You'll stop when Ken or Jim says you stop, not until then."

"I don't believe you understand. I said, I need to stop." Leonida held her chin steady and glared at the man.

"And I said..." He reached for Leonida's wrist but she jerked, causing the horse to side-step.

"What's going on here?" James Sattler trotted his horse back to where Leonida sat glaring.

"This woman decided she was going to stop," the huge man said, pointing at Leonida.

"That right, Mrs. Garcia?"

"Not really. I said I needed to stop. There is a difference, Señor."

"What she is saying, Jim, is that she needs to heed nature's call." Loretta moved her horse closer. "In fact, I believe I could use a little break myself."

""Might as well get down and relax, Frank. The women need to take a break." The huge man glared at Leonida and mumbled something under his breath as she slid from the saddle.

"You could help me down instead of standing there like a stump, seeing as you're the one who hurt my arm," Loretta said.

"Get your own self down, bitch." He turned his horse toward the river.

"You're such a nice man," she yelled.

"I'll help you, Ma'am." The youngest of the group slid from his saddle and offered Loretta his hand. "I want you to know I don't cotton to treating women this way."

"If that is true, you have befriended the wrong people, Señor." Leonida glanced over her shoulder from where she was tying her horse to a bush.

"They ain't my friends, Ma'am. I just needed some money, so I came with them. I didn't know the Mexican they was going to steal from was a woman."

"If it was a man, that would make it all right? Señor," she continued as he helped Loretta to the ground, "I supposed they did not tell you who I am, did they? I am Doña Leonida Garcia, daughter of General Jose Flores. He will take it very badly if Señora McDougal or myself are harmed in any way. There are more than one hundred vaqueros on this property. Quite a few of them are Indians, and their leader is Ildefonso Baca. He is a great warrior who reports to my father. I have two other vaqueros, Juan and Paco, who are pistoleros. They have ridden with Jack Slade and Chico Cruz. I understand they were also friends with Joaquin Murrieta. Señores Hanky and Tex were both Texas rangers before coming here. What I am trying to say, Señores," she shrugged and glanced at the men who were now listening, "I don't see how any of you believe you will ever leave Rancho Manantial Escondido alive."

"Nice speech, very nice." James clapped his hands. "You should have become a solicitor. In fact, we could have become a team, arguing our cases together inside the courtroom. The only problem is, you forgot to mention the part that we are holding you and Lady McDougal as hostages. None of those men you mentioned...not even your father...will even come close as long as they think there is the slightest chance of your getting hurt. Am I right, Doña?"

"Sí, I suppose that might be true, but even if you do get away, where will you be able to hide? My men will hunt you no matter where you go." James tilted his head and laughed.

"Damn, you don't think highly of yourself, do you? Once we split the money and turn you loose, they'll be so happy, they'll forget about us in a day or two." He was still chuckling as he pointed toward the bushes. "Go do what ever it is you need to do, and let's get back on the trail."

Leonida found a large stick and stood guard as Loretta took her turn behind the brush and rocks. She raised her weapon with both hands as one of the men stepped forward. "Aw, come on, Lady. Can't I have just one little peek?" She lowered it again as he retreated laughing.

"Your turn." Loretta appeared, straightening her skirt the best she could.

"Here, watch them." She handed her the stick.

"What in the world are you doing?" Loretta whispered as Leonida gathered a pile of fist-sized rocks.

"I am going to make things a more even." She turned with a grin. "Do you see that huge oak tree sitting all alone on that hill?" Leonida pointed west.

"Yes. What about it?"

"I want you to run toward it as fast as you can. On the other side, you'll find a small cabin belonging to a family of Yokuts. Apolinar Leija and his family have a herd of goats, and they understand enough English for you to tell them what has happened. They'll get you to safety."

"What about you?" Loretta shook her head.

"I will hold them off as long as I can with these rocks. Now go." Leonida motioned with her head.

"Hey, what's going on back there," Frank yelled.

"Aw, keep your shirt on, ya big lug," Loretta yelled. "She's having trouble with her clothing." She turned back toward Leonida as the men laughed. "I can't leave you here like this. They'll kill you."

"No, not until they have their gold, and they'll have to take me to the hacienda to get it. Now, go. Run as fast as you can."

"You sure?"

"Sí. I'll be all right. Now go with God."

Loretta dropped the stick and stumbled as she bolted past Leonida across the rocky ground. She regained her balance and scampered down the hill.

"Via con Dios, mi companera," Leonida caressed the stone in her hand with her fingers.

"What the hell?" one of the men yelled.

"They're getting away. Get after them." It was Ken Edwards' voice.

Saint Michael, come with your angels now, Leonida popped up as the men charged. Her first rock ricocheted off Frank's forehead with a dull thud. The huge man fell face-forward with a groan. Her second rock thudded against Black Jack's chest, causing him to grab his mid-section and stagger back toward the trees. Leonida turned as a rock sailed past her head to strike one of the men in the shin. Loretta grinned and raised her eyebrows.

"I can't run in these shoes. You'd better go."

"Too late." Leonida flung another rock as the men drew closer. It sailed past its intended target as the man ducked and struck another man in the arm. He drew back cursing as Loretta's victim continued rolling on the ground holding his leg. Loretta's second rock bounced harmlessly in the dirt as her target danced away laughing. Leonida grabbed another rock as James Sattler drew his pistol and fired two shots into the air.

"That's enough, ladies. I think we've had enough fun for one day. Although I must admit, you've entertained me more in one afternoon than anyone has in the past year. Go ahead and throw it, Loretta," he pointed his gun and cocked the hammer, "and I'll blow your damned head off." Loretta shrugged and tossed the rock to the side.

"That's better. You too, Doña Leonida. Drop the rock and come on out." He motioned with the gun.

"Hey, Ken. I think she killed Frank," someone yelled.

"Really?" Ken Edwards finished lighting his cigarette before walking toward them.

"Yeah. He's still breathing, but he's not coming to. His head's kinda sunken in where her rock conked him."

"So, you killed another one, Doña Leonida. You're compiling quite a record. How does it make you feel to know you're a killer?" James grinned.

"Sick to my stomach. How does it make you feel to treat women the way you do?"

"Me? Good, actually." His eyes widened as he laughed. "Now, come on," he motioned, "let's get going."

"What about Frank?" The kneeling man glanced up at the two leaders.

"We'll have to leave him, unless you want to try holding him in the saddle while we're making our getaway." Ken shrugged and tossed the butt on the ground.

"Don't seem quite right, that's all." The man shoved his hat down tight and walked away, leaving Frank lying face-down in the dirt.

"Well, come on, Billy. Let's rustle." Ken yelled at the man holding his leg. He was the same young one who had helped Loretta from the horse moments earlier.

"Na, I ain't going." He shook his head.

"Whadda ya mean, you're not going?" Ken put his hands on his hips.

"Just like I said. Ya'll go ahead. I'm gonna rustle cross the river and head somewheres else."

"Oh, what's the matter, Billy-boy. Am I offending you by treating these women rough?" James snickered.

"Some, but it's your firing that hogleg the way you did that caused me to change my mind. If there's any truth to what this woman said about having a hundred Injuns or so running around," he shook his head, "there ain't an Injun or Messkin within a hundred miles that don't know exactly where we are or what we are up to. They's probably watching us right now. Ya'll go on and get yerselves scalped. Me? I'm gonna fork my horse and ride outta here while I still got my hair." He shoved his hat down tight and limped toward his horse.

"I didn't say you could go." James cocked the revolver.

"Don't even think about it, Jimmy-boy." Billy pointed a finger at him. "I'll bore you three times a'fore you can pull the trigger."

"He's right, Jim," Ken said. "Why do you think I had him along?" They watched as Billy led his horse behind several trees. Seconds later they could hear him urging the animal onward as they splashed into the river.

"Okay, now what?" Ken grinned at James.

"So, we're short a man."

"Two men. Don't forget Frank." Ken motioned toward the prostrate man.

"Okay, two men. We've still got the women. We go on and do exactly what we planned."

"What about the Injuns?" One of the men glanced around.

"What about them? They won't do anything while we have the women. Let's go."

Chapter 44

The gunshots caused Hanky to glance at Jose Flores. "That was down by the river. Come on, let's rustle." He dug his spurs into the dun's flanks and shot into the lead. They were about a quarter of a mile from the trees lining the banks of the Mokelumne River when Ildefonso Baca suddenly appeared. The Indian stood calmly in the middle of the trail while Hanky brought his horse to a halt.

"Dammit boy. Ain't you're liable to get yerself run over doing that." He reined the mare to one side as the general's horse began to pitch. Hanky slid from the saddle and double-checked the loads in his pistol as Jose addressed the Indian in Spanish.

"Ildefonso says there are eight white men over by the rocks holding Leonida and Loretta hostage. He said the women were throwing rocks at them. That is why one of the men fired two shots in the air. They've started moving again, further down river." He paused as Ildefonso spoke again.

"Por que?" The general pushed his sombrero back on his head while several of the vaqueros laughed.

"What's he saying?" Hanky turned toward Paco who had paused in the middle of rolling a cigarette.

"He says Doña Leonida threw a rock that hit the big man in the head. He didn't get up and they took his horse and left him for the coyote. Ildefonso thinks maybe she killed him. Pablo took another horse to go bring him here." He licked the paper and propped the cigarette in the corner of his mouth and struck a match. "He also says that one of the men argued with the leader and left. He crossed the river by himself. Ildefonso sent several Miwoks to get him and bring him back. Only six men watch the women now."

"Ya don't say." Hanky holstered the gun and adjusted his belt. "Looks like yer woman ain't lost none of her spunk, Doc."

"My little Spartan." Jose laughed and shook his head.

"Yer what?" Hanky cocked his head to one side.

"Spartans were Greek soldiers, tough as horsehide and uncompromising like you Texas Rangers. I had just finished reading about King Leonidas and the battle of Thermopylæ at the time of her birth. I'll tell you what, Señores, my daughter came into the world with a struggle, fighting against change. As I held her for the first time," he cradled both hands in front of him, "all I could think of was, what a fine little soldier you are. So I named her Leonida after King Leonidas, who led a couple of hundred Spartans against the invading Persian army at Our Lady of Lourdes. She has never disappointed me."

"Didn't Leonidas die at Lourdes?" Sean took a swig of water and shoved the cap back onto the canteen.

"They all did, but they bought enough time for the rest of Greece to prepare for battle. Leonidas and his Spartans might have lost the battle, but the Persians lost the war. Our job today, Señores, will be to win both the battle and the war, without losing our Spartans.

"Ildefonso says one of the women has been wounded. The man my daughter hit with the rock hurt your wife earlier, Captain." Jose studied the crooked line of trees following the river.

"Loretta? How badly?" Jonathan pushed his way through the crowd of armed vaqueros.

"He says it is her left arm. He thinks it might be broken, but she was still able to throw rocks and fight beside my daughter. He says to tell you he is proud of both women. He will hold a ceremony to make them Paiute after he has killed the men."

"Well now, the ceremony's fine, but me and Tommy might have a thing or two ta say about who does the killing." Hanky growled. "There ain't a Texan alive that would tolerate treating a woman like them varmints are doing."

"I might be a Kentucky ridge-runner, but I ain't never allowed fer hurtin' of no woman." Bear spit and wiped his mouth with the back of his hand. "Besides, I wuz Miss Loretta's friend a'fore any of you knowed who she wuz."

"Frankly, I don't care who gets to tie and hull those men. You can hang everyone of them yourselves. I just want my wife and the general's daughter back safely." Jonathan's hand trembled as he checked his revolver. He jammed the gun back in his belt before mounting his horse. "You can stay here and talk, if you want, but I'm going after my wife."

"Hold on there, now." Hanky grabbed the reins. "Use your head. You just can't bust in there and ask them to hand her over."

"I wasn't planning to be nice." The captain glared.

"The Scotchman's right, for once," Sean said as he leaped aboard the bay. "I'm going after Leonida myself."

"Not without me." Bear led his horse toward a clearing before climbing into the saddle. "I ain't missing the fun."

"Alto! All of you. One step further, and I'll shoot." General Flores pointed his riding crop at the angry men.

"You go to blazes." McDougal turned his horse in a tight circle. "That's my wife down there."

"Si, and the other woman is my daughter, but we need to focus on which is the better way to get them back."

"Better listen to him, before ya go getting them women kilt," Hanky said. He waited until the grumbling men dismounted. "What's inside that head of yours, General?"

"Ildefonso has men following them, and says they are moving toward the road leading to Dogtown. We will stay close to them for until we feel it is safe to attack."

"Makes sense." Tex nodded. "They want a bridge crossing the river and easy access to the hacienda."

"The hacienda? Why would they want to go there? They would be like riding into a box they couldn't get out of," Sean said.

"They don't see it that way. Besides," Tex crushed his cigarette and reached for the reins as his horse took a bite off a manzanita bush. "They think the hacienda's got something they want."

"The gold," Sean said.

"Exactly, and plenty of it. Looks like yer new patient is arriving, Doc." Tex put his foot in the stirrup and swung into the saddle as Pablo appeared leading a white pony with a large man draped across its back.

"Ya know, General," he said as Sean untied his bag, "Baca's got these Injuns pretty well trained. The way I see it, they can get pretty close to the women without anyone knowing they're there. Like Pablo did just now. Weren't none of us here, except maybe Baca hisself, that even guessed that Injun was right on top of us."

"We think alike, Señor Tex. Come, let's ride."

~   ~   ~

Billy James slid from the saddle and hung onto the pommel as his palomino lost its footing in the swift current of the Mokelumne. The point he had chosen to cross wasn't the best, but he wanted out. His first inclination was to blow James Sattler's brains out, but that wouldn't have been smart either. He would have had the element of surprise on his side and might have been able to take two or three more, but he would have certainly gotten himself shot by one of the others. Besides, Black Jack was good with a gun...real good. If he wasn't able to kill him with the second shot, it would have been all over then and there.

They were drifting now. The trees and brush on the bank whipped past as if they were in a hurry to get someplace. The palomino snorted as he struggled against the current. Billy. had to adjust his grip on the pommel as his boots filled with water. The horse suddenly lunged forward as his hooves found some footing. He snorted again and took two bolting strides, pulling Billy with him.

"Easy, boy, easy." He caught his own footing and patted the horse's neck. "Don't blame you none. That was a hell of a way to cross a river, wasn't it?" He cleared a path through the thick brush.

"But even if we did get wet, it was better'n hanging around with them yeller coyotes." He found a flat rock and sat to empty the water out of his boots. He spied a hole in the toe of one of his socks and wondered when he'd last changed them. Maybe when he got to the next town and built up his money poke, he'd buy a new pair.

"Come on, boy." He pulled his boots on and climbed into the saddle. "Let's you and me find out where the next town is." He drifted south, following the path of the Mokelumne, knowing that sooner or later he would run across a gold camp or settlement. There was plenty of gold elsewhere, but the prospectors followed the water where the hunting was easier, and no matter how greedy someone might be, they still needed a drink of water. He reined the palomino to a halt as a group of Indians suddenly appeared. He quickly counted ten, and they all had their weapons pointed at him. The Colt hanging in his holster only carried six rounds and was wet. His odds were even worse here than back across the river.

"Okay." He smiled and raised both hands. One of the Indians trotted his pony forward to remove the pistol and the rifle from where it hung on his saddle. The leader motioned him forward with his lance.

"Where're we going?" The Indians urged their ponies into a gentle lope and rode silently.

"Just thought I'd ask, that's all." Billy shrugged. The only thing he knew for sure was that they were heading south, following the river.

~   ~   ~

The sliver of sun peeking over the top of Mt. Diablo cast a red and yellow glow across the cloud-scattered sky. James Sattler brought the group of riders to a halt and slid from the saddle. "Okay, we'll stop here and rest our horses for awhile. Roy, you take Frank's horse and ride to Doña Leonida's hacienda. Make sure her father gets this message." He handed a folded piece of paper to the man.

Loretta's body trembled, and she let out a whimper as Leonida helped her to the ground. "Señora, are you all right?" She led her to a seat on a fallen log. Loretta first nodded, then shook her head.

"No, my arm hurts so much I think I'm going to vomit." She hung her head between her knees.

"Señor Sattler. Señor," she called louder, finally getting his attention.

"Yeah, what is it now?"

"I don't believe Señora McDougal can go much further. She is in terrible pain."

"Really? Well, I suppose I could cure that for her here and now." He pulled a large pocket knife from his coat and clicked open the blade. "I could cut her throat and not have to think about her or listen to her whining any longer." He grabbed her hair and jerked her head backwards.

"No!" Leonida grabbed his wrist. "No, por favor." She shook her head. "I'll do anything you ask. Please don't."

"Anything?"

"Sí."

"That could be a big order. You should find out what someone's demands are before promising. I mean," he closed the knife and returned it to his pocket, "I could ask you to disrobe and allow all of us to take our turn with you. What would you say to that, Doña?" Leonida's mouth felt dry as her eyes darted from one grinning face to another.

"If...if it actually meant saving Señora McDougal's life, I would be willing, Señor, but how would I know that you would keep your promise?"

"Ah-ha!" James nodded. "A very wise question. You couldn't know, could you? You would have to be willing to take my word, but if I insisted on making that a condition of her staying alive right this minute, and all you had was my word, what would you say then? Would you still be willing to meet my demands in order to save her life?"

"Sí, I believe so. I am praying you would never make such a demand, but to save this woman's life, I would have to." She suddenly felt nauseated.

"Why?" James shook his head. "She's nothing but a whore. Why would you become a whore to save one?"

"Because it is what Dios would want from me."

"God." James snortrd. "I might have known. You really believe that stuff about God and the angels, don't you?"

"Sí. Have you never heard the story of Saint Martin?"

"No, but I suppose you're prepared to tell me."

"Martin was a soldier in France in the fourth century. One evening, he noticed a near-naked beggar shivering by the city gate. Everyone ignored the poor man," she raised her voice for the others to hear, "but Martin was so moved with compassion that he slashed his own cloak in two with his sword, giving one part to the beggar.

"Our Lord came to Martin in a dream that night, wrapped in the beggar's half of the cloak. As you did it to one of the least of these, my brethren, he said, you did it to me.

"From that time on, Martin gave himself completely to Jesus Cristo. He wholeheartly served Dios and helped those less fortunate. After his death, Martin of Tours was canonized as a Saint by the Church.

"The cloak was enshrined. The Latin word cappa was created because of that cloak, and the word for that shrine is cappella, or what you Americanos call chapel. Your word chaplain literally means "keeper of the cloak". That is what I am, Señor Sattler. A keeper of the cloak."

"Beautiful." James clapped his hands slowly. "A marvelous story, but I have my doubts that Saint Martin would have considered sacrificing himself for a whore, like you're wanting to do."

"I never said wanted to, Señor. In fact, I'm praying you won't it. If that was the only way to save her life, I would have to do. Why do you keep calling Señora McDougal such a dirty name?"

"Why?" James roared with laughter. "You don't really know, do you?"

"Know what?" Her eyes darted from James to Loretta and back.

"He's right. I am a whore." Loretta's voice was weak.

"What are you saying, Señora?" She sat on the log and an arm around her shoulders. "Do you know what you're saying?"

"Oh yeah." Loretta sighed deeply. "I know perfectly well what I'm saying. Isn't that right, Jim?" She glanced at the man before lowering her chin to her chest.

"Yeah, you're a whore all right, but don't worry, it's almost over with. There's the bridge and the road leading to the hacienda. Roy's going to see if Doña Leonida's daddy won't negotiate somesettlement and take you off our hands. I might have to keep Leonida a little longer to insure our getting away, but I do aim to be shed of you soon, one way or the other." He turned and walked away.

~   ~   ~

"Well, whadda ya think, Tommy?" Hanky asked as Tex joined them under a grove of scrub oaks on a rise overlooking the river. They could see the men milling around the horses, with their hostages seated on a log in a small clearing.

"Looks like they're gonna make camp. Got themselves into a fix all right. Think Baca's got his men close enough?"

Tex and General Flores nodded in unison. "How many's he got down there?"

"Nearly all of them. Place is crawling with Injuns. Ain't a one of 'em out watching cows. We jest don't see 'em," Tex said.

"What's the plan?"

"Well, the way I see it, you and the General work out some sort of signal. Or, better yet, pass the word. The instant they hear me pick off the leader with my needle gun, they're to jump up and get the rest at close range."

"Yeah, might work at that, if they was close enough," Hanky said.

"Only as a last resort." General Flores shook his head. "It would only take one stray bullet to harm the women. It would be too risky."

"Yeah, but didn't ya say that one of them done hurt Miss Loretta?" Bear growled. "What makes you think they ain't gonna hurt them more? Let me see that buffal'r gun of your'n." He reached for the Prussian made rifle hanging on Tex's horse.

"Better listen to the general, Bear. That's the captain's wife and general's daughter down there," Hanky said.

"Exactly. I ain't aiming ta shoot either one of 'em. I'm gonna take the head off that son of a buck holdin' em." Bear lay under one of the trees to sight the gun on James Sattler.

"Señor Bear, do you actually think you could hit a man from this distance?" General Flores grabbed hold of the barrel.

"Not with you holding onto the gun like that."

"But Señor, that is several hundred meters. Think of what might happen to my daughter and Señora McDougal if you miss."

"I ain't aiming ta miss, if you'll let go of the gun. Aw hell, now look what you've done." Bear scowled as James Sattler entered the grove of trees with one of the men leading a horse. "Had myself a perfect shot."

“He's just worried that you might miss and they'll hurt one of the women,” Hanky said.

“I know what he's worried about.” Bear handed the gun to Tex. “But me or you or Tex could pick a tick off a dog's ear at this distance with that gun. Hell,” he stopped to spit and wipe his mouth, “I ain't one of them soldiers you been used to ordering 'round, General. I've hunted buffal'r, mountain lions and Injuns all over these here United States, and I ain't used to missing what I aim at.” He pointed a finger at the general's nose.

“Sí, and I believe everything you say is true, but there has to be a better way. One that will insure the safety of the women. Where's Baca?” General Flores glanced around angrily before raising his voice. “Will someone get me Ildefonso Baca?”

“He's at the bottom of the hill having a confab with those braves.” Tex motioned with his head. The general brushed past them with a muffled “bueno” only to pause and stare at Sean and Jonathan as they slid down the hill toward a clump of bushes. He pointed at the men as he gave orders in Spanish to a group of vaqueros. The vaqueros quickly forced the men back up the hill.

“The general says we are to tie you to a tree if you try this again,” Paco said as he gave Sean a shove. He quickly scampered away as the angry doctor raised his fist.

“Still coulda done it.” Bear glared at Hanky.

“Well, it's too late to argue now. Let's mosey on down and see what Baca thinks. Well, now would ya look at that.” Hanky pointed as they caught up with Jose. A single rider had left the grove of trees and was headed toward the hacienda. “Looks like they's sending someone in to have a confab with you, General. Want us to head him off?”

“No, he'll return once he finds there is no one there but the women. In the meantime, we shall see what the man Broken Tooth is bringing has to say.” He walked toward the Indians escortin Billy James.

Chapter 45

"Why did you agree with that man when he called you names?" Leonida crinkled her brow as she sat beside Loretta. James Sattler had joined the men as they passed a bottle around the small campfire they had built.

"You really are a dear, aren't you." Loretta took Leonida's hand. "I guess it's time I told you my story."

"Bueno, I would like to know everything about you."

"Okay." Loretta inhaled a deep breath as sadness swept across her face. She massaged Leonida's hand as she talked.

"There are things about me I should have told you the first day I came to your ranch, but I was afraid."

"I'll admit that I have a bad temper, and what I did when you followed me this afternoon was not ladylike. But there is no need to be afraid of me, Señora."

"Just listen, okay? This is going to be hard enough as it is." Leonida stared as tears flooded the woman's eyes.

"Do you have any idea where Doctor Kilkenney and I first met?"

"In San Francisco."

"San Francisco is a large city." She choked back a sob. "Do you have any idea where in San Francisco?"

"Sí," Leonida glanced toward the men as they burst into laughter, "Señor Kilkenney said you met at some place called The Silver Palace."

"The Silver Slipper," Loretta corrected.

"Sí, that was its name. He said you were an entertainer...a singer, if I'm not mistaken."

"Well, that's putting it nicely. He is a darling, isn't he?"

"Why, is that not true?"

"Let's just say, it's partly true. I did sing, but not the type of songs you're used to hearing around the ranch or inside the chapel. I sang songs the miners and sailors wanted to hear. I wore a lot of lip-rouge and painted my eyes. I wore my skirts above my knees and black stockings to show off my legs. The higher I kicked while dancing, the louder the men clapped, and the more money they threw on the stage. I got paid extra for any favors I performed off the stage."

"I don't understand." Leonida shook her head. "Señor Kilkenney said you sang beautiful music. Ballads and opera."

"Yes, that's what I studied back east, but, you see, I wasn't employed as a singer at the time. When I saw an advertisement in a magazine, saying they needed singers out west, why I jumped at the chance. What I found was, they wanted bawdy-house singers, and girls who were willing to take care of men's urges in the bedroom. I refused to do either for several weeks, but I didn't have enough money to get back home, and the rent on even a small room costs a fortune in that city. It didn't take long until my money was gone, and they threw me out onto the street. A girl doesn't last long on the streets, and I was nearly starving to death as it was. So, I finally gave in."

"You were?"

"That's right." Loretta sniffed as she nodded. "I think what Rosa called it was puta. Oh, but don't worry, Doctor Kilkenney and I were never that way." She squeezed Leonida's hand. "We were simply friends. Whether you believe it or not, all he ever talked about when we were together was you."

"Oh, Señora, that is hard to believe." Leonida shook her head. "How could any man be alone with you and choose only to talk about me?"

"You'll have to ask him that question. But he did...a lot." Loretta scrunched her eyebrows. "It used to make me angry. Here I was, trying my best to get him to really notice me, and he's telling me about this beautiful woman who owns half of California."

"I'm afraid that's an exaggeration. There are many ranchos larger than mine."

"Not in his mind. Yours is the best, and you are the most beautiful woman in the whole world. That's why I had to come. You sounded too good to be true, and I wanted to at least see the competition, even if I had already lost."

"I don't think I'm so wonderful." Leonida shook her head. "I do have a bad temper, and I am not as beautiful as you are."

"You are something else." Loretta leaned to kiss Leonida's cheek. "You're possibly the nicest woman I've ever met. Now, you know about me." She grimaced and grabbed her arm.

"Sí, but why tell me this? Why tell anyone? No one needed to know. What about your husband?"

"Jonathan already knows. I wasn't aware of it at the time, but he used to listen to me sing at The Silver Slipper, and he still loves me. Isn't that amazing?" She choked and covered her mouth. "Rosa and Angela knew right away. We're sort of like sisters in that respect, and, of course, James Sattler knows. After all, he had to defend me in court, remember? But the main reason for my telling you is, no matter what happens...how this all turns out...you don't have to worry about Sean Kilkenney having ever loved me. I tried everything I knew to make him fall in love with me, and none of it worked. He always did love you, and always will. He's all yours, honey."

"But you loved him, didn't you." Leonida took one of Loretta's hands and began rubbing it in much the same way she had done hers earlier.

"Oh yeah." She nodded. "More than I ever thought I could love anyone. I still do, but he's more like a brother now.

"I finally got to know my Jonathan, and I'm positive I couldn't love anyone or anything more than him. It would be impossible. I know it might be hard for you to understand, him being older and you being who you are, but my husband and Sean, were the only men I've met since arriving in California who treated me more than something to poke in bed. Sorry for being so crude." She covered her mouth and turned away as tears flooded her eyes. "Well, there was Bear, but he's just that...a big stuffed bear."

"No need to apologize, señora. I am sorry you've met with so much sorrow in your life." Leonida pulled her close and leaned her head against Loretta's shoulder.

"You're the one who's seen trouble. You lost your husband, and now that slug over there is going to steal you blind."

"Gracias, but what can he take that can't be replaced? The gold? This rancho with all its cattle? They are only things, but your wounds run deep. You need to let the Holy Father heal you as He has done for Rosa and Angela."

"Thank you, but I think He's already done some of that." She sighed. "That's the part I didn't tell you. I realized while I was in San Francisco that God hadn't totally forgotten me. After Jonathan and I were married, I found this little church and we would go there and pray nearly every day, and the rest is history."

"Bueno." She kissed Loretta's cheek. "Everything has worked out as the Father had planned."

"I just wish He would have worked it a little different. Here I am, at the happiest time in my life, about to have a baby, and now this." She glanced toward the men.

"You're pregnant?" Leonida scanned her with wide eyes. "Oh, that is so wonderful!" Her squeeze caused Loretta to cry out in pain. "I'm so sorry. Are you all right?"

Loretta nodded. "Just my arm." She took a deep breath. "Yeah, it is. I mean my being pregnant. Jonathan wants a baby real bad, but, I'm afraid he'll never get one. At least not with me."

"Señora, you're young and healthy, and..."

"You don't honestly think Jim's going to let me go, do you? It was my testimony that caused Judge Baker to start checking the records." She shook her head. "He's going to kill me the same as he killed those other girls in San Francisco."

"He has murdered someone?" Her voice was barely audible.

"I thought you understood that. Remember me saying he had been cutting girls? He's killed three girls that we know of. Maybe more, and I'll go before this is all over. He said he was *going to be shed of me one way or the other*, and you can be sure he's not going to allow you to walk away either. He'll slit your throat as soon as he gets his hands on your gold."

"Madré de Dios." Leonida crossed her breast. The sound of pounding hooves caused them both to look toward the road. A single rider turned into the grove of trees and dismounted and joined James Sattler by the campfire.

"Ain't nobody there 'cept a fat maid and couple of kids. She said everyone was out looking for the women. I told her I wanted to help and asked which way they went." He laughed. "She said they headed west. We got the whole place to ourselves."

"I guess we shall find out soon. Won't we, Señora McDougal?" She squeezed Loretta's hand as James rose from the rock he'd been sitting on and headed their way.

~   ~   ~

Ildefonso Baca and Broken Tooth crept silently through the tall weeds, approaching the two women from the rear. They had Armando Rohas and Jesus Rivas, two trusted Yokuts at their sides. Baca had chosen these men specifically because they were more experienced in battle. It would be their job to help shield the women from danger with their own bodies. They, along with Baca himself, would position themselves between the women and their captors while the remaining vaqueros captured and disarmed the men. He doubted very much that the men would give up that easily. Some of them, especially the leader, might have to be killed, but that was of no concern to Baca. The vaqueros could kill them all once he had the women to safety.

They paused about twenty feet from the women as a single rider turned into the grove dismounted near the campfire. He began talking to the leader in a hurried tone. Baca glanced toward Broken Tooth, who shrugged. Baca motioned with his head and the men inched forward. They were about ten feet away, when the men by the campfire turned and walked toward the women. He cringed as they stopped in front of the women to talk. They were too close. If they attacked now, the women would be used as shields. Baca and his men melted back into the weeds to wait.

The leader grabbed the Leonida by the arm and shoved her toward her horse while another man helped Loretta onto the mule. She cried out in pain during the process and sat slumped in the saddle. Now was not a good time to make a move. Baca shook his head as the captors ushered the women out of the woods and onto the road. The grove was suddenly filled with Indians coming from behind trees and rocks. Baca rose from the ground and motioned with his arm. The men vanished as quickly as they had appeared, racing toward their ponies. They would be waiting by the time the women reached the hacienda.

~   ~   ~

"Na, I ain't saying I'm lily-white. All I'm saying is, I don't cotton to anyone treating a lady the way they're doing. Only a Yankee would do a woman that-a-way." Billy paused to stare at the soggy cigarette papers he'd pulled from his shirt pocket. "Hey, y'all wouldn't have something to smoke, would ya?"

"Sí." Juan licked the fresh cigarette he'd finished rolling and passed it to the young man.

"Thanks," Billy accepted a light from Paco, "both of you."

"Por nada." Juan shrugged and rolled another smoke.

"Then tell me, Señor Billy. If you did not agree with the way they were treating my daughter and her companion, why did you choose to ride with them in the first place?"

"Well, I didn't know they was gonna do something like that. All I was told was, they planned on robbing some rich Mexican of some of his gold. I didn't know that Mexican was a lady, and I didn't know they planned on hurting any women in the process. In fact, I didn't know anyone was gonna get hurt a'tall. Na, I just couldn't cotton to an idee like Sattler's got cooked up." He shook his head.

"Who'd you say he was?" Jonathan McDougal grabbed his arm.

"Sattler. Jim Sattler. Why?"

"Great God in heaven." Jonathan turned white.

"What's wrong?" Tex clasped a hand on his shoulder.

"James Sattler is a madman. He enjoys killing people, especially women. We have to get them out of there, or he'll murder them both."

"Baca's taking care of that right now."

"Ya say yer name's Bill? Got any idee who I am?" Hanky glanced up from packing his pipe.

"No sir. I can't rightly say so."

"Well, son, let me tell you." Hanky paused lite the pipe. He blew a cloud of smoke as he spoke. "I'm Josiah Russell. Duly appointed sheriff 'round these parts. You might not know it yet, but your being with them skunks makes you one of them. You're in a heap of trouble, boy, and if one of them women gets hurt any worser, you might get yerself hung beside a Yankee. Whadda ya got to say about that?"

"Don't reckon I cotton much to the idee." He studied the smoldering butt in his fingers before taking one last drag and tossing it to the ground. "William Franklin James of Beaufort, North Carolina, getting hisself hung next to some damned Yankees and buried in Californy." He shook his head and grinned. "Nope, don't sound too good, especially seeing as how we are at war with them Yankee aggressors back home. Any way I can get myself outta this mess?"

I might put a word or two into Judge Hansen for you, if ya cooperate. I don't cotton ta hanging a good ol' southern boy like you either. Now, what can ya tell me 'bout them?"

"Nothing much. Only one I really knowed was Ken Edwards, and the reason I knew him was because I set in on one of his card games and got fleeced outta all my money. He promised I'd get it back plus a whole lot more if I take this little ride with them. That's the honest truth."

"That ain't much," Tex sniggered. "We ain't asking for no names or addresses or nothing like that. What we'd like to know is what you seen with yer own eyes. What do you feel inside yer bones? A southern boy like you knows what I'm talking about."

"What I seen is, Frank over there," he nodded toward the prostrate man Sean was examining, "was mighty happy to twist that lady's arm. He was shore gonna twist her head clean off before this was over. And Sattler was tickled all the way to his backbone watching him do it."

"Bastards." Jonathan wiped his face with a trembling hand.

"Yes Sir. The way I see it, they crawled out from under a rock. Sattler plans on killing both them women before he's through. The others don't know it yet, but he does."

"What about the others?" Hanky puffed deeply on the pipe.

"Well, Ken's a gambler. He's along for thrill. You know, seeing if he can get away with pulling it off." Billy shrugged. "Black Jack's the one dressed like he's going to a funeral."

"He is," Hanky said. "His own. Go on."

"Well, he's kinda hard to figure. He don't say or do much. My guess is he's a hired gun. Some sort of bodyguard to Ken, and I'd watch him real close. The other three are kinda like me. They was picked 'cause they need the money, and they can use an iron. They might put up some sort of tussle, but if they figured the odds were agin them, they'd drop their guns and take the easy way out."

"Much obliged. That's what we wanted to hear."

"If you were so taken aback by their actions Señor, why didn't you try to do something when you were with them?" Jose scowled.

"Because my mamma gave me a little more sense than that. Even with yer daughter bonking ol' Frank on the head, there was still six others. I might of bored two, maybe three of 'em myself, but I didn't like the idee of dying for a couple of women I don't even know. Sorry."

"Most unfortunate. Perhaps most men would feel that way." Jose shrugged. "Now we must rely on the cunning of our Indians to rescue our women."

"Well, you can give up on that idee right now." Bear pointed toward the line of riders leaving the small campsite. "Looks like Baca didn't have time to pull it off. Looks like their going to the house."

"There's Baca." Tex pointed toward the Indians running toward their horses. "Bet he's gonna shadow them all the way to the hacienda, unless you say something different, General."

"I don't know what else we can do. He has men front and back, and on either side of the women. It would be impossible to shoot without hitting one of them." Jose shook his head. "Paco, you and Juan race back to the hacienda and get everyone to safety, especially the women and children. Make them hide in one of the casas outside the wall. If they are looking for gold, they will search the hacienda first, and that is where they will make their last demands."

"Bueno." Both vaqueros scrambled down the hillside toward their horses.

"Well, I'll tell you what," Bill hitched his empty gunbelt, "you give me my iron back and let me ride down there and rejoin them. Then, y'all get yerselves ready to back me up. I'll take Sattler and Black Jack out myself, just because I owe it to them. But y'all need to be ready ta finish the game, 'cause like I said, I'm not aiming ta die for women I don't even know."

"He might have a point, old man." Tex grinned.

"No, no," Jose waved them off, "it would be too dangerous. The women might get hit by a stray bullet."

"We might not have much choice." Hanky checked the loads in his gun. "Besides, they're out in the open now. It won't be so easy once they're inside."

"Sí, you have a point, but only as a last resort. If we make them think they are getting what they want, we may rescue the women. Besides, how do we know we can trust this man?"

"Now, you take that back!" Billy squared off to face the General. "I gave my word and William James ain't no liar."

"Not now boy." Hanky gave him a shove. "We got us better fish to fry. You two can settle this later. Come on, let's rustle or them Injuns will have this thing settled and we'll miss all the fun."

"You might be some sort of General, but you ain't got a lick of sense if you're thinking Sattler's gonna let them go," Billy growled. "I told you he plans to kill both them women."

"I said later." Hanky shoved Billy harder.

"How's he doing, Doc?" Tex stared at Frank's bloody face.

"Not too good. If he pulls through, I don't think he would ever be the same." Sean wiped his palms on his pant legs.

"Hell, that ain't so bad. He weren't nothing but a snake in the first place. Besides it wouldn't make much difference seeing as Hanky plans on hanging his sad ass first chance he gets. Come on, leave that critter with the Injuns and let's rustle. Yer liable ta have some easy bullet holes to patch before this dance is over."

Chapter 46

Evangelina's two dogs met them at the gate barking as they rode into the courtyard. James Sattler brought the small group to a halt near the fountain and dismounted. Black Jack grabbed Loretta by her injured arm and jerked her from the horse. She fell to the bricks with a cry of pain.

"Bruto!" Leonida leaped from her horse to hit him, but he caught her wrist in mid-flight and gave it a twist. "Leave her alone." She gritted her teeth. Haven't you hurt her enough?" Black Jack laughed and turned away.

"Where the hell's everyone?" James Sattler asked as he stared at the empty courtyard. The place looked deserted excluding the heavy-set woman standing in the doorway. "What kind of a host are you anyway? No welcoming party, or dancing girls?"

"I was praying my father would have a welcoming party for you, Señor." She helped Loretta to her feet.

"Hell, I told you we was gonna have everything to ourselves, Jim. Her pa and them vaqueros are combing the countryside, looking for us," Roy said.

"Makes me kinda of antsy," one of the men said. "You'd think they woulda caught up with us by now."

"No one's ever accused Mexicans of being intelligent," James said. "Come on, let's get inside."

"Digame Doña Leonida. Cómo esta?" Maria scampered to help Loretta through the door.

"Maria, Señora McDougal esta lastimada. These beasts continued hurting her all afternoon. May Dios judge them rightly."

They helped Loretta to one of the kitchen chairs, where Maria dashed to the cupboard to retrieve a bottle of brandy and filled a glass.

"Here, drink this Señora. It will help the pain." She held the glass to Loretta's lips, only to have James Sattler jerk it from her hand.

"Hell, that's good brandy." He sniffed the aroma before taking a sip. "Too damn good to waste on a whore." He drained the glass and slammed it on the table.

"Come on, where's the gold? We didn't come here to nursemaid a whore."

"No," Leonida shook her head, "you will receive nada from me, Señor. Not until someone has seen to Señora McDougal's injuries."

"No?" James grinned and slapped her hard across the cheek. Leonida clenched her jaw and glared back.

"Want some more?" He hit her twice more. The second blow caused her to stagger and brought tears to her eyes. But once again she straightened herself to glare.

"Nada, Señor."

James took a step toward her, but Ken Edwards caught his arm. "Come on, Jim. You can hang around beating the hell out of her later, if you want. But me and the rest of the boys want to grab the gold and get the hell outta here before her papa gets back with all those Mexicans."

"Yeah, sure," James snickered and turned toward Maria. "Give the whore some brandy so your Doña will quit acting stupid."

"Sí." The neck of the bottle rattled against the glass, as Maria poured. "Here, Señora, let me help you." Her hand trembled as she held the glass to Loretta's lips. The woman took several sips before nodding.

"Okay, let's get this over. Where're you keeping the gold?" James grinned. "In your desk drawer?"

"Some of it." Leonida nodded.

"What'd I tell you." James turned to Ken with a laugh. "Come on." He bolted from the room. Leonida could hear her desk being taken apart as she helped Loretta from the chair. She was pale and leaned against Leonida as they made their way into the den.

"Hell, I only found this one little bag." James tossed the bag of coins on the desk. "Where's the rest?" Leonida scanned the scattered drawers and papers.

"I said I kept *some* of the money here, Señor. You didn't have to make such a mess. I would have gotten it for you."

"Where is it?" James pointed his gun at her.

"Easy, Jimmy-boy." Black Jack eased the hand holding the gun toward the floor. "Don't kill her until we know where she's got it hid. This is a mighty big place here."

"I will show you where it is, if you will take the money and leave us alone."

"I promise we'll do exactly that, Ma'am." Black Jack said.

"Bueno. It is in my bedroom. Come, I will show you."

"Well go on, you too." James prodded Loretta with his gun. "You can have the fat maid help you, if you want. I'm not that mean." They followed the Doña up the steps.

~   ~   ~

General Flores brought the group of riders to a halt fifty yards from the open gate and dismounted. He frowned at the jingle of Paco's spurs as the vaquero joined them.

"You sound like one of Apolinar's goats. Take those things off. You too, Juan. Everyone," he ordered in a hoarse whisper. "Pronto." The men crouched behind the wall surrounding the hacienda and unbuckled the riding gear.

"They are inside the hacienda," Paco whispered as they peered around the gatepost.

"What about the others? Were you able to get everyone to safety?"

"Sí, all but Maria. She says she will die with Doña Leonida. The others are at Juan's casa with Angela."

"Bueno." Jose sighed. The men glanced at each other as Baca appeared at their side.

"Damn, I'm glad he's on our side." Hanky chuckled.

"I'll say," Tex mumbled. "I know it's dark, but take a good look around you. We've got ourselves surrounded by Injuns." They listened intently as the general and Baca spoke softly in Spanish. The Indian rose quietly and motioned with his lance. The Indians darted through the gate and split into two separate lines. Their moccasins whispered against the sand and bricks as they slid through the darkness.

"How many entrances they got to the place?" Billy leaned over Hanky's shoulder to peer through the gate.

"Five. The front door, and one through the kitchen. Three more on the second story veranda."

"The trick will be getting inside without being seen. They'll kill women if they do," Tex said.

"There's more than one way to enter a house," Salty whispered. "You blokes give me a minute to scale those vines to the second floor, then come a running."

"No," Jose waved them off. "That is exactly what we do not want. A fire-fight at close quarters will be more dangerous for the women than attacking them in the open."

"Well, begging your pardon, Mate, but what do you expect us to do? Wait until they've cut their throats before we knock on the door?" Salty raised his eyebrows.

"No, I expect you and Baca and several other Indians to work yourselves inside just as you suggested. But I also expect you to follow orders."

"And what might that be?"

"I want you to wait for an opportunity to get the women to safety before we enter the building. At this point, I have no idea what that might be. Lock them inside one of the bedrooms or something then give us a signal. The rest of us will come the instant we know they are safe."

"Ya won't have ta try very hard getting 'em inside a bedroom." Tex pointed as someone lit a lamp. "Looks like they're inside the Missus' bedroom right now."

"That's where she keeps the gold hidden." The general nodded slowly. He stared at the gravel and took a deep breath. "Get going." He clapped Salty on the shoulder. "One of the Indians is waiting."

Salty could see the dark figure slip over the top railing and press himself against the wall near one of the windows that remained dark. Two others had scaled the railing by the time he reached the vines. He pulled the knife from its sheath and clamped the blade between his teeth before latching onto the vine. *Just like climbing a ship's rigging.* He crawled quickly up the side of the hacienda. *We're going to slit James Sattler's bloody throat just like he did Sara's.* He had almost reached the railing when three men ran out the front door and rounded the corner of the house toward the chapel.

Maybe they've had a change of heart and are going to pray. He snickered as he grabbed another handful of vine. That was when he heard the first shot.

Chapter 47

Leonida waited until one of the men had lit both lamps before entering her bedroom.

"Okay, show us where the gold is." James ordered.

"I keep it hidden over here." She crossed the room to the fireplace and removed one of the bricks. "There is no need of keeping it hid, because no one living on Rancho Manantial Escondido has ever stolen anything."

"That's nice, but we don't live here, do we? Show me the gold."

"It's inside the chimney, Señor."

"Oh, no," James chuckled, "I'm not sticking my hand in there. You first."

"Okay." Leonida shrugged and shoved her arm inside the opening halfway to the elbow and withdrew a small leather pouch filled with gold and tossed it to him. "You are being frightened por nada, Señor. I would not keep poison snakes or dangerous things hidden inside my own bedroom."

"No, you're dangerous enough." He motioned with the gun. "Keep digging. I want it all."

"Sí, I thought you would." She pulled three more bags from the fireplace. "You have been like this from the start. You wanted more from the first time I saw you. You have no regard for the feelings or needs of others. It only matters what concerns you."

"You've got that right, lady."

"Doesn't love for Dios or your fellow man mean anything to you?" She paused before retreaving another bag.

"Let me tell you something, lady. Ideas of God and love are overrated. Even family relationships are nothing but cultural constructs. Take it from an expert. I never knew my father because I don't think my mother even knew who he was. She was a real bitch who treated me like dirt. I used to lie awake nights, listening to her take care of her customers. If I wanted to, I could peek through the curtains separating my bed from the rest of our one room apartment, and watch her spread her fat legs for the drunks who wandered in there.

"But I rose above it. I made something of myself, with no help from anybody. I worked my way through Harvard by waiting tables and cleaning the slop left by those rich boys. They had their skinny, perfect wives and doting parents. All I had was me. James Sattler." He thumped his chest.

"I found out the hard way that love makes people soft. But not Jimmy-boy. Not anymore. I was hard back then, and I'm hard now. That's why I'll not only survive, but I'll prosper." Beads of sweat worked their way down his cheeks as he waved the gun wildly. "I don't mind leaving San Francisco, either. In fact, I like it this way. It'll give me a chance to take time off, to relax and go some places I'd like to see. But no one's ever done a thing for me that I know of. I've had to fight for every scrap every inch of the way."

Leonida shook her head. "You seem to have forgotten, Señor. I believe I came to you in my hour of need and begged your help. I also paid you well for work you never performed. I seem to be the one who has given, and you are the one who has taken."

"Maybe, but you'll be surprised at what those who come after me are going to take. You won't have a ranch or even a single cow when they're through, lady. There's no way you're going to keep this place, and it doesn't matter what I could have said or done inside that courtroom. Now, come on," he motioned with his free hand, "quit talking and get the rest. Like I said, we want it all."

"That's all there is." Leonida shrugged.

"All there is?" James smirked. "This isn't a good time for a religious woman like you to start lying. You've got an entire gold mine, and you're telling me these five little bags are all you have?"

"Sí, check for yourself." She stepped away from the fireplace as one of the men rushed forward to shove his hand inside the hole.

"She's right, it's empty."

"All right, where's the rest?" James yelled.

"I've given you all there is. There is no other gold."

"Dammit," he swung the gun toward Loretta's head, "do I have to kill her in order to make you talk?"

"She is telling you the truth, Señor," Maria said. "The gold they take from the river belongs to the people. Doña Leonida keeps only a little to help run the hacienda."

"What?" James lowered the gun as the men glanced at each other.

"I could have told you that Jim, and saved you a lot of trouble," Loretta snickered. "She's such a darling, she honestly believes that since the people working for her found the gold, it should belong to them. It doesn't make any difference they were working for her on her land. She gave it to them. She only takes a little bag every now and then."

"You can't be serious." James squinted at Leonida.

"I don't need gold. I have the land and the cattle. Señor McDougal gives me what I need from his ship in exchange for hides and tallow. Why should I take their gold when they found it and do all the work taking it from the ground?" She stared as Ken Edwards leaned against the wall laughing.

"What the hell's so funny?" James glared.

"Nothing, actually. Only that we rode all the way out here for this." Ken bounced one of the bags in his hand. "Hell, I've made more sitting six hours at a card table."

"No, they're lying." James grabbed Loretta's hair and jammed the pistol against her temple. "Either you tell me right now where the rest of the gold is, or I'm going to splatter her brains all over your bedroom."

"She's telling you the truth, Señor, por favor." Maria fell to her knees begging. "The people give her the gold, but she only keeps a little for herself. The rest she gives to the priest to buy medicine and books for the people."

"Maria!" Leonida glared.

"Perdon a me, Doña Leonida, but he will kill her."

"That's better." James released Loretta's hair. "Now we're getting somewhere." He nodded toward the men standing by the door. "Why don't you guys go pay the padré a visit and take up a collection from him? Tell him Doña Leonida said it is okay." He grinned and pointed the gun at her nose. "The church is right behind the house," he added as the men glanced at each other. He waited until they had gone before turning toward Ken.

"You know something? I'd be willing to bet that there's a lot of things laying around she hasn't told us about. Things like jewelry, silver." He shrugged. "Why don't you and Black Jack take a look while I keep these women company?"

"Sounds like a good idea." Ken nodded. "I'll see what she's got in here, Jack. You can start in the next room." Black Jack nodded and backed out the door as Ken started rifling through Leonida's things. It only took him a matter of seconds before he had found her jewelry box and emptied its contents into his pockets. "Thank you, Ma'am." He grinned and hurried from the room.

"Well, now that you've gotten what you wanted, what's going to happen to us?" Loretta leaned heavily against the wall.

"You know, Loretta, it's actually too bad about us. With your looks and my brains, we made a pretty good team. But you had to turn moral on me. To make things worse, you told Judge Baker about our money-making enterprise. You probably flap your lips about the same as you spread your legs. I guess there is no way to trust a whore, is there?" He shook his head and pulled the trigger. Loretta whimpered as she clutched her side and folded on the floor in a fetal position. "Goodbye, bitch."

"Madré de Dios!" Leonida clutched the fallen woman in her arms.

"Mother Mary isn't going to be much help to you now, believe me." The lamp near the window exploded as James pulled the trigger a second time. Flames leaped up the curtains and across the French doors leading to the second story veranda. He then grabbed the lamp sitting on the night stand and paused at the door to grin.

"Welcome to hell, Doña Leonida." He pulled the door partway closed before dropping the lamp.

Leonida's eyes darted from the flames blocking the door to the ones eating at the curtains and French doors. The room was filling with smoke. *Welcome to hell, Doña Leonida. James Sattler. It was you all the time.* Maria's coughing brought her out of her daze. The maid was vigorously beating at the flames with a blanket.

"Maria, come here. Maria," she yelled a second time louder. "Come help me with Señora McDougal. We must get her help."

"But Doña Leonida. The fire..."

"Forget the fire. It's too late. The house will burn and there's nothing we can do about it. Open my closet and come help me carry her. Now," she yelled Maria stared. "Hurry!"

Maria jerked open both closet doors.

"Now, push my clothes aside and you will find a small door leading to the next room. Open it and help me get her through the opening." Instead of pushing the clothes aside, Maria grabbed double-handfuls of clothing and tossed them on the floor. She jerked the door open and ran to grab Loretta under the arms.

"You take her feet, Señora. Wait." She quickly laid Loretta on the floor and dashed to the dresser where she shoved Leonida's wedding picture in her apron pocket. "You will have it to show your grandchildren someday." She readjusted Loretta in her arms. "Come." She backed toward the closet. The house had suddenly turned into a war zone with the sounds of gunfire and men yelling. Leonida cringed as someone fired a gun in the hallway right outside her door.

~   ~   ~

"No!" General Flores yelled at the sound of gunshots coming from the bedroom. He bolted toward the house as flames appeared in the window.

"Sonofabitch." Tex almost knocked Hanky to the ground as he dashed through the gate. "Come on, old man," he called over his shoulder.

"You heard him. The ball's open. Let's dance." Hanky pulled his .44 from its holster and ran after them.

Two of the three men who had headed for the chapel were now backing through the front door firing their guns. One of them had an arrow sticking in his shoulder, while the third man lay dead in the courtyard from a lance wound.

"Hold on there." Tex drug General Flores to the pavement beside the fountain. "I know it's yer daughter, but use yer head. You ain't gonna help her none by getting yerself kilt." Hanky paused beside them long enough to fire his gun at the open doorway.

"Of course you ain't gonna have no fun staying glued to the bricks either." He fired again. "Go on, I'll keep you two covered 'til you reach the porch. Then you can cover me."

"You got it, old man. Come on, General." Tex bolted forward as the ranger fired the .44 several more times.

~   ~   ~

The instant the second gunshot rang out and flames leaped up the curtains, Salty Moran followed the Indians through the doors leading to the darkened bedroom next to Leonida's. *Bastard is trying to burn them alive.* He stumbled over a small table in the darkness and fell to the floor. It was the fall that saved his life. The braves were met with a hail of gunfire as they dashed into the hallway.

Dammit, he crept across the floor on all fours to pause behind the open door. He could hear James Sattler laughing as two other men exchanged angry words.

"What the hell are you doing? We needed those women to make our get away."

"Hell, we're not getting away, Ken. The son of a bitch is crazier than an opium-smoking Chinaman. That woman's been telling us the truth. This place is crawling with Indians. Listen to the commotion downstairs. I ought to blow his brains out right here and now."

"Save your ammunition." Salty could hear the voices fading down the hallway. "We'll leave him for the Indians to scalp. I'm going downstairs to join the others."

He was positioning himself to pounce on the laughing madman, when the closet door suddenly burst open. Maria's silouette was outlined by the orange glow of the fire as she backed into the room holding Loretta in her arms. Leonida appeared, a second later. *Dammit!* He could see Sattler's back as he eased the door shut. *Save the women first, Salty.*

"Shhhh," he whispered as he closed the closet. The smoke from the next room had already begun to sting his eyes. "Get some air." He took Loretta in his arms and moved toward the veranda. Once out in the fresh air both women began coughing and wiping their eyes.

"Paco," Leonida leaned over the railing and yelled. "Paco. Somebody help!"

Que, Señora?" the vaquero called from his vantage point by the fountain.

"Toss me your lariat. Hurry."

"Bueno." He disappeared into the blackness.

"Begging your pardon, Ma'am, but you'd better keep it down." Salty leaned close to her ear to whisper. "That son of a sea serpent is right out in the hall."

"If that man can hear us over the yelling and shooting, Señor, he has better ears than I do. Besides, if we don't get down from here, we'll burn to death." They scooted toward the opposite end of the veranda as the windows in her bedroom exploded, sending a shower of flames and sparks toward the sky.

~   ~   ~

"All right." Hanky finished shoving new shells into the .44 and snapped the cylinder shut. "Same thing. Juan and I cover while y'all make it to the porch." Pieces of wood and glass leaped into the air as the two men riddled the front of the hacienda with bullets. General Flores and his companions fired randomly as they dashed onto the porch to press themselves against the adobe walls. Hanky waited a long second for the general to signal with a wave of his gun.

"Ready?" He glanced at the vaquero beside him.

"Sí." Juan finished loading his weapon with a nod.

"Let's dance." Hanky let out a rebel yell and fired into one of the windows as he dashed across the courtyard. Juan flew past on his left, firing in midair as he leaped the porch railing and rolled to a halt under the living room window.

"Damned showoff. If I wuz younger, I'd show you a thing or two," Hanky growled.

"Hell, you couldn't a done that, no matter how young you wuz," Tex sniggered.

"Smart aleck kid. Who wuz it who taught you how to use that iron in the first place? Better move over there, next to Bear." he motioned toward the opposite side of the doorway. "Don't want you shooting me in the foot when they decide to play the next tune." He leaned and snapped off two quick shots as Tex dove at the huge man's feet.

"General, wanna ask them if they wanna quit, or keep playing?" Hanky said.

"Señores," Jose yelled, "it is hopeless for you to continue. Please drop your weapons and come out with your hands raised. We have our trained vaqueros covering every window and exit to the hacienda. It is impossible for you to survive unless you surrender immediately."

"Damn, he makes it sound polite." Tex laughed.

"Go to hell." Someone inside yelled and fired. The bullet whined mournfully as it ricocheted off the fountain.

"Guess he still wants to dance." Tex said.

"Well, let's quit waltzing and strike up a Texas hoe-down." Hanky leaned to fire down the hall. Bear let out an ear-piercing yell and fired over their heads. The men riddled the living room walls and lower stair casing as they charged through the doorway.

"Whadda ya think, General," Hanky said as he pressed against the living room wall. "Think they're all holed up inside the study, or scattered out some?"

"The latter, I'm afraid. I can still hear that madman laughing upstairs."

"I think yer right. Hey, y'all inside the study," he leaned close to the door and yelled. "We know yer in there, 'cause we can see a trail of blood on the floor. How bad ya hurt, anyways?"

"Not so bad we can't fight."

"Well, this wing-ding's getting boring, so why don't you toss yer guns into the hall and come on out. We can have doc look at them scratches and whip up a pot of coffee."

"Why don't you come and take our guns?"

"Ifin you say so." Hanky nodded toward Tex and cocked his pistol. "My turn. Y'all fill the place with lead." The men slid against the wall toward the study and paused as the door swung shut.

"Hey, that ain't too hospitable. How ya expect me to come in when you slam the door in my face?"

"Well, it isn't locked. Open it and come on in."

"Okie-dokie." He nodded and Bear gave the heavy oak door a kick. The hall was filled with gunfire as the men inside fired their weapons.

"Caramba," Juan said as Bear pressed him against the plaster next to the door. Hanky counted silently with his fingers. One...two...three, then dove through the door as Juan, Tex and Bear fired rapidly. Someone screamed and cursed in pain as Hanky slid across the wood floor, firing under Leonida's desk.

"Okay, we quit." A pair of hands rose above the desk.

"Toss the guns out first, then come out trying to scratch the paint off the ceiling," Tex yelled.

"Better do as he says, or I'll shoot another leg off. I can see y'all under the desk," Hanky said.

"Hold your fire. We're coming." Two guns hit the floor in front of the desk, followed by a third, seconds later. "You've got a couple of men hurt real bad back here." Ken Edwards motioned with his head.

"Well, y'all drag them out from behind the desk and maybe we'll have doc take a look at them," Hanky said. Ken helped Roy to the center of the room. His right leg hung limp and was covered with blood from the knee down. The other man staggered from behind the desk with an arrow embedded in his left shoulder. They were immediately surrounded by Indians.

"I think you shot his kneecap off," Ken said.

"Hey Doc," Tex called down the hallway, "wanna take a look at this hombre before he bleeds to death?" Sean quickly poked his head through the open door and frowned.

"No, wrap a tourniquet around it. I'll see him later."

"What the hell kind of a doctor are you? The man's hurt," Ken yelled. Sean paused to glare over his shoulder.

"I'm the kind of doctor that's interested in finding the woman he's engaged to marry, and another man's wife who happens to be pregnant. You and the other two bastards who are responsible for them being trapped inside a burning building will have to wait."

"You heard him." Hanky motioned with his gun. "Tie his leg off with a belt and do exactly what these Injuns say. 'Cause they'll kill ya if ya don't."

"What about Nevada? He's got an arrow stuck in him."

"He'll keep." The wounded men cried out in pain as the braves drug them from the room. "Bunch of crybabies." Hanky joined the men at the base of the stairwell. Smoke billowing from the second floor stung their eyes.

"Whadda ya think, old man? We going up there?" Tex checked the loads in his gun.

"Hell yeah, I am. There's still two varmints on the loose, and they've got three women up there."

"Well, there ain't gonna be no women or house or nothing left if we wait much longer." Tex cocked the hammer on his .44 and led the way, one step at a time. The men paused halfway up the stairs as another shot rang out and a woman screamed.

Chapter 48

Salty caught the end of Paco's lariat and looped it once around one of the posts holding the roof of the veranda. He then carefully secured one end under Loretta's arms, using his sweater as a pad, and hoisted her over the railing.

"Both of you hold onto that end and keep the rope tight as I let go. We don't want to hurt her any more than she already is. Ready?" He glanced at Leonida.

"Sí." Leonida blinked against the smoke bellowing from her bedroom.

"Okay, lower away, slowly." He released his hold. Loretta whimpered as her body swung like a slow pendulum in the breeze. "All right I got her now." He grabbed hold of the leather rope. "You can let go." He kept his weight into the rope, using the post for friction, easing her lower, an arm's length at a time. Loretta was halfway to Paco when the door to the bedroom burst open.

"There you are. I wondered why you weren't screaming your heads off. You're just full of surprises." James Sattler laughed as he pulled the trigger. Salty groaned as the bullet took him in the left side, knocking him into the railing. Leonida screamed as she dove for the rope holding Loretta above the pavement.

~   ~   ~

At the sound of Leonida's scream, Tex dove to one side as Sean Kilkenney leaped past him. He grabbed at the doctor's right foot, causing him to fall face-first against the carpeted steps as someone at the top of the stairs fired a gun.

"Stupid sonofabitch." He blinked as plaster flew from the wall where Sean would have been. "Keep down."

"Hot damn, ya spoiled my shot," Hanky said as he and General Flores fought for position on the crowded steps. The man fired again as Tex rolled to his left. The bullet ripped splinters from the handrail above his head. He grabbed the pickets with his left and swung to his right to snap off a couple of shots, but three quick shots from the base of the stairs caused the figure to clutch his chest and stagger before falling. Tex let go of the pickets and rolled on his back to see Billy James lower a smoking gun as he joined them on the stairs.

"How'n the hell'd you get that hogleg?" Hanky growled.

"It belongs to Budger lying in the courtyard. I didn't figure he would mind me using it, since he's dead."

"No, I don't guess he would. Make sure you keep it pointed in the right direction. Who'd you just kill?"

"Black Jack. I think Sattler's still up there."

Tex grabbed Sean by the hair and shoved his face hard against one of the steps as he tried scrambling up the stairs.

"I told you to keep down. I want you around to patch me up in case I get myself bored." He scrambled past the doctor to peer over the last step. He could barely see Sattler inside the smoke-filled hallway, standing inside the doorway to Rosa's old room. Tex raised his gun and yelled.

"Drop the gun and come out of there, or, I'll blow you to hell." Sattler swung quickly and fired. The bullet hit the wall lamp at the top of the stairs, showering the stairs with sending flaming lamp oil.

"Oh, hell...son of a bitch." Tex beat at the tiny drops of burning oil on Sean's back. He sent a wild shot down the hall before sliding lower on the stairs to put out the flames on his own pant leg. General Flores had his jacket off, beating at the flames on Juan's face and arms as the men retreated down the burning stairwell.

"Well, Doc, looks like you and me's got ourselves cut off. We only got us one way to go, and that's down the hall. Got a gun? Or wuz you just planning on beating him to death with your bare hands?"

"The latter would give me more pleasure." Sean peered over the top step. "But if you insist." He made a quick lunge and came back with Black Jack's pistol as another bullet crashed into the plaster behind them.

"Nice move. How many rounds left?"

Sean opened the cylinder and snapped it shut. "Four, but I've got these." He removed the fifty-caliber pistols from his belt."

"Yeah, I'd say that's enough. He's moved across the hall to Maria's room, now. When I say, I want you to send all four rounds from the revolver at her doorhandle. I'm gonna try for Loretta's room, then I'll cover you. Got that?"

Sean nodded.

"Good. Now!" He slapped Sean on the back and bolted forward. Sean fired four times at the door. He could hear Tex fire twice more as he disappeared inside the room.. That was when Sean chose to bolt for the open door.

~   ~   ~

"To the fountain, quick." General Flores grabbed Juan by the arm and rushed him through the front door. He could hear the others cursing and complaining as they followed. Hanky grumbled something about having to abandon his son and the doctor on the burning staircase as the general splashed cold water against Juan's scorched face and arms.

"I'm sure they will take care of themselves." Jose soaked his scarf and held it against Juan's cheek.

"Yeah, but that ain't the point. Hey, Julio," Hanky yelled at the stableboy. "Y'all better get a bucket-brigade going and try putting out that fire, or Mrs. Garcia will have yer hide."

"Sí." He dashed toward the bucket hanging on the bunkhouse wall, yelling for help. In a matter of minutes there was a line of men, women and children dipping buckets in the fountain and passing them toward the front door.

"That ain't gonna be enough. That place is a tinderbox." Bear shook his head.

"I know, but it'll make 'em think they at least tried." Hanky paused as Captain McDougal let out a cry.

"Oh, Mother of Christ and the holy angels." The large man staggered before bolting across the patio.

"Jesus!" Hanky said as they stared at Loretta's limp body. It was covered in blood and hanging by a rope over the balcony. Paco was pushed aside as Captain McDougal readied himself as she inched closer toward his waiting arms.

"Papa!" Leonida screamed over the gunshots coming from inside the house. "Where is Sean? Señora McDougal is hurt. So is Señor Salty."

Hanky jumped on the fountain's edge for a better look. He could see the sailor struggling to his feet while holding a bloody hand to his side. The flames coming from Leonida's bedroom were licking the eaves while smoke poured from Loretta's old bedroom in billowing clouds. In a matter of minutes it would be too late to worry about James Sattler. The people trapped on the varenda would burn to death waiting for someone to save them.

~　　　~　　　~

James Sattler stood inside Maria's bedroom wondering why he hadn't killed the Doña and her fat maid when he had the chance. Na, shooting them would have been too quick and easy. She needed to suffer like he had suffered.

The pretty Mexican had confused him from the moment she entered his office almost a year earlier. He hated most women and only tolerated the others at best, but Leonida Garcia was different. He found her not only pretty, but pleasant to be around. They had laughed and talked about her ranch compared to life in the big city, as they discussed business over dinner. He had gone to bed that first evening thinking that things might have changed for the better. He liked her...liked her a lot.

Come here, sonny, and I'll show you what a woman's for. The scene leaped to his mind as quick and fresh as it had happened that night. Just like it had nightly for the past twenty years. The smelly man with a gray-speckled beard and missing tooth laughed as James crept closer.

That's right, Jimmy. Come closer. You can watch if you want. Maybe you'll learn how to keep a woman happy. His mother laughed as the man climbed into bed with her.

No, the six-year old boy shook his head. He could never do any of those things with any woman. He found it disgusting. He didn't understand how she could stand to do something like that. He closed his eyes and turned away from the laughing couple in bed. The man stank and she stank. The pretty Mexican on the veranda had been married and done those same things. What if it caused her to stink like his mother? What if she was still doing those things now? She could be inviting men to her room like his mother did. The thought of her spreading her legs caused his stomach to churn. He picked one of Maria's dresses from the wardrobe and ran his fingers across the pattern. Blue with white dots. She was almost the same size as his mother.

~   ~   ~

"Hold still." Sean had torn Salty's undershirt into rags and was wrapping his mid-section tightly. "We're sending you down next." He reached for the end of the lariat as it snaked over the railing.

"No you don't. There ain't a sailor worth his salt that would sneak to safety before a lady. Women first, Mate."

"You're wounded, Señor. You should be the one..." Leonida trailed off as Salty struggled to his feet.

"Don't I know that, M'lady? But either you and Mrs. Sanchez go first, or we'll all stay here and burn to death."

"Okay." Sean nodded. "I didn't think you'd have it any other way." Salty knelt beside Tex as Sean secured the rope under Leonida's arms.

"Getting a little smoky, Mate." He coughed.

"Yeah, makes you wonder what hell must be like." Both men cringed as something fell, and flames and smoke billowed inside the room they were guarding.

"Reminds me of the time I was aboard the frigate Royal Resolution in the Spanish Seas. A British battleship," he added after Tex glanced at him. He paused as Leonida climbed over the railing and clung onto the rope. She swung into midair as Sean and Maria began lowering her toward the patio.

"We got attacked in heavy fog by a Spanish warship. They caught us napping. The first volley ripped our hull wide open. We were, sitting in the middle of the ocean, with fog so thick you couldn't see your hand in front of your face, and flames leaping from our deck."

"You were on fire?" Tex glanced at him.

"Oh yeah. Anyways, we knew we had only a few minutes to abandon ship before she blew. But I stayed right beside my ten pounder," he grinned at Tex, "because I knew those Spanish blokes were going to pull real close in order to see just how bad we were damaged. And sure enough, just as the last of our crew were climbing over the starboard side into the longboats, she pulls up along side of us broadside." Salty coughed as he started laughing.

"Even people you think are smart can do stupid things. That captain should have known better. The instant they turned broadside, I touched off my ten pounder. The ball cracked open their hull just below the waterline. Last I seen of them, they was scrambling to save their own bloody hides as we made off in our longboats. We were picked up by another British frigate the following afternoon."

The door on the opposite side of the hallway jerked open, and James Sattler poked his head through the opening to grin. "Yoo-hoo." He waved his fingers before firing a shot their direction and slamming the door.

"The bloke's bloody mad." Salty shook his head.

"I'll say." Tex glanced over his shoulder as Sean jerked the lariat back over the railing. "Looks like Mrs. Garcia's made it. Here," he handed his pistol to Salty, "keep an eye on mister locoweed while I help Doc lower Maria."

"Aye-aye, Mate." Salty saluted. The door swung open and shut once more as James continued taunting them.

"That's it, you bloody squid. Keep it up." The fire had eaten away the wardrobe and flames were licking the curtains and wooden beams inside the room. He shoved the pistol in his belt and grabbed the lamp from the night stand. Lightin the lamp and turning the wick up high, he pressed himself against the wall just inside the door to the hall. The door hiding James Sattler was not more than four feet away.

"Come on, you son of a sea serpent, open the door."

~   ~   ~

Leonida ran across the patio to where Jonathan McDougal held his wife in his arms. Father Ramon was already hovering in front of them, checking the wounded woman much the same as Doctor Kilkenney would have been. "Come," he was saying, "we had better get her inside. We can use my quarters in the rear of the chapel. I have plenty of water and clean bandages, and it is a safe distance from the hacienda." Leonida followed halfway across the patio before suddenly stopping.

"What's wrong, Doña? Aren't you coming?" Angela took hold of her arm.

"The medical kit. Sean keeps his medical kit inside his room." She glanced toward the hacienda. The flames leaping toward the sky cast a red glow across the worried faces surrounding her.

"Sean." She ran toward the hacienda. "Sean!"

"Niña," the general chased after her, "it isn't safe."

"No Papa," she pulled away, "I must. Sean," she yelled and waved both hands. "Your medical kit. We need your medical kit."

"Find Cathy." Sean leaned over the railing and yelled, "it's tied to her saddle."

~   ~   ~

Sean turned toward Tex. The cowboy was leaning into the lariat, with Maria suspended between the railing and the patio. "Can you handle her by yourself?"

"Hell, I got her now. Why?"

"I've got a lot of medical supplies inside my room that we might need before this thing's over."

"Well, go on get 'em before this place falls around our ears. "Go on," He fed more rope over the railing.

Sean dashed into the smoke-filled room and paused as he spied the sailor crouched near the door holding the lighted lamp in his hand.

"I heard. Go fetch your supplies. I got you covered." Salty withdrew Tex's pistol from his belt.

"What that for?" Sean motioned toward the lamp.

"A little present for our friend across the hall. Go collect your things before Lady McDougal and I decide to bleed to death."

"Right." Sean bolted through the door and down the hall. He had a hold on the door handle when a loud crashing sound caused him to turn. Part of the stairwell had given way, causing a display of dancing sparks and smoke to bellow toward the ceiling. He shoved the door open the exact instant the door to Maria's room jerked open. James Sattler smiled and pointed a gun at him. Something flashed across the hall to explode against the door. Sattler was engulfed in flames.

"Holy Christ!" Sean crossed his breast as the man ran screaming down the hall. Sean dove through the door as he bounced from wall to wall past his room, leaving droplets of burning oil in his path. He hit the wall at the end of the hall and reversed his path. Sean grabbed a blanket from off his bed and dove back through the door, hoping to smother the flames, but the wild man was already passed him.

"Wait." Sean chased after him. "Oh, Jesus." He crossed himself again as Sattler became air born in the empty stairwell and fell screaming to the floor below.

"Get that kit of your'n and let's rustle." Tex yelled.

"Huh?"

"Forget about him. He's done for. Get your grip."

"Yeah." Sean bolted back toward his room.

Chapter 49

Leonida covered her mouth and sobbed. Sean and Tex had lowered Salty Moran, and now both men were descending the lariat toward safety. The vaqueros had abandoned fighting the fire and were crowded opposite the fountain watching the once great hacienda being reduced to a pile of rubble. General Flores and Ildefonso Baca were shouting orders as Indians passed buckets of water to men dousing the roofs of neighboring homes and buildings.

"I know it's a huge loss, but I thank God you are all right, my dear." She felt Dorothy Baker's arms around her shoulders. She choked back another sob as Clara wrapped both arms around her waist and buried her tear-streaked face against her stomach.

"Gracias, both of you." She ran her fingers through Clara's , "but the hacienda and the things inside were just that...things. I can replace them. It is my people I cry for. For Señora McDougal. I fear for her, and for Señor Salty."

"For Loretta?"

"Sí, she is hurt very badly."

Sean reached the pavement and handed the bundle of medical supplies to Angela, who dashed toward the chapel. He then said something to several men, who scooped Salty Moran off his feet and rushed him toward the rear of the chapel. Sean stared at them a long minute before trotting toward the fountain where they were standing.

"Well, we made it." He gave Leonida a weak grin before splashing water on his face and arms.

"Sean? I am glad you are alive. Are you hurt? Are you..." He grabbed her trembling hands and kissed them.

"I am fine." He kiss her cheek. "I have to go."

"She told me." Leonida grabbed his shirt. "Señora McDougal explained everything. Can you forgive me?"

"There's nothing to forgive." He pulled away and put a finger against her lips when she started to speak. "Later." He dashed halfway across the patio and turned to yell. "Please pray. All of you. I'm need all the help I can get."

"Sí, I will, mi amante. Sí," she shouted as he turned away.

"Come," she grabbed Clara's hand, "both of you. You can be my prayer warriors. I'm not sure Dios will be pleased to hear from me. Señora McDougal needs prayer."

~   ~   ~

Hail Mary, full of grace; the Lord is with thee; blessed art thou among women and blessed is the fruit of thy womb, Jesus. Holy Mary, Mother of God, pray for us sinners, now and at the hour of our death. Amen. Leonida knelt before the cross in the front of the chapel, clutching her rosary in her fingers. Dorothy and Clara, being Protestants, had chosen to kneel between two pews, facing the rear.

Glory be to the Father, and to the Son, and to the Holy Spirit. As it was in the beginning is now, and ever shall be, world with out end. Amen.

Pray for us, O Holy Mother of God. She bowed her forehead to the cold stone floor as a huge sob escaped her throat.

Oh, what is the use, Holy Father. You know my heart, and there is no use in pretending. I have been angry, cold and bitter, but it is not for me I pray. It is Señora McDougal and that funny little man called Salty. I am praying for them. I am sorry I felt that way about her, Jesus. Can you forgive me? I didn't know you had chosen her to bring Señor McDougal happiness. I was jealous about Doctor Kilkenney's attention toward her. I did not understand or trust you. I am as Father Ramon says I am, prideful and arrogant. Thank you for sending him to us...to me...to teach such things.

But now, Holy Father, I ask that if it is in your will, that you will heal Señora McDougal. I don't care what she did in the past. She is a good woman. I'm sure of that. She loves her husband, and I'm sure she loves you, even if it is in an imperfect way. And who am I to talk? Is the way I love you perfect? I don't think so. Only you are perfect.

And for Señor Moran. He was wounded trying to help me. Guide Doctor Kilkenney's hands and give him wisdom.

Please forgive me for talking so familiar Father, but I ask one more thing. I ask you to forgive and heal those who have caused this sorrow. Heal their wounds and give me the grace to forgive them. I can't do this in myself. You'll have to help me.

Had she been aware of what was happening, Leonida would have seen the building gradually fill. Mexican, Indian and white people alike knelt beside each other and spoke their own language. They were her people. She had loved and cared for them through the loss of her husband and his brother. They had seen her cry over the grave of Father Franco and the graves of Julio and Lupe Perez. She had been there when they were ill or suffered a loss. Even now, she was praying for someone else, while everything she owned smoldered in the middle of the courtyard. She was their Doña, and they loved her.

~   ~   ~

Leonida had no idea when she fell asleep. She didn't even know if she had finished her rosary. She woke in the middle of the stone floor clutching the beads. Someone had taken care to cover her with a wool blanket and slip a folded jacket beneath her cheek as a pillow. A bird fluttered in the open window and chirped at her. It was morning.

She arched her stiff back and stepped out into the sunlight. The Rodriguez children paused in the middle of chasing their dog to stare, but continued with their play after receiving a smile. Vernon Blackstone was rummaging through the charred remains of the kitchen with Maria in search of anything of value. His wife Catherine was bent over an open fire cooking breakfast for the hungry workers. Several Indians were herding cattle toward the corral, while dozens of vaqueros loaded chunks of mortar and brick into a carreta to be hauled away.

"Quite a sight, ain't it Ma'am?" Hanky was seated a few feet away on a bench. "They're fixin' ta rebuild the place right where it wuz. If ya got any changes you want made, ya better let 'em know right pronto."

"I can see, but where are they going to get the things to build? Rudolfo said his father had to have lumber cut and brought from the mountains, and bring other things in by boat. He said it took months...more than a year to build this hacienda. The furniture took even longer."

"Well, I can't say about most of them things, but Ruby says seeing as her and Bear are leaving fer Utah, y'all can have what wood ya want out of The Rusty Rail. Yer pa's done took a bunch of vaqueros into town to tear the place to the ground. And Paco says Armando Segoviano used to make brick, so they got themselves a crew down by the river whipping some up right now. Looks like yer gonna be in business right soon, Ma'am. Ya got yerself a pretty good bunch of folks around here."

"Sí." She blew and wiped her nose on a soiled handkerchief. "I had better go and see about them."

"Oh, Ma'am? One more thing." Hanky scrambled to his feet.

"Sí?"

"Baca says this belongs to you." He dropped a large chunk of melted gold in her palm. "They found it at the base of where the stairs used to be. That Sattler feller musta had a sack of your gold on him when he fell."

"Yes, he did." Leonida shivered. "Gracias." She dropped it into the pocket of her riding skirt. "Buenos dias, my friend." She squeezed his hand.

"Yeah, you too," he said as she turned away.

"Doña Leonida," Angela rushed toward her as she rounded the corner of the chapel, "come, I have made some tea. Drink it while it is still hot." She grabbed a mug from a make-shift table of boards and sawhorses. The table was spread with breads and pastries.

"No, gracias," Leonida waved the girl off, "I must find out about Señora McDougal..." She came to a halt at the sight of Sean sitting on bricks outside Father Ramon's living quarters with his head buried in his hands. "Madré de Díos." She crossed herself.

"What is it, Doña Leonida?"

"Señora McDougal...is she...?"

"Señora McDougal is fine, Doña. Señor Sean says she will be weak and have to stay in bed, but she is okay. Here," Angela shoved the steaming mug toward her, "take the tea, por favor, and go talk to him."

"Gracias, mi niña." The term caused Angel to grin.

"I am almost your age, Doña Leonida, and will soon be having a niña own." She patted her stomach.

"Sí, but you are still *my* niña." She kissed the girl's cheek before squatting on her heels in front of the doctor.

"Por que, mi amante? Angela tells me the woman and her child are going to live. Why are you sad?"

"I don't know. Sometimes I hate my job." Sean tried to smile but his lips trembled instead. "She came awfully close to losing her baby, you know that don't you?"

Leonida nodded.

"In fact, she almost died. The baby is so tiny and the bullet came that close." He held his fingers apart for her to see. "Dirty bastard." He sighed and covered his face with both hands.

"Sean? Look at me, mi amour." She tugged against his fingers. "You are not responsible for what that man did."

"Yes, but I almost lost you again, and that thought frightens me. I should have been there to protect you and her both and Maria, but I wasn't."

"You're upset because you weren't there? I hope you aren't going to say that every time something goes wrong after we are married. I will be very angry if you do." She took a sip of tea and smiled. "I am sad that Señora McDougal got hurt, and I prayed for her and Señor Salty. And I'm terribly upset that everything I own has been turned to ashes." She glanced toward the smoldering pile in the middle of the courtyard. "But I did not shoot them and set fire to my hacienda, and neither did you. Besides, you were inside that burning room with us. By the way, how is that funny little man doing?"

"Salty?"

"Sí."

"He lost a lot of blood, but he will recover. He says it takes more than one bullet to kill a sailor, and I believe him. The bullet didn't touch any vital organs."

"What about Señor McDougal? How is he?"

"He worried himself sick last night, be's asleep beside Loretta now. You can see them later."

"And the others?"

"Juan's burns are minor and will heal quickly. The three Indians Sattler shot inside the house are dead, and three others suffered minor scrapes and bruises. Your father believes we managed well, considering."

"What about those other men, the ones who tried to..." She shrugged and took another sip of tea.

"Well, they are another story altogether." Sean shook his head. "The one you hit with the rock has a concussion, but he's starting to come around. He has one thick skull, I'll tell you that," he snickered. "He'll pull through and stand trial. Hanky's going to send him and Ken Edwards back to San Francisco, so he won't have to bother hanging them himself. The other two are going to be laid up for awhile, especially the one Hanky shot in the leg. The bone was shattered so badly I had to remove his leg from the knee down. I'm sorry," he added after seeing her cringe.

"No, it is okay. I'm just sorry you had to go through this. I love you very much." She studied the mug in her hands as her eyes began to water. "I want to apologize for causing this."

"Causing what?"

"This trouble. If I hadn't been suspicious at seeing you and Señora McDougal yesterday, and run off angry, none of this would have happened." She snapped her head upright as Sean laughed.

"I'm sorry." He wiped his palms on his pants before reaching for her. "James Sattler was insane. You didn't see what we did up there."

"I saw plenty."

"Yes," he nodded, "more than you deserved to see, but not what we saw. Believe me, he would have attempted the same, no matter what. He would have found a way. As far as getting upset seeing me kiss Loretta, you had every right. I'd be upset if it hadn't bothered you. I was completely wrong. We all were." He stood and helped Leonida to her feet.

"Loretta was wrong for keeping her marriage and pregnancy a secret. Everyone made mistakes. That's life. But no one is to blame for James Sattler's actions but James Sattler. I'm sorry for kissing another woman when I'm engaged to you, no matter how innocent it was. Can you forgive me?"

"I don't know," Leonida shook her head slowly, "that mistake will cost you dearly. I may insist that you marry me now instead of waiting for the Dons and their families to join us. What would you think of that, Doctor?"

"That's acceptable. Would this afternoon be soon enough?"

"Perhaps, if I can find a place to bathe and something to wear." She grinned with a shrug. "Every piece of clothing I owned seems to have disappeared."

"Oh, but I still have your wedding dress at my casa." Angela scampered from the make-shift table to grab her by the shoulders. "Perdoname, but I could not help overhearing. I will chase Juan out of the house so you can bathe and get rested before the wedding. Oh, this is so wonderful." She kissed Leonida on both cheeks.

"Niña." She grabbed for the girl's arm.

"Sí?"

"Mañana. My father went to Dogtown to fetch wood. I cannot get married until he returns. Mañana."

"Sí." She dashed across the brick with a squeal.

"Well, it looks like that is settled. We're getting married tomorrow afternoon," Sean chuckled.

"Sí, but where are we going to live? We have no where to sleep. There isn't a place to cook our food or food to cook. It's all gone." She walked toward the smoldering ruins of her home.

"Ah, on the contrary, my dear." Sean raised his voice Angela rang the courtyard bell. "We'll pitch a tent right under the oak tree where we enjoyed our first kiss. Or, better yet, we'll borrow the Blackstone's wagon. I believe we can somehow squeeze it in there. As for cooking, Angela and Catherine Blackstone have proven we can make tea and cook over an open fire right in the courtyard. And there's tens of thousands of cows wandering around this place. We can eat them."

"But you don't like eating cow three times a day."

"I'd eat snakes and lizards, to be with you."

"Being married to you will be a challenge, Sean Kilkenney. The tent or wagon will be okay for a day or two, but I will have a casa built next to Angela's until we can rebuild the hacienda. I don't think I would like eating snakes and lizards. We can find something better than that, Doctor." She smiled before covering his mouth with hers.

End

About The Author

MAJOR MITCHELL is the author of seven novels and two children's books. He lives with his wife, Judy, in Northern California. A member of The Western Writers of America and a frequent guest speaker at historical meetings and schools on the West Coast, he has also written several songs, and takes the stage on rare occasions as a singer.

More about the author, his books and photo gallery may be found at www.majormitchell.net.

Correspondence should be addressed to:
Shalako Press
P.O. Box 371
Oakdale, CA 95361-0371

For your reading pleasure, we invite you to visit our Trading Post bookstore.

Other books by Major Mitchell:

The Doña
Poverty Flat
Dusty Boots
Manhunter
Joker's Play
A Reason To Believe
Charlie Shepherd (children's)
The Witch On Oak Street (children's)

Shalako Press

http://www.shalakopress.com